Sampson [...] aid. "This is [...] you know why [...] so I'll dispense with introductory matters and allow Mr. Cuyos to get to business."

"Thank you, Governor," Cuyos said. Sophia had to lean forward to hear him. "I wish I could report that the situation on my planet has improved. While the rioting seems to have calmed for the moment, the governor believes that's only because the rioters have run out of targets. Much of the planet still remains outside government control. Our militia is next to powerless—many troops have rebelled, others have simply gone home. In short, Governor Sampson, Zurich is rapidly falling into anarchy. We need aid."

"That much is clear," Sampson said in his customary even tones. "What I have difficulty understanding is why you are here instead of in the capital. Surely they are the ones who should organize the distribution of troops in the prefecture. We have only our own militia at our disposal, and we face the same concerns as you, if not to the same extent. It would not seem wise to part with any of our forces at present. I'm sure you understand."

In the blink of an eye, Cuyos lost his composure. He jumped to his feet, and his chair rolled backward into the wall. He waved his arms, and for the first time Sophia noticed sweat stains on the armpits of his jacket.

"Understand?" he yelled. "I understand that the house I grew up in, my family's house, burned to the ground the day I left my planet! I understand that hundreds of my people are dying every day! And I understand that *there is no more Republic*! At the very least there is no more Prefecture VI! New Canton is the capital of *nothing*! I came to you because we are neighbors. If we do not act together in this universe, both of us will fall. We *need* your help. We are your countrymen. We are your friends. And we are falling apart."

Sophia was impressed at Cuyos' passion, but it did not change a thing. In the time it would take for reinforcements to get from Aldebaran to Zurich, the rioting on Zurich could end while new tension broke out on Aldebaran, and the militia would be more than a week away from being able to come back and help. Nothing could be spared.

MechWarrior™
DARK AGE

PRINCIPLES OF DESOLATION

A BATTLETECH™ NOVEL

Jason M. Hardy and Randall N. Bills

A ROC BOOK

ROC
Published by New American Library, a division of
Penguin Group (USA) Inc., 375 Hudson Street,
New York, New York 10014, USA
Penguin Group (Canada), 90 Eglinton Avenue East, Suite 700, Toronto,
Ontario M4P 2Y3, Canada (a division of Pearson Penguin Canada Inc.)
Penguin Books Ltd., 80 Strand, London WC2R 0RL, England
Penguin Ireland, 25 St. Stephen's Green, Dublin 2,
Ireland (a division of Penguin Books Ltd.)
Penguin Group (Australia), 250 Camberwell Road, Camberwell, Victoria 3124,
Australia (a division of Pearson Australia Group Pty. Ltd.)
Penguin Books India Pvt. Ltd., 11 Community Centre, Panchsheel Park,
New Delhi - 110 017, India
Penguin Group (NZ), cnr Airborne and Rosedale Roads, Albany,
Auckland 1310, New Zealand (a division of Pearson New Zealand Ltd.)
Penguin Books (South Africa) (Pty.) Ltd., 24 Sturdee Avenue,
Rosebank, Johannesburg 2196, South Africa

Penguin Books Ltd., Registered Offices:
80 Strand, London WC2R 0RL, England

First published by Roc, an imprint of New American Library,
a division of Penguin Group (USA) Inc.

First Printing, August 2006
10 9 8 7 6 5 4 3 2 1

PUBLISHER'S NOTE
This is a work of fiction. Names, characters, places, and incidents either are
the product of the authors' imaginations or are used fictitiously, and any
resemblance to actual persons, living or dead, business establishments, events,
or locales is entirely coincidental.

The publisher does not have any control over and does not assume any
responsibility for author or third-party Web sites or their content.

To my sisters, Lindy, Elissa, Megan, Gretchen, Katrina and Jenica. If there's anything accurate about the female characters in this book, it's because I lived with them for so long.

—Jason M. Hardy

Prologue

Genève, Terra
Republic of the Sphere
9 May 3135

The Republic of the Sphere was spread out across the floor of the grand ballroom like a buffet, and most of the people present seemed interested in taking a slice or two for themselves. The planets stayed in their engraved places while the most powerful individuals in the Inner Sphere orbited around them. Taffeta and silk flashed and ruffled as people danced. Some of them moved to the music being played by the orchestra, others to the quieter but more powerful song of politics.

Politics was not supposed to be a topic of discussion in the room, by decree of the exarch. He followed his own order by diligently discussing thirtieth-century baroque revisionism with whoever tried to buttonhole him. Most people, being interested in meatier fare, quickly moved out of his orbit.

They would spin away from Exarch Levin into the middle of the floor, where dancers twirled gently near tables filled with people who were ready to spring to their feet as soon as they saw someone they needed to talk to. Traffic, dictated in part by the uniformed servers carrying trays that never stayed full for long, was generally clockwise and steady. Entering the outermost circle of the crowd was easy. Penetrating the other layers, moving toward the core, was much harder.

Low-level functionaries, carrying in their heads a list of questions or demands or requests, bobbed through the crowd, waiting to see someone significant enough for them to grab. The important people had functionaries of their own, clinging to them like barnacles. Their job was to keep other minor functionaries away.

A diplomat spinning through the room's outer orbit would see Coordinator Vincent Kurita standing with his left foot planted firmly on the engraved representation of Savannah, a planet on the opposite side of the Republic from where his forces were whittling the Republic down, planet by planet. On the other side of the Inner Sphere map, Chancellor Daoshen Liao rose above the throng surrounding him like a needle poking through uneven fabric, and he surveyed the image of the Republic and those who stood on top of it with equal disdain. Prince Harrison Davion stood near the representation of Yangtze, tolerantly listening to the governor of that very planet regale him about local difficulties.

These were the people shaping the Inner Sphere's fate, people who might make plans to attack one another's holdings immediately after the end of this ball. The level of power in this room was intoxicating.

But most of the participants knew they couldn't let it overwhelm them. They needed to stay alert, to see who was talking to whom, to eavesdrop on conversations where important deals were being struck, or to pass along rumors about what others had heard. Questions darted back and forth between the minor functionaries as they worked to stay abreast of what was happening. Who's that talking to Tara Campbell? Does Daoshen Liao always look that angry, or did something specific rouse his ire? What's going on between Alaric Wolf and Caleb Davion? And where was that woman who entered the reception behind Daoshen Liao, the one with the burgundy dress and the swept-up hair?

Attendees at the ball were playing other games besides political ones. Power wasn't just an intoxicant, it was an aphrodisiac, and the sheer number of glamorous, attractive men and women—plus the fact that many envoys and nobles were currently quite far from their homes and families—only encouraged those who wished to turn the Exarch's Ball into the largest, most expensive singles bar on the planet. Or in known space, for that matter. Several attendees had been the targets of multiple advances, both clumsy and graceful, but the strange disappearance of the woman in the deep red dress after her grand entrance had only heightened her already considerable desirability.

Most of the rumormongers had attached a name to their target—Danai Liao-Centrella. The name was enough to scare many of them off. As the youngest sister of the Capellan chancellor and the champion of the Ishiyama Open on Solaris VII, she was out of reach of all but the highly noble or the vastly deluded.

However, as the night wore on, the latter group surged in numbers, and more and more suitors tried to track the woman down. Soon, rumors of a few confirmed sightings made their way around the room. She had been seen on a balcony, and the son of a senator of the Republic bellowed a proposition up to her. She responded by draining her wine glass on his head, a perfect hit from eight meters in the air. But what else could be expected of a 'Mech champion?

A noble from the Federated Suns told of finding her near the orchestra, and engaging her in a long, entendre-filled conversation. While no conclusive plans had been made, the noble said he had every reason to believe their sparring would continue later that night, and would be more than verbal in its nature.

So when the son of the chief of staff of the legate of Lipton chanced upon Danai leaning against the east wall, he prepared himself for an extended battle of wits that, if he had his way, would end up with her succumbing to his charms.

He strolled up to her while she sipped from a champagne flute, pretending (he guessed) not to see his approach. When he got close enough to be heard over the noise of the orchestra and the chatter of hundreds of guests, he spoke.

"Did you ever turn a cartwheel in a 'Mech?" he asked.

Danai continued looking at her glass. She might have said something, but her suitor couldn't make it out. So he just kept talking.

"I've heard some people have tried it, pulled it off even. Seems impractical to me, but I guess it would give you the advantage of surprise. It'd better—or else any enemy watching would blast you to kingdom come while you were heels over head."

A mild grin flickered on Danai's narrow mouth, and a few words worked their way past her lips. "Yes. I suppose."

The suitor looked at her curiously. These brief, distant replies were not what he'd been led to expect. Danai still hadn't looked directly at him, or even in his direction.

"There's something to be said for distractions," the suitor continued valiantly. "Look at what you're doing to us in the Republic now. Or what your brother is doing, at least. When was the last time the Republic struck any sort of blow against his efforts? Levin's just too distracted. Interior problems, Jade Falcon problems, Dragon problems—his whole realm's turning one big cartwheel. Works out well for you, doesn't it?"

If anything, Danai looked more removed from the conversation. She shrugged. "I suppose."

The suitor made a few more volleys before he finally gave up and took his leave of the lovely Danai. Either her wit and intelligence had been greatly inflated by a considerable number of people, or she disdained him too much to have a real conversation with him. Either way, he wasn't getting anywhere.

Danai watched the young man go, feeling a twinge of regret at how poorly the conversation had gone. But only a twinge. She didn't enjoy talking politics with any-one, and having some useless bureaucrat try to talk to her about the Confederation's ongoing incursion into former Republic territory didn't help. So she was less than gracious to the boy, mainly because she couldn't find a way to be interested in his chatter, until he merci-fully left.

She'd been looking for isolated spots where she could wait out as much of the ball as possible, but no location stayed empty for long. The balcony, the little nook be-hind the orchestra, this plain spot on the wall—everywhere she went, people found her. And they all wanted something from her.

There was one person at the ball she wouldn't avoid if he came looking for her, but she'd only seen Caleb from a great distance a time or two. She thought they'd made eye contact once, but Caleb had quickly broken it off. He hadn't come looking for her, and she wouldn't blame him for staying away. She was still trying to get her mind around what she'd learned tonight—that the Caleb she'd had several dinners with on the journey here was Caleb *Davion*. Possibly the last person (besides Har-rison Davion) she should be socializing with. She'd been clumsy, relaxing her guard on the journey here. If Dao-shen ever caught wind of it . . .

Anyway, she certainly couldn't go anywhere near Caleb tonight. What good could come from a Davion and a Liao flirting in full view of the collected powers of the Inner Sphere?

She knew that in most of her conversations this eve-ning she'd sounded as engaging as a baboon, which, in hindsight, was as good a strategy as any for pushing away unwanted attention. Still, many of the people pes-tering her had no interest in her verbal skills, and while her mumblings might have disoriented them briefly, they kept after her. So she kept avoiding them, kept moving.

She'd had her eye on one possible spot for much of the evening, a tiny alcove where a fountain ran down the high wall into a small pool. The sound of the water discouraged conversation, and that, along with the drops that tended to fly out of the pool, was enough to repel most of the attendees. Danai would have settled there earlier, except there were always one or two other people perched on the pool's rim—apparently she wasn't the only one hoping to avoid talking to other guests.

She glanced at the fountain again as she passed, and was once again disappointed to see two people occupying the spot she wanted. She turned her head, ready to look for a new safe perch, but then stopped and looked back. She recognized the posture of the two people, and her sympathies were raised. A woman in a jade green dress was backed against the low wall of the pool, throwing quick glances back and forth as she sought an escape path. But the man in front of her—a rather attractive man, though quite a bit older than the woman he had pinned down—had cornered her quite neatly. She needed help. Danai, who had spent the entire evening feeling directionless, suddenly had a purpose.

It only took three strides for her confidence to return. She wasn't caught in politics anymore. She was back on the battlefield—the oldest battlefield in history.

Thanks to the noise of the fountain, Danai didn't hear a word of the conversation until she was just behind the older man in the jet-black suit.

"You wouldn't even have to adjust to a new last name!" he said in a jocular tone. "You'd still be a Marik. Or you could hyphenate. Marik-Marik." Danai couldn't see the man's expression as he spoke, but she caught a glimpse of the increasing horror in the woman's eyes.

She knew who the woman was. Once she heard the last name, the face fell into place. Nikol Marik, fifth in line for the throne of the Oriente Protectorate. A neighbor of the Confederation and therefore, in the eternal tradition of Capellans, a likely rival. For the moment, though, Danai put aside politics, preferring to help someone who needed assistance.

She'd tried to think of a line of attack on the way over, but hadn't come up with one. Her warrior blood was up, so she decided to take a physical approach.

Walking at a good clip, she let her left shoulder catch the older man firmly in the back. He lurched forward, and Nikol alertly dodged him by stepping to her right.

Danai grabbed the gentleman's arm. "I'm *so* sorry," she said. "I don't know what's gotten into me tonight. It's possible that, well, I think I might have had a little too much to, well, you know, what *is* it that they're serving? It's spectacular, but it seems to have me somewhat off my balance. I'm really, really sorry. Did I already say that? Then I should say it again. I'm really very really sorry."

The man stood stiffly, pulling on his jacket to smooth it. "Think nothing of it. Now if you'll excuse us . . ."

"Oh, no no no, excuse *me*!" Danai said, deliberately missing the man's meaning. "I'm the one who bumped into you!" Then she assumed a confused expression. "That's what happened, right? You didn't back into me? Did you?"

"No, I did not," the man said stiffly.

"I just couldn't remember. I . . ." Danai suddenly grabbed her stomach. "Ooooo . . ." she said. "I don't feel too . . ." Then she doubled over.

"For God's sake," the man said, but Nikol, seeing an opportunity, stepped forward and put an arm around Danai's shoulders.

"Let me give you a hand," Nikol said, then glanced at the man with an expression that actually looked regretful. "I'm sorry, Frederick, but this poor woman needs some help. We'll have to continue this conversation some other time."

"Of course," Frederick said, and shot Danai a look that made it clear he hoped she would suffer from a powerful hangover in the morning.

"Come along," Nikol said, and steered Danai along as Danai maintained her stooped posture.

"You're a lifesaver," Nikol said once they were out of Frederick's earshot.

"Perhaps I'm really sick," Danai countered, making sure to keep looking pained.

"Perhaps," Nikol said. "But I saw your face as you approached Frederick, and you did not look like a woman who had drunk too much."

"What did I look like?"

"A soldier going into battle."

Danai laughed. "That happens," she said. "That expression just kind of comes up."

"Where am I taking you?"

"We'd better go to the ladies' room, just to keep our cover intact. After that, you can join me looking for a nice, quiet place."

"That would be heaven," Nikol said.

Half a dozen balconies overlooked the interior of the ballroom, but only one of them had an adjacent outer balcony. The night air had grown cool enough to keep most people from wanting to be outside. Nikol and Danai shivered a bit, but they were alone. And they had a fine view of the fireworks that had been going on all night.

"Quite a display," Nikol said. "Do you think many people in there remember we're here for a funeral?"

"Many would view the death of Victor Steiner-Davion as a cause for celebration," Danai said, then decided she didn't like the tone of her own voice. "He wasn't a great friend of the Confederation," she said. "Daoshen—I mean, Chancellor Liao—has subjected me to many lectures about his shortcomings. But he was a warrior. I can respect him for that, at least."

"I think if you made a complete survey of ball attendees, you'd find people who worshipped Steiner-Davion and people who hated him. And just about every emotion in between. Only thing you wouldn't find is people who don't care."

Danai shook her head. "That room—it's exhausting. A thousand people who don't agree on anything, each of them convinced of their own superiority. And willing to do whatever it takes to make others see how superior they are."

Nikol smiled. "Isn't that the point of the Solaris VII

tournaments? Pummeling people until they admit you're superior?"

"Now that you point it out, yes, it is. But at least there are clear winners and losers there."

"Oh, you get that in other parts of life, too. Take the nice man you saved me from, Frederick Marik. Clear loser."

"Yeah, he sure seemed to be."

"No, no, I didn't mean like that. Well, I kind of did. But look at his situation. His ancestors ruled hundreds of planets, and what's he got? A broken realm and an older brother who may be the most disliked paladin in the Republic. He's been scraping around for years, looking for some way to get a piece of the old Free Worlds League back. It's sad. Does life present you with too many clearer losers than that?"

"But in 'Mech combat you lose because of what you did on the field," Danai countered. "Not because your family got blasted in the Jihad. Life is just . . . sloppier."

Nikol laughed as she turned and looked back inside the grand hall. "You can say that again. Do you know how many things are going to happen that shouldn't before the night is over?"

"Like what?"

"I don't know . . . like senators making a deal with a House outside of the Republic for protection. Like minor nobles from House Kurita seducing a member of Chancellor Liao's entourage."

"Not likely," Danai scoffed.

Nikol motioned her back inside. "Come here." They walked back onto the inner balcony, where Nikol scanned the shimmering forms on the floor for several seconds. Then she pointed.

"There," she said. "Look."

Danai followed the line of her arm. "That couple?"

"Right. The two who'd better find a private spot quite promptly or they're risking public indecency. Recognize either of them?"

Danai squinted, a somewhat embarrassing thing for a warrior to have to do, but then she normally didn't try to pick out objects in dim ballrooms with erratically flashing lights. She stared at the couple for a minute or two before one of the faces registered.

"The woman," she said. "She was in the group I walked in with. I forget exactly who she is—daughter of an executive secretary to one of the chancellor's assistants?"

"Something to that effect. And the man she's wrapping herself around is Ken Hasagawa, nephew of the duke of Sutama."

Danai stared at the entanglement for a few moments. "It could be worse," she finally said. "He could be a Republican."

Nikol laughed again. It was a sound that obviously came easily to her. "That sort of coupling may be happening somewhere else on the floor, for all I know. It's that sort of night—the power on display, the flow of champagne, the fact that most of these people will likely never see each other again—all kinds of strange dalliances are going on down there."

Reflexively, Danai found herself scanning the floor for Caleb. If everyone else was getting into questionable situations . . .

"Almost makes me want to go back down," she said.

"You have a particular target in mind?" Nikol asked lightly, and Danai felt herself starting to flush. Thankfully, Nikol didn't press the subject. "If you decide to reenter the fray," she said, "remember that Frederick might have you in his sights next."

Danai assumed her most regal, fearsome attitude. "He wouldn't dare."

Nikol waved her hands frantically. "Don't look powerful!" she said. "That's just what he's looking for!"

Danai smiled and deflated back into her normal posture. The memory of other conversations she'd had that night that she'd managed briefly to forget came back, and she remembered why she was hiding.

"You're right," she said. "I'll stay up here for a while."

They talked for a good long time, neither one of them

bothering to bring up the fact that they probably shouldn't like each other. As with many of the other people down on the ballroom floor, political tension should have trumped personal friendship. But for the time being, it didn't.

1

Genève, Terra
Republic of the Sphere
1 July 3135

Daoshen Liao had ordered a complete remodeling of the Capellan Cultural Center in Genève as soon as he arrived. He needed a place to receive visitors (or, to use his word, "supplicants"), and the academic-looking office in the embassy did not fit his needs. The changes he ordered were extensive, especially since he did not intend to be on Terra long and, once he left, would likely not return for quite some time. But the chancellor needed appropriate surroundings, and he dedicated significant sums of money to adjusting his reception area as quickly as possible.

Danai didn't hear the sounds of construction as she approached his office—or, as he called it now, the Hall of Celestial Purity—so she assumed the work was nearly complete. She was interested to see what the hall looked like, though she had a good idea of the effect Daoshen wanted to deliver.

He didn't have high ceilings to work with, so he couldn't quite pull off the sheer imposing grandeur Danai knew he'd prefer, but given that fact he had still done quite well. Soft light spilled from gold wall sconces, and green marble columns lined a thin black carpet that led to the commanding throne Daoshen had designed. The top of the chair stretched a full meter higher than Daoshen's head, and above that hung the seal of the Capellan Confederation, in glossy green and black, a full two meters in diameter. Light from throughout the room seemed to gather around the throne, and the chair's burnished metal made a halo around the chancellor. Danai was certain the effect was intentional, to highlight his divine status as God Incarnate.

Guards stood by the door, and Danai half expected them to act as medieval heralds announcing her entry into the chancellor's presence. Instead, they stood still and silent, leaving Danai to make her own way to her brother's throne.

When she drew near it, she bowed—she'd neglected to do so once, and Daoshen's remonstrance still rang in her ears—then waited for Daoshen to speak before she said anything. She felt the back of her right knee tremble, and she willed it still. But it kept moving, so she leaned a little to her left to hide it. She could not remember a time when her body had not responded that way to being in her brother's presence, and she didn't understand it. When she was a teenager, summoned to the Confederation from the safe cocoon of the Magistracy of Canopus, the fear had made some sense. Now, as an adult and an accomplished warrior, there was no reason to be nervous in front of her brother. But her earliest memories of him, ingrained from a time before she knew how to count her own age, were steeped in primal fear.

"We welcome our honored sister," Daoshen said in the still, formal drone that was the only tone Danai ever heard him use. "You are a valuable treasure to the state, and we are grateful for the honor you have brought to our house."

Danai bowed again. "You honor me," she said.

"We understand you are preparing to leave, to return to the struggle on New Hessen. While we have enjoyed your presence here, we also admire your dedication to the Confederation's military campaigns. We are convinced you will be quite useful on New Hessen, and we look forward to reports of your future victories."

"My only desire is to add to the great glory of the Confederation and its chancellor, and I am confident that the might of the Confederation will lead to exploits that will cover the realm in glory."

She knew how artificial she sounded, and she hated herself for it. She tried, every time she saw Daoshen, to speak like she always did, to put simple sentences together like a normal human being. But instead these flowery utterances came out, matching or even topping Daoshen's own formality. She strained to control it, but she never could.

Daoshen nodded in response. "You will do well. However, before you depart, we feel compelled to offer you a warning. You have proven your abilities as a warrior repeatedly, particularly on the gaming fields of Solaris VII. The glory you have gained is great. Yet too often, it seems, the glory you obtain—the glory you seek—is glory for yourself.

"We wish to remind you that the individual cannot surpass the state. Individual glory is meaningless next to the glory of the state. Whatever triumphs you gain on New Hessen—and we remain confident that you will gain many—be sure they are for the betterment of the Confederation, not for the satisfaction of any personal goals or the acquisition of individual fame. We have seen this weakness in you, this part of you that loves the acclaim of the masses. Remember that at the end of a truly glorious battle, the victors should not be shouting your name, but the name of the Confederation."

And the name of its chancellor, Danai silently added.

"Yes, Chancellor," she said.

Daoshen stood, unfolding to his full height. His eyes glowed like coals set inside a withered skull. "For the glory of the Confederation," he intoned.

"For the glory of the Confederation," she repeated,

and bowed again. Then she was excused, so she hurried away.

The way Ilsa Centrella presented herself couldn't have been more different from Daoshen's custom-made throne room. Cushions and pillows filled every corner and horizontal surface. Steam drifted lazily from a bone teapot on a small wooden table. Even though she was reclining on a pastel blue divan and occasionally eating from a plate of biscuits, Ilsa's every move seemed to contain far more grace than Daoshen's entire chamber.

Ilsa stood as soon as Danai entered and enfolded her in a hug. Even though her features often seemed to belong on a marble statue amid some ancient ruins, she still managed to look warm and friendly when she wanted to.

She drew back from her embrace to get a good look at Danai. "Ah, Danai," she said. "High-ranking members of the Republic should die more often so we can see you."

"They should die more often just on general principle," Danai said brightly.

Ilsa cocked her head. "Not the kindest sentiment, perhaps, but not necessarily untrue." She sat back on her divan, then gestured toward the many cushions strewn across the room. "Please, find a place to sit that suits you."

Danai chose the softest silk pillow she could find. It might be a while before she had truly comfortable surroundings, and she knew she should enjoy it while she could.

"Did Daoshen put on a nice show for you?"

"Of course. Regal, imposing and self-centered. All the classic Daoshen hallmarks. And, of course, the reminder that I'm nothing and the Confederation is everything. He sure knows how to make a girl feel special."

Ilsa laughed, a gentle sound. "We all have our eccentricities, but Daoshen's aren't entirely . . . well . . . *human*. He doesn't always have an easy time attempting to deal with mere mortals."

"He should try it from our side once in a while. It's not exactly easy for us, either."

"I know," Ilsa said. "Remember, I spend much more time with him than you do. I'm fully aware of his quirks."

"Quirks," Danai said. "That sure sounds a lot nicer than 'signs of dementia.' "

Ilsa's face hardened a touch, and her resemblance to a piece of sculpture became more keen. "I know Daoshen is difficult, but remember that he is our brother and the chancellor. Remember all he has accomplished, all he has done for the Confederation. He deserves our respect—and even a little sympathy now and then."

"I suppose. You would have been proud of me, actually. I played his game very well, very respectfully."

"I'm sure you did," Ilsa said, her demeanor warming again. "And I know you'll take his advice seriously, even if his personal bearing leaves you cold."

"I'm guessing that means you know what advice he offered."

Ilsa laughed again. "Daoshen doesn't have the widest range of advice to give in the first place, and I've heard him talk about you often enough that I know his concerns."

"Fair enough. He doesn't need to worry. If all I wanted was personal glory, I'd still be on Solaris VII. The state has my loyalty."

"I know it does," Ilsa said. "Just be certain you always remember how many ways there are to serve the state. How much you have to offer."

"I'm putting my life on the line!" Danai said, growing impatient with Ilsa's echo of Daoshen's concerns about her. "What more does he—do you—want?"

"I'm not being critical, Danai. You needn't be defensive. I'm fully aware and appreciative of the risks you're taking, but you must remember that dying for the Confederation is not the only service you can give. Death, in fact, is often the easiest gift—you give your life once and it's over. There are other kinds of sacrifice, both more difficult and more lasting, that the Confederation may need. You must be willing and able to offer them when the time comes."

"I'm going to help take New Hessen," Danai said with a confused note in her voice. "What more can I offer besides my willingness to fight? What else is there to put on the line besides my life?"

"Nothing, in this battle. I simply wish to remind you that there may be others. I have complete confidence in your ability to survive this one—what concerns me is your ability to fight future battles of an entirely different nature."

Danai shook her head. "I'm sorry, Ilsa, but I don't know what you're talking about. I have a battle in front of me, and that's the one I'm going to fight. With everything I have. These 'future battles' you're talking about—I don't know what they are."

"I know," Ilsa said. "And there's little I can say here to fully prepare you for them. I simply want you to be ready to offer what is required when asked. We owe that to the Confederation. That's how the Confederation survives."

Danai still didn't understand what Ilsa was asking of her, but she knew what Ilsa wanted her to say. So she said it, if only to close off the topic.

"I am ready to offer whatever I can, whenever I can. I will always offer what is needed."

Ilsa nodded. Her expression was mostly opaque, and Danai guessed Ilsa was not entirely convinced by her vow. But for now, it was all she would get.

3 July 3135

Danai felt like a child at the end of a school term. She'd been locked up for too long with people and subject matter that she didn't necessarily care for, and now, finally, it was time to go do what she did best. What she loved. It helped that the summer air in Genève was warm, the sun was bright and the trickling of water off the snow-capped mountains down into the lake seemed audible everywhere.

Yen-lo-wang awaited. Soon she'd be back in its cockpit, going toe-to-toe with the Federated Suns. Exactly what a good Capellan warrior should be doing.

It would be a good mission. A worthy cause—taking New Hessen, a former Capellan world and a stepping-stone to the coveted planet of Tikonov and its prized 'Mech-production facilities. A direct body blow to the Federated Suns and the Davions. She couldn't wait.

She couldn't help but think of the glory that would come with the conquest of New Hessen, and of the pleasant prospect of having her name attached to such a battle. She couldn't help but remember what Daoshen and Ilsa had warned her about, but it wasn't as if she was advancing her own name at the Confederation's expense. If this worked out like it was supposed to, her personal glory would advance in lockstep with the glory of her nation. What could be wrong with that?

Daoshen might not like her perspective, but she couldn't recall Daoshen ever really enjoying anything. Deep in her mind, when she pulled up her earliest memories of her older brother, she could only picture him as stern, imposing, critical. She could not imagine him laughing. She could not imagine him doing anything for his personal enjoyment. Perhaps that made him the perfect servant of the Confederation—that was why he wanted her to be more like him.

But at present, subsuming herself into the Confederation wasn't in her nature. Danai fully supported spreading the glory of the realm, but she wasn't above having a little fun while she was at it. And in truth, even without the noble goals of reclaiming a Capellan planet and opening a route to Tikonov, Danai would have been excited by this mission. Taking a shot at the Federated Suns while she had the chance was always worth the effort.

She'd been on Terra for two months, and most of the time she hadn't had any idea of what she could do on behalf of the Confederation—or even of what she could do to amuse herself. Left to her own devices, she'd flirted with a Davion and struck up a friendship with a

Marik of the Oriente Protectorate. Neither development would please Daoshen, but thankfully she had no reason to let him know about them. Her Great-Aunt Erde had told her numerous times to make sure some parts of her life remained irrevocably hers.

"Do you want a cinnamon roll?" Nikol asked. "I want a cinnamon roll."

Nikol, the catalyst for what little fun she'd had on this planet, had come along to the DropPort to see her off. The scent of cinnamon filled the wide corridor they were passing through, and Nikol reacted the way the merchants expected her to act.

"Then get a cinnamon roll," Danai said.

"You want one?"

"No. I hate boarding with sticky fingers."

Nikol threw her a curious look. Danai shrugged.

Two minutes later, the cinnamon roll was half gone and they were near the customs line.

"Give me a bite," Danai said.

"The odor," Nikol said. "You can't fight it."

"Give me a bite!"

"What about the sticky fingers?"

"Hold it for me."

Nikol obliged.

Danai savored her bite, then turned toward the long, winding line. "Time to whip out the pass."

"Be sure to hold your nose in the air as you walk by the great unwashed masses," Nikol said. "They love that."

"The little people are grateful for my mere presence. No matter how I hold my nose."

"Little Capellan people, maybe. Little Republic people . . ."

"Good point," Danai said. "Maybe I should crawl by them."

Nikol waved her hand. "Ah, just walk. There have been so many dignitaries coming and going the past few months you'll just blend into the background."

Danai pulled herself to her full height. She arched her back a little and unbuttoned her jacket, letting it fall open. Immediately, at least ten nearby males started to gape, then quickly turned away so their stares would not be noticed.

Danai returned to her normal posture. "I *never* blend into the background," she said firmly.

Nikol laughed. "I suppose not." She grasped Danai in a quick hug. "You'd better go. If you're ever in my corner of the Inner Sphere . . ."

"Where else would I be?" Danai said. "We're neighbors."

Neither of them mentioned that, most of the time, they'd be at least several weeks' travel apart, and that they'd have little reason to run into each other. Their future meetings would be rare—if they occurred at all.

"Give 'em hell," Nikol said.

"You too," Danai replied, then turned and walked by the crowd in the customs line. She noticed one of the men who had looked at her earlier still shooting her surreptitious glances, and she aimed a broad wink at him. He reddened and turned the other way. Danai smiled back at Nikol, and Nikol shook her head and laughed again.

It was good to be back in control, Danai thought. But then she turned a corner to walk up to the DropShip. Nikol disappeared from her sight, and there was nothing she could do to keep her friend with her. Control was never total.

2

Sian Jump Point
Capellan Confederation
21 September 3135

No one should ever notice how hard he was working.

That was one of Daoshen Liao's rules of conduct. His bearing, his poise, his confidence should look effortless. The authority he gave to every word he spoke should seem completely natural. The aura he possessed should seem a part of who he was, rather than the result of a relentless effort to embody the most glorious sovereign nation in the Inner Sphere.

He owed his ancestors and his realm nothing less.

He knew there were those who sneered at him, at the way he carried himself, at the materials with which he surrounded himself. It was good to travel out of the Confederation on occasion, to directly encounter those who did not understand him, who belittled his efforts. If he spent all his time at home, he would be surrounded only by people who worshipped him and the Confederation he ruled (two things that, in truth, were one and the same). Journeys away from home allowed him to encounter such oddities as Exarch Jonah Levin, a plainspoken man whose distaste for the trappings of his office

was evident in every public gathering. At times when
Levin should pull glory into himself and bask in the wor-
ship of his people, he shrank. Or worse, he fell into
tactics of logic. Of persuasion. Of attempting to *convince*
his people to follow him.

The man's lack of dignity was appalling. Yet Daoshen
knew that several subjects of the Republic of the Sphere,
accustomed to rulers such as Levin, expected all leaders
to behave like Levin. When such people saw Daoshen,
whose every move incarnated true nobility and leadership, they did not know how to react, and so they fell
back on the reflexive contempt of those who lack understanding. They called him arrogant and they described
his surroundings as ostentatious, all because they did not
understand the true nature of power. They had never
been ruled by someone who had entirely given himself
to his position, who lived as an embodiment of the state
he served. People like Levin were so wrapped up in
politics that they had no time to *lead*. That was what
Daoshen's trappings meant. They had no personal value,
as Daoshen had no need for such luxuries. The trappings
existed to further the state, to exude the appropriate
aura, to inspire loyalty and dedication. They, like everything else about Daoshen, existed for the good of the
Confederation.

Daoshen meticulously ensured that he had proper surroundings everywhere he traveled. He had heard grum-
blings from some of the hired Terran laborers about the
work performed on his throne room, saying it would be
complete just in time for him to depart, and that, relations being what they were, Daoshen might never return
to use the room they were creating. But their complaints
only showed their ignorance.

It had taken time, but eventually the Cultural Center
became an appropriate backdrop for him. Now he was
on his executive JumpShip, in quarters whose every centimeter was designed for the effect he intended. His
quarters took up nearly the entire gravity deck, because
those who traveled with the chancellor should always

remember how the state and its leader must take priority over their own selfish desires for comfort.

The domed ceiling of his throne room was ten meters high and dotted with representations of Capellan Confederation planets—the Confederation as it should be, as it was in the days of the original Star League, not the crippled version inflicted on it by the long Succession Wars and the upstart Republic of the Sphere. Below the dome stood six black granite pillars, trapezoids that widened as they reached from floor to ceiling. The walls bore red-and-black murals of great Capellan leaders, each with a two-meter-high character naming a defining virtue of that ruler. By the throne was a picture of Daoshen's father, Sun-Tzu Liao. Next to him was the character for "rebirth." An apt reminder of all that Daoshen's father had done for the Confederation, and all the work left to Daoshen to restore the Confederation and build on his father's efforts.

A subtle chime sounded from near the ebony doors. Daoshen's posture, already stiff, did not change. Around the room, four guards dressed in styles that had not been functional for well over a thousand years shifted into an attentive stance. The layered metal of their armored skirts rattled, and their swords cut the air with unified swishes.

The doors opened and a herald in a red silk jacket with embossed yellow characters walked in.

"Ilsa Centrella, magestrix of Canopus, has come in response to a summons from the chancellor," the herald said in tones designed to reach far beyond the top of the dome.

"We are ever honored when our beloved sister comes to our presence," Daoshen replied. "She may enter."

Ilsa flowed in, and Daoshen watched her with admiration. While he could not approve of all of her actions as a ruler—the casual air of her administration reflected the laxness Daoshen believed was all too common in the Magistracy—he could not help but admire her regal air. She had the bearing of a true sovereign, and as ever, he thought her the epitome of grace. Her flowing robe displayed her straight, well-defined collarbone to good advantage, and she walked as if carried by a light breeze.

Daoshen's herald followed her, carrying a small, padded stool. The stool was a concession Daoshen still privately deplored, but after repeated gracious requests he had allowed his sister to bring her own chair to audiences with him. He knew it revealed a special preference for her, but she was his sister. He assumed any observers would understand.

A lesser ruler would dread the conversation he was about to have, but only lesser rulers allowed themselves to be overcome by the emotions of their subjects. A good ruler must care for his subjects, of course, but he must never let their feelings stand in the way of the business of state, to which everything is secondary.

"Couldn't we have done this over dinner, Daoshen?" Ilsa asked, speaking before Daoshen had a chance to begin the conversation. Several of the guards flinched, for they had heard Daoshen's vociferous reactions to breaches of etiquette in his throne room.

He surprised them all by smiling. She was his sister, and she was, in her way, magnificent. In her presence, Daoshen could afford to be tolerant.

"Matters concerning the realm are best discussed in the proper places," he said. "We are confident you understand that."

"I *understand* it, of course," Ilsa said, shifting uncomfortably on her stool. "I'd just be more comfortable elsewhere."

A long lecture about the insignificance of a ruler's personal comfort sprang into Daoshen's head, but he had delivered a similar speech to Ilsa earlier in the week, so he saved this one for later use and instead continued with business.

"We have received the latest news from New Hessen," he said. "Our troops have acquitted themselves admirably, but the numbers and nature of the opposition are larger and stronger than we expected. We have considered dedicating the appropriate resources to win the planet for the Confederation, but at present we believe other targets are more important. Therefore, we will shortly pull our troops away from the planet."

Ilsa frowned. "We lost."

Daoshen scowled. He had thought his description clear enough not to require restatement. "Our armed forces will be leaving the planet for the time being."

"How bad are our losses?"

"No more than are required."

"Daoshen!" Ilsa said, anger flaring across her face. Again, several guards flinched at this breach of etiquette; but again, Daoshen chose not to respond to it.

Ilsa calmed quickly. "I'm sorry, Lord Chancellor, but the answers you are giving me are not helpful."

"The exact numbers of our losses are not important," Daoshen said. "Those who died lost their lives for the Confederation, and there is no greater honor. The outcome as it affects the Confederation matters more than the outcome of individual lives. In this case we—as you said—lost." Daoshen spat out the last word. "But we will bring our forces off-planet and marshal them for another attack. We may not approach New Hessen again, but we will continue our progress. In the end, there can be only one result—the Confederation will advance."

"What news of Danai?"

"Danai is not accounted for," Daoshen replied.

Ilsa stayed silent for a long time. Her mouth trembled, and despite all his poise Daoshen briefly considered standing to give her comfort. He didn't, of course. A ruler did not indulge in that sort of emotional behavior.

Ilsa finally spoke. "Not accounted for?"

"She is not in the ranks and her body has not been recovered. She is not accounted for."

"She's missing."

Ilsa's need to restate the obvious grated on Daoshen's nerves. "Yes," he said through clenched teeth.

"What efforts are being made to find her?"

"None."

Ilsa stood up so fast that her stool clattered to the floor. "None? Daoshen, this is your . . . your sister!"

This was one breach too many. Daoshen stood—not quickly, like Ilsa, but slowly, unfolding himself to his full height, allowing his black robes to drape smoothly in front of him.

"Such reminders are not necessary," he said, his raspy voice swirling around the room like an aural tornado. "We know who she is. Yet we also never forget our duty. Our responsibility is to the state, not to any individual. It is not our place to risk lives to discover a single missing soldier. If *Sang-wei* Liao is worthy—and still alive—she will find her way back to the main body of troops in time to leave the planet. It is up to her. The army cannot reconsider its tactics and cannot delay its movements simply because of one soldier, no matter how high-ranking or how personally dear she may be to us."

Ilsa put her hands on her hips. " 'If' she is worthy? How dare you! You know her worth! You know her abilities! And you stand here and insinuate that if we lose her, it's her own fault—because she wasn't 'worthy'!"

Daoshen kept his calm. "We know our sister has demonstrated considerable skill on Solaris VII. Yet history has often demonstrated that skill in tournaments does not always translate to skill on the battlefield, and it certainly is no indication of skill in command. She was sent to New Hessen in part to show how well her skills can be applied to the real world. If she does not return, we will have our answer."

Ilsa pulled her chin up, and Daoshen suppressed a small shiver that tickled the base of his spine. "If this is a measure of her skill—if this is some sort of a *test*— then she will pass. She will return. She will never disappoint you."

"We certainly wish that to be the case," Daoshen said, then eased himself back down onto his throne.

Ilsa was already on her way out of the room, her gown

swaying behind her. Though Ilsa's methods differed from his, Daoshen could not help thinking, as he watched her go, that she was a queen indeed.

DropShip Sword of Justice, *New Hessen Outbound*
Federated Suns
22 September 3135

There was a shuddering, then the slow lifting as an enormous weight pulled itself into the sky. The speed increased, and Danai was pushed into her chair. She felt a heavy weight on her chest, but the g-force had nothing to do with that—she'd been feeling that for days.

She wanted to forget. To forget the whole series of events. She had come with such high hopes . . .

It wouldn't be much—she'd just have to erase a few months of memory, to find a way never to think of it again. Then she could proceed as if her defeat—her entire series of defeats—had never happened.

It was impossible. Everything, every moment, was seared into her memory, as easy to replay as a holovid. Easier, even—over the past few days, it had often replayed without her intent. It was starting again now.

She saw Caleb and his knife. She heard the battle crashing around them. She felt the warehouse floor under her back, felt Caleb pawing her . . .

When she came back to her senses, the ship had left New Hessen's pull. Her skin felt clammy and she was shaking in her seat. But she was gone. Away from that planet.

Except for the part of her that would never leave New Hessen.

She took a shuddering breath. She knew she couldn't continue like this for long. Her Great-Aunt Erde had long ago taught her the futility of evading herself. There was, her great-aunt had told her solemnly, an old saying with much truth to it: "No matter where you go, there you are." To a young Danai, the words had sounded like nonsense. She now knew that was intentional, that her great-aunt had found it amusing to plant wisdom in a silly phrase. Erde had meant that you can run and run, but you can never escape yourself. Cross a star system or two or a hundred, move as fast as your legs or a Kearny-Fuchida drive could carry you, but the moment you look in a mirror—well, there you are.

She would face it someday. She would take Caleb's violation of her and find a way to live with it, to move beyond pain and hurt and anger and make herself whole again. And then she would castrate the Davion son of a bitch.

She would do it soon. Just not today.

The DropShip moved toward its rendezvous point, where it would dock with the JumpShip that would take Danai home so she could stand in front of her brother the chancellor and tell him how badly she had been beaten.

3

Danai had been traveling for four weeks, and she had spent very little of that time outside her own quarters. There had been debriefings, of course, and a medical checkup (thank God for rank, Danai had thought during the visit to the doctor—the poor med had meekly suggested that maybe someone else should know about what he was seeing, but Danai snapped at him to mind his own business and swore him to secrecy on the name of her brother the chancellor). Other than that, she had stayed secluded. She accepted no invitations to other quarters and she invited no one to hers.

Any passersby who knew of her self-imposed isolation might have been surprised to hear a voice coming from her quarters almost constantly. It spoke in a long monologue, sometimes full of sorrow, other times bursting with rage, still other times managing only to sound befuddled.

Danai had spent the entire journey to the New Hessen jump point recording, editing and rerecording a holovid for her Great-Aunt Erde.

The editing was principally for clarity as she tried to ensure that what she was attempting to say came across. She didn't remove parts that might make her look bad, or weak, or vulnerable. She wasn't making the holovid to put forward a brave face, to tell Erde that everything was okay. She was making it so she could say out loud all the thoughts that were racing around inside her head and try to communicate them to the only person who might understand them.

She found organizing, cutting and rerecording her thoughts painful, especially having to watch herself in the video looking so weak and scared. The words came out of the holovid like bursts from a needler, each sentence a nest of stings. But she hadn't flinched while she said it all, and so she didn't flinch when she played isolated snippets, trying to find a way to integrate them into something coherent.

" . . . and I just lay there, and I struggled a little, of course, but not enough, I didn't fight hard enough, and I tell myself now that it was because he had a knife and I wasn't armed, but since when was a *knife* enough to paralyze me? And when it was over, he walked away. I let him walk away! He should have been lying on the ground, rolling in pain, his hand grabbing for the bloody mess where his balls used to be. But he walked away, and I just whimpered on the ground like some damned *dog*. How could I?"

"Daoshen will never feel any blame for what happened on New Hessen. It's not in his nature. He would never admit to any mistake, especially a military mistake, so in his final evaluation, he will come off as exemplary. As always. So who gets the blame? Me. I'm sure of it. I could try to apply to him, saying I'm sorry we couldn't deal with the Swordsworn when they came in to help out, but gosh, I was busy being raped at the time, but will he care? Will it make any difference? Of course not."

"I see it now, the nature of men, more clearly than I ever did. Not that I ever doubted you, Erde. I always believed what you said, and of course I've had plenty of chances to see the baser instincts of men at work. And sometimes those instincts work out well for us. But I'd never seen it like I saw it in Caleb . . . his complete and total *weakness*. A slave to his instinct and passions. Barely above an *animal*. Everything that's flawed about his gender. But somehow, he and his kind convince so many realms that they, not women, deserve to reign, simply by virtue of their viciousness. When, how, when did savagery become a virtue?"

"I know. I know, I know, I know. I know who to blame for this. I know who did this. But still, I know what I did, what I didn't do. I know my mistakes. I didn't fight hard enough. And I flirted with him, and I was—well, wasn't there a time when maybe that was where I wanted things to go? So they went there. Isn't that, isn't some of that, my fault?"

She had watched that last part, frozen the playback, walked into her lavatory and thrown up. Her own image revolted her. She wanted to grab the floating duplicate of herself and shake some sense into it. Such a mewling little *victim*. So pathetic.

The recording and editing process continued until the first jump to Buchlau. While the JumpShip was recharging, Danai made arrangements with a courier she trusted to get the holovid to Sian. She encrypted it using every technique she knew to make sure Erde was the only one who would see it, then she let it go. And it was gone.

For a day or two after she sent it off, she kept thinking of something else to say, something she should have added or something she should have expressed differently. But before long she resigned herself to the fact that she could make no more changes. The final holovid was what it was. Now she had to do something else with her time.

It took a few days before she felt like leaving her quarters, but after spending enough time walking in small circles around her berth, she finally got stir crazy.

So four weeks after leaving New Hessen, as her JumpShip sat recharging in the Ningpo system, Danai left her quarters to see what else the ship contained.

After a quick walk, she already missed the private JumpShips she'd taken to and from Terra. Military JumpShips seemed to carry four times as many people, with an equivalent reduction in amenities. This ship had no five-star restaurant on board—instead, it had a military mess and an officers' club. Since she felt more like drinking than eating, she headed for the officers' club.

Most of the JumpShip's interior looked utilitarian. Pipes and vents were left exposed, metal handrails were painted primer gray, and most of the walls were actually wire-mesh fences. The echoing voices of soldiers two or three decks away, and the noise of them pulling themselves along the handrails toward the gravity deck, sounded as if they were right behind her, making the near-empty corridors seem crowded with ghosts.

She returned the salutes of the few soldiers she passed without saying anything, or even glancing in their direction. After a few more turns and an ascent up a narrow staircase, she stood at the hatch of the officers' club. She took a deep breath and walked in.

The club was nicer than the ship's corridors, but still far from luxurious—this was a Capellan military vessel, not a Canopian pleasure circus. The bar was dark stone on burnished gray metal, brown industrial carpeting covered the floor and the chairs had black padding on the seats but only hard metal on the backs. Danai found an empty table near the bar and waited for someone to bring her liquor.

A young man in a black jacket buttoned up to his chin walked over. "How may I serve you?" he murmured. The club was only a quarter full and quiet, so she heard him easily.

"Mao-tai. Straight," she said. "Make it a double."

The waiter bowed quickly and walked behind the bar. He was back in thirty seconds with a glass half full of dark brown liquid.

Danai's hand jumped toward the glass. She wanted to

throw every last drop of the liquor down her throat in a single, pleasurable gulp. The alcohol content of mao-tai, however, made that seem like a bad idea unless she wanted to spend her first moments out of her cabin plastered on the floor of the officers' club. The last thing she needed was humiliation, so she contented herself with a good sip.

The drink tasted a little salty, a little sweet, a little earthy and quite fermented. The alcohol went right to work in her system, and she felt mild goodwill toward the universe. She hadn't felt that way in a month.

It wasn't right. She shouldn't feel good. She took another sip, then another. She didn't want to down the drink too quickly, but she was anxious to get to the part of inebriation where she became belligerent and angry.

A shadow fell across her table. She didn't look up. The shadow didn't move. She hoped it was just the waiter hovering nearby, and that he'd move soon.

A voice, a little raspy and edged with amusement, addressed her. "Insert cheesy pickup line here."

The words were so odd that Danai couldn't help but look up. A man with black hair, green eyes and a cocky, sideways grin stood over her. His face was narrow and convex, as if a normal head had been put in a large vise and squeezed. The blue triangle on his shoulder indicated that he was a *sang-wei*, like her.

"Pardon?" she said.

"That's all I've got," he said. "I thought of a bunch of lines, but they all sounded stupid to me, and I couldn't choose between them. So I thought maybe you could pick for me. Just pick a stupid pickup line, pretend I said it and then we'll move on."

"Go away," she said.

"That's it!" he exclaimed. "That's the spirit! Right, that's exactly what you'd do. Now, I grin my charming grin"—he grinned, apparently attempting to turn on the charm—"and I apologize for being inept, but then I say it must mean something if I was willing to look so idiotic just to meet you. That has to be worth something, right?"

"Go away," Danai repeated.

The man frowned. "Hmm. Okay, disarming honesty didn't work. How about . . ."

Danai stood quickly. Her chair toppled onto the carpet. She pounded the table with her fist. The metal top rang.

"Go *away!*" she yelled.

All noise stopped. All eyes looked at Danai. She righted her chair, sat back down and stared at her drink, but didn't grab it because her hands were still clenched into fists. *Ah, there it is*, she thought. *There's the belligerence I've been waiting for. The mao-tai's doing its work.*

She listened to the ragged rhythm of her breath and stared at a single bead of water running down her glass. She didn't see the man leave, but she assumed he didn't stay long after her outburst. She also didn't know how long the other people in the club stared at her, and she didn't care.

She sat for a while, her back hunching more and more until she was slumped on the table. She felt nauseous, stiff and angry, but at least she was out of her berth. She knew this was supposed to represent progress, but she couldn't remember why.

13 October 3135

She eventually drank herself into oblivion, which, she finally recalled, had been the point of the endeavor. Or at least, if it hadn't been the point when she entered the club, it quickly became the point when the first drops of mao-tai rolled over her tongue. She'd made it back to her berth somehow, collapsed on her bunk, plunged into unconsciousness and stayed there for a good, long time.

It had worked so well that Danai was tempted to repeat the whole performance today, but she had two good reasons not to. First, drinking herself into a stupor didn't conform to her great-aunt's advice about confronting problems head-on. Second, she had a briefing to attend, and it wouldn't do to be tipsy. Being hung over was bad enough, but she was pretty sure she'd manage to lick the worst of the headache by the time the eleven o'clock briefing began.

Sure enough, when eleven o'clock rolled around, Danai's mind felt fairly sharp, though still veiled by a difficult-to-locate ache. It would be enough to get through the meeting.

The briefing room wasn't far from the officers' club, and she felt a slight twinge when she passed the club entrance. But she soldiered on.

The briefing room held about a dozen people, most of whom she knew quite well, along with a few new faces. One of them was the dark-haired man from the club last night. He didn't look at her when she entered, so she didn't bother to look at him.

Chairs sat around a white holovid projector, and Danai found a place between two of her fellow officers. She nodded politely at each one but did not exchange pleasantries.

Sao-shao Leong entered the room and commenced the briefing without wasting a moment on small talk. At other times Danai had found Leong's businesslike air off-putting, but today she felt grateful for his direct approach.

"The Confederation's military has been busy since our involvement on New Hessen," Leong began in his deep monotone. "Our journey should provide all the rest we will need, for it seems likely we will all be thrown back into action shortly. McCarron's Armored Cavalry is never left to rest for long."

He turned on the holovid, and an image of the systems in the Inner Sphere appeared. Most of the planets were navy blue, dim and hard to see. Capellan planets, by contrast, showed up in bright red.

Danai saw it immediately. The shape of the Confederation had changed, extended on the coreward side. Daoshen had been on the move.

Of course, she couldn't be sure what criteria were used to mark a planet as Capellan on the map. Knowing

Daoshen, it might mean nothing more than that someone of Capellan blood had managed to land on the planet and stay alive for longer than a week.

"The military buildup enabled by the chancellor has come to fruition," Leong said. "We have launched attacks across our coreward border, and seen success on almost all fronts. Ningpo is ours. Genoa, Algol, Azha, Slocum, Acamar and Nanking have been hit, and all are bound to fall." As Leong spoke, the holovid of the Inner Sphere seemed to move forward, planets growing larger as the image zoomed in on the recently expanded border of the Confederation. The scope of the offensive impressed Danai, as it struck much closer to the heart of the Republic than she had thought possible.

"What was once Prefecture V of the Republic of the Sphere is increasingly returning to our hands, where it should have been all these years," Leong said. "These attacks are largely the natural result of the chancellor's efforts, and the events of yesterday will only encourage our own efforts to rebuild our nation. Most of you have not seen this yet. I urge all of you to pay close attention to an announcement that was recently released across the Inner Sphere."

The image of a planet blinked away, replaced by Exarch Jonah Levin of the Republic of the Sphere. His face looked drawn, his eyes exhausted. *Just the way he should look*, Danai thought.

Still, as Levin spoke, Danai felt a peculiar sympathy for him. He had inherited a mess not of his own making. Enemies on all sides were closing in on a state that never should have existed. The Republic was an oddity, an anomaly, and soon it would be nothing more than a blip in recorded history. Yet Levin clearly cared for it, obviously hoped that somehow it might still have a future. She could imagine what it felt like to have huge portions of your nation seized out from under you—as a Capellan, she was all too familiar with that feeling.

The content of the speech amazed her. The Republic was in full retreat, locking down in its core. Crawling into its shell like a turtle. The vulnerability of all the planets not included in that shell left a gaping void, and Danai fully expected Daoshen to rush headfirst into the opening left by the Republic's weakness.

Levin finished speaking and his image disappeared. The map, still zoomed on the volatile Capellan-Republic border, reappeared.

"Do not let this speech deceive you," Leong said. "The Republic may be concentrating forces inside its core, but the remaining planets are far from defenseless. By all appearances there simply was not enough time to pull all forces into the core, even had Levin wanted everything beyond the core to be abandoned. Many forces, some of them elite, remain, and they seem determined to preserve what scraps of the Republic are in their possession.

"They will make staunch foes, but weakened ones. The chancellor intends to use this opportunity to take back what the Confederation never should have lost. You will all be a part of this effort. Specific assignments will be forthcoming shortly.

"Officers should maintain the following protocols as we draw nearer to battle territory. First, all enlisted personnel should . . ."

Danai let Leong's voice gradually fade from her consciousness as she stared at the map. Her brain shifted gears, and all the hours she had spent studying tactics in the academy and on the battlefield became useful. The planets, she thought, would tell far more about Daoshen's plans than Leong would, and the cold act of analyzing them would make a welcome change from what she had been doing up to this point on the journey away from New Hessen.

It didn't take her long to see it. The pivotal acquisition seemed to be Nanking. The other planets being attacked might be nothing more than stepping stones to that prize, a planet with 'Mech production facilities that lay quite close to the border of Prefecture X—the border behind which, according to Levin, the Republic had sealed itself.

With Nanking and the other nearby planets in hand,

much of Prefecture VI would be vulnerable. A small pocket of a half-dozen planets scattered around New Aragon could be isolated, left to wither until they finally surrendered. The Confederation could reclaim worlds such as Aldebaran and Zurich, worlds that rightly belonged to it, worlds that had played a crucial role in the rise of the Liaos and of the Capellan state. Then, with so much of the Republic of the Sphere in his pocket, Daoshen could once again take aim at the prize that, due in part to Danai's failure at New Hessen, currently lay out of reach—Tikonov. The current offensive push, if sustained, could net the Confederation two prized 'Mech-production facilities.

As she pondered the map, grasping what Daoshen must be up to, she felt like fighting again for the first time in a month. She wanted to climb into Yen-lo-wang's cockpit and take part in this wave of attacks, to take back planets that had a deep connection and long history with the Confederation and with House Liao. She could see herself on the battlefield, envision herself pushing her enemies—the enemies of the Confederation—back, watching them stumble under the force of her charge, watching them flee. She could, for the first time on this particular journey, imagine circumstances where she wasn't being overwhelmed. Where she was victorious. The vision of conquest had a tenuous hold in her mind, and she saw dark edges around it as other forces gathered to cloud the image into darkness. But she could see it now, and she would hold on to it as long as she could.

Returning her attention to the map, Danai noticed at least two big hitches in Daoshen's plan, or at least in the version of it she had cobbled together. First, going toward New Canton would mean opening up a new front in the war, and that often led to trouble, even against a foe as battered and disorganized as the Republic. Second, New Canton still contained a strong military presence, including the Triarii Protectors. Sometimes scorned as nothing more than a colorful parade unit, the Triarii were nevertheless highly disciplined, and each prefecture's regiment was led by some of the most promising minds churned out by the Republic's military academies. New Canton lay only a jump away from Zurich and Aldebaran, two jumps from Nanking. Any move toward New Canton would bring out the Triarii, and that would keep the invading troops occupied. If the battle didn't go Daoshen's way, he might even end up losing Nanking, as the Triarii would surely press him as far back as they could if they gained any advantage. Daoshen might want to reclaim Zurich and Aldebaran, but those battles would likely have to wait.

Danai saw several possible solutions to the problem, but at the moment, based on the limited information emanating through Leong's drone, she couldn't pinpoint which option Daoshen might choose. Whatever he decided, though, she would be a part of it. She'd see to it.

The briefing ended and Danai joined the others filing out, her head high. The dark-haired man from the previous evening slipped into line just behind her. She kept her gaze locked ahead, straining to believe that nothing out of her line of sight actually existed.

"Look," he said, in open defiance of her attempts to deny his existence, "I'm sorry about yesterday. If I had known you didn't want to talk, I wouldn't have talked. I was just, you know, being sociable. I just saw you and thought I should . . . well, don't get the wrong idea, it wasn't all just that you looked good or anything—not that you *didn't* look good . . ."

This will end, Danai thought. *This will end right now.* She turned and held up her palm. "Stop," she said.

The man stopped.

"Talking doesn't seem to work for you," she said. "Try something else."

The man furrowed his brow. "Like . . ."

"See, you're talking again. Try *anything* but that." She turned and walked away.

The dark cloud in her brain had fallen, and her vision dimmed. She didn't hear anyone behind her, and she was grateful. If the dark-haired man kept after her, he'd end up with a broken neck in short order.

She remembered the DropPort on Terra, walking past

the disgruntled travelers, making them look at her. She had sought the attention, courted it, and that certainly hadn't been the first time in her life. Slender, teenaged females in the Magistracy of Canopus don't have to look far for people willing to pay attention to them. But now the thought of someone looking at her turned her stomach. She wanted to kill the dark-haired man, or herself. Or both. Or neither.

She'd be better off alone right now.

4

It was the blackest night Legate Sophia Juk had ever
seen. Aldebaran's moon was dark, and somehow even
the stars seemed to have dimmed. She had always drawn
reassurance from the stars, from the knowledge that a
mighty nation surrounded her. Now, as the Republic
seemed to be flaming out, everything else in the Inner
Sphere seemed to be fading as well. Every celestial body
for hundreds of light-years was slipping into a common
blackness.

At least Aldebaran was relatively calm. There had
been minor disturbances and a few demonstrations, all
quite understandable in the light of recent events. Most
of those events had slacked off in the past few days, as
the planet's population settled into stunned inaction.

On nearby Zurich, things were much worse. Full-scale
rioting, some of which placed members of the planetary
militia on the side of the insurgents, consumed much of
the planet. A large portion of the population had given
in to the sense of betrayal that had followed Exarch
Levin's announcement of the closure of Prefecture X,

and for two weeks had let themselves become rage personified.

Governor Melvin Gulvoin had tried to keep the peace, making continuous media appearances and dispatching his planetary militia anywhere and everywhere trouble broke out. But no one was watching the news anymore, and the militia had its hands full battling itself. They had little time to spare for anyone else. The last straw was the death of Legate Corl Burton at the hands of his own personal secretary. Shortly after that, Gulvoin went into hiding. His last known order was sending an envoy, Lieutenant Governor Ferdinand Cuyos, to Aldebaran for a "strategic planning session." Legate Juk had little doubt that the meeting would be nothing more than a long plea for help.

The envoy had landed only fifteen minutes ago, and Juk was immediately summoned out of bed to the governor's mansion. Her close-cropped hair required little maintenance, and she always had at least one uniform pressed and ready to go, so she managed to be on the move within minutes of her summons.

She didn't know why the meeting had to take place so quickly—even if Aldebaran had substantial help to offer, it wouldn't arrive on Zurich for more than a week. Would it make that much difference if the meeting were delayed until morning?

She hated herself for the thought. If her home were going up in flames, she wouldn't want to wait a single moment to work on the problem. It didn't matter if hurrying would help get the problem solved; it would be better than sitting around.

Her driver pulled into the large circular drive in front of the mansion. The governor's house looked like a block of iron that had been heated and then pummeled with gigantic sledgehammers. A few windows were visible here and there, but for the most part the facade was odd angles and drooping metal. Sophia had been here several times, but it always took her a moment to remember where the main door was.

Once she found the door, she had to wait in front of

it for a moment while cameras verified her identity. Then the door slid open.

She went through two more security checkpoints before she was admitted to a windowless room somewhere in the bowels of the mansion. She'd had to ride two elevators to get there, one up, one down, so she was never sure if she had ended up above or under the ground.

The room was a simple oval, lit by a glowing tube that circled the ceiling. Four large screens, one on each wall, played constant updates of news, troop locations, and—in case the governor cared—stock and commodities prices. A heavily lacquered black table took up most of the floor space.

Governor Sampson, flanked by two aides, sat at the head of the table. What hair he had was smooth and moussed, his shirt was wrinkle-free and his eyes looked alert.

Seated to Sophia's right was a short man with black, slicked-back hair. He sat absolutely still—Sophia assumed he was breathing, but she had no way to be sure.

Sampson stood as she entered. "Legate Juk," he said. "This is Lieutenant Governor Cuyos of Zurich. I'm sure you know why he's here, so I'll dispense with introductory matters and allow Mr. Cuyos to get to business."

"Thank you, Governor," Cuyos said. Sophia had to lean forward to hear him. "I wish I could report that the situation on my planet has improved. While the rioting seems to have calmed for the moment, the governor believes that's only because the rioters have run out of targets. Much of the planet still remains outside government control. Our militia is next to powerless—many troops have rebelled, others have simply gone home. In short, Governor Sampson, Zurich is rapidly falling into anarchy. We need aid."

"That much is clear," Sampson said in his customary even tones. "What I have difficulty understanding is why you are here instead of in the capital. Surely they are the ones who should organize the distribution of troops in the prefecture. We have only our own militia at our disposal, and we face the same concerns as you, if not to the same extent. It would not seem wise to part with any of our forces at present. I'm sure you understand."

In the blink of an eye, Cuyos lost his composure. He jumped to his feet, and his chair rolled backward into the wall. He waved his arms, and for the first time Sophia noticed sweat stains on the armpits of his jacket.

"Understand?" he yelled. "I understand that the house I grew up in, my family's house, burned to the ground the day I left my planet! I understand that hundreds of my people are dying every day! And I understand that *there is no more Republic*! At the very least there is no more Prefecture VI! New Canton is the capital of *nothing*! I came to you because we are neighbors. If we do not act together in this universe, both of us will fall. We *need* your help. We are your countrymen. We are your friends. And we are falling apart."

Sophia was impressed at Cuyos' passion, but it did not change a thing. In the time it would take for reinforcements to get from Aldebaran to Zurich, the rioting on Zurich could end while new tension broke out on Aldebaran, and the militia would be more than a week away from being able to come back and help. Nothing could be spared.

The governor sat quietly as Cuyos stood over him, panting. Sophia saw no sign that anything Cuyos had said registered with Sampson. He certainly didn't appear swayed.

The silence stretched into discomfort. Cuyos' breathing evened out. He wiped sweat from his brow, looked at Sophia, then back at Sampson. Then he slowly reached back for his chair, rolled it forward and sat down.

Sampson did not speak until Cuyos was firmly in his chair, and when he did his tone was unchanged. "I admire your passion on behalf of your people. As you might imagine, I have the same loyalty to the people I serve, and you must understand that I am required to take care of my people first. With the many threats that surround us, it would be criminally irresponsible of me to remove security from my planet."

Cuyos' head drooped, but Sampson was not yet done. "However, allow me to point out that there are other ways we may assist you besides sending troops. Permit me the rest of the night to gather some of these resources, and in the morning we can talk more specifically about what we can offer you and the best way to move our contributions to Zurich."

Cuyos nodded. "Thank you," he said, his voice returning to a thin whisper. "We will talk in the morning."

A young lady in a gray jacket and black skirt walked into the room, summoned by some signal sent out by Sampson. "Quarters have been prepared for you," Sampson told Cuyos. "Lira will show you to your rooms."

Cuyos nodded silently, then shuffled out of the room. His body looked weary enough to sleep for an entire day, but his eyes seemed too haunted to allow even a moment's rest.

Sophia, knowing Governor Sampson liked to have an extra word after most such meetings, remained in her chair. Even if Sampson had nothing more to say to her, she had at least one thing to say to him.

Sampson spoke as soon as the door closed.

"I apologize for calling you out at this hour," he said. "You may think I could have handled this matter on my own, and you may be correct. However, whenever I make pronouncements about the state of the planetary militia, I feel it's wise to have the legate present so that we may demonstrate a unified front. All this is to say that, though you may not have spoken at the meeting, I found your presence valuable."

"Thank you, Governor. And I was happy to present a 'unified front' with you, since I agree with what you said—we can't send our military anywhere."

"Indeed. The situation here is stable, but tenuous. It's best not to tempt fate."

"It's more than just internal trouble," Sophia said. "It's worse than that. We're going to be invaded."

A small crack appeared in Sampson's normally composed face, a sight Sophia rarely saw. It was nothing more than a small tic, a twitching in his cheek, and then his expression returned to normal.

"Do you have some intelligence information I'm not yet privy to?" he asked.

"Nothing specific, no," Sophia said. "But it's only a matter of time. Daoshen Liao has taken Nanking. He's right on the border of the Republic's new iron curtain, and no one's come out to cause him any trouble. The exarch made it clear that no one's to cross his new border, but it's equally clear that no one's coming out.

"So Liao's got position. What's he going to do with it? Take New Canton. And the best way to do that is to go through us. The Capellans are coming. I just don't know when."

"Are we strong enough to withstand them?" Sampson asked.

Sophia stifled the urge to laugh at the question. "I have total faith in the loyalty, skill and determination of our militia. But before things fell apart, we weren't a border world. Our forces were never designed to withstand an invasion, especially from one of the major Houses of the Inner Sphere. If they come—when they come—we will give them a battle. But on our own, we won't win it."

Then, for the first time, Sophia saw Sampson's composure break completely. His posture sagged, his chin drooped and he ran his hand through the tuft of hair over his left ear, leaving it bedraggled.

"We are completely on our own. There is no help available." Sampson's voice, normally calm and aristocratic, had become a low, flat drone. "You heard about the conditions on Zurich—they will be no help. If we approach our neighbors like Cuyos approached us, we'll get the same response—they'll be apologetic, but they'll tell us they need to look out for their own. Our only hope was New Canton, but I can't believe they'll send aid. Nanking received nothing, and I have no reason to believe we would be any different. We'll be left alone."

"We need to at least *ask*," Sophia said. "There still is a Republic, no matter what Cuyos thinks. New Canton is still the capital of the prefecture. They still owe it to us to participate in our defense."

"They owed it to Nanking, too," Sampson said flatly.

"Then we can argue it's in their self-interest to send aid. They're going to have enemies at their doorstep sooner or later. If it's not the Capellans, it could be the Oriente Protectorate. They might as well put up a fight here, with the help of our militia, rather than wait for enemy forces to land on New Canton, where they'll have to battle them without our help. They leave us alone, they'll just be leaving an open road that the Capellans or the Protectorate will run over to get to them."

Sampson sighed. "That argument would persuade me," he said. "I'm just not convinced it will persuade them."

"We have to at least *try*!" Sophia said. "We can't just sit here, waiting, not looking for help!"

Sampson's shoulders briefly moved up and down in a weary shrug. "Do what you will," he said. "Find help if you can." But he already looked defeated.

20 October 3135

The first DropShip of the morning, the merchant ship *Brigham's Wagon*, was scheduled to leave at 5:20. Chaos was increasing across the Republic as its borders collapsed, but that didn't remove the need for trade—if anything, the demand for goods to be shipped from planet to planet only grew as military activity increased and people kept seeking safe havens.

It was already five o'clock, and the captain of the ship wasn't in his command chair. He wasn't even on the ship. He looked at his watch, then at the ship, then at his watch again. Three seconds had passed. Time might be moving slowly, but there was still no way the launch would take place on time.

The captain wished the delay had a single cause, because then he would have a clear target to yell at. But everything seemed to be dragging behind in unison—the last shipment of crates had arrived late, ship's maintenance was behind schedule and three members of his crew were in their bunks, rolling around in the grip of a nasty virus. And he couldn't really yell at the virus, could he?

He was left to sit in the captain's lounge of the DropShip port and watch a holovid 'Mech joust in which he had no real interest. He couldn't even have a drink, as that sort of thing just before liftoff was frowned upon. Two other people were in the lounge, but both of them seemed to have just finished a trip instead of being on the verge of starting one, and they looked quite content to drink alone and talk to no one.

The lounge door slid open with a squeak. *Someone should oil the damn thing,* the captain thought, turning toward the door because whatever entered was bound to be more interesting than the holovid.

Or maybe not. It was just a couple of gorillas in militia uniforms. The captain thought about asking them how they got clearance to enter the lounge, but then decided not to bother. Military people usually could get clearance for any place they wanted to go.

The uniformed men kept their hands on their sidearms as they entered. They positioned themselves on either side of the door and made a quick visual scan of the room. Then one of them poked his head back through the door and nodded once.

The next person who entered was immediately the most interesting thing in the lounge. By a wide margin. She sported a more formal version of the uniform worn by her escorts, gold braids on her shoulder where the others simply had red bands. Streaks of gray ran through her short black hair, and her oval face was composed. She looked singularly unintimidating, unless you took account of the fact that she had the entire planetary militia at her command.

Legate Sophia Juk was moving briskly and decisively, heading right for the captain. An impulse to run came over him, but he had nowhere to go. He imagined that was part of the reason Juk had brought her two companions. Not knowing what else to do, he stood.

Juk started talking before she stopped walking. "Captain," she said. "I have a data chip for you. You will take it with you to New Canton and bring it to Prefecture VI Military Command. Give the chip to the guards at the entrance, but don't let it out of your sight. As soon as they've given it an initial scan, they'll summon Edmund Barkes." She anticipated his question before he could speak, raising her hand to tell him not to interrupt. "Never mind who he is. He'll meet you at the entrance. You can turn the chip over to him.

"Now, some things you should know. If you refuse this mission, you'll be placed under arrest for treason. Do not attempt to read the chip on your own—you won't be able to crack it, and if you try, I'll find out, and you'll never be able to enter this system again. That's the stick. Here's the carrot—once Barkes has the chip, ten thousand C-bills will be transferred into your account as payment for your service."

She pressed the chip into his hands. "Aldebaran thanks you."

She turned away abruptly, obviously not interested in anything the captain had to say. He knew he should remain silent, knew he wasn't supposed to know anything about what was in the chip. But he couldn't keep the words from flowing out of his mouth.

"What is this?" he asked.

Legate Juk didn't turn back or break stride. "A fool's hope," she said, then led her two soldiers out of the lounge.

The captain squeezed the chip with white knuckles. Now he had something he could curse at.

5

Lianyungang, Liao
Capellan Confederation
1 November 3135

If there was anything worse than being humiliated by a commanding officer, it was waiting to be humiliated.

Sang-shao Shaiming Tao, commander of the Second McCarron's Armored Cavalry, had summoned Danai as soon as she had disembarked. She was fairly certain he'd be meeting with all the senior officers, but as she walked out of the DropPort, she looked at the other officers and none of them seemed in a hurry to get anywhere. She'd made it to the head of Tao's interview list, and she didn't think that was a good place to be.

She had been ready for Tao to tear into her as soon as she entered his office, but instead he made her wait while he studied something on his noteputer. She looked around the office a few times, taking in the tapestry depicting a Davion-Capellan conflict from the Fourth Succession War, a sadly neglected Zen garden, and several military and history texts, all bound in red leather covers. Even after she lost interest in her surroundings, Tao still stared silently at his noteputer. His expression hadn't changed since Danai entered, and that wasn't good. His broad forehead was deeply creased, and he had drawn the tips of his eyebrows so close together that they almost touched. The right side of his narrow mouth drooped farther than the left, seeming ready to wrap around his jaw. The effect was accentuated by the fact that Tao had very little chin space.

Finally he looked up. "*Sang-wei* Liao-Centrella. I am pleased to see you healthy."

Danai couldn't help but note that Tao did not say, "Thank you for coming," "Welcome back," or any such niceties. He was happy she wasn't dead, but that seemed to be as much enthusiasm as he could muster.

"I have a complete report of the activities on New Hessen," Tao said. "While I am not convinced the loss there merits disciplinary action, I am disappointed. More than disappointed." The volume of his voice started climbing. "Caught from behind. From *behind*! You realize, don't you, that your 'Mech is equipped with *sensors*! You allowed yourself to get sloppy. Careless!"

Danai let her head sink, a combination of real shame and a desire to put on the appearance of shame. It didn't seem to help. Tao's lecture continued.

"Avoiding rescue simply to find your 'Mech! Yes, your machine is a precious item, but is abandoning your duty to reclaim it the best way to serve the Confederation? Or is it another example of you putting personal preferences before the good of the state?"

Danai assumed the question was rhetorical, and didn't answer. She could have responded, though, at length and with eloquence. Yen-lo-wang was not just a simple machine, and even calling it a "precious item" was a grievous understatement. It was a gift, a gift bequeathed to her by a legend who had believed in her potential when she was barely more than a toddler. It was a 'Mech she'd given a year of her life to make just right, a year where she'd traveled to parts of the Inner Sphere no one knew she'd been to and met with people no one knew she'd talked to. People who never would have spoken with her if she wasn't piloting Yen-lo-wang. After all that, how could she ever consider abandoning it?

But she hadn't told anyone the details of how she'd made her machine what it was, and she wasn't going to let Tao be the first to hear the story. She sat silent and let him talk.

"And then leaving the planet. Fleeing. With nothing. Your mission was a complete failure, and the road to Tikonov is more difficult to traverse than ever. All the loss of life and equipment meant nothing."

So now Danai was to be held responsible for the actions of Erik Sandoval-Groell in declaring for House Davion and bringing the Swordsworn to New Hessen. The interview was going even worse than she had expected.

"As I said previously, while your mission was clearly deeply flawed, I do not believe there was anything in your actions requiring discipline. However, there was also not anything in your actions that deserves this." He pointed to his noteputer. "This order arrived just before you did. From the chancellor himself. You are to be promoted."

Danai blinked, then blinked again. Perhaps, she thought, Tao had suddenly switched to another language, one where "promoted" meant "severely punished." She sat quietly, waiting for him to explain what this "promotion" entailed.

But Tao wasn't in the mood to spill any details right away. "I want you to understand that this is not my doing. I am following my orders, but without those orders a promotion for you would be the last thing on my mind. Is that clear?"

"Yes, *Sang-shao*," Danai said, feeling impressed and mortified at the same time. It was quite rare for high-ranking Capellan officers to show anything other than total unity with their superiors. For Tao to feel he had to underline his disagreement with the orders meant he had a lot of independence for a Capellan officer (something MAC officers had assumed ever since their mercenary days)—and also that he was extremely upset with her. She'd have been angrier about his disapproval, except that she agreed with it.

"You are being raised to the rank of *sao-shao*. Third Battalion is yours."

"Thank—" The words died on Danai's lips. After what Tao had just said, thanking him for the promotion didn't seem appropriate.

"You have little time," Tao continued, ignoring her aborted attempt at speech. "Chancellor Liao also orders you to prepare an attack."

"Yes, *Sang-shao*. Where?"

"Aldebaran. You are to choose two warriors to join you in your command lance, plan your attack and depart as quickly as possible. Your orders are simple—invade and secure Aldebaran for the Confederation. Understood?"

"Yes, sir—except for one thing. Why only two others in my command lance?"

"Because a third member has been chosen for you. You need someone who has experience with the Third Battalion, who knows its members and capabilities. *Sang-wei* Jacyn Bell has been assigned to serve in that capacity, to ease your transition into the unit. He knows the battalion quite well, and is considerably skilled. He will be an asset to your lance."

Jacyn Bell—it was a name Danai thought she had heard, but she couldn't recall if she had ever seen his face. She thought she had heard mostly positive things about his skills, which hopefully would make up for any inherent male weakness he brought into the command.

Tao stood, and Danai moved quickly to her feet as well.

"Rewarding failure is not the way of the Confederation." Then, abruptly, his voice softened. "The main consolation I have in presenting you with this promotion is that you have shown your worth in the past year. You are a capable warrior. My concerns about this promotion are tied to its timing, not to any doubts about your abilities. I have hopes you will grow into your position, and I'm sure I do not need to tell you that the chancellor's impatience for failure far outstrips my own. He has high expectations of you—though I trust he has made that known to you over the years. You know what you must live up to. You are dismissed."

Danai saluted her *sang-shao*, turned smartly and marched out of his office. She made sure to keep her spine straight and stride swift until she was out on the streets of Lianyungang. Then she stopped dead in her tracks and tried to absorb what had just happened. The sun shone from a deep blue sky, cloudless and cool. The light breeze was welcome, cooling the sweat that had broken out on her brow as soon as she left Tao's presence.

Her first thought was a good one. She had her own battalion and she was taking it to Aldebaran. That, taken by itself, was exhilarating.

But she'd already thought about Aldebaran during the briefing on the JumpShip. She'd ruled it out as a current possibility, because New Canton loomed nearby. A journey of little more than two weeks would land reinforcements from the capital of Prefecture VI on Aldebaran. If her victims somehow managed to get word of her approach before she arrived, the New Canton forces could be right on her heels. The Republic was in chaos, breaking up on all sides, but she couldn't assume the break was so severe that New Canton couldn't help its neighbors. When she planned her invasion, she'd have to take into account the reinforcements.

This wasn't going to be easy. But since Daoshen had ordered it, it was what she had to do.

At least she had the support of her commander. Kind of. His reaction to her promotion, while unpleasant, was not surprising. After every battle, every raid, he seemed to have a long list of her failures ready to rattle off the top of his head. Pleione, Shensi, St. Andre—all successful operations, but to hear Tao's version, all victories put at risk by Danai's blunders. To hear him now admit she had shown her worth was something like having a resurrected Hanse Davion appear and say that, on second thought, maybe he should have just left the Capellan Confederation alone. The profound disappointment and the unexpected praise he had uttered mere sentences apart set her off balance.

So she had stumbled into the best opportunity of her career, and she well knew that the bigger the opportunity, the bigger the risk. At this point, a second consecutive failure could put her career—not to mention the Confederation's fortunes in Prefecture VI—on a steep downward slope.

In short, she had a lot riding on her skills as a warrior and her ability to command a group larger than any she'd ever led.

If anything could help her get back to her old self, that was it.

6

Jojoken, Andurien
Duchy of Andurien
2 November 3135

The russet vines hung from every tree, sometimes looping all the way to the ground. Autumn flowers bloomed along most of the ropy plants, covering much of the dark red with blues, greens and purples. The trees themselves had leaves so light and sun-touched that they appeared almost blue. It looked quite exotic, Rickard thought, and stunning. And that was just one corner of the vast gardens that stretched below him.

The window in front of Rickard was eight meters long and two meters high. It curved gently outward, allowing a beautiful panorama of the botanical gardens from twenty-three stories in the air.

It was a wonderful setting for a waiting room, impressive and calming. Anyone who spent enough time here would more than likely be positively disposed toward the duke once an audience was finally granted.

Rickard had been waiting a mere seven minutes. He figured he had anywhere from eight to twenty-three minutes left before the duke sent for him. Any shorter time and Duke Humphreys wouldn't seem busy enough.

Much longer than a half-hour wait would seem rude and could lead to a minor diplomatic incident if Rickard felt so inclined. Surely, with so many dangerous neighbors on his borders, Duke Humphreys wouldn't risk offending the representative of one of them.

As it turned out, Rickard waited exactly twenty-two minutes before a rosy-cheeked receptionist told him the duke would see him now.

Rickard, able to play the game as well as Humphreys, set himself on a nice slow saunter to the duke's office, even stopping to admire an impressive green-and-blue piece of abstract holoart mounted on the corridor wall. Then he walked into the duke's private sanctum.

The room gave the impression that the entire building had been designed around this particular space. The wall behind the duke's desk bulged outward, pushing over the spectacular gardens below. Birds of every color and variety flew in and out of trees, the birds and the trees both brought to Andurien from planets across the Inner Sphere. A better view of the gardens did not exist anywhere on Andurien, and the duke had perched himself directly in front of a broad series of windows displaying his planet's crowning glory.

The rest of the office was deliberately muted, dark woods and subtle colors acting in concert to keep the focus on the view. It was a brilliant strategy except for one thing—Duke Ari Humphreys, perched in front of the windows, looked small, mild and unassuming. He, like the rest of the room, tended to shrink in relation to the gorgeous display of nature behind him. His tall leather chair dwarfed his 1.6-meter frame, and his small, round face on top of his squat body was decidedly unimpressive.

He stood as Rickard entered, his expression bland. "Ambassador Rickard. Your visits are always looked forward to."

Rickard noted the duke's careful use of the passive voice—in effect, he was saying *someone* looked forward to Rickard coming by, but he wasn't about to reveal who that individual was.

Rickard's mission for this meeting allowed him no such evasions. He had instructions to be as direct and gracious as circumstances allowed.

"I appreciate your making the time to see me," Rickard said. "I know there are plenty of things on your mind at the moment."

"As it should ever be with the ruler of any great realm," the duke said, striving for grace and magnanimity. His high, thin voice couldn't quite pull it off. "Of course, seeing as how the realm you represent is one of my many concerns, it would be irresponsible not to receive you, wouldn't it?"

Again, Rickard could find a way to be insulted by that remark, but his orders didn't allow for it.

"If the Magistracy is a concern to you," Rickard said, "then I hope it is a concern we can lay to rest before this meeting is over. As you well know, the Magistracy has never been an aggressive nation, so you can be assured that our intentions toward our Andurien neighbors are peaceful."

The first part of Rickard's statement was not strictly true, but since the most notable act of Canopian aggression had come as part of a joint effort with the Anduriens, he was fairly certain the duke wouldn't bother to correct him.

"And as I'm sure you remember," Rickard continued, "a long history of friendship exists between the Anduriens and the Magistracy. I want to assure you that, in light of the growing chaos in the Inner Sphere and the recent dissolution of much of the Republic of the Sphere, our friendship will continue. We will not let shifts of power compromise our loyalties."

Humphreys sniffed, his short, narrow nose twitching. "Dissolution. Funny word for it, isn't it? You make it sound like the Republic dissolved solely through executive fiat. 'Disintegration' would perhaps be a better word. Or 'shattering.' Such words capture the event better, don't you agree?"

Rickard wasn't about to get dragged into an argument on semantics. "Certainly, your grace." Whatever words one chose to describe it, the battle over the far-off Republic had its effects on the Duchy of Andurien. As neighbors like the Oriente Protectorate and Capellan Confederation moved to claim the remains left on the Republic's table, they would grow more powerful while the Duchy essentially stood pat. Long ago, when the Free Worlds League was still a political entity, the Duchy had been protected from Capellan aggression by the strength of the many worlds behind it, all united in a mighty state. Now, the Duchy had not only lost the support of its former neighbors, but had gained a second insecure border on its coreward side.

"I am, of course, well aware of past cooperation between the Magistracy of Canopus and the Duchy of Andurien," the duke said. "However—and please, Ambassador, correct me if I am mistaken—I believe such cooperation was directed against the neighboring Capellan Confederation, a nation that has always posed a threat to both our states. Situations have changed—haven't they?—in the intervening decades. Specifically, the Magistracy does not seem to feel the same antipathy toward the Capellans that your nation used to possess."

"Times have indeed changed," Rickard said smoothly. "While the Magistracy has entered into a new era of understanding with the Confederation, that does not mean that—"

Rickard got no further. Duke Humphreys could not contain himself any longer. His composure, his formal speech and his bland expression all dropped away as he jumped to his feet.

" 'New era of understanding'!" he yelled. "What the hell kind of language is that? Bloody hell, man, call a spade a spade. You have a Liao on the throne. A *Liao*! I could call you an ally of the Capellans, but even *that* would be wrong. You're a damned *suburb*! You *are* Capellans, only with more sex and better hors d'oeuvres! 'New era of understanding' my *ass*!"

The duke sat down. His blank expression returned, like the curtain falling across a stage at play's end.

Rickard fervently wished he could take self-righteous

offense at the duke's remarks, but his mission didn't allow it. He was forced to act as if he had not just received one of the gravest insults of his diplomatic career.

"We have a Centrella on the throne," he said mildly, "as we have had since our founding. Yes, she is also the daughter of Sun-Tzu Liao, but can she be held accountable for her mother's romantic decisions? I assure you she is as complete a Centrella as any who have ever sat on the Canopian throne."

"Your assurance means little when your magestrix is the sister of the Capellan chancellor. When the two of them travel the Inner Sphere in tandem, practically arm in arm. Ilsa cannot help but differ from her predecessors. Her family necessitates it."

Rickard leaned forward. "May I be candid, your grace?" The duke waved his hand in what Rickard assumed was a gesture of assent. "A fair number of people in the Magistracy share at least a portion of your reservations. Capellan society and Canopian society are . . . different. Incompatible, really. So the new closeness between the two nations is quite disconcerting. But let me tell you something—with each year that passes, the alliance gets easier and easier for our people to accept. The muttering grows quieter. Would you like to know why? Because each year, our people see two things. First, the Magistracy is still the Magistracy. Our people are still free, our pleasure circuses still roam the Inner Sphere, bringing in vast resources to the state. And second, the Magistracy is safe. One of our most intimidating enemies is now our friend, and not only are we safe from Capellan aggression, but we also have Capellan assistance against any other threats. Let me tell you—that's more than a little peace of mind. Look at your duchy, look at what's left of the Republic of the Sphere. Isn't a little peace of mind worth something right now?"

The duke frowned but did not speak for a moment. He steepled his index fingers and pressed them against his upper lip. He looked like a thoughtful grapefruit.

Finally, he spoke. "Your faith in Canopian resilience is admirable. But these kinds of political entanglements do not, cannot come without cost. It is impossible for two nations to have an exactly compatible set of goals and priorities, and where those goals and priorities differ, there will be a need for compromise. Or a need for one nation to subordinate its will to the other. You may justify this all you want, you may continually proclaim the value of safety, but your alliance does not come without a price. To all appearances, your magestrix is now the Capellan chancellor's subordinate. What you call an alliance looks to the outside eye very much like subjugation."

Rickard was careful not to smile. While the duke thought he had just made a decisive pronouncement against the possibility of an alliance, he had actually walked down the exact path Rickard wanted him to travel.

"The history of the Magistracy of Canopus," Rickard said, "is the history of outsiders underestimating the abilities of our rulers. I'd like to think that our long list of leaders would compare favorably, if not surpass, those of any other nation. They have preserved us and enriched us, generally against the odds, for centuries. They should never be easily dismissed—but it seems they always are.

"Don't dismiss Ilsa now," Rickard continued, purposefully using the magestrix's first name instead of her title. "She may travel with her brother, but she is no subordinate. And she has wiles, tricks and methods of which he knows nothing."

"Be that as it may," Duke Humphreys said, once again striving for magnanimity. "I haven't seen those methods, either. Until I do, I have no reason to consider an alliance."

And that was it. Rickard had fulfilled his instructions, almost to the letter. "Meet with Duke Humphreys," his orders had said. "Have him ask to see some sort of gesture from the magestrix before he considers an alliance. Once he has made that request, conclude the meeting."

Having followed his instructions perfectly to this point, Rickard saw no reason to deviate from them. He stood.

"I understand," he said, "and I will convey your sentiments to the magestrix."

Duke Humphreys rose and stretched out his hand. Rickard bowed, grasped the duke's hand and touched the Andurien sigil ring on the duke's finger to his forehead. Then he straightened. "Thank you again for your time, your grace."

The duke nodded curtly, saying nothing, and plopped down in his seat. He looked, Rickard thought as he walked away, like a man who needed a friend.

7

The invitations had gone out within an hour after Danai's interview with Tao concluded, and they had all been accepted almost as quickly.

Not invitations, Danai corrected herself. Orders. Reassignments for her command lance.

They were not the first orders she had given in her career, but they were the most satisfying. This mission was hers and hers alone, and she had the complete freedom (well, almost complete—this Bell character was being forced on her) to surround herself with the right people to get the job done.

Even Bell seemed acceptable, based on some quick recon work she had done. He'd trained in the Magistracy, so she'd have that much in common with him. It hadn't taken him long to figure out that a male could only rise so far or so fast in the Magistracy, though, so he'd managed to get a transfer to the Confederation. Capellan military leadership thought well enough of him not only to grant the transfer but also to put him in McCarron's Armored Cavalry. Clearly, he wouldn't lack for skill on the battlefield. And having someone who, like Danai, had spent some formative years outside the Confederation might be nice. Especially when Sandra Sung, who was as Capellan as they come, would be in the same command lance.

It would at least lead to an interesting mix of personalities, but that was pretty much the case any time you got four MechWarriors together. They would work together—her job was to see to that—and they would get the job done. That was all that mattered.

The three other members of her new command lance would be waiting in a room at the Liao Conservatory of Military Arts, a space that should hold all the readouts they would need on Aldebaran and surrounding planets. She was almost running to get to the meeting, full of adrenaline for the coming task. Nothing compared to actually fighting in Yen-lo-wang, but taking time to plan just what damage she'd inflict, and how, was a job with its own special delights. She was ready to grab this new assignment in a flying tackle, pin it to the ground and slap it around thoroughly.

An hour later, a fair amount of the excitement was gone. The first sign of trouble had come when she entered the room at the conservatory. The rest of her command lance was already there, and none of them looked happy. Clara Parks, her freshly minted executive officer, was on her feet, waving her arms, speaking emphatically, doing everything short of standing on her chair to get her point across. The trouble was, even after listening to her for a good two minutes, Danai couldn't be sure what her point was. Something about seniority and ancestry—Clara's grandmother had commanded the First McCarron's Armored Cavalry—and a lot about respect and who should get it, but none of it was congealing into any kind of central argument.

Sandra Sung sat near Clara, arms folded, staring at the wall with her full Warrior House glare. She was making a concerted effort to not so much as glance at Clara, who didn't notice her subtle defiance. Clara had too much momentum worked up to pay attention to her surroundings.

Then there was the third lance member, the man she assumed was Jacyn Bell. He sat slumped in his chair, one arm flung over the back, a smirk on his face. He watched Clara's fervent speech, then glanced at Sandra to make sure she was still seething, then looked back at Clara. Each time his eyes moved back and forth, his grin grew wider.

His amusement at the expense of his lancemates was bad enough. Worse was Danai's recognition of him. Jacyn Bell was the dark-haired officer who'd tried to chat her up on the JumpShip from New Hessen. The one she'd slapped down hard, twice. And now he was supposed to serve as a liaison to help her integrate into her first battalion command.

Her stomach sank. So much for her hope that he might be a welcome addition. Dammit, if men could just *contain* themselves once in a while, life would be so much easier.

But she didn't have time to worry about Bell. She needed to get Clara settled down first. No one seemed to have noticed her entrance, so she spoke up in her loudest, most authoritative voice.

"Sorry I'm late," she said, "but it looks like you started without me." She'd served with Sandra and Clara for a while and knew how much they'd bring to her lance. But she also knew their quirks and weaknesses, and she had known from the start that a run-in like this would probably happen sooner or later—though this was sooner than she expected.

Clara and Sandra turned. They looked surprised to see Danai, and immediately stood at attention. Bell, who did not look surprised at all, drummed his fingers on his leg for a moment, then stood as slowly as he could while still exhibiting some degree of movement.

After an eternity, the entire lance saluted. Danai returned it briskly. "As you were. Except for Clara's yelling."

The three of them sat. Clara and Sandra looked like conservatory students—Clara especially, her oval face quite youthful—while Bell looked like a truant in detention.

"I'll do the official welcome in a moment," Danai said, "but first let's take care of Clara. Clara, was that all you needed to say, or would you like to continue your speech?"

Clara shot an angry look at Sandra, then composed her face. Her mouth and jaw seemed to stretch downward when she wanted to look serious, giving her a vaguely equine appearance. "No, *Sao-shao*," she said.

Clearly that wasn't the truth, but just as clearly now was not the time to resolve whatever issue had come up. Danai pressed ahead.

"All right. As you might have guessed by the tone of your orders, you're not in this lance to sit around. We're moving out, and soon. We've been ordered to take and hold Aldebaran for the Confederation, restoring one of our homeworlds to our rightful possession."

Danai paused, hoping to hear surprised gasps or appreciative murmurs at her announcement. She heard nothing. She reminded herself that there were only three other people in the room, and they were not likely to react the same way a crowd would. She'd just have to continue her speech without the theatrical flair.

"Aldebaran will resist us, of course, but their militia is not likely to pose much challenge. Latest intelligence reports put no more than two 'Mech companies around the capital, along with some infantry and battle armor units. I expect Third Battalion to be more than a match for them."

The other three remained silent, but at least Sandra and Clara nodded agreement.

"Aldebaran isn't our only target. Intelligence reports tell us the situation on Zurich has moved from abysmal to cataclysmic. The militia is essentially eating itself. We might be able to take the capital with a single 'Mech, but to be on the safe side I'm sending in a company of 'Mechs, along with some support."

"Leaving us two companies for Aldebaran," Sandra said.

"Right. That should be enough to deal with the forces currently on the planet, but there's a hitch."

"New Canton," Sandra said. She sounded like an eager-to-please student.

"Right again," Danai said. "They sat out Elnath, Second Try and Nanking, but now we'll be knocking on their front door. A double-pronged attack might bring their forces out of hiding."

"Where will they go?" Clara asked. "Aldebaran, Zurich or both?"

"Good question," Danai said. "And I can only guess at the answer. We have to be ready for them to hit either planet, with a light blow or a swiftly descending hammer."

"That's a little vague," Bell observed dryly. "Tough to prepare for that."

"That's why you're not my tactical officer," Danai said. Her tone sounded harsh, but she didn't care. "Sandra, you and I will work on some specific contingencies."

"I'm already planning," Sandra said confidently, while Bell made an obvious effort to keep his eyes from rolling.

"I've got one element worked up already," Danai said. "If attacking two planets will put them a little off balance, what will attacking three planets do?"

The question hung in the air for a minute before Bell finally answered, likely saying what all three of them were thinking.

"Attack three planets with a single battalion?" He didn't bother to hide the scorn in his voice. "Don't you think that might be spreading our forces a little thin?"

"If the third planet was a real invasion, yes. But it's not. Take a look at the map."

Danai turned on the projector. The thousands of inhabited planets of the Inner Sphere appeared in the air, color-coded by nationality. Just like every other time Danai had looked at the map recently, the several borders seem to have shifted, with planets bouncing from one nation to another.

"We have an opportunity," she said. "Zion is about as close to our border as Aldebaran, but it's antispinward of New Canton. Think of how they'll react when all three planets—Zurich, Aldebaran and Zion—get hit at once. They'll have to respond. If all three planets fall, New Canton becomes a border planet."

"But all three planets won't fall!" Bell insisted. "We'll have one company per planet—that's not enough."

"No," Danai said. "We'll have two on Aldebaran, one on Zurich."

Bell opened his mouth for another scornful reply. Then he saw what she was driving at. He gaped wider for a moment, then spoke. "A feint. With, I'm guessing, aero units?"

Danai nodded. Thank God Bell wasn't a complete idiot. "That's right. I'm not too worried about aerial support, at least not at the beginning of the fight, so I think we can spare them. They go to Zion and wait for us to start our assaults on Zurich and Aldebaran. Once the news has gone out that we've landed, the aerial units attack Zion, doing their best to make it look like they're softening up the place for a third invasion. They don't have to do any real damage, though I wouldn't mind if they did. They just need to stay long enough and make a big enough fuss to get New Canton's attention. As soon as New Canton troops land on Zion, our aerial forces can leave. They'll have done their job."

"What if New Canton doesn't send troops to Zion?"

"Then the aerial units stay. They get more aggressive, hitting more and more strategic targets. If they keep it up, eventually we'll have a pretty easy time landing there. So we take Zion, too."

She was rewarded with more nods, but Sandra still looked concerned. *Good,* Danai thought. She should be concerned. A good tactical officer should always worry about plans and strategies, even in her sleep. And she shouldn't sleep that much.

"Sandra, you don't look completely satisfied. What's on your mind?"

"I like the Zion plan," Sandra said slowly. Her short, wide face was compressing itself into rough horizontal lines. "It doesn't cost us much and could gain us a lot. But I'm not sure it will be enough."

She sat up straighter in her chair as she talked. The more she went on, the more her voice changed, until she no longer sounded like a subordinate addressing her commander. She sounded like a professor lecturing to a class. Danai had heard that tone many times before, and she'd always written it off as the cost of knowing Sandra. You don't befriend someone who's eyeing a spot in Warrior House Hiritsu without learning to put up with a certain degree of arrogance.

"I want to be clear that I don't consider two companies of 'Mechs to be an insignificant force. It's not insignificant in anyone's terms, particularly when the companies contain Capellan 'Mechs and Capellan warriors. However, the fact remains that New Canton is—was—the capital of Prefecture VI, and it held the military forces you'd expect it to have. True, they're somewhat reduced—we already defeated some of them in Prefecture V when they came to give assistance, while others seem to have disappeared between Levin's wall. Still, a fair amount stayed behind as we've been whittling away the prefecture around them, and we cannot expect them to stay away when we attack. I firmly believe two Capellan companies can take and hold Aldebaran, but I am hesitant to say two companies can withstand whatever New Canton decides to throw at us. The Triarii Protectors are not Capellan, and they are partially built for show, but that does not mean we should underestimate them."

Those remarks, coming bare moments into her first command briefing, put Danai into her first critical moment as battalion commander. Sandra had a point, and the expression on Clara and Bell's faces showed that they knew it and were interested in what their new commander had to say. The trouble was, she was just as much in the dark as they were. She'd been asking the same question ever since she'd received her orders.

Briefly, she thought of how *Sang-shao* Tao would handle the question. He'd slam his hand on his desk, bark that the orders had come from the *chancellor himself*, and that they should be *honored* to receive the assignment, instead of wasting time *questioning* the will of their leader.

The flash came and went and, as it faded, Danai saw a different path.

"I can tell you two things," she said. "First, the chancellor is well aware of the threat New Canton poses. Second, our attacks are only one part of the chancellor's larger plans for furthering the glory of the Confederation. I think we can be confident that among the other aspects of the plan are measures that will help ease any pressure New Canton might want to place on us." She took a breath, and then surprised herself with what she said next. "I'll be honest with you—I don't know what the chancellor's other plans are, and I wish I did. Knowing would make it easier for us to anticipate what we might face. But we know what we know, and in the chancellor's eyes that's enough. So all that's left is to live up to his expectations."

It worked. The three of them nodded. Bell even sat up a little straighter.

Danai had noticed an odd thing as she spoke. The middle part of her remarks, the part she hadn't planned on saying, the small admission of her own frustration at being kept in the dark, was the part that really sparked the attention of her lance. She had seen a lot of leadership techniques in her time, and she knew there was still a place for the one she'd seen most often in the Capellan military—intimidation. But now she had a new tactic to call on when she needed it, and any warrior knew that two weapons were better than one.

"Now that we know what we need to do," Danai said to her attentive lance, as she made the planetary map zoom in on Aldebaran, "let's talk about how we're going to do it."

8

"I'm not taking any bets on military maneuvers!"

The hall was nearly empty. The worn strip in the middle of the red carpet, covered by the feet of the crowd in better times, was embarrassingly visible. The instability of the past month had people on edge all the time, and so far not enough people had decided to dull that edge through the joy of gaming. Gartin Krauss had laid off so many employees he was forced to take on more and more duties each day—including, today, manning the sports betting window.

"It's all everybody's talking about!" said the lumpy man in the stained sweatshirt. "When's it going to happen, who it's going to be. Even the news people are getting into it; I heard Phillip McConnell laying odds on what's going to happen."

Krauss pulled at his tie in a too-subtle reminder that patrons used to dress up when they came to his establishment. "What'd he say?"

"Five to two that the Cappies will come get us before anyone else. They're closest, right? But he kind of hedged his bets, saying you never know, some power on the make like Oriente may want to make its move before the Cappies come in."

"Did he put any odds on Oriente?" Krauss asked, running some numbers in his head in spite of himself.

"Naw, he was just talking, you know? Off the top of his head. But the point is, he was interested. *I'm* interested. And since when does a fine establishment like yours not want to take the money of people like me?"

But the moment of temptation had passed. "No!" Krauss said. "You're talking about war! That's not some game for us to pass money back and forth on. It's life and death. I won't have it!"

The lumpy man smirked and waved his hand in a gesture that took in the slot machines with the scratched displays, the tables with the felt peeling in the corners, and the bar empty except for one person who had been running a tab all month and hadn't paid anything yet.

"You worried about the reputation of this place?" the lumpy man said. "Worried that bets like the one I want to make will bring you down in society?"

Krauss opened his mouth to respond, but before he could make a sound, a piercing wail filled the air. It rose, fell, rose again. The whole planet had been waiting for that sound, while hoping it would never come. Krauss didn't know exactly what was happening, but the sound gave him the general outline.

Outside, engines roared to life and people shouted as they ran past the casino's entrance. They didn't need to be told twice to get the hell out of there.

Krauss walked to his terminal so he could see his evacuation instructions and get the joint secured. As he passed the lumpy man, he did his best to match the fellow's smirk.

"Sorry," he said, "but I can't accept a bet once the event in question has started. Game's up."

The evening sun had settled behind some distant, low-lying clouds, lights in nearby Wen Ho were coming on and the wind was blowing through Danai's hair as Yen-lo-wang strode forward. All in all it was a lovely way to start the night.

Of course, the wind came from the cooling fans in Danai's cockpit, but for the time being she could pretend she was in the open air. Once the missiles and lasers started firing, she'd be happy to let go of her fantasy and enjoy the shelter of her armored surroundings.

The landing had been easy. The two companies and Danai's command lance had hit land only ten kilometers away from the small city of Wen Ho, and the planet's defenders had decided not to venture too far out of the city's protection. A quick march, less than twenty minutes, brought them to the suburbs with no sign of resistance. Buildings here were long and low, seldom rising beyond three stories, with broad, flat roofs that often stuck out five meters or more beyond the walls. Danai could understand why the militia wasn't making a stand here—few structures rose high enough to offer a 'Mech any real shelter. If this was going to be a street fight, the locals might as well choose a place with some buildings they could hide behind.

She understood why they weren't here, but she wished they were. She felt impatient. Her fingers wouldn't stay settled on her control sticks, and she kept shifting them, moving to new grips and occasionally rubbing them against the sticks to relieve her itchy palms. Her feet were fidgety too. She hadn't been in Yen-lo-wang for too long. She'd spent all that time on the ground of New Hessen looking for it, only to find Caleb and . . .

When Danai's eyes refocused, she saw she was about to run into a house. She quickly veered right, back onto the road, and took a series of controlled breaths to get her heartbeat under control. Clearly, reminiscence was a danger. She needed to stay focused on the present.

She took a minute to touch base with Harris Yun back on her command DropShip, where he had been tracking a large JumpShip that had entered the Aldebaran system only a day or so after Danai's battalion. The initial impression had been troubling—the ship was a big one, *Star Lord*–class—but the IFF signal said it was just a merchant vessel. If so, it might turn around, or at least stay in place, while events in the planetary system resolved themselves. But six DropShips had detached and were heading toward Aldebaran with an apparent strong sense of purpose. They were still claiming to be merchants, but Danai had trouble taking their IFF signature seriously.

"Have our friends decided they'd be better off turning around yet?" Danai asked Yun.

"Naw. They're coming to greet you in person, looks like."

"Great," Danai sighed. "Keep an eye on them. Once we're convinced they're hostile, don't engage them orbitally—you don't have the firepower for that. We'll do the fighting down here. Keep yourself in good enough shape to go fetch us a new planetary government once we've taken care of this place."

"You got it, *Sao-shao*."

While she talked to Yun, the rest of her command lance had jogged ahead of her. Bell was directly in front, loping along in his large but fast *Yu Huang*. Few machines could compete with Yen-lo-wang in Danai's eyes, but Bell's was one of them. Bigger than her machine, reasonably fast and with a set of weapons that packed a punch from almost any range, it was an impressive piece of work. It didn't have Yen-lo-wang's ax, though, or its impressive appearance, so Danai was grateful to put a few points into her 'Mech's column. Still, if Bell ever got put out of commission while his machine was in working order, she might need to take it out for a test drive.

Sandra, in her *Marauder II*, was left and a little forward of Danai; Clara's *Tian-Zong* held a parallel position on the right. Danai happened to be looking at Sandra, getting a visual fix on her position a few blocks over, when she saw a blue flash, followed by smoke rising from a spot on her elevated right shoulder. Danai squinted and thought she saw armor running down from the wound. Sandra had been hit.

Danai readied her weapons. If smoke would help conceal her in this battle, then smoke was what she'd make.

Zi-jin Chéng, Sian
Capellan Confederation

The message had traveled quickly, in the inimitable fashion of bad news. Erde had already watched the message several times, but she'd known what she'd needed to do after the first viewing.

She had hoped to go home. She'd spent too much time away, too much time with Capellans and politicians and others who at best had very vague understandings of what it meant to enjoy life. Not that her fellow Canopians were perfect in that regard—some mistook the pursuit of simple pleasure for a well-lived life—but by and large they were more enjoyable company than the people she'd been surrounding herself with for too long. She had lived many years, traveled to many, many places and she still hadn't found one that appealed to her as much as her home. And, as there likely weren't too many years left to her (how could there be?), she was anxious to spend as much time on Canopus IV as possible.

But now she knew that would have to wait.

One of the doors to her private chambers opened soundlessly, and a servant in a shiny black silk jacket and matching pants slipped into the room. He stood quietly by the door, his head slightly bowed, waiting for Erde to issue a command or dismiss him.

They did this every hour on the hour. It hadn't taken much investigating for Erde to discover that Daoshen had so ordered, and it also didn't take much to discern that she could do little to stop it. The servants would look out for her well-being whether she wanted them to or not.

At first she had believed the servants were acting as spies for Daoshen, but as time passed she considered that idea increasingly unlikely. Surely Daoshen would realize that she'd quickly identify the servants as his eyes and ears, and that she'd make sure not to say or do anything in their presence that would provide them with a single interesting report. Since Daoshen should know the servants were not likely to come away with anything of value, he would not waste manpower on so trivial a task.

Another possibility was that the servants were there to check on her health, an hourly inquiry to see if she had stopped breathing. Concern for her well-being didn't seem to be part of Daoshen's nature; concern about having a dead body lying in his guest rooms seemed more in character. So now, whenever the servants entered, Erde made a show of looking lively to ensure they knew she was alive and well. Except, of course, when she was asleep. Erde didn't know, nor did she want to know, what they did to check on her health during the nighttime.

She said nothing, showed no emotion while the servant was present. She did not allow herself to look the least bit sad, even though the message from Danai had left her heart in pieces. Her regret at having to stay on Sian, the heavy burden of the tasks she now had in front of her—none of these appeared in her actions, her bearing, her face.

Her mind, though, was actively plotting. She needed to reestablish some sort of relationship with Daoshen. In recent weeks she'd been content to keep her distance, to let Daoshen and Ilsa take care of governing while she planned her trip home. But if she meant to help Danai—and Danai needed help, not just because of what happened on New Hessen, but because of what Erde believed was certain to come—she needed to be in closer communication with the chancellor.

She needed a pretext. Something positive. No complaints, like relating tales of the nonstop harassment of Canopian pleasure circuses when they passed through Capellan space. She had to pay a call on Daoshen to compliment him on something he'd recently done. And her discussion could have nothing to do with Danai, since bringing up that topic at the beginning of what she intended to be a series of conversations would only invite suspicion of her motives.

Sadly, finding reasons to complain to Daoshen was much easier than finding reasons to compliment him. But she found it, eventually, after scanning Capellan and Canopian news and the high volume of correspondence that always found her, no matter where in the Inner Sphere she placed herself. It was a simple matter, a trade agreement that would allow a greater flow of meat products from the Canopian world of New Abilene to the Capellan world of Joppa. Normally it wouldn't be worth noticing except that a close friend of Erde's had just invested in cattle futures, and this agreement would make her retirement much easier.

Daoshen, of course, would maintain that he had made the agreement for the good of the Confederation, and he had little interest in whether friends of his family benefited from his nation's actions. It wasn't much of a pretext, but it was enough to let Erde talk to Daoshen—which, for the time being, was all she needed.

9

Yen-lo-wang stomped forward, nearly at a run, into a broad plaza. Ferrocrete at her feet, nothing but a few benches and an eight-meter-tall statue for half a block. Black steel-and-glass buildings rose on all sides of her, but for this moment she was free of their confines. She had room to swing her right arm.

She rotated her right control stick in a pattern she'd deployed dozens, maybe hundreds, of times. She knew each position she had to hit like numbers on a clock dial—six, four, then threetwoonetwelveeleven. Then down, hard, to seven-thirty.

The *Ocelot*, with a dire break in its relatively thin upper right leg, had nowhere to go. The pilot had stayed in too long, possibly hoping for mercy, but Danai refused to let up as long as his weapons were still functioning. The enemy 'Mech's shoulder laser could still fire, though mostly in random blasts.

The *Ocelot*'s pilot finally ejected as the dark gray blade of Yen-lo-wang's ax buried itself deep in the torso.

Danai found the crunch and scream of metal deeply sat-isfying. The blow nearly shattered the *Ocelot*'s entire left arm, and no more energy came from the shoulder gun.

Danai yanked her ax out of the *Ocelot*'s corpse and stood above it, striking a victorious pose as if surrounded by the cameras of Solaris VII. Normally the battlefield was no place for that sort of posturing, but this fight, which had been a rout from almost the first moment, was about over.

"Command lance, check in," Danai said. "Anyone need help?"

Clara's only reply was a short bark that might have been a laugh. Apparently she hadn't seen much that her *Tian-Zong* couldn't handle on its own.

"Good hell, could they send out a 'Mech bigger than forty tons?" Bell said over the comm. "I feel like a high school bully beating on kindergarteners."

"How do you think I feel?" Sandra asked, her voice good-natured. Her disposition was always at its most pleasant right after a victory—her customary arrogance dropped away, as if she felt no need to verbally prove her superiority because the fighting had done that for her. "I should've walked into the city on my knees. Would've made for a fairer fight."

The mental image of the backward-jointed *Marauder II* trying to scoot along on its backside made Danai smile. "All right. Sorry there weren't enough challenges for everyone. Any losses to report?"

"I think I chipped a nail," Bell said somberly.

"Besides that."

"One of Kuang Nu Company's *Blades* is hobbled," Clara reported. "Pilot's fine, the thing could probably move if we needed to retreat, but that doesn't seem likely."

"Field repairable?" Danai asked.

"The pilot thinks so. Crew's on its way."

"Fine. He can catch up to us when he's able. Leave a few groundpounders with him, but not too many—I don't think they're in danger of being overwhelmed."

Bell laughed. "Right now, I could stand downtown with a hold-out pistol and not be in danger of being overwhelmed."

"Let's move on, then. Might as well do another city while the night is young—assuming everyone's up for that?"

Her sensor showed the three other 'Mechs of the command lance already jogging north toward Daipan. That was answer enough for her.

It was dark. All dark, until they came. No cars were out driving. No lights shone from within the buildings past which the 'Mechs strode. Even the streetlights were off. The only light came from the reddish moon above and the sweeping spotlight beams on the invading 'Mechs. The spotlights' glow glided over the tops of houses, down long, straight streets and through the tight spaces between buildings. Grass went from black to green to black as the lights stayed in motion, taking color with them wherever they went.

The city had heard about Wen Ho's recent fate and had taken the short time available to get ready. Their unity, Danai thought, was impressive. They would make good Capellan citizens.

"Slow it up," she said to all units. "They know we're coming and they've planned for us. Be alert for an ambush."

She looked at the city map on her secondary screen, evaluating her position. Following Sandra's tactics, her command lance had split, with Sandra and herself on the left while Bell and Clara stayed on the right. They were all at the backs of the lines, a position Danai was loathe to assume, but she knew the demands of leadership sometimes meant having to stay away from the front. For a time, at least.

"Okay, fly the Kites," she said. "Probes on. Don't get farther than three kilometers away from the main force."

"Roger, starting our scan now," said Kay Cheung, leader of the battalion's Kite reconnaissance company.

Danai kept her pace at a solid walk as the Kites did

their work. While she had a moment, she checked in with Yun back on her DropShip.

"Yun, give me a report on the incoming DropShips."

"Still coming."

"Still reading as merchants?"

"Yup."

"Have they sent a message to you, saying, 'We mean you no harm?'"

"Not yet."

"Have they sent anything?"

"Not yet."

She sighed. "Okay. At this point we have to assume they're reinforcements and they're coming for us. I want you to keep a read on their location and send me an ongoing estimate of their probable landing spot. Or spots."

"Yes, *Sao-shao*."

"They approach you, you move back. I don't think they'll pursue—the real game's down here."

"I'll keep you posted," Yun said.

"Okay." Danai switched to her command channel. "Sandra, reinforcements are coming. Probably a full regiment's worth. We'll need to be ready for them."

"Yes, *Sao-shao*. I'll get some options together."

"Thanks." Danai wished she could do more about the likely approaching threat, but for now she had a force in front of her to worry about. She settled herself in to wait for word from the Kites.

It didn't take long.

"Got 'em," Cheung said. "Moving south, concave formation. Line looks like it's eight kilometers long."

"Numbers?"

"Low, from what I'm seeing. We've got the upper hand there."

The Kites were more than a kilometer in front of her now. That meant she had a little more than five—maybe five and a half—kilometers before the armies met. A few minutes, at best, before the firing started.

She couldn't see the enemy on her radar, but she could see it all in her head. The cluster of buildings downtown, the arc of the Aldebaran militia moving ahead, the line of her units. And she knew exactly what to do. Sandra had already laid out the basics of the battle plan. Now Danai laid down the particulars based on the info from the Kites.

Her words came with the speed of autocannon rounds. "Artillery, stop. Lay down fire the moment you get a chance. *Sang-wei* Parks, take Kuang Nu Company west. *Sang-wei* Bell, take Rang Yu Company east. Five kilometers, both of you. Outflank the enemy, then collapse. Armor companies, split up, two with Kuang Nu, two with Rang Yu. Infantry, advance in the middle. *Sang-wei* Sung and I will support you."

A simple plan. Artillery to soften them up, slow their approach, the wings collapse on the arc, then Danai and Sandra smash the center. Should be short work.

It wasn't long before the thundering behind her let her know the artillery had begun firing.

"Kites, come on back," she ordered, though she guessed Cheung had already turned them around. "Drop back and keep an eye on things. Watch the skies particularly, in case they bring in some aeros." The fact that she had no aero support of her own made an aerial attack by the defenders a particular worry, but she didn't think they'd drop many bombs on their own city.

She continued stomping forward, firing a single heavy laser blast to get Yen-lo-wang's heat up. She didn't think she'd hit anything significant, but the shock value of the large beam flying through enemy lines was usually enough to cause a little unrest among her opponents. Seeing a Clan weapon on a Capellan 'Mech was a distraction, to say the least. Danai could still remember the day she'd had it installed, sitting in front of what looked like a junkyard on a planet deep in the Periphery, watching one tech mount the weapon on Yen-lo-wang's shoulder while another applied new armor to cover the scars she'd earned in the fight to obtain that weapon. Good times.

The laser discharge had another purpose besides

intimidation—heat. It got her triple-strength myomer working, and she started sliding through the air like a hard wind was blowing at her back. She had to keep herself from getting too far ahead of her battalion's central group, including Sandra's plodding *Marauder*. She slowed down, deactivating a heat sink to make sure the slow pace didn't reduce her heat too much. She needed to be ready to run when the time came.

She pressed forward for a few blocks, then saw the first holes in the ferrocrete and broken windows in the surrounding buildings, traces of artillery shots that had fallen short. It was time to get serious.

She saw units on her sensor now, the top of the Republican arc moving down toward her. Nothing showed up on her HUD, though—the street ahead of her was empty. She dashed left a block, turned (working hard to keep Yen-lo-wang balanced on the slick ferrocrete), took a quick laser shot, then watched to see where it hit. Nothing. All the enemy units shifted when she did, staying out of her sight. Cowards.

She stood still for a moment, feeling her machine cool while she let the rest of her group catch up to her. She'd let them herd the militia troops to a spot where she could take some nice clean shots.

A slight tremor, growing heavier each second, told her that Sandra was coming near.

"Impatient?" Sandra said over the comm as her *Marauder* drew near.

"Yes, dammit."

"Just save some of them for the rest of us," said Sandra, sounding oddly jocular before battle. Like the rest of the battalion, she clearly didn't think this conflict would amount to much.

"Artillery!" Danai barked. "How soft are they getting?"

"Like soggy tofu," Cheung said. "We've got the range measured and are hitting them regularly and hard."

"Keep firing for fifteen more seconds," Danai replied. "Then we'll engage at close range. Maneuver around after that, and put spotters on some rooftops. Keep dropping shots on the rearward units for the rest of the fight."

"Yes, *Sao-shao*."

Danai switched her comm to the channel for her entire battalion. "Center group, artillery's about to concentrate its fire on the rear, so the front will be open for us. Be ready to move forward hard on my mark."

She grabbed her control sticks tight, and her feet tap-danced on her pedals in anticipation. Time seemed to stand still for a good long while, but then the wait was over.

"*Now!*" she said.

She moved ahead, quickly leaving Sandra and her *Marauder* behind. If Sandra wanted some action, she'd need to hurry up. Danai was easily outpacing most 'Mechs her size or bigger, with only the smaller *Wasps* and *Blades* able to keep pace. She got glimpses of them, particularly the distinctive long legs of the *Wasps*, as she crossed east-west streets.

Then there was no more time to look anywhere but straight ahead. The militia, which had stayed out of the north-south streets to take shelter in the cross streets, opened fire. The lines had met.

Danai made a left turn and was greeted by an *Ocelot* with its right arm firmly extended, lasers shooting from its arm and chest. Danai kept her turn wide, feeling her feet skid lightly, her raised ax gouging a hole in a building's concrete facade. The beam from the *Ocelot*'s arm laser went wide, while the chest laser was harmlessly absorbed by Danai's vast rectangular shield.

If the *Ocelot*'s pilot had kept his head, he probably would have had time for another shot, which might have done some actual damage. But Danai knew full well the intimidating effect Yen-lo-wang could have, especially on a smaller 'Mech, and she used it every chance she got. She raised her ax higher, her machine tilting slightly left as she wheeled it around. The carapace over Yen-lo-wang's cockpit gave the 'Mech an almost Neanderthal visage, and the sight of a 50-ton caveman bearing down with a five-meter-long ax blade unnerved many warriors more hardened than a simple militia pilot. The *Ocelot* seemed to tremble as the pilot tried to move back and make a fast turn to get away. But he couldn't move fast enough, especially without good traction.

Danai didn't bother with the more rounded swing this time—she went from five o'clock to eleven o'clock in a swift, direct line. The ax came down in a straight, slashing line, catching the rotating *Ocelot* in the chest, just above its laser. Metal cracked and whined, and the force of the blow staggered the militia 'Mech. Knowing he couldn't run, the pilot tried to bring his right arm laser back into play, but Danai pivoted, pulling her ax back and stepped forward, extending her shield arm and slamming it into the *Ocelot*'s laser. The militia MechWarrior absorbed the blow by letting his right arm swing back limply, while his left arm, a closed fist, came swinging up at the same time.

"What are you going to do, slap me?" Danai muttered. She took her ax arm out to the right and aimed a low, crossing blow at the *Ocelot*'s midsection.

The blade buried itself deep. The *Ocelot* bent at the waist, off-balance and falling. Through the darkness, Danai could see all kinds of lights blinking inside its cockpit, and she could almost hear the klaxons that must be filling the pilot's ears. She'd hit something good.

With a terrible screech, she pulled her ax out of her enemy's side as it crashed to the ground, lifting the machine slightly before the blade finally came free. She raised it up again, intentionally holding it high for an extra few seconds, before she got the result she wanted. The top of the canopy flew away, and the pilot ejected. The two blows he'd received were all he wanted from the ax.

Danai straightened herself and turned, surprised that no one had come to aid the *Ocelot* while she had been pummeling it—its pilot undoubtedly had been calling for help. The militia must be badly undermanned.

The streets immediately around her were clear. Time to check in with her lance.

"Sung, Parks, Bell, what's going on? Sandra, did you manage to catch up yet?"

"I've got two kills," Sandra said with pride.

"All right. Clara?"

"They're tenacious, but their line's thin. We've got at least three breakthroughs, but they keep trying to re-group and come at us. No retreat yet, but just say the word and I'll make it happen."

Danai smiled. That was one reason she'd wanted Clara in her command lance. Clara would willingly charge into just about anything without much of a hint.

"They're masochists on a suicide mission," Bell said, without waiting for a prompt from Danai. "Normal troops would have run when we first hit them."

That meant one of two things. "All right, they're either fanatics or they want to hold us here for a reason. I'm not discounting the former, but it would be a good idea for everyone to shift a little in case they're trying to pin us here. Try to push things to the north at least half a kilometer. Make them chase you if you need to."

Unfortunately, as far as Danai's battalion was concerned, her order came too late.

Danai walked to a north-south street, heading for a skirmish one block north and a half block east, when it happened. She saw the light first, orange flashes like lightning in a humid sky, except too low. She heard the explosions next, a series of concussions that shook the ground and blew out hundreds of windows. The flashes of light continued, seeming to rise higher into the air. Glass fell across the streets like icy snow.

Danai had been whirling, looking for the source of the flashes, then finally saw it two blocks to the south—a tower at least 150 meters tall, with orange fire envel-oping its corners. The explosions continued for a half minute, then stopped, leaving a severely damaged build-ing filled with fire.

"All units, get away from that building!" Danai yelled. "Get away *now*."

It was perhaps the most unnecessary order Danai had ever given, as troops had started clearing the block when the first explosion occurred. By the time the fatally damaged building started falling on itself, most of her people were clear, except for one 'Mech that lost its footing in the panic.

Dust billowed through the streets and over buildings, and Danai immediately saw the Aldebarians' purpose in destroying one of their own structures. Any Capellan units actually damaged by the explosions and the collapse would be just a pleasant side effect. The militia troops wanted the chaos, confusion and poor visibility.

Danai couldn't see more than a few meters in front of her, and her sensors were cluttered with static and false images. Certain blips were larger and brighter than any other images, and she knew what they were.

"Center units, use your sensors and head toward the biggest, clearest blip you can find. Those'll be the 'Mechs. We give them enough trouble, the support troops will come running to them. Move!"

Blood thundered in Danai's ears. This was her fight now. It would be a close-quarters battle, and she was convinced no one else on the field could match her there. She didn't appreciate the Aldebarians blowing up a piece of their city just to throw her off guard, and she would make sure they felt every bit of her wrath.

She let her sensors guide her, little caring when her ax or shield took a piece off a building's corner as she ran toward her target. Nothing she did to the city would match the damage its residents had inflicted on it.

She leaned forward in her harness, straining, as if the force of her body could add to Yen-lo-wang's speed. In an urban fight, she became almost strictly a melee brawler—it was tough to get enough of a bead on an enemy to justify the heat expenditure of firing her heavy laser, and the high amount of cover made it equally difficult for her Artemis system to obtain and hold a target lock. Her ax was easily her most useful weapon in this kind of fight.

Now, thanks to the dust filling the air, her ax was even more useful. Drawing a bead on a target from as little as half a block away would be difficult, so no one would be able to get a good shot at her while she charged. Her speed would put her on top of her targets, swinging hard, before they could do anything about it.

The brawl she targeted was a good one, a *Ghost* and a *Hellstar* grappling with one of her *Phoenix Hawks*. The *Hellstar*'s size, together with the rounded, clublike PPC mounts on the end of each arm, gave it the advantage, and it rained blows on the Capellan 'Mech. The *Ghost* moved into and out of view as the dust clouds blew and shifted, looking for opportunities to fire small laser bursts at the *Phoenix Hawk*. They glowed fiery red through the thick cloud of particles in the air. Danai saw the *Ghost* get off three shots—one miss, one hit on the leg of the *Phoenix Hawk*, and a wild ground shot that sliced through the pavement.

Clearly, the *Hellstar* was the real threat here, and that was the way Danai wanted it. She positioned her shield and swung her ax in one motion, bringing it crashing down on the *Hellstar*'s back. But either her aim was off or the militia 'Mech shifted. All she managed was a glancing blow.

The *Hellstar*'s pilot was too smart to panic. Instead of turning on Danai and giving up his advantage over the *Phoenix Hawk*, he brought his right arm down in a punishing blow that took his opponent to the ground. His left arm already in position, he leveled a devastating PPC shot at the *Phoenix Hawk*'s head. The bolt slammed the head to the ground, splintering the cockpit's ferroglass, making the remnants glow red. The Capellan 'Mech remained where it fell.

"*Ta ma de!*" Danai yelled. She didn't care if the *Hellstar* was twice as big as her own machine and had help behind it. It was going down.

Her hands moved in a blur while her feet worked the pedals, keeping Yen-lo-wang pressing ahead, not wanting the *Hellstar* to get into a firm stance. She was going to give the *Phoenix Hawk* one last chance to strike back.

She led with her shield, pushing the militia 'Mech, then wielded the ax twice, once in the back, once in the shoulder. The *Hellstar* tried to use its weight, leaning into her, but she didn't give a centimeter. Her shield came up, pushing on the *Hellstar*'s arms, not letting it take any aim, giving it no chance to inflict more than glancing blows. Of course, the "glancing blow" of a 95-ton 'Mech was enough to send shivers down the length of the shield arm and into her cockpit. Once the *Hellstar* even managed to fire its right shoulder PPC into her shield. The blow set off a cockpit alarm or two, but she didn't care. She leaned forward, pressing her attack.

Then the *Ghost* shuffled into view, waiting for a clean shot. Danai made sure he didn't get it, sliding to her left to put the *Hellstar* between herself and the *Ghost*. She used the same move to give her next ax swing a little extra pop. The *Ghost* tried to circle for a clear shot, but then smoke and dust blew in and took it out of view. For a few seconds, at least, Danai had the *Hellstar* to herself.

She shoved her left control stick forward in a hard push, her shield arm straining against the big assault 'Mech. The giant machine didn't give much ground, but it gave enough.

The *Hellstar*'s feet came into contact with the motionless *Phoenix Hawk*, and it stumbled. Danai was waiting for that moment, and she took full advantage of it. Yen-lo-wang's ax came down with all the force she could muster. The blow shook her entire 'Mech, but did a lot worse to the *Hellstar*. It nearly severed the assault 'Mech's left arm, and the force of it sent the *Hellstar* even more off-balance. With the *Phoenix Hawk* below it, the *Hellstar* had no place to get firm footing. It went down, sprawled across the Capellan machine's corpse.

Danai's ax came down, once, twice, three times. The dust outside her cockpit was gray, but all she could see was red. The *Hellstar* tried weakly to bring its right arm and shoulder weapons into play, but a crossing slash of her ax put an end to that.

Then the *Ghost* emerged, ready to get off a clean shot with no *Hellstar* in its way. But Danai was ready—she'd kept her shield arm up for just this purpose. She only had to turn slightly and press the trigger to sent a blast of energy from her shoulder laser into the *Ghost*. Surprised and hurt, the *Ghost* disappeared back into the dust.

Danai returned to the motionless *Hellstar*. She swung again and again and again, sparks flying with each impact, slowly turning the once mighty 'Mech into rubbish. The red drained from her vision as she chopped and chopped, and it went from an act of fury to an act of anger to cold, remorseless battery. She didn't notice that the *Ghost* hadn't returned, and she couldn't say how long she stood there dismantling her enemy.

"*Sao-shao* Liao-Centrella?" A static-filled voice broke into her head. *Oh, yeah,* she remembered. *I'm supposed to be commanding a battle.*

The voice belonged to Clara. "Yes?"

"The militia has been routed. They are in full retreat, heading to Jifang Po City."

"Then we will meet them there. Have the troops regroup as quickly as possible so we can advance. I don't want to give them time to recover."

"Yes, *Sao-shao.*"

The dust had begun to settle a little, and visibility was improving. Then a gust of wind cleared out most of the block where Danai had been fighting, and she was surprised to see Clara's *Tian-Zong*, its weapons giving its shoulders an oddly hunched appearance, standing above her. She looked at her sensor. Sure enough, it indicated a large, friendly 'Mech only meters away. She should have noticed it sooner.

She lowered her ax and shield as she straightened, and she imagined Yen-lo-wang looked as abashed as a 50-ton king of the underworld could. She thought about asking Clara how long she'd been there, how much she had seen, and if she wondered why her commander was so intent on reducing a single enemy to little chunks, but then she decided she didn't owe anyone, even her XO, an explanation. She pulled her ax back up and prepared to head to Jifang Po City.

Jifang Po City
Aldebaran

The news from Daipan was not good. Legate Juk knew it wouldn't be, of course, but this was worse than even her low expectations. She knew her forces would lose the battle, but she had hoped the confusion caused by the collapsed building and her troops' advantage of fighting on their own turf would help them slow the Capellans down. For God's sake, she would have accepted two-to-one casualties in favor of the Capellans if that at least meant her people had *hurt* them. As it stood, her forces had inflicted little more than a flesh wound on the advancing elements from McCarron's Armored Cavalry.

She was in a round room on top of the planetary defense headquarters. Two hundred meters in the air, she had a perfect view of the surroundings, which, like the nearby cities of Wen Ho and Daipan, were almost entirely dark. The evacuation, at least, had gone relatively well. The residents of her planet took the Capellan military very seriously, and they had no desire to be present when the invading troops arrived. Government personnel and other related residents had remained behind, but they were all squirreled away in bunkers and shelters. Only the army was out to greet the soon-to-arrive guests.

Neither the tower's sensors nor the relays from the militia's scouting vehicles nor Legate Juk's own eyes registered any Capellan troops yet. When they came in sight, Legate Juk would likely have to abandon her lofty perch. As commanding as the view was, it didn't seem like a good idea to be perched high in the sky, surrounded by ferroglass, as the troops below came to grips. Before long she'd take an elevator that would shoot her 250 meters down, into a bunker well underground, where she'd monitor the battle.

This, then, would be her last glimpse of a whole, intact Jifang Po City. The only positive result she had gleaned from the battles so far was that the structures of Wen Ho and Daipan were relatively intact—in fact, her troops had done more damage exploding the building in Daipan than the Capellans had done in both cities combined. Jifang Po City, though, was not likely to be so fortunate. Conquering it would, for all intents and purposes, mean conquering Aldebaran. The Capellans would want to make a show of force here, to make Jifang Po City an example of their might for the rest of Aldebaran to see. When the sun next rose on her city, the place would likely be unrecognizable.

She wished she could do more for it. She wasn't entirely without resources—the planet's conventional fighters, a last-ditch measure, would hopefully make life uncomfortable for the Capellans (and provided another compelling reason for her to leave her high tower)—but her tricks wouldn't be enough. In the end, she was facing a force with more 'Mechs and more skill than she could hope to put on the field. Her city was doomed.

There were, of course, the incoming DropShips. She kept waiting for them to hail her, to tell her they were reinforcements coming to chase the invaders away. But they had remained stubbornly silent. She knew of no other reason a group of DropShips would be inbound at this moment, and so she clung to a slight hope. In the end, though, if they didn't hurry, the reinforcements might do no more than batter the Capellans after the Capellans had routed her militia.

She looked at the sensors and at the horizon, waiting for the first signs of the invasion to arrive. She wished briefly, irrationally, that some of the residents of Jifang Po would come back, would turn on the bright lights of the city and make even a small section of it look like it was supposed to, for one brief moment, before the city fell.

10

"The middle of your shield looks like an old candle," Clara said as the battalion tramped along.

"I know," Danai said regretfully. "I don't know when I'll be able to get it sculpted right again."

"Why bother?" Clara asked. "Just hold a lump of unfinished metal in front of you. It's going to look like that eventually—why spend time on a temporary cosmetic fix?"

"It's called 'panache,'" Danai responded archly. "If you drove a machine that looked like something other than a hunchback with elephantiasis, you might know something about that."

"At least I don't call myself king of the nine hells each time I take the battlefield."

"That's only because no one would take you seriously if you did."

Clara guffawed. "I guess some of us are gods, and others are just destined to be handmaidens."

"I'm glad you finally understand the chain of command."

The lightness of victory always eased the burden of battle. Later, the damage would be evaluated, the lost soldiers mourned. Later, she would feel the weight of command more. Now, though, Danai and her command lance felt only triumph, and it made them almost giddy as they traveled from Daipan to Jifang Po City.

It was a longer journey than the trip from Wen Ho to Daipan, and Danai was letting her troops take it a little slow so the techs could make minor repairs on the fly while they marched. The talk had been almost entirely banter and battle stories, and Danai didn't mind in the least—a battalion, like a muscle, couldn't stay tight all the time. A little relaxation on the journey would make them that much more ready for the next fight.

For her own part, she was ready now. Her feet kept twitching, wanting to break into a run and charge the Aldebarian capital on her own if everyone else couldn't keep up, but she'd already been incautious enough today when she'd pummeled the *Hellstar* and disregarded everything else.

Actually, that fight had been yesterday. The battalion had needed to cover two hundred kilometers to reach the capital, a journey that, at their current pace, would take them just under seven hours. It was now early morning—by Danai's estimate, they'd reach Jifang Po City an hour or so before sunrise. Since it was a new day, maybe that meant she could commit another rash action.

She sighed. That would be a very un-commander-like thing to do. Daoshen would be furious if he heard about her indulging in impulsive acts, and he undoubtedly would get the news eventually—it was a rare Capellan battalion that didn't have at least one or two troopers feeding information to the Maskirovka about the conduct of high-ranking officers. Plus there was the small matter that a lone charge would likely be suicidal. For some reason, though, imminent death didn't bother her as much as possible dishonor.

"Kites, what are you seeing?" she asked for the twentieth time since they left Daipan.

"Nothing yet," Cheung said. "We're getting closer to the outskirts of the city, though. It won't be long." She had the soothing tone of a parent calming a grumpy child on a car trip.

"All right," Danai said.

The countryside around her, like most of the planet she had seen since she landed, was dark. A thin moon had risen as they traveled, casting a greenish-gray light over the highway and surrounding farmland. She saw silhouettes of silos and massive garages housing Agro-Mechs, but no signs of life or movement. Either the people of Aldebaran were extremely sound sleepers, or they'd cleared out long before the Capellan battalion came through.

Danai had run through several battle plans in the past seven hours, trading notes with Sandra, but there were too many variables for them to fix on a specific plan yet. Would the militia meet them inside or outside the city? What exact numbers would they face? Should they expect another imploded building, with the ensuing dust storm, or not? If she split a 'Mech's cockpit with her ax, would it fall backward or crumple straight to the ground?

The last question was the only one she could conclusively answer (naturally, the final resting place of a 'Mech depended on its momentum before the blow landed, but for the most part they tended to fall backward). Too much guesswork went into the others, so she was left to simply move ahead and react to whatever she found.

Then her comm crackled to life to tell her what was waiting for her.

"We have them, *Sao-shao*," Cheung reported. "They're on the outskirts this time. Plenty of artillery; they're already firing at us. They're in a straight line—a series of lines, really. Looks like three layers of troops, four in some places."

"Numbers?"

"Hard to say. From what I'm seeing, they may equal us, probably have a little more. But I doubt I'm seeing everything—they must be keeping some troops in reserve inside the city."

"Okay. Thank you. Keep those arty units guessing on range while we get a little closer."

"Yes, *Sao-shao*. We'll serpentine until we're dizzy."

Danai grinned, then set her mind to specific tactics. She got in touch with Sandra and brought her up to speed.

"I'm not worried about having to take out more of them than they do of us," Danai said. "But we have to keep our losses as minimal as possible. We can't assume beating the forces on the outskirts is all we have to do."

Sandra heard Danai's information without reply, and Danai assumed that meant she was thinking things over. Danai allowed her silence.

She didn't have to wait long. "We can't just charge straight in," Sandra said, thinking out loud now. "They'll have too much time to get the measure of us with their artillery and long-range weapons. We'd be taking on senseless damage."

Then Sandra had it. Danai could hear it in her tone immediately. Her words came quicker, her excitement mounting as she visualized what she wanted. "We'll have the infantry scatter, make themselves individual targets instead of large groups as they move forward. Fast units will go up front, divided into three groups—left, right and jump. The left and the right will head out on diagonals, the jump will continue charging toward the middle. They'll draw the most fire. As soon as it looks like it's getting too intense, they jump. All of them at once, making a series of timed jumps. They give a signal that they've started, and left and right turn back toward the center, blasting the enemy down with cover fire. All three groups try to break the middle of the line. Once we're through"—Danai appreciated Sandra's assumption of her plan's success—"we wreak havoc on their back lines, while our infantry and slower units keep the pressure on the front. We keep on them until they're routed."

"Excellent," Danai said. The plan seemed like a good combination of textbook planning and clever improvisation based on the circumstances. "You're already justifying my faith in you."

"Thanks." The word was the vocal equivalent of a shrug—Sandra was clearly happy with her plan, and she apparently didn't need a compliment from Danai to prove the worth of her ideas.

Danai passed the plan on to Clara and Bell. Clara replied with a simple "Yes, *Sao-shao*," but Bell, naturally, couldn't leave it at that. She'd told him he would be in command of the middle group—he and Sandra both had jump jets, but his superior speed made him the better choice to lead that group—and he responded with mock surprise.

"A good assignment in only our third battle!" he said. "Does this mean you really like me after all?"

A sharp reply about personal likes and dislikes sprang to her mouth, but she let it die on her tongue. Instead, she matched his tone.

"No," she said. "It means I hope you'll be a really big, inviting target for the militia."

Bell fell silent. Was he actually tongue-tied? Then Danai thought back on all the things she'd ever said to him, and this most recent remark counted as the nicest. Clearly, any friendly gesture from her confused the hell out of him.

The front line of the militia was growing closer. Time to concentrate.

Danai had assigned herself to the right wing of the attack, so that when they veered back to the left she'd be able to lead with her ax hand as she charged. Her heat was relatively low, which kept her triple-strength myomer inactive. For the time being, she was only slightly faster than most 'Mechs her size.

Clara was with the left wing of the attack, having to command it from behind because she couldn't keep up with the smaller, faster 'Mechs in her group. She was the easiest target in her wing and was drawing the most fire. Danai couldn't tell how many hits the *Tian-Zong* was absorbing, but since it was still moving and Clara hadn't yet called for help, she assumed it wasn't too bad.

The fire in the middle of the field came in faster and faster. A few shells were fired from her own artillery units, but most came from the stationary militia guns, whose shots were growing more and more accurate. Holes kept appearing in the ferrocrete where rounds landed, and Danai saw at least one battle-armored trooper catch a gauss slug in the head, leveling him. So far, though, the overall damage was manageable. And the range to the front lines was dropping every second.

Bell's voice came over the comm. "Center units, prepare to jump on my mark. Five . . . four . . . three . . . two . . . one . . . *mark*."

Dozens of pairs of orange flames burst into life as the center units, almost in unison, leaped into the air. One *Phoenix Hawk* was unlucky enough to jump right into a large shell from the militia artillery, but the rest of the units flew clear while shells and laser beams harmlessly passed them by.

Danai and her unit had already wheeled to the left. She put Yen-lo-wang into a run and fired her shoulder laser into the militia units clustered at the center of their line. She scored a hit on an opposition 'Mech, and she felt the welcome heat from her weapon's discharge flood the cockpit. The myomer was ready for action, and now Danai had all the speed she wanted.

She pounded ahead, earth shaking beneath her, keeping pace with a *Wasp* that was less than half her size. In her unit, only the speedy *Blades* could outrun her, but they hung back a little—at thirty-five tons, they usually weren't anxious to be the first ones to reach enemy lines.

Unlike the last battle, Danai had a fair amount of open space between her and her enemies, so she wouldn't have to rely solely on her ax. It was time to bring some long-range weapons into play. Using her eyes and her sensors, she scanned the lines in front of her for an appropriate target. The militia troops had stood fairly still when her battalion started its charge, but became more active when the Capellans reached their firing range. They were advancing slowly while zigging and zagging, not letting themselves become easy targets for Capellan weaponry. Then, behind the shifting militia troops, Danai saw what she wanted to see—the big barrel on top of a Regulator hovertank hurling slugs deep into her lines. Time to put an end to that.

Her Artemis system drew a bead on the Regulator, and Danai fired a cluster of missiles that should put a damper on the vehicle's enthusiasm.

The LRMs streaked out of her chest-mounted launcher, exhaust contrails twisting out of their tails as they flew toward their target.

The Regulator detected the incoming missiles and started to move back, but it had nowhere to hide. The Artemis system guided the missiles home, and eighteen of them slammed into the side of the Regulator. Another one, defective, bumped off the top and then exploded harmlessly, while the last of the flight caught the arm of a nearby *Cougar* and detonated there instead. Flame enveloped the Regulator, which for the moment quit firing. Then militia 'Mechs and support vehicles closed in front of the wounded vehicle, laying down cover fire to keep Danai from finishing it. Lights flashed and an alarm buzzed, warning Danai that she had incoming missiles of her own to worry about.

She grinned, ready to use every weapon at her disposal. Nothing like a good, open fight. Everything was going perfectly—except for the continually updating information from Yun that showed the approaching DropShips were in Aldebaran's atmosphere.

DropShip **Exarch's Pride**
Over Aldebaran
Republic of the Sphere

Major Bennett Anderton carefully drummed his egg on his white linen tablecloth. He shelled it delicately, making sure no piece of the hard exterior remained on the white. Once he had removed enough shell, he scooped out the egg with a spoon and let the gleaming white orb slip into his china bowl.

He ground two peppercorns and sprinkled them over his egg, then threw on a dash of salt. He cut through it with his spoon, observing with pleasure that the white was solid but the yolk still flowed outward. Cooked to perfection.

He carefully chopped off a small piece of white, coated it with yolk and was raising it toward his mouth when a crisp knock sounded at his door.

He managed to call out "Enter!" before the spoon reached his mouth, so he could chew and swallow the bite without interrupting his motion.

One of the DropShip's crew entered his stateroom. "Sir! All machines are prepared and your battalion is ready to land!"

Anderton nodded, taking another bite. "Excellent," he said. "Thank you." He continued eating.

The crewman didn't leave. He stood straight, fidgeting slightly as Anderton ate his egg.

After a minute of this, Anderton sighed. "Is there anything else?"

"No, sir."

"Then why are you still here?"

"I am available to conduct you to your 'Mech preliminary to your insertion on the planet."

"That's quite gracious of you, but I believe I can find the way myself."

The crewman's fidgeting was becoming more obvious. "Yes, of course, sir. But . . ."

Anderton raised an eyebrow. He generally did not approve of enlisted men saying the word "but" in the presence of an officer. However, his sense of decorum (as well as the inner calm he needed to maintain if this morning's activities were to go as planned) prevented him from barking at the crewman. Instead, he humored him.

"Yes?"

"I just thought that you would want to go to your

'Mech as soon as possible. Once it was ready. For the fast deploy."

Anderton sighed, very quietly so the crewman wouldn't notice. It seemed he was always having to deliver lessons in time management.

"Generally speaking, it will take my battalion anywhere from twenty-seven to thirty-eight minutes after completing the initial checks to be ready to move forward. Walking to the bays, getting the necessary clearances, ensuring everything inside one's machine is the way one wants it, et cetera, et cetera. Now, I know from experience that it will only take me twenty minutes to perform those tasks. That means I have at least seven extra minutes. I could use that time sitting idly in my machine, or I can use it enjoying a small breakfast that will provide necessary nourishment for the coming fight. I assure you I will be ready to drop before the rest of my crew. That will be all."

The crewman saluted. Clearly still out of sorts, he turned too quickly and stumbled through the hatch out of Anderton's berth.

Anderton shook his head as the door to his quarters closed. *Efficiency*, he thought, *is a lost virtue*.

Anderton was perched in his *Thunderbolt*, the LRM-15 launcher a comforting presence just off to his right. He had tested the grips of his control sticks and the grip of the pads on his pedals, he'd put on his combat gloves and stretched his hands exactly six times to make sure the leather settled itself properly. The cockpit hummed quietly with power, ready to do whatever he asked.

Time to check on the rest of the battalion.

"Alpha Company, please report on your status." When he'd taken command of the Second Battalion of the Triarii Protectors, the companies within the battalion had names he found fairly ludicrous—Hyena Company, Hangfire Company, Wolfsbane Company—and making sure those names were dropped had been one of his first matters of business. He had nothing, of course, against colorful nicknames, and he by no means wanted to trample on the individuality of the men who served beneath him, but the last thing a commander needed when issuing orders was to waste time trying to remember the eccentric appellations the soldiers had chosen. There was a reason simple labels like Alpha, Bravo and Charlie stood the test of time—they were clear and straightforward. They did not impede the business of combat.

"Alpha Company prepared and ready," responded Lieutenant Marcy Breen. The redundancy of the answer briefly annoyed Anderton but, since it was clear enough and to the point, he let it pass.

"Bravo Company, please report on your status."

"Bravo Company ready." That was Lieutenant Fisher Cowen—direct and efficient. *A good lad,* Anderton thought.

"Charlie Company, please report on your status."

"In the saddle and itchin' to ride!"

Anderton didn't respond. He'd reviewed protocol enough times with Lieutenant Gaffney that he felt no need to repeat the lecture now. He let his silence do all the talking for him.

When Gaffney finally spoke again, he didn't sound quite as much like a character from the *Dead in the Ancient West* holovid series.

"Ready, sir," he said, giving the last word something that might have been an insolent twist. Anderton paid it no mind.

After reviewing his supporting units in similar fashion, Anderton gave the clearance for the operation to proceed. In the blink of an eye, he went from the harsh white light of the ship's 'Mech bay to the dim pinks and purples of the first traces of sunrise over Aldebaran. He could see explosions and smoke in the distance, traces of the battle with which he meant to interfere. The grass well below him looked easy enough to land in, and the enemies in front of him should be surprised and hopefully discomfited by his unit's jump jet–aided arrival.

All in all, the morning looked to be just as satisfying as a perfectly shelled egg.

Jifang Po City, Aldebaran
Republic of the Sphere

"*Sao-shao*, the reinforcements are officially on the move."

Danai blinked in midslash. The *Locust* she had pinned thought it was being granted a chance for escape, but her hesitation was brief. Yen-lo-wang's right arm continued its downward swipe and crushed the middle window of the 'Mech's cockpit. The poor little beast shuddered and collapsed.

She pulled her ax out of the wreckage and let the momentum of the move spin her to the right, where a battle-armor platoon was getting annoyingly close. A single blast of her heavy laser made them think better of approaching her.

Now she could take a moment to concentrate on what Harris Yun had to tell her.

"All right, Yun, how much time do we have? Do you know who they are yet? And how many they've got?"

"Everything besides the IFF points to them being Republic troops, probably from New Canton, and that means probably Triarii. Looks like a battalion, coming down in a fast deployment. They'll hit the ground running and come right to the back of your lines."

"*Ta ma de!*" Danai swore. "How long?"

"They're a ways east. Maybe fifty kilometers. You've got an hour, maybe a little more."

Danai and Sandra had talked earlier, when it was clear that reinforcements were coming, and they'd decided their best option was to push through the militia troops and get a defensive position inside the city. But they had less time than Danai wanted, and the reinforcements were larger in number than she'd hoped. The sooner they could get secured inside Jifang Po, the better.

"*Sang-wei* Parks—how scattered are we?"

"More by the minute," Clara said briskly, "but that's because the militia's scattering." The Aldebarian forces had fallen back inside the outskirts soon after the start of the battle, trying to gain concealment behind the low buildings of the suburbs while leaving Danai's forces out in the open. All it did was slow down the inevitable—the militia troops gained some shelter, but at the cost of ruining their own sight lines. They could do little more than wait for the Capellan troops to track them down and take them out. It had been a sloppy battle, filled with individual skirmishes, but Danai wasn't bothered because she was getting the results she wanted—her disciplined troops were easily outperforming the militia, and the Aldebarian casualties were much higher than her own.

"Call off the chase," she told her XO. "We need to move into the city center. You and Bell lead a punch through the middle of the militia lines. Hold the hole open long enough to get the whole battalion through."

"Yes, *Sao-shao*."

"Sandra, come with me. We're going to head up the rear guard for this action."

Sandra's *Marauder* was only a kilometer away, laying down heavy cover fire while faster units mounted their pursuit. She was tromping at Danai's side a bare minute later.

For a time they had little to do besides watch the troops gather in front of them. Clara and Bell easily punched a hole in the militia line, and Bell in particular seemed to have fun holding the gap open practically single-handedly. Before long he began delivering a play-by-play of his actions over the comm.

"Wait, wait, this could be trouble. Couple of Kelswas, cleverly coming at me from two different directions. But whoops, I've got a laser, that one's going to have to swerve for a minute, and hey, look at that, an autocannon! I've got an autocannon too! And the Kelswa just isn't the best-armored vehicle in the universe, and it's taking it right on the chin. And the nose, ears, whatever. Shredding like paper in, well, a shredder."

Danai was glad Bell couldn't see the small grin that kept tugging at one corner of her mouth against her will. "Bell!" she said, making her voice sound much harsher than she felt. "Can we keep this channel open for official business, please?"

"This *is* official," Bell insisted. "I'm relaying my experiences for posterity. So when historians write about this battle, they'll know how a *Locust* tried to sneak up on me and, *oh*, took a PPC right up the guts! That's *gotta* hurt!"

That stupid grin persisted, and now it seemed to be sneaking into her voice. "Bell, don't make me order you."

"Wouldn't dream of it, *Sao-shao*. I'll conduct my heroic defense of this gap in noble silence."

Danai rolled her eyes. At least his morale was good.

The battalion had gathered itself promptly, and Danai was pleased at its discipline. That would be vital for the tougher opponents charging toward them.

The last units were moving toward the gap. Sandra stomped forward, each step a minor tremor. Between her gauss rifles and her extended-range PPC, she was deadly at a distance, and she kept a steady stream of slugs and bolts flying toward anyone attempting to move on the rear of the battalion.

While the *Marauder* moved forward in a more or less straight line, Danai took Yen-lo-wang on a darting course, back and forth through the occasionally winding streets of Jifang Po's outskirts. Her shoulder laser rose above most of the buildings in this part of town, and she fired a few shots over the rooftops. The Artemis system locked on to a few militia 'Mechs and a tank or two as she weaved back and forth. She launched volleys at the units that looked the most threatening. The sight of the missiles exploding upon impact and the excitement of intimidating units by her mere appearance was fun, but the whole time she kept her ax upright and unused. Plenty of units on the field had missiles and lasers, but she appeared to be the only one with an ax. She hated to keep it out of play for long.

Soon she and Sandra were passing through what had once been the militia's line. Clara and Bell fell in with them, Bell offering one final flourish.

"And the battalion is through! History will debate whether this was a fantastic display of individual combat prowess, or a brilliant example of two 'Mechs exhibiting team tactics, but either way this battle will likely be a part of military academy texts for decades to come."

Danai almost smiled again. Then, for no good reason, she thought of another MechWarrior she knew who clearly thought highly of his own abilities, and she spent the rest of the advance into the heart of Jifang Po City trying to resist the urge to fire her heavy laser into Bell's back.

11

Jifang Po City, Aldebaran
Republic of the Sphere
28 November 3135

The sheets had not been changed. Room service was not available. The holovid worked, but no signal came through—none of the channels in the city were functioning. Water flowed, but power was erratic, and Danai was calling in techs every few hours to keep as much juice flowing to her second-floor room as possible. Under normal circumstances she would have registered a firm complaint to management and refused to pay her bill until she received satisfaction. However, since management had fled and she wasn't paying anything for the room, she supposed it was acceptable.

After her forces made it to the heart of Jifang Po City, Danai had stood ready and waiting for the militia and their reinforcements to push them out. The new arrivals had come just close enough for Danai to get a look at the insignia on the shoulders of their lead 'Mechs—a curved rectangle that looked like the front piece of a column with the Roman numeral III on it. They were Triarii Protectors. Not the most fearsome unit in the

Inner Sphere by any means, but not one to be over-looked, either.

The first part of the battle had gone fairly well for the Capellans, but they had still suffered losses. She had lost a little over ten percent of her 'Mechs and one of her three artillery pieces. Her infantry had suffered similar reductions, though some of the troopers were only wounded and would recover in time. All told, she'd come onto the planet with about two-thirds of a battalion, and she now had about half a battalion still functioning after three battles. Her reports had the Triarii at a full battalion, including air support, plus whatever was left of the militia. This meant Danai was sitting at two-to-one, maybe two-and-a-half-to-one odds. Odds much more suited to defending than to attacking. So she looked for a good position—including placing her surviving artillery units and many of her infantry troops in buildings with good views and decent protection—and waited for the attack to come.

It didn't. Her troops got a few good shots at the *Spider* that led the Triarii pack, and it promptly turned around and headed out of downtown. A pair of Capellan *Wasps* ran out in pursuit, but cover fire from the bulk of the battalion discouraged them, and they returned to downtown Jifang Po City.

Then, except for the occasional crash of artillery shells through skyscraper windows, there was silence. Silence for more than two days.

If the Republic troops were trying to starve the Capellans out, they'd picked the wrong venue. Civilians fleeing from the city's interior had left behind a wealth of food, and Danai had no compunction about taking whatever her unit could find—and that included taking over the hotel kitchen and its cavernous walk-in freezer.

Foraging for supplies kept the troops occupied for a time, but it was nothing like combat, and after two days they were getting restless. Especially Bell, who had already told everyone he could find about his heroics on the front lines. He was eager to write another chapter in his glorious biography.

Danai wanted some distraction, any distraction, that could keep her from reviewing her unit's losses in her head. When she was young, she had played a game with her friends, an old, old game. Pieces moved around a circular board, buying properties and charging opposing players rent when others landed on your spaces. You won by bankrupting your opponents.

One girl she had played with, Reenie, took losing particularly hard (and, because she tended to hoard her money rather than buy properties, she lost often). After one defeat, Reenie, near tears, had taken out her frustrations on the victorious Danai.

"I hope you're happy," she had said. "You and all your money. Did you ever stop to think of the families you've ruined? The people who don't have a home to go to anymore? Just so you can have more money? You must be so proud."

Danai was, in fact, quite proud of herself, and she said so, leading to a protracted argument. She had laughed off Reenie at the time, since it was only a game, but on further consideration (and much pushing by Reenie), she had been forced to admit that if it hadn't been a game, her actions would indeed have been particularly cruel.

The heat of battle was thousands, millions of times more exciting than that old game. It got her blood moving like nothing else in the world, and while she was fighting she wanted to be utterly triumphant, no matter the cost.

But then it was over, and she was left with the dead and wounded Capellans who had suffered because of her orders, and it was like winning the game she'd played with Reenie and subsequently being forced to shake the hands of each and every victim of her heartless quest for money. Only the aftermath of battle was thousands, millions of times worse.

She had been at this long enough to have a series of preconstructed arguments in her head, and she ran them in a constant stream in the days after a fight. *This is war. It's harsh, it's brutal, people die. That's the way it is. People sign up for it, just like I did, knowing what they're getting into. They know the potential cost. It's not my job to baby them, to protect them. It's my job to use them. To further the glory of the Confederation, to secure our borders, to vanquish those who would conquer us. If I didn't do it, I'd be shirking my responsibility, or worse— I'd be a traitor.*

All those arguments helped somewhat, and she knew that time and activity would force her back to her normal self. But in the immediate silent aftermath of a battle, the voices of the people she had sent to their deaths were not easy to drown out.

The distraction she sought finally came—a transmission into the Capellan comm center, with a code that the techs passed on to Danai. Danai put the code into the video comm in her commandeered hotel room and saw the image of an elaborately handsome man in full Triarii dress uniform. He had the kind of face normally seen on store-bought frames for holovid stills, the clean good looks to which everyone, according to retailers, was supposed to aspire. His dark brown hair was wavy, his chin slightly cleft, his nose strong but not too bold, and his eyes green and intelligent. For a moment, Danai was convinced the code she had received had dialed her into a Triarii recruiting ad.

Then the ad spoke.

"Good evening," he said. "I asked that this code be conveyed to the commander of the invading Capellan forces, so I assume you are she."

"That I am."

"Splendid. I'm Major Bennett Anderton, commander, Triarii Protectors Second Battalion. We have been dispatched to assist in the defense of Aldebaran."

He fell silent, clearly expecting a reply from Danai. Not quite knowing what he wanted to hear, she said, "Good for you." Then there was another moment of awkward silence.

Anderton sighed. "May I ask your name?"

Danai shrugged, deciding it mattered little if this man knew who she was. "*Sao-shao* Danai Liao-Centrella."

He showed no reaction to the name, remaining blankly

composed. "A pleasure, *Sao-shao* Liao-Centrella. I wanted to arrange this meeting to take a measure of your intentions. May I ask what your plans are?"

"Only if you'll be satisfied with vague, general statements."

"Naturally," Anderton replied smoothly. "I wouldn't expect you to compromise your defenses."

This man, Danai decided, had been Triarii for too long. He was like a human show pony.

"My plans are to take and hold this planet for the Capellan Confederation," she said.

Anderton nodded slightly. "As I thought. It's a pity, really. If you were here on a raiding mission of some sort, perhaps we might be able to come to some sort of agreement that would end this standoff peacefully. But it seems you want more than just a portion of Aldebaran's material wealth."

"Yes, it seems," Danai said. "But you can still get out of this without any more fighting. If you and the militia surrender to me, everything's fine."

"I'm afraid that's not one of our options," Anderton said, puckering his lips slightly. "In fact, I might suggest the reverse—with the way the forces are currently aligned, you may want to consider surrender."

Danai put her index finger to her lips and looked up, as if concentrating. Then she looked back at the comm. "I considered it. No. We're not surrendering. Not now, not ever." She wasn't sure what had gotten into her— she usually wasn't this flip in diplomatic matters. But something about Anderton—maybe his formality, maybe his smugness, maybe just his *maleness*—made her want to needle him as much as possible, to get under his skin.

Anderton shrugged, looking much like a wealthy patron of a tropical resort who has just been informed that his preferred vintage of wine is not in stock. "Very well. I expect to encounter you on the battlefield shortly, where hopefully our physical jousting will be more conclusive than our conversation. Good evening, *Sao-shao* Liao-Centrella."

His image disappeared before she could respond.

His confidence unnerved her a little. He seemed sure that his force could subdue hers—but if that was the case, why had he waited two days? It was time to check in with Cheung.

"Yes, *Sao-shao*?" Cheung said promptly when Danai hailed her over the comm.

"Is anything going on out there I should know about?"

"Funny you should ask," Cheung said. "We've been picking up some vehicle activity on the edge of our sensor range—support vehicles, looks like a column. No 'Mechs yet. They get close enough to get in sensor range, then dart back out. We've picked them up three or four times now. They were north of us, heading west, first time we saw them. They seem to be circling—last time we saw them, they'd shifted their direction to southwest."

Danai instinctively knew what was going on, but she needed proof—and a definite head count of the opposition. "Push your vehicles a little farther out," she said. "Try to get a complete picture of what's out there and let me know as soon as you do."

"Yes, *Sao-shao*."

It had to be more reinforcements, coming in on a roundabout path, avoiding Capellan sensors as long as they could. This was not good. She didn't figure the amount of militia forces coming in would be huge, but it could easily worsen the imbalance of the situation— make it three to one, maybe even three and a half to one. While the general consensus among Capellan warriors held that one Capellan was worth five or even ten troops of any other given army, Danai didn't wish to put that notion to the test, especially when she was hemmed in on enemy ground. Nothing would be improved by sitting here in the city. The longer she waited in her commandeered hotel room, the more likely that a sizeable Triarii/militia force would come in to make her life miserable.

She was already feeling pretty miserable. Her big gambit, spreading out her forces across three planets to con-

fuse the troops of Prefecture VI, seemed to have gotten
her nothing. That didn't make her happy, but it wouldn't
have mattered much if she had succeeded on Aldebaran.
Unfortunately, the situation here was looking grim, and
she found herself wishing she had aerial support to help
her take the planet. She never liked being wrong, especially when the stakes were so high.

But the fight wasn't lost yet. She summoned her command lance to her room. If the Capellan forces meant
to take the planet, they first needed to get safely out of
Jifang Po. Then they could regroup, and give that smug
Triarii what he had coming.

29 November 3135

It had been worse than Danai expected. The militia, with
good reason, seemed to have decided that there was little point to guarding the rest of Aldebaran at the moment. If Jifang Po fell, whatever happened elsewhere
would be largely irrelevant. So they had stripped most
of their garrisons and brought the bulk of their forces
to the capital. When Cheung finally tallied up all the
arriving forces, it came to two full battalions of reinforcements. The actual worth of a Capellan soldier compared to a Republican trooper seemed likely to be
tested.

The planning meeting for the upcoming battle had
gone against most of Danai's instincts. She was no
stranger to improvising a retreat when the situation
called for it—New Hessen had been good for that, at
least—but sitting down and planning an entire battle
whose only goal was retreat was a new and unpleasant
experience. She tried to assuage the discomfort by referring to the action as a "retrograde movement" throughout the planning meeting, but in the end the effect was
similar to saying someone had passed away instead of
saying they had died—it sounded more pleasant, but the
choice of words did nothing to bring the individual in
question back to life.

She comforted herself that this movement did not

mean defeat—they were merely regrouping, buying more time to make a stronger assault. She wasn't giving anything up yet.

It also helped that Sandra's plan for the movement gave her a plum assignment due to Yen-lo-wang's speed. Kuang Nu Company held the fastest 'Mechs in her command, so Sandra had plucked the two quickest lances, thrown in a few Enyo strike tanks for good measure, and put Danai at the head of this group. It was the only reasonable choice—none of the others in her command lance could hope to keep up, and they had other assignments anyway.

She was in the heart of the movement, walking down a broad avenue behind a pair of *Blade*s. With their speed and smaller lasers, she was counting on them to do a lot of the heavy lifting on this part of the battle plan. But she'd pick up a little weight of her own as well.

The *Blade*s were already peppering the buildings and street ahead with autocannon fire, their thick, awkward lower legs belying their considerable speed. They weren't hitting anything—no Triarii or militia units had been foolish enough to come out of hiding—but that wasn't the point. The point was to make noise, and they were doing plenty of that.

She walked by broken windows and chipped facades where limestone cladding fell away and exposed the brick clinkers underneath. A few traffic lights remained in operation ahead of them, but the *Blade*s finished them off by walking through the ones that overhung the street, tearing them off as if they were tall blades of grass in a meadow. Every little bit of destruction made Danai feel better about the planned retreat.

She checked her sensors. They were getting in pretty deep now. The units directly to their west had backed up a little as Danai's group advanced, putting a small pucker in the defenders' lines. If they wanted to, they could collapse on Danai from three directions at once. Danai suspected they would want to do just that fairly quickly—in fact, her plan hinged on it.

"Halt the advance," she told her group. "We get in any

deeper, we'll have trouble getting out. Deng, Chow, I want you two stationed at the park we just passed. That should give you some open space to fire across when the attack comes. The rest of you, stay put and keep firing. If you actually hit something, so much the better."

Lasers traced through the streets, autocannon rounds clattered everywhere and a few artillery rounds whined overhead. Danai didn't have much to do—firing her missiles without a target lock was pointless, and rapid, random firing of her heavy laser would lead to overheating in short order. She stayed put, wiggled her ax menacingly and fired an occasional laser blast to keep her heat up so that her triple-strength myomer would be ready when needed.

The uniform gray of the sky blended well with the smoke and dust rising from the efforts of Danai's group. The tall buildings of downtown Jifang Po funneled the cold autumn breeze, blowing it directly into Yen-lo-wang's face. *That's okay*, Danai thought. *If the wind cools me down enough, I can take an extra shot or two.*

Then the preliminaries were over.

Klaxons sounded in her cockpit, lights flashed and movement on the sensors showed that the Triarii and the militia were on the move. Missiles snaked toward Danai's group, while gauss slugs flew in straight, terrifyingly swift lines. The enemy was charging from all three directions. It was time to move.

"Here they come!" Danai called. "Keep moving, but don't move back yet. They need to think we're on the offensive. We have to hold this line for a while."

Danai turned and started north, stopping with a short skid as a single missile—either defective or jammed—passed right in front of her cockpit. It broke through a shattered third-floor window, hit an interior wall and exploded. Flames shot out of the building.

Danai ran past, hoping the whole thing would burn enough to become a minor distraction. Her steps, faster and faster, punished the ferrocrete beneath her, opening cracks and enlarging existing divots. She glanced at her sensors to see what was coming at her, ran another block, then took another right. Two more blocks, then left, north again. As she passed through an intersection, several energy beams flew out, but the attacker hadn't judged her speed correctly. The weapons fire passed harmlessly behind her, and she continued north.

One more block, then west again. Then south, and there were the 'Mechs that had fired at her. Two of them in the intersection, an *Ocelot* and a *Cougar*, waiting for her. They had five pulse lasers between them, and it looked to Danai like they'd let loose with at least four.

She couldn't avoid them all. There wasn't enough room. She let the momentum of her turn carry her to the west side of the street, moving her clear of the *Ocelot*'s fire, but not the *Cougar*'s. She caught one beam on her shield, melting some of it away. Soon it would be about as effective a defense as Swiss cheese.

The second beam from the *Cougar* caught her in the right leg, just below the knee. Her damage monitors showed the leg actuator to be singed but functional. It had better be—the last thing she could afford to lose was her legs.

Because her enemies were using their lasers, Danai decided it was only fair to return the favor. The *Cougar* stood right in front of her, so she let it feel a full blast from her heavy gun.

Her aim was a little off. She got the enemy 'Mech mostly in one of its extra-wide shoulders, cooking off its Triarii insignia but doing no significant damage.

Swiftly, she assessed the situation. Street-level visibility remained good, and these two 'Mechs had a wider assortment of short-range weapons than she did. Dancing with them in a melee slugfest was asking for trouble. Better to use the skills she had available.

She kept Yen-lo-wang running down the block, ax held high, shield covering her vitals. The two 'Mechs in front of her were preparing their next shots, but the sight of the tall, low-browed Capellan 'Mech bearing down on them caused a crucial moment of hesitation. As that moment ended, she was on them.

She swept her ax down and to the side, carrying it

almost perpendicular, with a slight downward cant to offset the lower height of her opposition. She let her speed do most of the work as she made a quick move to her right, placing her between the two 'Mechs. Her ax caught the *Cougar* firmly in the midsection as she passed, while she flung out her shield arm and smashed the *Ocelot*'s chest-mounted laser. She didn't think the blow would break the laser, but it would at least knock the *Ocelot* off-balance.

Her ax stuck in the *Cougar* as she passed, pulling on her right arm. She let her torso swivel, straining to stay upright, then held Yen-lo-wang on its right foot, letting the inertia on her right side and the momentum on her left swivel her around. While she turned, she brought her shield back in front of her, just in time to extend it and deliver a sharp blow to the *Cougar*.

The Triarii 'Mech stumbled back. Danai fired her heavy laser again, this time catching the *Cougar* full in the torso. She saw no spike on her IR sensor—the *Cougar*'s engine was damaged but still working.

She wasn't in prime condition, either. Two heavy laser shots in rapid succession, combined with the effort of running and the hits she had taken, had spiked her own heat. The air in the cockpit felt oppressive, and Danai realized she was panting. Time to cut off this skirmish.

She was already pointing north, so she ran in that direction. The *Ocelot*, which had been turning toward her when she caught it with her shield, was left to awkwardly stumble around and try for another shot. It succeeded, but again it underestimated Danai's speed. A beam clipped her back, but the shot had no effect other than slightly raising the already-high cockpit temperature and making her heat alarms whine even more insistently.

She turned right at the next corner, checked to see if any opponents had a clear shot at her, then slowed a little when she saw they didn't. She could envision the waves of heat that Yen-lo-wang must have been trailing as she walked back east, then south, drawing closer again to her group.

"How are we holding up?" she asked over the comm and got varying reports. The park, being one of the only open blocks in the immediate area, had attracted a lot of attention. Two pilots with her, Deng and Chow, had held their ground under swift and heavy pressure, then thrown the Triarii and Aldebarian troops back when the other 'Mechs from their lance came to lend a hand. Deng had borne the brunt of the initial assault and could barely move. Danai ordered him to fall back and get ready for what would be a very slow retreat—for him, at least.

"Stay near *Sang-wei* Sung," Danai advised Deng as he fell back. "Now that you're crippled, you may be the only unit we've got that's as slow as she is."

The group had also lost a strike tank, but other than that they seemed to be holding together. Even better, the first wave of the attack hadn't broken them, so the Triarii/Aldebarian force was calling for reinforcements from other sections of their line to drive off this menace. Just what was supposed to happen.

That meant Danai had a little more time, but not much. She could check quickly on the two 'Mechs she'd just met and see if they were ready to play a little more. She'd paid attention to the buildings on the street one block east of where she'd met the *Ocelot* and *Cougar*, and she had an idea.

Both her opponents were moving south. She'd hit the *Cougar* with a pair of pretty good blows, but not enough to keep it down. *Soon enough*, she thought.

She'd have to move quickly for this to work. She was now a block south and a block east of the pair of 'Mechs. She slowed her pace and headed west.

She traveled about a quarter of the way down the block, then turned back east as her two opponents rounded the corner to the west. Seeing her, they sprinted forward and fired their lasers, but Danai was ready. Already on the move when they started their turn, she had gone around the next corner and headed north before they could get a clear shot.

Now she needed to move fast. She edged over to the

right side of the street as she ran at full speed, battling to maintain her traction on the smooth ferrocrete. Before long the two pursuers rounded the corner behind her and tore after her. Danai went into an erratic run, heading northwest, then straight north, then northwest again, changing her direction at irregular intervals to throw off their fire. A number of their beams went astray, but not all of them. Her rear armor absorbed at least three shots. Luckily, her preference for charging meant her rear armor hadn't taken much damage in combat recently. Sensors flashed, alarms blared, but Yen-lo-wang held together.

Then she was where she wanted to be. She'd opened up nearly a block and a half lead on her pursuers, which should be enough. She turned west, ran a quarter of a block, and turned south again.

The building she approached had a tremendous glass atrium in front of it, with windows stretching thirty meters into the sky, slowly curving back until the glass formed a partial roof, then met with the gray granite office building behind it. The atrium sat at an angle, with one wall on the north-south street, another on the east-west.

Danai crashed through the glass about as easily as the *Blades* had moved through the traffic signals. A few exotic trees fell in front of her, thanks in part to a sweeping blow with her ax—*the king of the nine hells*, she thought, *is not above occasional work as a lumberjack*—and then she was tearing across a white tile mosaic floor. Her passage left it unrecognizable.

It was possible the two 'Mechs chasing her didn't realize what she was doing, didn't check their sensors to see what kind of turn she had taken. It was equally possible that they knew exactly what she was doing but, when it happened, the sheer spectacle of it overwhelmed them. Either way, the end result was the same.

She barreled through the atrium and crashed through the glass wall on the other side. She held her shield in front of her, pushing plenty of glass forward as she burst through.

The two 'Mechs still faced north, and she was coming from the northwest. The odd angle of her approach, bad visibility caused by flying glass and the surprise of her emergence threw them off balance. They turned on her, but too slowly, and she was on top of them. Her eyes stayed on the wounded *Cougar* the whole time. She swung; an uppercut, diagonal, under the left shoulder. Thirty-five tons of metal lifted three centimeters off the ground, then slammed down as Danai pulled the ax back. In a single, smooth motion, her arm wheeled around and came down hard on the off-balance *Cougar*'s head. The cockpit shattered. Leaning to its right, with no pilot to stabilize it, the 'Mech went down.

The *Ocelot*, meanwhile, had taken a few steps back. It let loose with its lasers as the *Cougar* fell, and Danai could not move her shield around quickly enough. Catching her full in the chest, the shots did more than melt away armor. Her chest missile launcher suffered a hit, and a few missiles detonated. The concussions shook her 'Mech, and status lights showed that her launcher was compromised. She'd have to do without it for the remainder of the battle.

Luckily her engine was okay—the LRM was close to it, but the armor held. Still, she couldn't afford to take too many more hits in that area.

The *Ocelot* was going to pay. She came at it in a flurry, her ax arm slashing an *x* in front of the retreating 'Mech. The *Ocelot* squeezed off a few more shots, but now Danai was ready, and her shield took the damage. She leaned forward harder, her ax moving menacingly, and the *Ocelot* hastened its retreat.

But Danai's feet didn't move. She had them planted, set, ready. While the *Ocelot* panicked, she blasted it with her laser. A head shot. The *Ocelot*, like the *Cougar* before it, reeled.

Danai waited, but it didn't go down. She'd made a mess of the cockpit, but the machinery still functioned and the pilot was alive. Pity.

She plunged forward again as the *Ocelot* regained its

footing, and once again it was time for the ax. Danai aimed a crossing blow at the machine's waist. She caught it, and the *Ocelot* stumbled again.

Another ax chop, then another. The *Ocelot* kept feinting, as if waiting for another blow from the laser, but the blow didn't come. Instead, Danai kept her ax working on the enemy 'Mech's relatively thin waist.

Metal groaned, then screamed. The top of the *Ocelot* fell over while its legs remained erect. The pilot extended the machine's arms to absorb the impact of the coming crash, but that was likely the last useful thing the arms would do for it.

The comm crackled to life. "*Sao-shao!* The pressure is getting too heavy! We'll have to fall back."

Danai glanced at the bisected *Ocelot*, mentally chalking it up as a kill even though the arms were still scrambling. She turned and ran back to her group.

By the time she crossed the few blocks to join with them, they were gathered and ready to move. They had taken more losses—a tank and a *Phoenix Hawk* were gone. But it sounded like the Triarii/Aldebarian losses had been worse. If the rest of the plan worked, that imbalance should only increase.

Danai took her group back east, toward the bulk of her battalion. Now they needed their speed.

The enemy had gathered an impressive pursuit, with light tanks running ahead of more *Ghosts, Spiders* and other light 'Mechs. They moved well, but Danai's hand-picked group moved faster. They made north/south shifts when needed to avoid rear fire, though that brought the risk of running into another group as they shifted streets. But their speed served them well, and they soon approached the spot Danai had made sure they would all remember.

They were about two blocks ahead of their nearest pursuers when they reached it, and they had strict instructions to keep their course straight for at least a kilometer afterward. That meant they had to endure a steady stream of Triarii fire for a block or so, and Danai took more damage to her rear. But then the ambush opened up, and the pursuers had a whole new set of problems to worry about.

Infantry troops positioned in high windows, tanks hidden in underground garages and spotters on low roofs directing artillery fire turned a single block into a blaze of gunfire and energy. Explosions flared here and there, but it was impossible to tell in the fast-appearing cloud of dust and smoke how much damage was critical and how much merely annoying.

The ambush stopped the militia and the Triarii in their tracks, making them fall back and regroup for a moment. They had more than enough numbers to blast away the Capellan forces on the block, which was why Sandra's plan called for a second wave to counter them.

After traveling a kilometer, Danai and her group veered south to make way for the force moving west toward the ambush site. Led by Bell and Sandra, the heaviest 'Mechs in the battalion were moving forward to make life miserable for the ambushed opponents. Bell was laying down PPC fire while Sandra kept a steady stream of gauss rounds flying through the block. These hit the Triarii-militia forces just as they were trying to regroup, throwing them into more disarray.

Bell and Sandra planted themselves a few blocks away from the ambush site. Together with the other 'Mechs in their groups, they provided cover fire to let the ambushing units withdraw.

Everything moved quickly, as Danai had known the ambush wouldn't hold for long. Once the planet's defenders got over their stubborn desire to overwhelm any units they encountered with numbers, they would realize it made more sense to go around the ambush, and all the units on that block would no longer be much use.

The artillery units were positioned so that they could put some cover fire onto nearby blocks, but they alone couldn't hold off the wave. Plus, they were under orders to move out with the rest of the ambuscade. Their firing soon died down, leaving Bell and Sandra's group to hold off the Republic troopers' advance as long as they could.

They managed to keep the enemy at bay for a good half hour, launching shells and bolts over and through buildings to keep the advancing units off guard. The Triarii and Aldebarians kept pouring more units into the contested area, and finally they reached critical mass. The fire from the Capellan 'Mechs was not enough to fend off the advance, and they were forced to retreat.

That had been the plan from the beginning. Bell gave the signal by saying, "We're moving south," an unusually brief comment for him. Then he and Sandra led their group away as quickly as they could.

Once sheltered from enemy fire by a few buildings, they turned back east. A few blocks ahead of them was a street Sandra had pointed to during the planning yesterday, jabbing at it repeatedly, saying, "Here. That's how we get out of here."

She couldn't have designed a better street for their escape if she'd tried. It started just southeast of downtown, meaning any units on the other side of downtown, or even in the heart of it, wouldn't have a clear shot at the Capellan battalion. About three kilometers away from downtown, the street bent to the south, once again making life difficult for pursuers looking for a good shot. The only problem Sandra anticipated was breaking through the enemy lines on the way out, which was why she had designed the whole rest of the plan. The concentration of forces to the west after her feint should have thinned the other lines, making them easier to break through. Or so Sandra had hoped.

Once Danai received Bell's signal, she started the rest of the battalion moving (some of the units had spent the past thirty minutes making whatever fast field repairs they could in preparation for the next charge). She kept the 'Mechs with her to a walk, giving the lumbering assault 'Mechs to the rear a chance to draw closer. She couldn't keep up a slow pace for long, though. The planet's defenders were bound to see what she was doing and would collapse whatever forces they could on her planned breakthrough point. She hoped to get through before that happened.

Bell, Sandra and the 'Mechs they led caught up to her surprisingly quickly. Danai didn't bother to question their exceptional speed; she just ordered her battalion to move out as fast as possible.

The run toward the city's outskirts was uneventful for the first three kilometers, when they reached the bend. The militia had set up a roadblock about a kilometer farther down the road, and their long-range weapons opened up as soon as the first units made the turn. But the Capellans had long-range units of their own, and Danai was convinced she had more of them. She was content to pound away at the roadblock (though she wished her LRMs were functioning) while maintaining a full-speed charge, waiting to see who gave first.

The Republic troops did. When she finished crossing the kilometer after the bend, the only thing left in the road was scorched, pitted ferrocrete. The defenders had fled; Danai's soldiers had broken the line. The plan had worked.

Danai would have felt better about that if this hadn't been a retreat. It was just the next step in the path toward victory, she kept telling herself. Just the next step.

12

Amur, Oriente
Oriente Protectorate
28 November 3135

Nikol grabbed a servant passing by her in the high-ceilinged corridor.

"Why is my mother summoning me to a meeting?" she asked. She pushed a stray lock of red hair to the top of her head. It fell back in front of her eye as soon as she moved her hand away.

The servant, who was a good fifteen years older than Nikol, looked at her warily. "I assume it's because she wishes to meet with you."

"Right. I'd figured that out on my own. But why?"

"I'm afraid the captain-general has not seen fit to inform me of the purpose of the meeting."

"Well, yes, of course, I understand that, but why summon me *this* way?" She waved the heavy piece of paper in front of the servant. "With an official notice! Why not just call me? Or talk to me the next time we're having dinner? Why *this*?"

The servant looked purposefully down the corridor, as if yearning after the tasks she would be accomplishing if Nikol hadn't stopped her. "In my many years with the captain-general," the servant said carefully, "I've found it wise not to attempt to guess her motivations."

Nikol sighed. "All right, all right. Sorry to have stopped you."

The servant, with much relief, hurried on her way.

The summons had come just that morning, interrupting Nikol's daily chore of diplomatic correspondence. A large electronic pile of it waited for her each day, most of it from within the Protectorate, some from outside, matters deemed not quite important enough for the captain-general's time but still needing a Marik name on the reply. Nikol had been groomed as one of the family's public faces for many years now, so this sort of work had become routine for her. Most mornings she would have welcomed any interruption—but the message she had received made her nervous. "Your presence is requested in Captain-General Jessica Marik's council room at 1 p.m. on the afternoon of November 30." That was all. It felt like the precursor to an elaborate dressing-down—as if the written summons had been proffered because Jessica Marik was too angry to talk directly to her daughter.

Nikol had thought briefly of fleeing, of finding some matter in her correspondence that she could use as an excuse for traveling halfway around the planet, but then decided that would only make her mother angrier. Nikol was a better diplomat than that. She'd best face up to whatever it was she had done at the time she had been summoned.

She approached the walnut double doors of the council room at exactly one o'clock. She tugged at her blouse, adjusted the waist of her dark wool skirt and waited to be recognized by security.

It didn't take long. There was a click, then the doors swung majestically outward, revealing a rectangular mahogany table. At the end of it sat her mother, out of uniform (thankfully) in a gray herringbone suit, and her father, Philip Hughes, who looked like he had just come in from a round of golf. Which was probably why, Nikol noted, the captain-general had scheduled this meeting for the afternoon instead of the morning.

Jessica surprised her by smiling when she entered. The captain-general stood and motioned for Nikol to come to her end of the table.

"Hello, Nikol. Sit here—we're not expecting anyone else at this meeting, so there's no reason to divide up."

Any reassurance Nikol received from her mother's smile instantly vanished. They were alone—her mother would not be fettered by decorum or propriety. Nikol meandered to the opposite end of the long table, not eager to start the meeting. But eventually she found herself next to Jessica, so she pulled out a high-backed chair with red satin upholstery and sat.

"Is something wrong, Nikol?" Jessica asked. "You look like a condemned prisoner."

So much for my poker face, Nikol thought. "No," she said. "Just a little after-lunch sleepiness."

"Ah. Well, I hope our conversation will take care of that."

Nikol wasn't sure about that—being lectured by her parents didn't tend to make her less weary. But she smiled and tried to look enthusiastic.

"I asked you here because you and Philip were present when I met with Daoshen Liao on Terra, and you are the only ones with whom I can speak freely. Additionally, this is exactly the sort of matter with which you've been gaining experience during recent years."

Nikol perked up. The conversation had taken a sudden 180-degree turn. Not only wasn't she in trouble, but she was about to take part in a confidential, serious political discussion. As Jessica's fifth child, she was usually kept at arm's length from the most sensitive discussions and decisions. She had been excited to go along to Terra for Victor Steiner-Davion's funeral, but at the same time she knew she had been allowed to come while her siblings stayed at home because she was expendable. All of them were needed to keep the Protectorate functioning in the captain-general's absence, but Nikol had little trouble delegating most of her diplomatic responsibilities to her staff for a time, leaving her free to travel. She liked to think her diplomatic experience was one reason her mother had brought her to Terra, but she could not escape the nagging feeling that the main reason she'd been chosen to go was that she would have the easiest time getting away.

But maybe that feeling was wrong. On Terra, she had been present when her mother met with Chancellor Daoshen Liao, and she had watched as they carefully negotiated an informal agreement between the Protectorate and the Capellan Confederation. She had heard the entire meeting, and she had the experience to understand the implications of most of it. The trip, it seemed, along with her background, had made her more necessary to her mother.

"I think it's pretty clear what Daoshen wants me to do," Jessica said. "A full charge into Prefecture VI, penetrating as far as Menkalinan. We would force New Canton to deal with us, leaving the Capellan forces free to do whatever they wanted in the sector with minimal forces, minimal cost and minimal loss."

"We would also be effectively putting an end to Prefecture VI," Philip added.

"Correct. And in return we receive the planets we conquer, some valuable military experience, but very little in actual concessions from the Capellan chancellor. If we're doing him a favor, it seems he should do a little more for us."

Nikol decided this might be the right time to venture a thought. "We'll be in Chancellor Liao's good graces, which is something. Not having to worry about the Capellans frees us up to concentrate on our other borders."

Jessica sighed. "Unfortunately, we *always* have to worry about the Capellans. Being in Daoshen's good graces is nice, but it means nothing if he decides we're in the way of the Confederation's destiny. He'll attack us just the same. The only difference is, he might offer us more generous surrender terms if we've been nice to him."

"What about his sense of honor?" Nikol asked. "Wouldn't that keep him from openly violating an agreement?"

"You live in what used to be the Free Worlds League," Jessica said sharply, "and we, more than anyone else, know how little restraint agreements like the Ares Conventions impose on the Capellans. Like any Liao, Daoshen's sense of honor bends itself to his sense of expediency. He will find a way to make what he wants seem honorable."

"Then why negotiate with him in the first place?" Nikol fired back.

Jessica opened her mouth to respond, then stopped. Her mouth closed, her head tilted to one side and she smiled. "You're quite right, Nikol. If Daoshen truly had no compunction about violating agreements and treaties, it would be pointless to form them. I overstated my case. I appreciate your correction."

Nikol nodded, pleased to be taken seriously. To this point, the meeting could not have been more different than what she had been dreading.

"Daoshen would indeed like to be known as a man of his word," Jessica continued. "That does not mean he won't violate an agreement or treaty, but rather that he'll need to have strong, clear reasons before he does it."

Philip, who for the past few moments had appeared to be pondering an errant golf shot from earlier in the day, spoke up. "Then we need to be careful to show Daoshen that keeping agreements with us is to his advantage, while breaking them is not."

Jessica nodded. "Right. That means we should have a clear understanding of what Daoshen expects to gain from our agreement. Then we can decide the best way for us to fulfill our end of the bargain."

Nikol thought back to the discussion on Terra with the Capellan chancellor. "Did we agree specifically to invade as far as we could? To hit Menkalinan?"

Jessica immediately understood why Nikol had asked the question. She leaned forward. "No. Menkalinan was simply named as an example. We agreed to get the attention of New Canton. And there are a number of ways to do that."

"Right," Nikol said. "There's a whole line of worlds between us and New Canton. We hit a few of them; there's no need to go as deep as Menkalinan. We'll get New Canton's attention, but we won't do all of Daoshen's work for him. Save some wear and tear on our people."

Philip looked alarmed, wrinkles filling the space between his eyes and his smooth, bald scalp. "Daoshen's not likely to be pleased with that. He won't enjoy having to work harder for the prizes he's after."

"Then he can make it worth our while to go in deeper," Jessica said dismissively. "We will fulfill our end of the agreement by distracting New Canton. If he wants more from us, he can offer us more."

Philip was not yet appeased. "The Capellans are already planning on sending forces into Prefecture VI," he said. "You're proposing making Daoshen angry when he has troops moving in our direction. Are you sure brinkmanship is the best approach here?"

"It's a tactic the Liaos have used dozens, if not hundreds of times in the past," Jessica said. "It's high time he had the barrel of that particular gun pointed back at him."

Nikol felt a surge of pride at her mother's words. The captain-general was pushing the Protectorate to be a true power in the Inner Sphere, not a loose coalition of planets that neighboring states could push around whenever they pleased. And standing up to the Capellan Confederation as part of this assertiveness felt particularly right.

Still, she was concerned. She didn't want her mother pushing the Protectorate to run faster than it had strength. If they overextended themselves, it would be all too easy for a foreign power to make their nation collapse upon itself.

She broached her concerns cautiously. "We need to be careful. It's probably best that we don't go too deep into the Republic's territory. With our forces being what they are, especially considering the low number of 'Mechs at our disposal, we'd best stick as close to home as we can."

Philip smiled broadly. He looked over at Jessica, who looked oddly girlish. She was gazing down at the table, her index finger tracing a random pattern on the dark wood. Nikol couldn't see her mother's mouth well, but she thought it, too, bore a smile.

She looked back and forth between them. "What? What's with these faces?"

Jessica looked up. She was definitely smiling. It made her look a dozen years younger, except for the crow's-feet that sprang up next to her green eyes. She looked back at Philip. "Well?"

"Your decision," he said. "You were the one who wanted to bring her this far in; you can decide what to tell her. But if you want her to be truly helpful, she'll probably need to know the situation."

Jessica nodded. "Our military strength is . . . somewhat beyond what is commonly assumed. Especially regarding 'Mechs."

"Irian!" Nikol practically jumped out of her chair. "Irian Technologies! The rumors are true!"

"Not all of them," Philip said. "People routinely overestimate IrTech's wealth and capacity." He grimaced. "Believe me, I wish some of the rumors were true. My family is far from poor, but if we really had the wealth some of the stories attribute to us . . . well, your mother wouldn't have to dress like such a peasant." He patted Jessica's hand.

Nikol knew her father was being facetious. She had been with Jessica when she bought the suit she was wearing, and she knew full well it had cost nearly three hundred eagles. The Hughes family might not be the wealthiest industrialists in the Inner Sphere, but "far from poor" was still a generous understatement.

"IrTech is making 'Mechs?" she asked, enjoying the sound of the words as she spoke them. "Making 'Mechs for us?"

"Yes," Jessica said. "We need them."

She sat back in her chair, and Nikol thought the meeting was about to reach a conclusion. And a good thing, too—she already had a fair amount of information to absorb.

But her mother wasn't done with her yet.

"Having 'Mechs, however, is only the first step. We now need to decide how to use them. You mentioned the worlds sitting between the Protectorate and New Canton. I'd like to hear your thoughts on which ones we should move against."

Nikol was too excited to be stunned. *This*, she thought, *is diplomacy*.

"I'd start with Park Place," she said. "Here's why."

It took a couple of days, of course—multiplanetary assaults were not organized at the drop of a hat. But things moved along, Captain-General Jessica Marik met with her military staff and discussed strategy and force strength and dozens of other variables, and before long the army of the Oriente Protectorate was on the move.

They had targeted three planets: Park Place, Holt and Bernardo. Nikol had named Park Place and Holt, and added Asuncion and Suzano. In a way, she was relived when the final target list was different than the one she had proposed. She had a fair amount of diplomatic experience, but military planning was a new field. She would have been worried if her mother fully adopted the recommendations of a novice. When she studied her map more carefully, paying greater attention to existing force deployments, she understood her mother's decision better.

Asuncion and Suzano lay too close to the Capellan border, which meant two things. First, their militias were likely to be on high alert and growing in size, as recent troubles in the Republic combined with Capellan belligerence had led to a recruiting boom on each planet. Second, should Daoshen decide to take offense that Jessica was merely observing the spirit of his agreement with him rather than the exact letter (as he saw it), he might well decide to lash out at vulnerable planets near his border, where the Oriente invaders had already been softened up by local militias.

In short, if you intended to tickle a sleeping wolf's belly, it was better to tickle and run rather than stand near the wolf to see how it would react. Nikol could easily picture Daoshen Liao as he had appeared at his discussion with Jessica—tall, sepulchral, with eyes that burned cold. Nothing seemed to amuse him, ever, and she could not imagine that Jessica's insolence would be an exception. The question was not whether he would respond, but what shape his response would take—whether it would be the extra concessions Jessica wanted, or a swift sword falling on the neck of the newly bold Oriente Protectorate.

13

It was a damn good thing her 'Mech had a global positioning system, Danai had thought more than once in the past few days. Without it, she was convinced she would either have become hopelessly lost or disoriented enough to stumble right into the nonstop pursuit that had beleaguered her since departing Jifang Po City.

There were no landmarks to speak of. She saw trees, grass and numerous farms, but they all looked like each other. She had tried once to remember a place, describing it in her head as the white farmhouse near the red silo and the three maple trees. As the day wore on, she passed at least four other white farmhouses with red silos and three maple trees. Without SatNav, she never would have known she wasn't passing the same place four times. She was harboring an increasing dislike for the planet, and becoming increasingly eager for the chance to grind down another corner of it.

But she couldn't stop and engage the forces behind her. She had run the numbers at least twice every day, and each time they looked very bad for her side. Her troops hadn't had an opportunity to make any real field repairs, because every time they stopped and tried to bivouac for an extended period, the Triarii troops—for it was mostly them, the militia staying back to protect Jifang Po—crashed toward them. Plus, now that they were out of Jifang Po City and there was no danger of damaging surrounding buildings, Triarii aero units had been particularly bold and annoying. Danai's LRM launcher was still nonfunctional, and likely would remain that way until she got off-planet or thoroughly crushed the Triarii forces and had time for full repairs.

She fervently hoped for the latter result.

Anderton and his troops were making it difficult. She'd finally spotted his command 'Mech two days after they left Jifang Po. She had first noticed it because of the way it reflected the sunlight—it was polished to an abnormal brightness. It was a *Thunderbolt,* modified to launch twenty LRMs instead of the normal fifteen, and it walked at a stately pace that seemed wholly consistent with the Anderton she had encountered on the comm. He stayed in the rear of his troops, firing missiles and gauss rounds occasionally, but for the most part surveying his lines and, Danai assumed, directing the battle rather than participating in it. To her that seemed like a waste of a heavy 'Mech, but each commander had his own style.

She hadn't seen him long. Her command had already mobilized when Anderton and his troops came in sight, and after a short skirmish Danai withdrew. She would have loved to engage Anderton head-on, but his first wave was closely followed by reinforcements, and—as had been the case all week—Danai needed to retreat or risk losing a substantial part of her forces.

She'd tried every maneuver she could think of to out-flank the Triarii and engage a small number of them instead of the whole battalion, but each time Anderton had responded quickly. He was maintaining tight control over his units, keeping them close together so they could respond to anything Danai attempted. The Triarii were not the most imaginative foes Danai had encountered—

for all their numerical superiority, Anderton hadn't yet managed to mount a serious offensive assault—but they were disciplined, moving well in unison and responding to orders with rapid precision.

Against Sandra's objections, Danai had tried to take advantage of the Triarii's lack of tactical sophistication by going against one of the prime lessons she'd learned in academy, dividing her force when outnumbered. She wanted to draw the Triarii one way with a feint by her faster units, then slam into the opposite side of the Republican forces with the bulk of her command. But Anderton's forces hadn't taken the bait—they'd simply stayed back, hammered the small Capellan 'Mechs with their artillery and long-range weapons, and remained cohesive to prevent Danai from making her planned second assault. In the end, she'd had to call back her entire force to keep the Triarii from advancing on her divided troops before she could bring them all back together.

All that would change soon. She'd put out a call to Liao as soon as she left Jifang Po City, stating her situation and asking for reinforcements. She had gone to great lengths to explain the opportunity at hand, saying that with a modicum of new troops she could reduce an entire Triarii battalion to rubble and secure Aldebaran. She hadn't received any official response, but what she *had* received was even better. A Capellan JumpShip had arrived in the Aldebaran system four days ago, and a DropShip had been making a beeline toward Aldebaran.

True, it was only a single DropShip—Danai had radioed Yun on her command ship a number of times to confirm that—but it was something. Even a single DropShip, especially one of the larger ones, would give her enough fresh forces to put together a more convincing offensive. Any time, she should receive information on where the forces planned to land. She'd connect with them, then teach Anderton and his Triarii how Capellan warriors fought.

But that was the future. In the here and now, she'd sought a place to stop for the past hour, someplace that might have at least a few meters of elevation above the surrounding countryside, or some sort of defensive value that would justify a halt. But the terrain was either flat grassland or farmland, and so Danai's command pushed on.

Finally, two hours after sunset, Danai told her units to stop. The terrain remained unchanged, but the Kite reconnaissance team reported that the Triarii had halted their pursuit, so the Capellans had opened up an acceptably large gap. Danai didn't want the gap to be too large—once she had her reinforcements, she'd want to be able to turn around and get on top of the Triarii in short order.

As had been her custom in the past eight days, she invited her command lance into her quarters for a debriefing on the day's activities and a little socializing. The latter aspect had gotten easier each day; while Sandra and Clara still occasionally acted like siblings vying for a mother's affection, and Bell still enjoyed poking holes in their egos whenever he had a chance, the trust warriors needed to have in one another had worn down some of their sharpest edges. Some rough patches remained, and Danai still didn't rule out the possibility of a fistfight between any of her lance members, but at least such a fight was far less likely to break out after a long day of marching and skirmishing.

The debriefing went rapidly, as they had spent most of their time moving over farmland, and soon they were on to socializing. Danai poured a round of drinks, including some mao-tai for herself, and the four of them stretched their legs as best they could around the small metal table in the cramped front room of Danai's mobile quarters.

"Did anyone else see that farmer earlier this afternoon?" Bell was saying. "The one next to the pile of hay? I think he was yelling at us the entire time we went by, but I couldn't make out any words."

"Curses," Clara said. "Extraordinary strings of vulgarity, really. He used one particular word as an adverb, adjective and noun in a single clause. Quite impressive."

"We should have set his entire farm on fire," Sandra said darkly. "Then he'd have something to curse about."

"Now, now," Clara said primly. "He's going to be our subject soon."

"Right," Bell said, "and we'll introduce him to the Maskirovka. That should put a smile on his face."

Danai and Clara grinned, while Sandra chuckled nervously.

"Maybe we shouldn't joke about that," Sandra said.

"Why not?" Bell said. "Are you Maskirovka?"

"No."

"Is it because you applied, and they didn't accept you?"

"No!"

Danai leaned forward. "No one here's Maskirovka. Especially not Sandra."

Sandra shot Danai a look, clearly worried that Danai was going to go into more detail, but Danai had no intention of revealing what she knew. Sandra and Danai had served in the same lance for a good while, and Sandra had spent a significant amount of time in the company of a "diplomatic liaison" whom everyone else had already pegged as a Maskirovka agent. Gossip claiming Sandra was Maskirovka as well had spread throughout the regiment, and that, combined with a particularly unpleasant breakup with the liaison, had pretty well soured her on the agency, even though she sympathized with their goals of supporting correct thought.

"The Maskirovka have no way of hearing this conversation," Danai continued. "I've seen to that as best I could."

To change the subject, Sandra asked the question that Danai felt certain was on all of their minds. "Any word from the reinforcements yet? Do we know where we're going to meet them?"

"I haven't heard a thing. Remember, for all we know, there are no reinforcements. We only know there's a DropShip on the way. We don't know if it's even military. It's not time to count our chickens yet." She said that despite the fact that she had been counting chickens almost constantly for the past four days.

"If it's not reinforcements, I say we revolt," Bell said. "Take this planet for ourselves, set up our own nation here."

Sandra's eyes widened. "I don't think . . ."

But Clara cut her off. "And we put Danai in as supreme executive, making you . . . what? Court jester?"

Bell shook his head ruefully. "No, no, no, I'm afraid we can't have that. Danai as chief executive, I mean. Really, does the Inner Sphere need *another* Liao-Centrella on the throne? It's just too much baggage. I'm afraid it would put a crushing burden on our new nation. I'm sorry."

"Quite all right," Danai said magnanimously. "In truth, having the three of you in my command is pretty much sucking all the joy of power right out of me. I'm happy to pass the title on to someone else. Any suggestions?"

Bell cleared his throat. "Well, now that you mention it . . ."

"What a surprise," Clara said dryly.

"Oh, come on, I'm the perfect candidate. I'm young, good-looking and not pure Capellan like the rest of you."

"I don't see what's wrong with being pure Capellan!" Sandra said hotly.

"Nothing, nothing at all," said Bell, holding up his hands defensively. "You know and I know that you're the noblest of the noble. But, you see, in everybody else's eyes, those of us with some Canopian background are widely regarded to be much more fun than you Capellans. I'm sure our *sao-shao* will back me up on this."

"We're a barrel of laughs," Danai said somberly.

"There you have it. So we're a little easier to accept than you. We're fun, and you're . . . well, you're . . . *not*."

"It's just jealousy. They envy our perfection," Clara said sardonically. Sandra nodded, missing the irony in Clara's tone.

"And, of course, I'd have roles for all of you. Clara, you can have the military. It's all yours. Sandra, you can be my Minister of Posture. Make sure all our people know how to walk like they have a broomstick lodged in their asses."

Sandra started to protest, but Danai waved her off. When Bell had a head of steam like this, it was pointless to protest or take offense. He'd shut himself up soon enough, if only to take a drink.

"So our beloved *Sao-shao* Liao-Centrella not only doesn't get the throne, but she doesn't get the military?" Clara asked. "You're not doing much to get her to buy into your plan."

"That's only because you haven't heard the entire plan," Bell said. "While Danai might not be the best choice for chief executive, I'll never deny her brilliance or political usefulness. That's why I've decided to make her my consort."

Clara laughed and Danai groaned. "You've just turned me into your first insurgent," Danai said.

"Just give me a chance!" Bell protested. "I'll treat you like a queen—okay, queen of only a single planet instead of sister of the chancellor of the entire Confederation, sure, but still—a queen! Chocolates every day! Foot massages! And in the bedroom—ah, in the bedroom . . ."

"That's enough," Danai said. She didn't think anyone could miss the sudden ice in her tone, but Bell did.

"I guarantee those are two words you'll never use again once we've spent our first night together as king and queen," he said. "I don't want to brag, but . . ."

"That's *enough*!" Danai banged her glass on the metal table, leaving a fist-sized dent in its thin surface. The echoing crack left everyone in the room silent for a moment.

Then, amazingly, possibly for the first time since she had known him, Bell let a subject go. "What's the weather look like for tomorrow?" he asked. It was the blandest, safest of subjects—Danai supposed it was a peace offering, and probably the closest he'd ever come to an apology.

The conversation drifted for a few more minutes until

it was interrupted by an intermittent buzzing. Danai, who had already downed three glasses of mao-tai, looked around helplessly before identifying the source of the noise. It was the comm, telling her someone was trying to reach her.

"Excuse me," she said, then stumbled over and flicked a switch on the comm. "Go ahead," she said.

Kay Cheung's voice replied. "Sorry to interrupt, *Sao-shao*, but there's an incoming vehicle. Another Kite, actually."

"Have you made contact?"

"Yes, *Sao-shao*. It's a courier looking for you."

Danai almost leapt to her feet. "A *courier*?" she exclaimed.

"Yes, *Sao-shao*."

Danai's hands, which had started trembling when she yelled at Bell, were shaking visibly now. She was ready to get into Yen-lo-wang and start hacking something, anything, into pieces.

"Send the courier directly to my quarters," she said, then flicked off the comm. She stood and paced around the small room, a fairly useless exercise since every other step she had to avoid tripping over a chair leg.

"Maybe the courier's here to tell us how many reinforcements are on the way and when they'll get here," Sandra ventured.

Danai stopped pacing and put her hands on her hips, willing them to stillness. She inhaled deeply, then exhaled. "Maybe," she said, though she didn't believe it. If reinforcements were on the way, they'd just *come*. There wasn't a good reason to go to the expense of hiring a courier to deliver a message that could be more easily relayed through laser comm from the incoming DropShip. This was something else. "All the same, the three of you better stay here in case the courier doesn't tell me what I want to hear and I decide to rip his throat out."

"Just so I'm clear on this," Bell said. "Are we supposed to stop you from killing him or help out?"

Danai glared at the door the courier was about to enter. "I'll let you know," she said.

7 December 3135

"The threat has ended," Major Anderton announced. "The Capellans have fled the planet."

He spoke as if addressing a multitude, and he paused as if expecting to be overwhelmed by thunderous applause. However, his audience consisted of Governor Sampson, Legate Sophia Juk and a few members of Sampson's staff. Legate Juk, for her part, kept her arms firmly folded across her chest.

Anderton did not look like he had been on an eight-day campaign harassing Capellan troops across the Aldebarian grasslands. Every strand of his hair was in its proper place, he wore his dress uniform rather than his field clothing, and he looked well fed and well rested. Ready for the cameras, which made it a shame none were there.

"We are in your debt, Major," Sampson said. "Your timely arrival averted disaster. I will be making a full report to the lord governor of the prefecture, and I will include our gratitude for the troops he sent and our admiration for the job you performed against highly skilled soldiers in a dark time. We could not be more appreciative."

Sophia gritted her jaw. She, too, was grateful for the Triarii assistance, and she had no doubt that without them, Aldebaran would have fallen. But aside from her instant personal dislike of Anderton, she didn't like Anderton and Sampson's assumption that the threat had ended. It was temporarily averted, but she did not believe the Capellan Confederation had set aside the goal of conquest quite yet.

"In my communication with New Canton, I shall also request your continued presence on Aldebaran," Sampson said. "You have already proven your worth to our planet, and we hope that keeping you garrisoned here for a time may avert any future hostilities."

"I certainly understand the motivation for that request," Anderton said, "as without us you would be helpless. However, as you well know, there are plenty of other disturbances throughout the prefecture at this time, and I can't guarantee that we will be left here to wait for hostilities when there are so many other ongoing battles where we can deliver immediate assistance. I would be pleased to stay here, but I must go where I am ordered."

Sophia was glad she had kept her arms folded, because her elbows were concealing her clenched fists. "I wouldn't characterize Aldebaran as 'helpless,' " she said. "As I recall, our units fought right alongside yours when we drove the Capellans out of the city."

Anderton smiled like a holovid anchorman. "Yes, Legate, but as I recall your militia was being pounded when we arrived. In fact, the only reason the Capellans managed to take shelter in the center of the city was that they shattered your lines. Had we not arrived, I can only imagine the military situation would have worsened from there."

Sophia dropped her arms to her sides, no long caring if Anderton saw her fists. "My troops gave everything they had! I'm not going to stand here while you casually dismiss their sacrifice!"

"I have no doubt your soldiers gave their all," Anderton said, his even tones not changing a bit. "That seems to be the problem—their all was not enough to hold off the enemy."

She turned to Sampson. "Governor, I have to protest the efforts of our troops being—"

Sampson raised a hand to cut her off. "This should be a happy time," he said. "Our planet has been delivered. We shouldn't be bickering over credit."

"Bickering over credit?" Sophia said. "This isn't about *credit*! This is about *respect*! This is about—"

"This is about to end," Sampson said. "I'm going to celebrate Aldebaran's freedom. You two may continue to argue if you wish, but I refuse to believe that's the best way to spend this glorious day."

Sophia unclenched her fists and smoothed her uniform. "I'm going to meet with my troops," she said. "We will take a final account of our losses, continue making repairs as rapidly as possible, and get ready for the inevitable return of the Capellans. We will be ready to hold off the Capellans with or without Triarii assistance."

"I admire the legate's passion on behalf of her people," Anderton said. "Still, Governor, I would send off that message you mentioned. If you want your planet's freedom maintained, it would likely be in your best interest to keep my battalion on it."

Sophia didn't listen to what he said. Instead, she pictured what he would look like with a black eye and a swollen jaw. It was satisfying, but not as satisfying as actually hitting him.

14

Zi-jin Chéng, Sian
Capellan Confederation
7 December 3135

Perhaps someday, if Erde worked hard enough and won Daoshen over, she'd convince him to meet somewhere besides his throne room. The fact that all the servants and hangers-on in the immediate vicinity insisted on referring to Daoshen as "God Incarnate" was bad enough; but the throne room was simply not built for comfort (at least, not for the comfort of anyone but Daoshen). This was now her third meeting with him, and on the second she had at least persuaded him to provide her with a simple wooden chair. She sat there, a good meter and a half below Daoshen, and attempted to hold a friendly conversation. It would be so much easier, more comfortable, if they could sit together at a table, sipping tea and simply chatting.

No doubt Daoshen would not share her assessment of the situation. There was no place in the universe more comfortable for him than where he was now, perched on his throne, surrounded by loyal servants, perpetually basking in his own glory.

So, despite the fact that looking up at him made her

old neck stiff, she put up with the surroundings. After all, she always made certain to travel with at least one highly skilled masseuse. Muscle stiffness could be dealt with later.

She was still figuring out the best approach to talking to Daoshen. Questions of a personal nature—"How are you? How is the stress of war affecting you?"—were meaningless. In his mind, he *was* the state. He fared exactly as well as did the state. He seemed to have no personal emotions, no desires, no anything beyond what the state needed and demanded. If he had ever had a distinct personality, Erde thought, it had long been swallowed up by the Celestial Throne upon which he sat. After all, what god worth his salt had a personal life to worry about?

So conversation was pretty much limited to matters of state, but even there she had to tread carefully. He did not seem to appreciate direct questions about his military adventures, and if she was too blatant with information she had picked up through her personal network of eyes and ears, he tended to close up. He liked to distribute information as he saw fit, and did not like his face rubbed in the fact that people could learn things without having to talk to him. She had to be circumspect, indirect and above all never appear to be questioning his wisdom.

It was exhausting and it made her passionately look forward to her neck massage.

Still, despite the difficulty of the conversation, she must be doing something right as he had now allowed her to come back for a third meeting. She wouldn't say he was beginning to like her, but at least he saw talking to her as something of use. For what reasons, she didn't know.

She was dressed simply in a sky blue gown that buttoned down the back. Her white hair was caught in a net at the top of her shoulders, and she thought she looked like a dignified elder stateswoman, though she would be happier if she could remove the word "elder" from that description.

It had worked the first time, so Erde was holding on to her strategy of complimenting Daoshen at the beginning of each discussion.

"I was just watching the news coverage of the demonstration outside the Forbidden City," she said after making the proper obeisance to the chancellor. "It was impressive—two hundred thousand people, by the most recent estimates, all engaged in a spontaneous demonstration of support for you. It must be extremely gratifying to see such concrete proof of your subjects' affection."

Daoshen gave a brief wave with his right hand. "It's a puppet show," he said. "Arranged by the Maskirovka. A public relations event, really." He paused. "Still, such a thing would be impossible to organize without people willing to attend it. In that sense, then, yes—it is gratifying."

Erde could not be sure if Daoshen was trying to fool her or if he had succeeded in completely fooling himself. She had no doubt the entire affair was engineered by the Maskirovka—she'd suspected that the moment the news coverage began—but she didn't for a second believe the Maskirovka simply found people willing to demonstrate and gathered them together. While some of the demonstrators clustered just outside the Forbidden City might have harbored genuine affection for the chancellor, many of them were motivated by fear—fear of accusations of disloyalty, fear of what would happen to them and their families if they weren't at the demonstration. Actual support for the chancellor had little to do with their attendance.

But Daoshen seemed to appreciate her pointing out her subjects' support, so she had started the conversation on the right foot.

"I imagine your recent military successes have much to do with that," Erde said. "Retaking the planets once owned by the Republic seems to be a popular move."

"It was, and remains, the right move," Daoshen said, his funereal voice seeping into every corner of the throne room. "These planets belong to the Confederation. They are the lands of our ancestors. They never should have been lost in the first place. It is my duty to reclaim them."

Erde blinked a few times, surprised. Daoshen, for a moment at least, had dropped his customary royal "we." Maybe she really was getting somewhere with him.

"I certainly understand that in the case of Aldebaran," she said. "That planet plays such a rich role in your history, I can imagine you wanting it back under Capellan control."

"Indeed," said Daoshen. "Its historical value is great. If its strategic value was as high, I would have retaken it long ago."

"I take it the current mission is going well, then?" Erde actually knew the answer to this question, but she didn't want to let Daoshen know she had heard something from someplace besides his own mouth.

He paused slightly before answering. "The first stage of the mission has gone acceptably well," he said. "However, there has been a small delay that might push back our final conquest of the planet for some short time."

"A delay? Really?" Erde sat up straighter. "I hope there's nothing wrong with Danai."

"*Sao-shao* Liao is fine," Daoshen said, adhering to his customary rule of ignoring the last part of Danai's surname. "She acquitted herself admirably. But for the time being she has been recalled."

"Recalled?"

"Yes. She will be returning to Sian shortly."

"Was she that badly beaten?"

"No," Daoshen said flatly. "However, there were other concerns that necessitated her return to Sian."

"Are those 'other concerns' something you could tell me more about?"

"No," Daoshen said.

"I understand. I just hope Danai will understand, too."

"She doesn't need to understand," he said. "She only needs to follow orders."

"Of course. But you know as well as I do that confidence makes a commander a valuable warrior. After Danai's involvement in the retreat from New Hessen, and now being recalled from her first assignment, I'm worried about how her confidence will be affected." Erde didn't mention all that had befallen Danai on New Hessen. As far as she knew, Daoshen had not been told about Caleb Davion's rape of Danai, and she did not intend to pass along that piece of information. Danai could tell him herself when she wanted to, though she suspected that day might never arrive.

"Her confidence should not be affected," Daoshen intoned. "As long as she holds her rank, she will know she holds the confidence of the chancellor, and therefore the confidence of the entire Capellan Confederation. If that is not enough to bolster a warrior, then perhaps that warrior did not have enough strength for command in the first place."

"That sounds harsh," Erde said. "How can Danai be sure she has your confidence if you pulled her away from her first battalion command task? Not that I'm suggesting you should not have done that," she added, backpedaling as she saw Daoshen's brow start to furrow in anger. "I'm just saying that when you bring her back here, you need to remember that she may be in a fragile state. That her confidence needs bolstering, not undermining. Just remember that when you speak with her."

Giving advice to the God Incarnate of Sian did nothing to assuage his wrath. Daoshen stood and raised his arms so that his black robes, flecked with threads of imperial gold, would unfurl in all their glory, and spoke in his most imperial tones.

"We will treat the commanders of our military as we see fit. They are warriors of House Liao, not infants. They will demonstrate their strength or they will be removed from our service. *Sao-shao* Liao will have every chance to prove herself, and we hope she proves worthy of the tasks we have for her, and of the journey that lies ahead of her. The way will not be made easy for her, as it has never been made easy for any Capellan warrior."

He sat back down, his face becoming an expressionless mask. Two servants arrived to take Erde's chair out of the throne room. Erde took this as a clear sign that today's discussion was over, and that she had quite spectacularly failed in her purposes.

Jojoken, Andurien
Duchy of Andurien

"*Who* requests *what*?"

Matthew Brand, the duke's chief of staff, read the request again. " 'Magestrix Ilsa Centrella of Canopus cordially requests the opportunity to extend her respects to Duke Ari Humphreys of Andurien at any time of the duke's choosing. I await the graciousness of your reply.' "

The duke shook his head. "And you say she's *here*?"

"Yes," Brand replied. "She sent this message shortly after landing."

"Why didn't she tell me she was coming?" he demanded. "I could have arranged a proper reception!"

"I think she's telling you now," Brand said. "So you can arrange whatever you would like."

Humphreys stood. He paced back and forth in front of his grand window overlooking the gardens, though he couldn't see much through today's fog and drizzle. He stopped at one end of the room and ran his hand through the few strands of hair left on top of his head, then patted the strands back into place.

"Perhaps we should have a formal reception," Humphreys said. "Bring in all the state officials to greet her."

"Sir, may I remind you that this is not just the Magestrix of Canopus we're talking about, but also the sister of the Capellan chancellor? What would your subjects think of you treating her to a formal reception?"

Humphreys blanched. This was why he kept Brand near him as often as possible. "You're right, you're right, of course you're right. That would never do. But I must do something. This is . . . this is . . . well, you know who she is. You've seen her—seen her on holovid. And now she's *here*?"

"Yes, sir. Might I suggest a private meeting with the magestrix would be the wisest course of action at present?"

Humphreys swallowed, practically gulping. "A private meeting. With Ilsa Centrella."

"Yes, sir. Is there something . . . wrong with that?"

"No, no," Humphreys said, shaking his head so rapidly he could feel the wiggle of his jowls. "Nothing wrong with that at all. Send a reply. Tell her tomorrow morning. No—this afternoon! Say I await her at her earliest convenience. Yes, yes, that should work."

Brand nodded and walked out of the office. Humphreys waited until the door had closed behind him before he took out his handkerchief and wiped away the beads of sweat that had sprung out on his brow.

As it turned out, Ilsa's earliest convenience was a mere two hours from the time Brand sent the reply to her inquiry. In the early afternoon, with the rain still slowly falling, Brand returned to Humphreys' office to announce that the magestrix of Canopus was there to meet with the duke.

Humphreys had taken some time to control himself, and though his insides still felt jumbled, his face was (he hoped) calm.

"Show her in," he said in his fullest tones. Brand nodded, walked out for a moment, then returned, followed by a woman who looked like she had stepped directly out of a classical painting of ancient Terran royalty. She wore a black dress of modest cut that still managed to cling to her waist and hips in a way that kept making Humphreys' eyes drift downward. He steeled himself to look only at her face—this was a diplomatic meeting, after all.

Besides, her face had plenty of features to occupy his attention. The thin, even nose, the wide brown eyes and the round, well-defined cheekbones gave her a distinct air of nobility. Duke Humphreys knew only too well what his own face looked like—features more suited to a neighborhood butcher, perhaps, than Andurien nobility. But he was what he was, and so he held his chin high and smiled graciously as Ilsa Centrella approached.

"Duke Humphreys," she said, gliding ahead and grasping his extended right hand with both of hers. "So good of you to see me on such short notice."

"Not at all," Humphreys said, trying to keep from sounding pinched. "I only regret that I could not arrange a reception more appropriate to your station. Please, sit down."

Magestrix Centrella perched on the edge of a chair in a smooth motion. She leaned slightly forward as she sat, looking eager to speak with him. Humphreys knew the pose was calculated, one of hundreds of tricks learned over a lifetime as heir apparent and magestrix, but it was effective nonetheless. He could not help but feel flattered at her clear interest in talking to him.

"You have nothing to apologize for," she was saying. "I realize my visit was unexpected. Honestly, I didn't even expect it myself. I was traveling from Sian to Canopus when I happened to receive a message from Ambassador Rickard detailing his meeting with you. While I fully understand and even sympathize with your position, I could not help but think that if we could get together and talk, just the two of us, without intermediaries, we might be able to work through some of the difficulties and come to a better understanding."

She had put a special emphasis on the words "just the two of us" that Humphreys had not failed to notice, and it had the intended effect. But Humphreys was still rational enough to realize that her speech was, to put it politely, a gentle shading of the truth. Leaders of large nations, even nations in the Periphery, simply do not happen onto another nation's capital planet on a whim. She was on Andurien for a specific purpose, but she wanted to pretend it was an informal social call. Humphreys hoped he'd figure out why before the meeting was over.

"I appreciate your persistence in seeking an alliance

with the Duchy of Andurien, but I'm afraid your trip might be for nothing," Humphreys said. "You may make any arguments you wish, but I can't imagine anything you might say that would change my mind. In any alliance, the stronger party seeks to bend the weaker to its will. It's inevitable. Now, in future years it may be possible to debate which is stronger, the Magistracy or the Duchy, but at this point I'm afraid it's indisputable that your state would hold the upper hand. The alliance would certainly benefit you, and so I can understand your reasons for seeking it, but I'm afraid the benefits to my state are less clear. At this time, an independent Andurien is for the best." His mouth felt dry by the end of his speech, and he wondered if he'd said too much.

Ilsa sat still for a moment and said nothing. Her eyes squinted in thought, as if she were considering his words. Then she spoke. "Well, if I leave here empty-handed, at least I won't be able to say you didn't give the matter plenty of thought. It's obvious this is something you've considered seriously. But perhaps there is one angle I can add to the discussion."

Not at all anxious to chase the magestrix away, Duke Humphreys nodded his head. "I'd be happy to hear you out."

"You're quite right in what you say," she began. "If my experience with my brother has shown me anything, it's that what you say is true. Whenever we speak in an official capacity, ruler to ruler, he does not let me forget that his state is larger, wealthier and more powerful than mine. He wields that particular weapon with abandon, and if I may speak frankly, it takes considerable effort to maintain even a modicum of independence. So I understand your concern and sympathize. Knowing the difficulty of my own situation, I wouldn't wish to impose a similar situation on anyone else.

"However, I must admit that, with all its apparent disadvantages, the partnership of the Magistracy and the Confederation has valuable benefits. As our other neighbors grow stronger and possibly more belligerent, you cannot underestimate what it means to have a friendly border with a nation as powerful as the Confederation. And if you look at your own borders, to see what the Oriente Protectorate and the Regulan Fiefs are up to, I think you can agree that having one fewer border to worry about, and one additional friend, is quite an advantage."

"Yes, yes," Humphreys said. "But making an alliance to maintain our independence is useless if the alliance itself takes away our freedom."

"Well put," the magestrix said, and Humphreys' cheeks grew warm. "But let me present something you may not have considered. You speak of alliances between two parties where one is stronger than the other. But what of a partnership between equals? An alliance where neither party has the upper hand, but both continually move toward a common good? In such an alliance, neither party is pressuring the other to actions that benefit only one partner, but rather both partners maintain their independence. They are free to act on their own, but they have the security of each other to draw upon when situations call for it. An alliance of equals can bring safety without compromising independence."

Humphreys had raised an eyebrow near the beginning of Ilsa's speech, and it only rose higher as she continued. When she fell silent, he felt as if the eyebrow was about to cross the top of his skull and start descending the back. He was certain his expression conveyed the appropriate amount of skepticism.

He chose his words carefully, moderating them so as not to entirely alienate the magestrix. "You present a fine vision of a partnership between two nations, but I fear such a vision is impossible. I know of no nations so equal that one would not seek to subvert the other to its will. There are always critical differences—in wealth, in military strength, in people—that set one state above the other. True equality certainly makes for some interesting possibilities, but it simply does not exist. What you present is, I'm afraid, nothing more than a beautiful pipe dream."

Ilsa showed no signs of taking offense at the duke's

dismissal of her ideas. Instead, she smiled warmly, almost in admiration. The power of the expression took Humphreys aback.

"You are, of course, completely correct," she said. "There are no nations, and never have been any nations, that are complete equals. There are always differences. But there is one thing you're overlooking—that, in the end, alliances are not made between the varying components of each nation, but rather are made between two leaders. It is not the nations that need to be equal—their leaders must be."

Duke Humphreys frowned. "I'm not sure I take your meaning."

Ilsa reached into the folds of her dress and came out with a simple piece of heavy white paper. She placed it face down on the duke's desk and slid it across to him.

His eyebrow arched again, this time in curiosity. He picked up the paper and read the formal language printed on it.

Blood dropped from his head to his stomach. He suddenly thought he could feel every bit of his planet's rotation. He wasn't sure how long he stared at the paper, but it felt like an embarrassingly long time before he could make eye contact with Ilsa again.

She did not appear impatient. Her eyes were warm, and she was smiling.

15

DropShip Silver Serpent IV, *Orbiting Sian*
Capellan Confederation
23 January 3136

Clang clang clang clang. Pause. Clang clang clang clang.
Danai had kept up that rhythm for a solid hour. Before that, she'd been pacing in her berth, but the DropShip's quarters were far too small to allow her to work up a head of steam. Even the corridors were too narrow and short to really allow her a long, continuous walk, so she was forced to turn or climb a ladder every few steps. But it was better than the small box of a room she'd been in for most of the past four days.

She'd be on the ground soon. Back on Sian. She assumed a summons from Daoshen would be waiting for her, but even if it wasn't, she was going to march right into the Forbidden City, barge into his throne room and rip out the God Incarnate's throat.

Recalled. *Recalled.* She had been strung out to dry by her brother. It wasn't that she expected any family loyalty from him—she didn't, she never had—but she at least expected him to do what was best for the Confederation. Yes, she'd taken some losses on Aldebaran, but she had inflicted far, far more than she'd suffered. She had swept through two cities and into the capital within twenty-four hours and had reduced the planetary militia to tatters. Only the timely arrival of the Triarii had saved Aldebaran, at least in the short term, and she could easily have countered them had she received reinforcements of her own.

Instead she had been recalled. She had never believed the Capellan Confederation would simply cut and run in the face of little more than a parade battalion, but that was what had happened. Prefecture VI of the Republic of the Sphere, which lay in tatters, had shown more support for its planets than had the resurgent Capellan Confederation. It was not only embarrassing on a personal level, it was embarrassing that the entire nation could be put off so easily. And she would make damn sure someone would pay for this humiliation. Finally— someone was going to pay.

She stopped stomping long enough to look around and figure out where she was. She had been striding around the grav deck with her head down, jaw clenched, eyes not really focusing on anything but the metal grating beneath her feet.

Whoops, she thought as she realized where she was. *These are officers' quarters. There's definitely no one I want to talk to here.*

She stalked away. Among the many puzzles of her withdrawal from Aldebaran was that while the bulk of her battalion—including the elements that had gone to Zurich and Zion—had been left behind at Liao, her command lance and first company had come with her. In all honesty she would have preferred to be alone, as the confusion and frustration of her lancemates only increased her own. She'd been avoiding them on the long journey back to Sian.

She made it away from the officers' quarters without anyone noticing her presence, then strode along in a meandering circle. A few crew members passed her, but noticing her face and bearing, wisely didn't speak to her, or even make eye contact. She glowered at them anyway.

She covered most of the grav deck at least once, some parts of it twice, before she decided she had used up enough energy. She could go to her berth and fume while sitting, rather than making another lap.

Clang clang clang clang clang.

She descended a ladder, walked down a short corridor, turned right, then turned completely around and tried to flee before anyone noticed her. But she wasn't fast enough.

"There she is!" Clara said. "We've been waiting here forever, *Sao-shao*. Where have you been?"

Danai sighed and turned back toward her quarters. Clara, Sandra and Bell stood in front of her door. There would be no getting by them. She trudged forward.

"I've been out," she said. "You better not be here to cheer me up or anything like that. Won't work."

"Wouldn't think of trying," Bell said with his customary smirk. While Clara and Sandra seemed just as upset about the recall as Danai, Bell seemed barely put out. That *really* made her wish she could have left him behind at Liao. Or on Aldebaran, for that matter.

"So what do you want?" Danai asked.

"Orders," Clara said. "We'll be on the ground soon. Where do you want us? We'll accompany you as far as you want us to go."

"We're here for you," Sandra said earnestly. "Whatever you need us for."

Bell waved his hand nonchalantly. "Yeah. What they said."

Great, Danai thought. *They can be witnesses when I disembowel the chancellor.*

"No," she said aloud. "I'll take care of things. Relax somewhere. Blow off some steam in a simulator. I'll find you when I need you."

She stood in front of them, waiting for them to understand they were not wanted and leave. The three of them exchanged glances, muttered some unintelligible words, then left her. Danai resisted the urge to shoo them along.

Clang clang clang clang clang clang. Three sets of foot-falls slowly faded away.

Danai stood outside her hatch for a moment, not anxious to face the drab cell that served as her quarters here.

Then she heard a noise that made her wish she'd dashed inside immediately and shut the door. *Clang clang clang.* A single set of feet quickly coming back to her.

She struggled to open her hatch quickly, but her fingers fumbled with the handle and she couldn't get inside before whoever it was turned the corner and saw her. Resigned, she turned to face the unwelcome visitor.

He became even more unwelcome the moment she saw who it was. Bell, for some reason, had left the other two and come back to talk to her alone. Just what she needed.

She lashed out. "I can't imagine you have anything to say that would be useful. Go away."

"I will," he said, drawling slightly. "In a minute. I just wanted to say a thing or two. Can I have permission to speak freely?"

"No."

"Well, I'm gonna anyway. The thing is, *Sao-shao*, you're taking this all wrong."

"Really? Thanks for the revelation. Go away."

"Look, I know why you're mad, okay? It doesn't take a genius. The chancellor's treating you like a pawn, yanking you here and there for whatever reason he wants, messing up whatever it is you're doing. It pisses you off. That's okay—it would piss me off too."

What he was saying pretty well echoed her own thoughts, but Danai was not about to let that fact slip. "Aren't you skirting the edges of treason there? You stay here, I'll find the onboard Maskirovka representative. I'm sure he or she would love to hear the rest of what you have to say."

He continued as if she hadn't spoken. "The thing is, you've been on the fast track for a while. Born to lead, right? So you sometimes forget what it's like to have your plans messed up, to have everything you're working for tripped up because some higher-up thinks it should be that way. You haven't had enough chances to learn how to roll with the punches."

"You have no bloody idea what you're talking about."

"Maybe. Wouldn't be the first time. All I'm saying is, this kind of thing is going to happen, even when you're not part of a regime that's as delightfully controlling as ours is. You just have to find the space where you can do your own thing, instead of getting all bent out of shape when the powers that be decide to be what they are. I know you think I'm not mad enough about being recalled, but I am. I was having fun down there, and I wanted to teach those Triarii a thing or two. But we can't right now, so we have to wait. It is what it is."

"That's deep."

Bell shrugged. "You can dismiss everything I say if you want. But I'm not the one stomping around the ship endlessly."

"You don't know a damned thing," she said. "This isn't just about me. This is about my nation. We showed weakness. We retreated in front of an inferior enemy. It's *not right*."

"Is the Confederation weak?"

"No!"

"Then why worry if Anderton and his Triarii think we're weak? They're wrong. No big deal. They'll find out soon enough."

"You know *nothing*," Danai said, frustration mounting. "Do you know what power is? It can be money, it can be guns, but the best kind of power, the power that really gets things done, is the power people *think* you have. If they see you as strong, you *are* strong. People, nations, react accordingly. Look at the Republic in the past few years. Look at how it moved from a mighty nation to a vulnerable one. Did their wealth change that much? Did their armies? No. Their neighbors started to perceive them as vulnerable, as weak. And so that's what they became. And now that's what the chancellor, the damned God Incarnate, has done to the Confederation. He's made us seem weak; he's given confidence to our enemies, not to his own troops. He's hurt the Confederation, and I can't just forget about it!"

To her infinite surprise, Bell did not respond with a smart remark. He didn't put on his sardonic grin. When he spoke, he actually sounded sincere.

"Okay," he said. "Okay. I forget sometimes. I spent too much time with the Canopians. They have a different way of seeing things. I forget the relationship between Capellan warriors and their state."

"I don't have the option of forgetting," Danai snapped.

Bell nodded. "All right. It is what it is. I'll remember that."

His sincerity started to take effect. Danai's shoulders, which felt like they had been hunched up near her jaw for several hours, lowered a little. Several other clenched muscles relaxed slightly. "Okay," she said.

He smiled as he saw her loosen up a little. "Good, good," he said. "Look, I'm helping, see? I can help sometimes."

"Right," she said. "Don't push it."

The accustomed cockiness returned to his grin. "Wouldn't dream of it. Just trying to score points with my commander by showing I'm not entirely useless." He glanced at his watch. "And here's another thing," he said. "By my guess, we've got at least another ninety minutes before we're on the ground. Your berth's right behind us, and if you give me enough time I'll show you ways to work out tension from plenty of other parts of your body. All you have to do is—"

She didn't think, she just reacted. Her right hand, in a tight fist, flew out in a straight line and made direct contact with Bell's nose. He staggered backward, his hands flying to his face, catching the blood that immediately flowed from his nostrils.

She felt like stepping forward and pummeling him

some more, but she restrained herself. She stayed on the balls of her feet, ready to spring forward again if given the slightest excuse.

Bell dropped his hands and looked at the bright red blood on his fingers. His nose was already swollen and discolored—she'd clearly given it a good break.

He took another step back, making sure he was out of her range, then put his insolent grin back on.

"Sometimes I help," he said. "Sometimes I don't."

He turned and walked away, employing an exaggerated limp even though he bore no wound on either leg. It was, Danai felt certain, one more way to mock her as he left.

She turned to enter her berth, the blank walls suddenly welcome as long as Jacyn Bell was not in there with her. Before the door closed, she heard the last of Bell's uneven footfalls as he continued on his way, no doubt stomping extra hard so she could hear him.

Clang CLANG, clang CLANG, clang CLANG.

16

Danai had filed her nails that morning. It was something she never did—combat in bouncing, jostled 'Mechs ruined any manicure in short order—but today it felt appropriate. It calmed her, sitting on the sofa in her chambers, watching her nails take shape as she carved a small point into each one. She could envision the red lines of blood that would spring up on Daoshen's cheek as she whipped her nails across it—assuming, of course, that the skeletal chancellor still had blood flowing in his cold veins.

She took one last look at the ten perfectly formed weapons on the ends of her fingers, and then she sighed. She wouldn't do it. Of course she wouldn't. He was the chancellor, the God Incarnate, and some degree of respect must be paid even though he was family. She could not attack him, especially in his own throne room.

That did not mean, however, that she would not rain down curses upon his head as soon as she saw him. If she could keep her courage up.

She was summoned within ten minutes of finishing her

nails, almost as if Daoshen had been monitoring her activities and waiting for her to complete her preparations. The two guards, wordless except for their greeting of, "The chancellor summons you," when she found them standing at her door, marched her to the throne room. Their archaic skirts of armor clanked as they walked, and their faces were invisible under the wide helmets they wore. Their armor had not changed for well over a thousand years, armor that unrelenting advances in weaponry had made useless many times over. But the armor meant something to Daoshen, and to Sun-Tzu his father, and to many Liaos before them, so it was worn.

Danai found herself becoming strangely composed as she approached the throne room. The ritualistic aspect of her approach felt soothing and familiar—probably the exact effect it was supposed to have. She still felt anger, like a boiling cauldron in her gut, but it no longer seemed to be in danger of erupting.

The herald stood in front of the entrance to the throne room, clothed in a Liao green silk robe, wearing the long, thin beard and mustache characteristic of a long-dead Terran emperor. He bowed slightly as Danai approached, and she responded with a deeper bow.

"Who may I say is approaching the chancellor?" he asked in a voice designed for proclamations, not conversation.

"Whoever you'd like to say," Danai said. "You can say Hanse Davion is here for all I care."

The herald turned his head slightly, making eye contact with Danai for the first time. "I will say that, if that is what you require of me," he said. "I suspect, though, that the chancellor will not be amused."

"Then say my name! You know who I am. Just go in and tell him."

The herald resumed his formal pose. "Who may I say is approaching?"

Danai rolled her eyes. She had gone through this little dance dozens of times with the herald, always trying to make him break, even slightly, from the well-established protocol. He never did.

"*Sao-shao* Danai Liao-Centrella of the Third Battalion of Second McCarron's Armored Cavalry."

"Please remain here," the herald said. "I will ascertain if the chancellor is available for an audience."

"Of *course* he's available!" Danai said. "He *summoned* me here!" But the herald had already slipped inside the throne room and the doors had closed behind him before Danai was finished speaking.

He returned promptly, his bearing still stiff, his face still expressionless. "The chancellor of the Capellan Confederation, the God Incarnate of Sian, bids you enter his presence. Please follow me."

Danai followed the herald, resisting the temptation to step on the heels of his shoes to make them slip off. It was only a quick flash of an idea, because soon enough she was walking the red-and-gold carpet that led her to Daoshen.

She walked past the columns at the far end of the room, then bowed deeply, as decorum demanded.

"You may rise, *Sao-shao* Liao-Centrella," Daoshen intoned. She straightened herself, much to her relief—folding at the waist did nothing to help the burning feeling in her gut—and walked closer to Daoshen. The back of her right knee began trembling.

"You have failed us," Daoshen said before she was even halfway through the room. "You have failed the Confederation."

So much for small talk, Danai thought. Bile rose to her throat, and her anger sprang loose. For once, the fear she felt in his presence couldn't keep it down. "The Confederation failed me!" she exclaimed. "The planet was *mine* if my request had been granted! All I needed—"

Daoshen's voice, usually little more than a sibilant whisper, became a roaring wind that filled the room. "You have not been asked to speak!" he said. "You will listen to the judgment and wisdom of your chancellor, and you will speak when we ask you to!"

Danai didn't want to obey. She wanted to shout him down, to explain how he had lost his chance to take

Aldebaran before the end of the year. But she couldn't speak. He wasn't just the Capellan chancellor—he was her brother. He had held a certain thrall over her for as long as she could remember, an aura of intimidation as natural as his skin. It had never failed to affect her, and today was no different. She could not respond.

Daoshen let his words settle in, then he returned to his normal voice. "You failed. You were asked to take Aldebaran with your battalion. You did not. Your orders said nothing about calling upon other forces. Only about doing it yourself, with the battalion that we gave you. The moment you asked for additional forces, you admitted failure. Compounded with your failure on New Hessen, we are beginning to doubt that your tournament prowess will ever translate into true military leadership. You must remember that your achievements on Solaris VII, while they brought you much personal glory, meant little to the Confederation. It is battlefield contributions that matter most—and there you have fallen far short of the hopes and expectations placed upon you.

"What is more, you have caused us additional trouble through your failure. For some reason we cannot fathom, you divided your force into three parts, sacrificing the valuable support your aerospace units could have provided by sending them to Zion. That played a crucial role in your defeat while also engaging a planet beyond the scope of your orders. You have caused me no degree of inconvenience through this."

Danai didn't understand this last remark. She saw his point about dividing her forces, though she didn't agree with it. It was a calculated risk that hadn't panned out. Besides, she wasn't convinced the aero units would have swung the balance of power on Aldebaran. They were useful, but usually not enough to make a difference in a battle involving dozens of 'Mechs—as long as the MechWarriors knew what they were doing.

But, as she did not yet have permission to speak, she couldn't say any of this.

"We had hoped, by this point in time, to be poised to take Tikonov away from the Federated Suns. Instead, our recent efforts have come to naught. While it is unfair to place all the blame for the slowed pace of conquest on a single pair of shoulders, it pains me greatly to say that your shoulders must bear a heavier burden for these failures than any others."

Danai stared at Daoshen's pale, drawn face. His burning eyes showed anger, but very little discomfort. *Yeah*, she thought. *It looks like you're in a* lot *of pain.*

"With all that has happened, one thing has become clear to us—the time has come for you to be relieved of your field duties."

Permission to speak or not, there was no way Danai could let that pass. "You can't . . ."

Daoshen raised a single imperial hand to silence her and, much to Danai's inner frustration, it worked. "We understand your passion for the battlefield. It is one trait you possess that helps us believe you may yet be salvageable as a commander. It may be of comfort to you, then, to know that this is only temporary. The Third Battalion of Second McCarron's Armored Cavalry is still yours. Your command lance will remain intact—in fact, you will need them, as well as your entire first company, for your next task. That is why they were ordered to accompany you to Sian.

"In the glorious history of the Capellan Confederation, many gains have been achieved through military conquest—I am confident I need not detail them for you. However, force of arms is only one way in which we advance our aims. If you are ever to move fully into your role as a member of the Confederation's ruling family, you must conquer fields other than those of battle. You have accompanied me on diplomatic missions in the past, and the time has come for you to embark on one of your own. You will lead a diplomatic mission to the Oriente Protectorate. Your command lance will accompany you to provide counsel and support.

"While we were on Terra, we entered into an agreement with Captain-General Jessica Marik of the Protectorate. In exchange for certain military favors, Captain-General Marik agreed to invade the worlds of

Kyrkbacken and Menkalinan. She has failed to live up to her side of the bargain. You are to persuade her to do all she agreed to do.

"The diplomatic art is a delicate one, requiring a far lighter touch than a warrior may be used to," Daoshen went on, assuming a professorial tone. Danai almost laughed—the idea that Daoshen applied a light touch to anything was ludicrous.

Her amusement soon faded under the weight of Daoshen's lecture on the art of diplomacy. It seemed to go on forever, and it contained many points of advice that Danai could never imagine Daoshen personally using. But then, he was God Incarnate and she was not, so she supposed different rules applied.

Thankfully, long hours of soldierly discipline allowed her to stand in place without showing discomfort. She thought she even managed to appear attentive, but she had no way of knowing for sure. Daoshen, lost in the wonder of his own wisdom, probably didn't notice anything about her.

Finally, the lecture seemed to be wrapping up.

"Remember that your command lance is present in an advisory capacity only, and your first company should do nothing more than act as a display," he said. "I realize that, with your warrior training and support, the temptation to resort to violence will be all too present. Do not give in to it, as that would be the gravest kind of failure."

If I resorted to violence as easily as you seem to think I do, Danai thought, *I would've strangled you with one of your own carpet threads by now.*

"We expect success. We will tolerate nothing less. You are dismissed."

Danai stood in her place, her mouth falling open. Knowing she was about to raise Daoshen's wrath, she spoke, the words tumbling out before Daoshen could silence her.

"You never gave me a chance to defend my actions on Aldebaran! If you had just left me on the planet, even without reinforcements, I would have found a way to reduce the Triarii to nothing! But you recalled me! How am I to blame for that?"

Daoshen's hurricane-level voice returned. "We did not ask for your defense because we are not interested in your justifications! The results speak for themselves, and your self-serving rationalizations mean nothing. You have your assignment, and your only concern is carrying it out, not engaging in vain attempts to save face!"

That was it. He was still Daoshen, he still had his odd power over her, but the accumulated slights and insults of the morning were too much to bear.

"Save *face*?" she exclaimed. "Coming from someone who has invented his own reality just so he never *has* to save face . . ."

And that was as far as she got. She hadn't heard the door open and she hadn't heard the clank of the approaching guards (probably because she had been yelling), but there they were. She knew she had two choices—keep yelling and be dragged out, or walk out on her own and retain some degree of dignity. She was too much of a Liao to completely forfeit her stateliness, so she cut herself off, whirled around and left the throne room before any guard could touch her.

She wasn't being fair to Erde. She knew it. But as soon as she saw her, as soon as Danai walked into the room full of cushions and pastel colors and bright sunlight and a plate of warm scones, she collapsed. She could not put sentences together; instead she just gasped out single words, heaving them out between spasms in her stomach, hoping somehow Erde would understand.

Erde walked to her. She did not take Danai in a full embrace—Danai was too hunched over, her body too given to twitches and jerks, for a hug to work. But she took Danai's hand and held it. Eventually the warmth of her touch got to Danai, and the words started coming out more smoothly.

She talked for a long while, some of it a recap of the message she had sent after New Hessen, some of it a summary of her frustration with her brother, some of it curses directed at the universe. Her aunt sat, took Danai's head on her lap as if she were a child, stroked her brow and listened.

Finally the stream of words started to dry up. Danai sat up, dried her eyes and tried to take back some of the dignity she was supposed to hold.

"I have a holovid," she said. "Something Daoshen gave me to watch just before I land on Oriente. I suppose it'll provide more information about what I'm supposed to be doing there, but I think I have most of it figured out. I thought I was going to Aldebaran to reclaim an important world of the old Duchy of Liao, but it wasn't about Aldebaran at all. It was about New Canton. I was supposed to provide one part of a pinch on New Canton, while Jessica Marik provided the other. But the Oriente forces didn't do what Daoshen expected, so the other half of the pincer never arrived, and for some reason I get the blame for that.

"I was used. He played on my patriotism and used me."

"You are a Capellan subject, my dear," Erde said. "In the chancellor's eyes, you are a vehicle that he can use as he pleases for the furtherance of Capellan glory. And since the chancellor and the Confederation are, effectively, one and the same, he can justify using any of his people for his own ends. It's the way it is and always has been."

"Between Daoshen blaming me for everything, Bell making fun of me for everything, Anderton acting pompous about everything and Caleb . . . well, and Caleb, I've had it. I could do completely without men for a good long while."

"Men are what they are," Erde said, and her words were so similar to what Bell had said on the DropShip that Danai felt a momentary surge of irritation. "They are too fiery, too prone to violence to be trusted with governance—why so many nations believe otherwise is a question that has always haunted we Canopians—but they still have their uses. Individually and collectively they have tremendous strengths and should never be casually dismissed. All the same"—and she smiled a gentle smile that did Danai a world of good—"I can certainly understand why one might need to spend some time outside their company for a while."

Danai smiled back and nibbled a scone. If she could arrange it, she'd stay right in this room until it was time to depart for Oriente.

"You've had a particularly bad run of it," Erde said. "But I have confidence you'll be able to handle most of the problems you listed. Daoshen's identity is well established and unlikely to change. He is frustrating you now, but you know how to adapt to him. This Major Anderton—well, if you have a chance to encounter him again, I suspect he'll suffer for any irritation he caused you."

Danai almost licked her lips at the prospect.

"And I imagine Jacyn Bell will come into line. Actually, it sounds like he already *is* in line—he likes the sound of his own voice, but you say he's never disobeyed an order and has carried out most of his assignments with skill. I suspect he's just hit you wrong at a bad time. In better circumstances, I'm sure his jabbering would be a minor matter.

"And that brings us to the one thing that truly concerns me."

At the mere mention of it—actually, Erde had only hinted at it—Danai felt a throb in the piece of ice that had sat in her chest ever since that day last September. She had poured out everything in her holovid to Erde immediately after the . . . event (she still did not like to call it what it was), and she didn't feel capable of returning to it again.

"I'm fine," Danai said, lying for all she was worth. "I was just frustrated when I came here, but I'm fine."

"You're not," Erde said. "And you shouldn't be. Not yet. I wish I could make it better in an instant, but of course I can't. There's only one thing of possible use I can talk about, and that's forgiveness."

The icy throb grew into a stab. Pain and fury filled Danai's head. "Forgiveness? I wouldn't forgive the Davion swine, ever! How could you ask . . ."

But Erde stopped her with her soft smile and gentle voice. "Not him, Danai. As far as I'm concerned you may hate him until the end of days. I certainly will. But you need to forgive yourself."

"For what? What did I do?"

"Nothing. You did nothing wrong. But you need to believe that's true."

"I do," Danai said. "Of course I do."

Her aunt kept looking at her with kind eyes, and Danai felt ashamed for lying to her. "Okay. I don't. Yet. But I'll keep trying."

"Blaming yourself is all too easy," Erde said. "When you lose on the battlefield, you look back at the mistakes you made, and you learn to fight better. This was not a battle, this was not a fair fight. This was cruelty, savagery that went beyond all the rules you live by. You did not lose because you were not enough of a warrior. You suffered because you did not know how savage your companion was. You had no way to know, and it's something you can't assume. If you look at every person you meet as a potential rapist—" Danai's face must have betrayed her when Erde said that word, and her aunt's eyes grew sorrowful. "It's a horrible word, I know, but it *should* be horrible. You cannot assume everyone you meet is capable of such things. If you do, the universe quickly becomes cold and lonely. It is no way to live. And if you want proof of that, look to your brother. He has removed himself from a universe that he mistrusts, and so he is the cold, remote person who made you so angry today.

"You could not have known. You could not have anticipated. And therefore you cannot be blamed."

With that, Danai's composure fell away, and she let herself be a child in her aunt's care until it was time to leave.

══ 17 ══

Danai had made a definite effort to fight isolation in the four weeks of her journey so far. She resisted the temptation to lock herself in her quarters again (which was even more alluring here in the roomier confines of a JumpShip), and she had let herself be seen out and about. When Clara or Sandra invited her out for a meal, or a workout, or evening drinks, she accepted. Her heart might not always have been in it, but she went out, and often she even had a good time.

She didn't know how she would have responded if Bell had asked her to a meal or some such activity, but to this point she hadn't needed to come up with a response. Bell smiled when he saw her and looked as insolent as ever, but didn't ask her to do anything with him. Which, she thought, was quite understandable. At least his nose was starting to heal—it didn't even look that crooked.

It had been like a four-week vacation, really. She had no battle or tournament to plan for, and she had a long journey on a JumpShip without Daoshen or Ilsa or anyone who might try to impose family duties on her. If she could have ordered the JumpShip captain to take an extra week recharging, she would have. But she couldn't, and the next jump would take them into the Oriente Protectorate. That meant vacation was over. Time to figure out what she and her crew would do once their mission started in earnest.

They gathered in the most formal of the JumpShip's three restaurants. The diplomatic life had its advantages, Danai thought each time she ordered a meal in a place that was not a military mess hall. Danai had requested a secluded table, tucked in a corner far from the kitchen, where they could talk in peace.

Sandra and Clara showed up in their dress uniforms (minus the *dao* swords and helmets), while Bell showed up in the same stained brown-and-green field uniform that, as far as Danai could tell, he wore every day. She thought maybe she should pay more attention to the location of specific stains—that might be the way to tell one of Bell's uniforms from the others.

She couldn't help but notice the difference in their bearings as they approached her table. Sandra, in her immaculate uniform, walked as if auditioning for the role of Ideal Capellan Warrior Number One in a propaganda video from the Department of Unity. She seemed to think that Warrior House Hiritsu, the House of her forebear Aris Sung, had eyes and ears everywhere, and they would always be watching to make sure her bearing and demeanor were proper. She moved accordingly, spine stiff, head straight, nose slightly raised.

Clara, on the other hand, moved into almost any room as if waiting for someone to challenge her to a fight. Her eyes took in the whole area as quickly as they could, moving back and forth, up and down, looking for any hint of a threat, and generally seeming somewhat disappointed when none materialized.

Bell moved like—well, how did Bell move? Like water in a small creek. He was smooth, unhurried and didn't seem to care if he was taking the most direct route to his destination. He babbled easily on his way, uncaring if people around him approved of how he was moving or not. And he did it in a uniform that looked more like casual clothing than any uniform Danai had ever seen.

"Nice of you to dress up," Danai said as he sat down.

Bell shrugged. "I figure I'm going to have to look nice for the folks down on Oriente. Don't want to break out the dress uniform now and risk getting food stains on it."

"You've seen how he eats," Clara said to Danai. "Stains are a serious risk for him and anyone sitting next to him."

"Besides," Bell said, smirking at Sandra, "it takes an awful lot to make me come out in public with a cape on."

Sandra, her spine stiff and straight as always, opened her mouth, most likely to deliver a discourse on the symbolism of the dress uniform and the many reasons she was proud to wear it. Danai cut her off.

"I guess if the maître d' let you in, then you're dressed up enough for me," she said. "Sit down, everyone."

They sat, pondered their menus silently as imitation candlelight flickered around them, ordered their meals and then Danai proceeded to business.

"As I told each of you, we're on a diplomatic mission, not a military one. But I've never led a diplomatic mission, and I don't think any of you have ever been on one—except maybe as security." She waited for any of the other three to contradict her. When they didn't, she continued speaking. "That means none of us has any experience on which to base our strategy. We're making this up as we go. But we all know military operations, and that's how our minds work. So I'm going to make this as much like a military operation as possible. Only without the violence."

"That's like having dinner, only without the food," Clara complained.

"I know. But the chancellor made it clear—if I resort to force on this mission, he'll consider it a worse failure than New Hessen or Aldebaran. My career, for the immediate future at least, will be headed right down the toilet. And, I hate to add, since you all are here to assist me, your futures wouldn't look too bright either."

"I'm healing a broken nose on a JumpShip many, many light-years away from home," Bell said. "My future's got nowhere to go but up."

Both Sandra and Clara looked away, embarrassed. They knew, of course, how Bell had gotten his broken nose, and to them his mention of it must have sounded like a reproach. But Danai was in a good enough mood to take it in stride.

"I could've kicked you in the groin instead," she said sweetly. "That would be worse."

She waited for Bell to take offense, but the man didn't seem capable of that particular emotion. He cocked his head to one side. "You make a good point," he said. "Has the chancellor been known to kick people in the balls as a punishment for failure?"

"You don't want to know all the things he's done to people's balls," Danai said.

"Hmmm," Bell said. "Okay. I guess I'm not at rock bottom yet. I'll try to be helpful from now on."

"That would be novel," she said, and watched Clara and Sandra raise their heads to rejoin the conversation now that the storm they'd feared would break turned out to be nothing more than a light breeze.

Their food arrived, steaming and succulent, and the meeting was briefly interrupted for each person to stuff a few bites into their mouths. After Danai chewed and swallowed her third bite of *ha gaw*, she continued with her plans.

"We're going to divide up, just like at Daipan. Sandra, I want you in charge of security. Anyplace we go, I want you to know where entrances and exits are, what kind of guards the Protectorate has there—things like that. I also want you to know where we can talk freely, where we can store sensitive items or files, and when we've got cameras watching us."

"Yes, *Sao-shao*," Sandra said, brightening. Having a specific assignment in an area she felt confident about seemed to ease any concerns she had about being a diplomat instead of a warrior.

"Clara, you're going to have my back. I want you with me at any meeting I go to, or whenever anyone from the Protectorate comes to talk to me—with one exception that I'll tell you about later. I'll be doing most of the talking in these meetings, so I want you to do a lot of listening and observing. If you see or hear me doing something that sounds ill-advised or stupid, I want you to shut me up as quickly as you can. Don't worry about correcting me then and there—just get me out of the situation before I do too much damage."

"I can do that," Clara said.

"Bell—you're going to find out everything that's going on that I don't see. I want you talking to anyone and everyone who'll talk to you, finding out any gossip or useful information you can. If the Mariks are planning some surprise, or have something up their sleeves, I want you to know about it long before they spring it on me. If you're half as charming as you think you are, this should be a good assignment for you."

"I'm *twice* as charming as I think I am," Bell corrected. "But I have a question."

Danai had a feeling she would regret this, but said, "Go ahead."

"How come I'm Bell?"

Danai blinked. "What?"

"How come I'm Bell? This is a nice dinner meeting, so you call Sandra, Sandra, and Clara, Clara. But you call me Bell. I don't think I've ever heard you say my first name."

"I think she used it as a curse once," Clara offered.

"I'm not going to count that. I want to know why you never call me Jacyn." He assumed a look of wounded dignity. "It's because I'm a man, isn't it? You Canopians—okay, I'm one too, but that's not the point—you're all the same. Judging us solely by our anatomy. Gazing at our shapely behinds as we walk by, but then not even deigning to treat us as people. We're mere cattle to be prodded by you, aren't we? But we're just a different gender, not a whole different *species.* Are we not human? If you prick us, do we not bleed?"

Sandra rolled her eyes. "Please."

"I just knew he'd work the word 'prick' into that monologue somewhere," Clara said.

"Are you done?" Danai asked.

Bell took a deep breath, raised one hand with his index finger as if he was about to launch on an extended oratory, then he abruptly exhaled and lowered his hand. "Yes," he said.

"A discourse that touching deserves an answer. You are Bell because that's what I feel like calling you. When I feel like calling you Jacyn, that's what I'll do. And since I'm your superior, there's not much you can do about it. Good enough?"

Bell nodded in mock respect. "Of course," he said. "Just as long as your reasons aren't, you know, totally arbitrary."

Danai figured she must really be in a good mood, as she was suppressing a smile instead of preparing a tongue-lashing (or another punch).

"All right," she said. "Do you think you can do what I asked you to?"

"Be charming?" Bell said. "Of course. I can't *not* be charming."

"Yes, you can," all three women said at once.

Bell's grin slowly spread across his face. "You make a strong case," he admitted.

"There's one more thing," Danai said. "When I met with the chancellor, he mentioned an oral agreement he had with Jessica Marik, but he didn't give me any of the details. While you're talking to people, try to find out what that agreement entailed. It would help me to know. I've got a holovid from the chancellor I'm supposed to watch before we arrive on Oriente, but there's no guarantee he'll give me the information I want. I may have to rely on you."

"In that case, God help you," Sandra muttered.

"God will help her or I will," Bell said. "Either way, the quality of the assistance is about the same."

The rest of the meal passed in pleasant conversation and light banter. It was only a few hours, but the failures of the past and the pressure of the near future faded for a time, and Danai relaxed. The ever-present icicle in her chest didn't go away, but there was at least a small thaw.

18

The time had finally come. She had put it off for as long as she could, but after nearly two months on the JumpShip, her cabin had run out of distractions. She'd written letters to everyone she could think of (including Nikol, hoping they could meet on Oriente outside of the normal diplomatic encounters), watched every ho-lovid the ship carried that seemed vaguely interesting, and planned fifteen different ways to take Aldebaran in case she ever had the chance to go there again. She didn't have much left to do except watch Daoshen's message.

She'd already waited until about the last minute. Or-bital insertion would be starting soon, and she'd be mak-ing her grand, official entrance into the Protectorate in a day or two. Just in case Daoshen said anything really important in the message, she'd need time to digest it.

She took a deep breath and cued up the holovid. Daoshen's spectral image appeared in front of her, his eyes dark hollows under his brow. Danai paused the vid briefly and slapped her brother's image around. As her hands did nothing but pass through him, she found it unsatisfying. She sighed and restarted the playback.

Daoshen said five words, and she paused it again. She looked quizzically at the machine. Something must be broken. Something in the audio output. She didn't just hear what she thought she had heard. There must be a glitch.

She restarted the playback, her hands shaking because her heart had started pounding.

She made it through twenty-two words the next time. Then her hand fell, heavy as Yen-lo-wang's ax, and stopped the playback. Her vision filled with multicolored stars, and she felt the JumpShip lurching beneath her. The only thing she could hear was a pounding throb in her ears.

Something's wrong with this, she thought. *Something's wrong something's wrong.*

She restarted it again, somehow managing to see the controls through a pinpoint of clear vision in the middle of the field of stars. She listened carefully to make sure she hadn't misheard anything.

She hadn't. It said the same thing as the first time she had played it, the same thing as the second time. It wasn't going to change.

She might have screamed. Her throat felt sore, as if wordless torrents had repeatedly ripped through it. She thought she could hear the echo of her own shriek in her ears, but she couldn't be sure over the sound of the blood. But there, there was Daoshen's voice. She tried to scream, intentionally this time, not a reflex, but only a hoarse rasp came out. Just enough to keep her from hearing Daoshen. She rolled on the floor—somehow, she'd missed her chair entirely—and yelled her near-silent yell as she tried to keep from ever hearing anything Daoshen said to her again.

Eventually, the playback stopped, and so did Danai's screams. She lay on the floor, panting. Her vision was returning. Everything—the bunk, the plastic table, the narrow desk—was right where it had been. But they shouldn't be there. The whole world, the whole universe, had just changed. Nothing should be the same. Nothing *could* be the same. But the furniture had remained the same.

She had no idea how long she stayed on the floor, gasping for air. She wasn't sure what day it was anymore, and she didn't really care. She finally pulled herself into a sitting position and looked at the holovid player. It sat there, innocuous, ignorant of the sentence it had just pronounced upon her head.

Then a curious thing happened. Danai's arm reached out. She didn't tell it to. It just moved on its own toward the player. Danai watched it curiously as it stretched, and when it reached full extension it pulled the rest of her body forward, like a small dog pulling a weary owner.

It was a strange sensation to be dragged, almost levitated, by one's own arm. The oddness of it all helped her ignore what her arm was doing, which was reaching for the holovid player. Her index finger extended and once again pushed the playback button.

Its mission accomplished, Danai's arm went limp. She collapsed, leaning against the desk that held the player. She heard Daoshen's voice again, and she was helpless to stop it. She felt too tired to move, too tired to scream, too tired to do anything but let Daoshen's whisper bore a hole into her head.

"Danai, product of my loins, it is time for you to embrace my personal heritage and accept the glory of my blood that flows in your veins in service to House Liao.

"I have had reasons for concealing my parentage of you in the past, just as I have reasons for revealing it to you now. Neither are your concern. All that must worry you now is the task in front of you, the goal I have set for you to further the glory of the Confederation. That goal should be of increased importance to you now, as you realize you are under the direction and guidance of, not your brother, but your father.

"I am well aware of your belief that I do not care for you as a person. You must now know that to be untrue.

You are my daughter. You are the heir of my glory. How could I not care for you?

"It is true that I have asked you to make many sacrifices, but that is the nature of sovereignty—to sacrifice for the state, which is greater than you. You—each of us—is only important as we strive to build the Confederation. We all make sacrifices toward that greater good.

"Of particular note at this time is the sacrifice being made by your sister Ilsa in the Duchy of Andurien. She has proposed marriage to Duke Ari Humphreys, a marriage that would bring the Magistracy of Canopus and the Duchy of Andurien into an alliance of equals—with both of them, naturally, acting in the service of the Capellan Confederation, whether they are aware of that fact or not.

"I assume I need not explain to you the worth of the alliance with Andurien. I give this to you as a wedge to use in your negotiations, though a wedge I hope you will use with prudence and foresight. Captain-General Marik must know that she is being increasingly surrounded by those loyal to the Confederation, and that her lofty goal of reuniting the Free Worlds League under the false Marik name is nothing more than an empty dream. Used properly, the pending nuptials of Ilsa and Duke Humphreys should prove quite persuasive in prompting the Protectorate to treat the Confederation with more deference than they have shown in recent months.

"You have my blood flowing in you. You have power. You will succeed. You will return to Sian in glory, because you have furthered the glory of the Confederation. And when you return, I will welcome you, my daughter."

The word "daughter" in Daoshen's voice was a sharp dagger in Danai's heart. Each time she heard it, she winced. But on this listen, she at least retained enough presence of mind to notice a few interesting facts.

The first, and to her mind the saddest, fact was that in all likelihood Daoshen was telling the truth. He was manipulative, he had little respect for individuals and in many ways he was unscrupulous, but he still valued honesty in his speech. And this was especially true when he spoke of something as sacred as the blood of Liao. To lie about such a thing would be a great dishonor to Daoshen and his ancestors. Or at least, to tell someone they were of his direct lineage when they weren't would be a grave dishonor—he did not have a similar compunction against telling someone who was of his lineage that she was his sister for more than a quarter of a century. In any case, she was resigned to the fact that her father was not the dead, distant Sun-Tzu whom she never really knew, but rather the quite living Daoshen whom she knew too well.

The second interesting fact was that while Daoshen was prepared to let her know the truth of her parentage, he did not seem quite ready to make the matter public. She noted his last sentence—"And when you return, I will welcome you, my daughter," not "And when you return, I will welcome you *as* my daughter." Apparently this was to be their little secret for a time.

And then there was the third fact, which was actually an absence of a fact. Daoshen had come forward as her father—who, then, was her mother?

She stayed on the floor a long time, contemplating that question and considering her new place in the universe. She hoped she would recover the will to move before she landed on Oriente.

Jojoken, Andurien
Duchy of Andurien

Just because the inevitable sometimes takes a little longer than you might have expected doesn't mean it was not, in fact, inevitable.

Duke Humphreys had consulted with his advisers. He'd made a military evaluation of the entire Duchy, together with an evaluation of the Magistracy of Canopus. He had taken Ilsa to dinner once, and once accompanied her to a visiting Canopian pleasure circus, where he had a grand time losing vast sums of money at the baccarat table. He had considered, pondered, then considered some more. And in the end, after three and a half months, he had done what Ilsa had known he would do the moment he looked at the proposal she passed to him across the desk. He had said yes.

Ilsa had already sent a courier to take a holomessage to Daoshen. She would be following it, but she did not want to engage in the JumpShip-hopping that most couriers relied on for speed—she preferred a more leisurely journey. After all, she needed time to prepare for her upcoming nuptials.

She wished she could be there when Daoshen received the news. In truth, she wished she could tell him herself. He would be pleased and . . . well, mostly pleased. Still, it would be worth seeing his face when the news came. He was expecting it, he was even hoping for it, but his reaction might be strong enough to actually provoke a flicker of emotion on his face.

He would recover his mask quickly, of course. He was a god, after all.

Ilsa smiled. She had watched the evolution of Daoshen's divinity with curiosity and amusement over the years. He had never lacked for self-confidence, even from his youngest days, but believing in oneself is not at all the same as believing oneself to be divine. She could pinpoint no single moment where he made the transition from human to god; it had been a slow growth, a boy growing into an oversized coat of armor. When he first became chancellor, it seemed he insisted he was God Incarnate because he needed others to believe in him so they would trust his word. Then, as his military adventures grew bolder and he took more risks, his need to believe in his own divinity increased, as a way to justify the blood he ordered shed and to boost his confidence after his failures. Finally, there came a time when he no longer pushed people, including himself, to believe in his divinity. He simply assumed it. He carried himself like a god, and he believed all those with eyes to see would recognize his divinity.

If he had been anyone but the Capellan chancellor, he likely would have been institutionalized long ago—

Ilsa was under no illusions about that. But he *was* chancellor, he was expected to act godlike, and so in context his actions and demeanor were perfectly appropriate. And the fact that the Confederation grew stronger under his direction could not be ignored. Whatever the boundaries of his sanity, he was a shrewd diplomat and a cunning general, and he served the Confederation with the entirety of his being.

As she had just shown here on Andurien, she did the same. Their methods and behavior might be different, but their dedication was equal. Daoshen would see that now, possibly in a way he had never seen it before and, oddly enough, he might feel a small pang of regret at that fact. Though that pang would be buried so deep in his godly heart that no mortal would ever notice it.

19

Amur, Oriente
Oriente Protectorate
23 March 3136

Spring rains had washed the air over Amur clean, and the sky sparkled. The sun shone warm, reflecting off the helmets of troops patrolling the DropPort.

Danai had spent the entire morning organizing her personnel. She was going to make as impressive an entrance as possible. If she had learned anything from accompanying Daoshen on diplomatic tours, that was it.

Daoshen. Her brother. Her father. Daoshen was her father.

Her legs trembled and her hands shook. This was exactly why she was busying herself with organizing her entourage—so she wouldn't think about the chancellor (she was trying to avoid even thinking his name).

She had her entire first company, including Bell, in dress uniforms. The chancellor had sent her with a fine group of aides and attachés, and Ben Wong, the Capellan ambassador to the Protectorate, had come aboard with some members of his staff. She had them all put on the finest clothes they had with them, splashing their outfits with as much Liao green as possible.

Still, with all that she only had bout twenty people. Not impressive enough. So she spoke with the DropShip captain, and enlisted him and half a dozen crew members to walk with her into the Amur Palace. Then she had the ambassador send for a few more guards from the embassy, putting her procession at thirty. She would arrive at the head of four columns with seven people apiece (with her at the head and one extra, maybe Bell, bringing up the rear). That would do.

Now the only trick was the timing. She clearly couldn't march toward the palace without being invited, as it seemed like a bad idea to cause a minor incident as her first official action. But she wanted to be on the move promptly once the captain-general sent for her, so she couldn't let her entourage go back to their quarters and lounge.

She thought of what the chancellor would do—he would organize his people near the DropShip exit and have them stand in place, ready to march out when the word came through. They'd all be uncomfortable and grumpy, but their fear of the chancellor (or, from his point of view, their respect) would keep them disciplined anyway, and they would march out promptly.

She rejected that idea. Instead, she invited all thirty members of her entourage to a large breakfast. She exhausted the DropShip's stores having the crew prepare a vast *dim sum* feast, wheeling bowls of steaming dumplings and other delicacies between the tables in the mess. She only put one condition on her people—they had to wear protective bibs to keep their dress clothes spotless. Beyond that, they were free to enjoy a meal that, if necessary, would continue for hours.

It wasn't necessary. The carts made a few circuits around the room, and then the announcement came. The captain-general was ready to receive the Capellan delegation.

Danai stood immediately. She was gratified to see her entire entourage stand with her and promptly follow her out the door. She might have been a good minute slower than what the chancellor would have accomplished in the same circumstances, but she found that gap acceptable.

Once her people had unloaded from the transports that brought them to the palace, Danai marched at the head of her columns, everyone keeping step, even the ambassador and his people. The marchers at the front of the left and right columns carried the colors of the Capellan Confederation, gently flapping in the breeze. They passed between two rows of Oriente soldiers who stood at attention, weapons resting on their shoulders. Danai kept her eyes fixed on the granite steps ahead, leading to the double doors of the Amur Palace.

She walked up the steps, enjoying the sharp click of her boots on the stone. Then she passed from the bright light of day to the relative dimness inside. Compared to the imposing stone exterior, the palace's foyer was a simple affair, low-ceilinged, plaster walls covered with historic artwork, subtly lit by fixtures hidden around the perimeter of the ceiling. Three uniformed men in Oriente colors stood in front of a sliding metal door opposite the entrance.

"Please continue this way," one of them said as Danai and her people entered. The door behind them slid open, and Danai continued through without breaking stride.

There were more stone steps on the other side, these ascending five meters to a long hallway with an arched ceiling. Sunlight streamed through windows set in the stone roof, falling upon a series of holograms and artifacts of the Oriente Protectorate's past and present. Danai was particularly impressed by a grand painting, at least seven meters long, showing the untamed rain forests of Oriente as the first settlers arrived. The smallness of the people compared to the vastness of nature shown in the painting said much about the stubbornness of the Oriente people and of their unwillingness to give in to intimidating and overwhelming surroundings. The chancellor had given Danai a little extra leverage in that direction, a way to make Jessica Marik feel as threatened as those first settlers in the jungle. But Danai thought the captain-general would be as likely to cave to the pressure as those settlers had been. Intimidation might not be the strongest weapon in her arsenal—and if so, she'd have to determine what her other weapons might be.

The hallway brought them to the Amur Palace throne room, which had a very different feel from its Capellan equivalent. The first things she noticed were the padded chairs, upholstered in purple, that lined the walls, indicating that people other than the captain-general were allowed to sit when visiting the room. Danai did not believe she would be taking advantage of the chairs on this visit, but it was nice to know they were there.

She also noticed that the throne, such as it was, looked only slightly nicer than the other chairs and was not elevated at all. Jessica Marik and her husband, Philip Hughes, stood in front of those chairs, both smiling warmly. The middle of the room had a thick burgundy rug that looked as if it was there for comfort rather than to impress visitors. All in all, the throne room looked inviting, a concept that likely would have given the Capellan chancellor fits.

Danai brought her procession to a halt, and was both pleased and somewhat embarrassed to see that her entourage outnumbered the Oriente folk in the room by a solid five-to-one ratio. Besides Jessica Marik and her husband, there were two soldiers by the door and two flanking the throne.

"Welcome, Danai," Captain-General Marik said, eschewing formality from the get-go. "We're glad to see you. We've made arrangements for you and your people to be very comfortable during your stay."

"Thank you, Captain-General. You're too kind."

"You know, of course, that I will be happy to speak with you at any time, but I imagine you would like to get settled first. I can have you shown to your quarters."

Danai had planned a formal greeting speech, but given the tenor set by Jessica Marik, she dispensed with it. "Thank you, Captain-General. That's very kind of you.

I look forward to our discussions later on. If you'd allow me to make some brief introductions—this is *Sang-wei* Clara Parks, my executive officer; *Sang-wei* Sandra Sung, my tactical officer; and *Sang-wei* Jacyn Bell, my sergeant at arms."

"I'm honored to meet you." Then a small corner of Jessica's mouth curled into a sly grin. "And who are all the rest of these people?"

Danai knew this was a light jab from Jessica, but she didn't feel the impact. Numb as Danai was from the revelation in the chancellor's holovid, Jessica Marik would have to hit much harder than that if she wanted to leave a mark.

"Some of them are my aides and staff," Danai said. "And some of them came with me to help me make a good entrance."

Jessica laughed. "It worked," she said. "You looked positively grand marching to the capital. I've always said making a good entrance is one of the keys to good leadership."

"I've never heard you say that," her husband said.

"Then I'm going to start saying it," Jessica said primly. "Anyway, Fern Beecher, my hospitality director, will show you to your rooms. We have space for two of you in the palace, while the rest of your group will be staying next to the DropPort."

"Thank you, Captain-General."

Beecher, a tall woman with a helmet of steel grey hair, entered the throne room on cue and showed Danai out. Once they were out of the throne room, everyone but Danai and Clara left the palace—the bulk of the retinue had left the DropPort only to return once the show was over.

Danai and Clara were shown to a matching set of pleasant rooms: a sizeable bed on a royal blue carpet, a sitting room with a square wooden table and a large desk with a terminal, and just about any amenity that could be squeezed into the space. The chambers were considerably better than the DropShip they'd come in on, and even a generous step up from her private quarters on the JumpShip. She was several jumps away from the chancellor, she had a comfortable place to stay and she would be able to get together with Nikol, who might be the only person in the Inner Sphere without ulterior motives when they spoke together. She knew she had to succeed in her mission, but the chancellor hadn't said anything about succeeding quickly.

Danai almost slapped herself. What kind of diplomat was she, so easily seduced by kind words and luxurious quarters? She had a job to do. She had the honor of the Confederation to uphold.

She sat at the room's terminal, the better to compose a few thoughts about the upcoming negotiations. But her mind wouldn't clear. Something had been bothering her since she had calmed down enough after the chancellor's message to think clearly. Erde, her great-aunt, had known Daoshen and Ilsa and even Sun-Tzu Liao since long before Danai was born. Erde had raised Danai until Daoshen ordered Danai to come to the Capellan Confederation and enter the military academy, pursuant to fulfilling her duties as a Liao. If anyone else besides Daoshen was in a position to know the secret of her parentage, it was Erde Centrella.

Erde. Her confidant. The one person she'd trusted with the truth about New Hessen and what Caleb Davion had done. Erde had been lying to her for her whole life.

Maybe. Maybe, somehow, she didn't know. Maybe Daoshen had pulled the wool over everyone's eyes. Not likely. But maybe.

She had to know. She had to know soon.

There was a command circuit functioning between Sian and Oriente, and Danai planned on using it to get any diplomatic materials back to the chancellor as quickly as possible. She had planned to send off a pouch tonight, detailing her arrival and providing a vague outline of her plans. She had time to dash off a quick note to Erde. It would go off with everything else.

Then she'd know. If she could hold on long enough to find out.

20

"**D**anai!" Jessica Marik stood, looking very much like a civilian except for the insignia on the shoulders of her charcoal grey blazer that identified her as captain-general. "Or, since this is a formal diplomatic meeting, I suppose I should say *Sao-shao* Liao-Centrella. I hope your accommodations have proven comfortable to this point."

Danai smiled warmly. "They're wonderful," she said.

In truth, she hadn't slept more than an hour the past night, but that was not the fault of her quarters. Every time she closed her eyes, two faces appeared in her mind—Daoshen and Erde. They were mouthing words, but no sound came out. Whatever they wanted to tell the weary Danai was not getting through to her, either because she could not or would not hear. Though silent, they still made it impossible for Danai to sleep. But she had a job to do today, so she had freshened herself as best she could, made her eyes look sharp and alert, and kept her bearing firm. If there was anything a Mech-

Warrior knew, it was how to function at a high level on little rest.

She had been summoned to a meeting, but in Jessica's private office rather than the throne room. With its floor-to-ceiling bookcases, stone fireplace and framed oil landscapes, it was an inviting room. The Marik's charm offensive was clearly continuing into day two.

Jessica's husband Philip was not present for this meeting, but Nikol was. Danai made a note of this. While Nikol might have been present as part of her diplomatic duties, Danai doubted it. Most likely, Nikol's inclusion in the meeting was yet another attempt to make Danai comfortable and get her to let her guard down.

Besides the two Mariks, a short, wiry man sat to the left of Jessica's modest desk, diligently making entries into a noteputer. Not a complete transcript, Danai thought—she assumed from the beginning that the meeting was being recorded—but rather notes on which parts of the recording might prove interesting at a later date. He probably had the additional duty of bringing a formal air to the occasion and, with his high-collared shirt and burgundy cravat, he performed that function well.

Danai had Clara in tow along with her own stenographer, one of the diplomats pressed on her by Daoshen. She couldn't remember the man's name at the moment, but he seemed to respond to any instructions Danai gave when looking directly at him, which was good enough.

Danai clasped Jessica's hand, then gave Nikol a hug. Her emotions almost threw her for a loop when she made contact with her friend—she suddenly wanted to giggle like a teenager and sob for hours on end at the same time, but she managed to keep herself steady and pull back without displaying anything more than a smile.

Once everyone was seated and comfortable, Jessica beamed at Danai—a motherly look, Danai thought, that the military under her command likely never saw.

"I must say, Danai—oh, heavens, I should say . . . well, maybe not. Could we just dispense with formality for these discussions, so I can be Jessica and you can be

Danai? I'm likely to keep calling you Danai anyway, so we might as well both be casual."

"That sounds fine," Danai said. She made herself sound grateful—no harm in letting Jessica think her unrelenting efforts to put Danai at ease were working.

"Good. Now, Danai, I was going to say how happy I was that Chancellor Liao sent you. My daughter Nikol has spoken highly of you since we left Terra, and from what I see I agree with her assessment. You seem capable and very bright."

"You're very kind," Danai said. She prepared herself for a blow, figuring that Jessica was laying on the praise in advance of some criticism. When she'd marched into the throne room with her retinue, she had expected a negative reaction sooner or later. The Mariks had opened the encounter with charm, while Danai had opted for a display of strength—a sign, Danai was sure, of the influence of her Liao blood.

The criticism started gently, but there was no mistaking the change in Jessica's tone. "I must say, though, I was rather surprised by the group you brought into the throne room yesterday. So many uniforms! It felt like an invasion."

"I'm sorry if I made you at all uncomfortable. I was just bringing the people the chancellor ordered along on the mission." It was a lie—Daoshen hadn't said anything about taking her company into the actual throne room—but a fairly harmless one, in Danai's estimation.

"No need to apologize," Jessica said. "It simply surprised me. Now, I assume most of the people you brought in are MechWarriors, correct?"

"Yes. It's my company from the Third Battalion of Second McCarron's Armored Cavalry."

"And I assume—well, I don't have to assume this, our scans have showed as much—your ships have your 'Mechs inside?"

"Merely as a convenience," Danai said. "I'm sure you know how nervous a MechWarrior gets if she is separated from her machine for too long."

"And I'm sure you know how nervous a ruler gets when sixteen large machines of war land practically in her front yard," Jessica said, her voice suddenly sharp.

Danai's opening move had worked—Jessica was angry. Now she had to figure out what to do next.

"I assure you, we do not intend to so much as arm our 'Mechs, let alone fire a shot, while we are on Oriente." Danai decided it was time for some flattery of her own. "Besides, we know the military strength of the Oriente Protectorate too well to believe sixteen 'Mechs would have any success in a hostile action."

"Oh, it's certain you would lose any battle you decided to start on Oriente," Jessica said, and Danai strained to find a trace of the motherly bearing Jessica had carried only moments before. "Still, there would be unnecessary death and destruction, which is intolerable. I will not have Capellan 'Mechs landing on Oriente and causing trouble. Your people will have strict orders about where they can be and when, and I expect those instructions to be followed to the letter. And, I should add, I do not appreciate the attempt to intimidate me by bringing them here."

Danai knew how she was supposed to feel—like a scolded child. That had been the whole purpose of the warm hospitality to this point, to make her apologetic, to make her want to grant any concessions Jessica thought to ask in return for her breach of etiquette. Unfortunately for Jessica, as the breach of etiquette had been entirely intentional, Danai didn't feel much of a need to make up for it. She did not quail in the face of Jessica's attack.

"I'm sorry you feel we were trying to bully you," Danai said. "I wasn't, of course. But if it helps, I can promise you that no one in my command will make an aggressive move while we are here."

"I appreciate your promise," Jessica said, though her tone had not grown any softer. "However, recent experience has shown that the word of the Liaos cannot always be trusted."

This was news to Danai; as far as she knew, she was

here because the Mariks hadn't lived up to their end of the bargain. Daoshen hadn't bothered to mention any promises he might have broken.

"I'm sorry, but which experience is that?"

Jessica slammed an open palm on her desk. Everyone in the room (except the Mariks' imperturbable clerk) jumped.

"Don't sit there and play games with me!" Jessica shouted. "You know full well what I'm talking about! It was your attack! Aerial units of your battalion making bombing runs over Zion!"

"Yes, but I'm not sure what that has to do with . . ."

"We had a specific agreement! The Capellan Confederation was only to take worlds that were traditionally part of the Confederation. Zion is not such a planet! You had *no business* sending your troops there! Now, as I said, I'm quite pleased the chancellor decided to send you on this mission, because now I can hear the explanation for your treachery from your own mouth. Why did you break the agreement?"

Danai had to think fast. Daoshen had done it to her again. This was the sort of thing that would have been nice to know before she came here. Hell, it was the sort of thing that would have been nice to know before she'd headed to Aldebaran. But again, he'd left her to drift in the wind. Made her a pawn in some game of his, rather than an informed player. Another way to see if she measured up to her family name—to see if she lived up to his blood. He'd thrown her into the deep end of the diplomatic pool for sport.

Danai knew Jessica wanted an explanation, but she didn't have a good enough one yet. If she wanted to live up to her bro—her father's example, she could start by playing a game of her own.

She flew to her feet. Her chair teetered a little, so she gave it a deliberate shove back with her calf. It fell with a thud.

"I am here as a diplomat!" she exclaimed. "A guest! And you ambush me like this? Accuse me of trying to intimidate you, call me deceitful? I will not sit here and listen to this!"

She turned and stormed out the door.

"Danai!" Nikol called after her. Danai would have liked to respond, but she had to let her anger carry her for the time being. She didn't look back.

She assumed Clara and Wiggins, her stenographer (his name came to her in a flash), had followed her out, but she didn't stop to check until after she had reached a turn in the corridor and passed out of sight of Jessica Marik's private audience. Sure enough, they were right behind her. Clara looked bemused; Wiggins looked stunned.

"That sure turned ugly in a hurry," Clara said. Wiggins just stood and shook.

"Don't they say that good diplomats shouldn't get caught by surprise?" Danai asked.

"I've heard that," Clara said.

"Well, I'm not a good diplomat yet. Come on, we need to talk to Bell. I think I know enough now to tell him the sorts of things he should be looking for. And then we need to sit down and strategize."

Danai continued on her way to her quarters. She'd managed to keep her voice calm when talking to Clara, even though she felt like her entire body was trembling. She'd given in to her rage in Jessica's office because it had been a good way to get out, but she would need a level head for the rest of this mission. She'd indulged in anger at Daoshen plenty on the DropShip. Now it was time to get things done.

"That wasn't nice, Mother."

"No," Jessica said. "It wasn't."

"You violated the agreement as much as she did—if she even knew all the details about it. But you made her feel like an oath-breaking pig, while you get to sit there in judgment."

"Yes," Jessica said. "I do."

Nikol sat silent for a moment, struggling for words.

"Anything else?" Jessica asked.

"No—yes! It's just . . . it wasn't *nice*."

"Yes, dear, we already covered that. I agreed. But

since the goal of the meeting had nothing to do with being nice, that point is neither here nor there."

"But she's my friend!"

Jessica said nothing, and Nikol felt as if she could actually see her weak argument disintegrating in front of her.

"All right, all right, it doesn't matter if she's my friend or not, I know. I just . . . I just didn't like to see her that way. And I don't like it that you asked me to be here just to soften her up. I didn't *do* anything in this meeting."

Jessica's face softened, and the expression she had worn at the start of the meeting with Danai returned. "I know. I didn't like to do it. For a Liao, Danai has many good qualities." Jessica paused. "She might even have a lot of good qualities for a normal human. But this needed doing, and I'm fairly certain you understand that. For what it's worth, I wanted you here for reasons besides your being Danai's friend. I won't deny that was a consideration, but it's important that you saw what happened and saw Danai's response, since it will shape our future meetings."

Nikol wasn't completely satisfied, but then she thought of all the times she'd called in favors to resolve some diplomatic dispute or another—she found solutions presented themselves much more easily when you could get friends talking to friends, instead of strangers to strangers. As she had used the same tactic herself that her mother had just used with Danai, she couldn't really resent her for it.

Nikol chewed on her bottom lip for a moment. "I'm a little worried about Danai. Something was wrong with her. She flew off the handle pretty quickly."

"I accused her of breaking a treaty—well, an agreement anyway. That can be enough to make people mad."

"No, there was something else. I can't exactly explain it, but she seemed . . . I don't know, off her game."

Jessica rubbed her right temple with her index finger. "If something is bothering her," she said, speaking slowly, "it would probably be wise for us to find out what it is."

"Mother!"

"Perhaps we could help her with it," Jessica said innocently.

"That's not what you were thinking! You want to exploit it, not solve it!"

"That may be."

"That's even worse than what you did in this meeting! Manipulating whatever's bothering her for your own good? That's low!"

"Nikol, I think you're forgetting who you are. And, perhaps more importantly, who I am. Do you know what I am trying to do here? The scope of the reunification I am attempting?" Jessica's words came faster and louder as she continued. "Do you think all I have to worry about is one person's *feelings*? I have a responsibility to my people, to my nation. I respect Danai, I even like her. But I have very little responsibility toward her."

"So ruling a nation means you no longer have to be a human being?" Nikol fired back, then instantly regretted it.

Her mother, though, seemed not to take offense. "No, Nikol. It simply means you need to become a different kind of human being. Hopefully, if you pay attention as I bring you into the world of ruling, you'll understand that more."

Nikol nodded, even though she wasn't sure she agreed.

"In fact, while you're here, you should learn one more lesson." She turned to her clerk. "Send for Major Ivan Casson, please."

The clerk didn't have to stand. He pressed a few buttons, said a few words and soon enough Major Casson arrived. He stood tall, but his head drooped a little and his face had a gray, pallid cast.

"Major Casson," Jessica said. "I understand I have you to thank for the scan of the Capellan DropShips."

"Yes, ma'am," Casson said in a flat voice.

"I'm glad to have you at the spaceport. I need someone qualified to keep an eye on the Capellans while they are here. If they so much as sneeze, I want you to clamp down on them, hard. And, of course, I want you to tell me about it."

"Yes, ma'am."

"I know this doesn't sound like the most glamorous assignment in the world, Major, but it's important to me. Crucial, even. If you succeed at this—if you can keep my mind at ease about this, prevent me from worrying about the Capellan 'Mechs that have landed on my tarmac—then any past difficulties will be forgotten. Your role in the events on Wyatt will be wiped from my memory. Do you understand?"

Casson raised his chin a little, and some color returned to his face. "Yes ma'am," he said, with what sounded like more conviction.

"Fine. You are dismissed."

Casson turned smartly and walked out of the office.

"Let me guess," Nikol said. "The lesson there was that every failure plants the seeds for future success."

Jessica smiled. "Perhaps not *every* failure," she said. "But an awful lot of them."

Nikol tried to return the smile, but the expression felt wan on her face. "So what happens now?" she asked. "We wait for Danai to calm down?"

"I do, yes," Jessica said. "I'd like you to talk to Danai."

"You want *me* to find out what's bothering her? Mother, can't you find out what's bothering her some other way?"

"Yes, I can," Jessica said. "I'm not asking you to betray any confidence between the two of you. All I need from you is to go to her. Be her friend. Help her get mentally ready for our next meeting. We will need her. If our plans are to work, we will need House Liao."

"That doesn't sound right. Mariks and Liaos needing each other?"

"No, I don't particularly like the sound of it either. But the opportunity has presented itself, and I'd be foolish not to take advantage of it. I fully expect our period of cooperation with the Liaos to be full of mistrust and double-dealing. But it should be profitable—for a time."

"Of course that still leaves us to deal with the Marik-Stewart Commonwealth—which could be the bigger threat."

Jessica looked steadily at Nikol, silent for a few moments.

"The Commonwealth should have other things on its mind," she finally said.

"Other things? Like what?" Nikol asked. But her mother just shook her head, and Nikol sighed. Naturally, she wasn't going to find out about all of her mother's confidential dealings at once.

"All right, back to the Capellans, then," Nikol said. "Just what is it you're hoping Daoshen will offer you?"

"The one thing a vast power can always offer. Pressure."

"I thought that might be the case. But on whom?"

"Ah, how to choose from all the stars in the sky?" Jessica said, laughing. Then she grew more serious. "For the time being, the Duchy of Andurien. A little pressure on them could not only keep them in check, but could also persuade them to help us discourage any adventurism by the Regulan Fiefs along our border. Once those two borders are secure, we can advance with our plans relating to the Marik-Stewart Commonwealth."

Nikol nodded slowly. "It would work," she said. "For a time. But isn't that a difficult line to walk? The Anduriens won't like being pressured, and neither will the Regulans. They may be held down in the short term, but that could just make them come back harder in the future."

"Then that's what they'll do," Jessica said. "But without this attempt, without this pressure, our move into Marik-Stewart territory can never happen. It's a risk—but when was anything worthwhile ever achieved without risk?"

21

The daughter of the Capellan chancellor strolled through the lush gardens in the late afternoon sun. The shadows of tall sunflowers stretched across the red-brown gravel path, which crunched with each step she took.

The daughter of the Capellan chancellor looked for a comfortable place to sit, passing a few stone benches that looked pretty but had no backs. Then she came to a metal bench, tarnished green-black, with many strands of twisted metal rising and intertwining to form a back. It wouldn't be as comfortable as anything in her quarters, but it would be better than the stone benches. And better than standing. So the daughter of the Capellan chancellor sat.

Danai had been at it for a week now, trying to force herself to accept her new identity. She applied the label to herself constantly, but it hadn't sunk in yet. It was like a bad organ transplant—every time she tried to internalize who she really was, the core of her being rejected it.

It had been a long week, and not just because she was trying to reshape her identity. She had met with Jessica four more times, and while the meetings had been more civil than the first, they had not been productive. Jessica clearly wanted Danai to offer some concessions, but she wasn't specific about what she wanted—it seemed she wanted Danai to suggest a long list of possible concessions, and then Jessica would tell her which ones she liked. That, of course, wasn't going to happen. In fact, Danai was entirely unmotivated to offer any concessions, as Jessica had yet to demonstrate any sort of leverage.

She suspected that was why the diplomatic wheels were spinning in place—Jessica was looking for some sort of stick with which she could beat Danai. Bell had confirmed as much. He didn't have a lot of concrete information yet, but he had been able to tell her that Jessica had her own intelligence operatives sniffing around—Bell kept running into them. Once they found something, Danai was sure the tenor of her meetings with Jessica would change, and the captain-general would become more demanding. So Danai had added counterintelligence to Bell's tasks, and she spread the word throughout the company to beware of Oriente agents poking around for information. She knew at least one or two items she wouldn't want Jessica to know about before Danai was ready to tell her.

For the moment, at least, that could remain Bell's concern. Not hers. She was going to sit in the garden and not think of Daoshen, or politics, or any of the many other things bothering her. She would just sit back and think of something peaceful—like Yen-lo-wang chopping the garden to bits with its ax.

She closed her eyes, letting the sun warm her face, listening to the trickle of a distant fountain. Then she heard the welcome sound of approaching footsteps, welcome because she knew who was approaching.

She didn't open her eyes as the person drew near. Partly because she was tired, but partly because she wanted to demonstrate trust, to show she did not need to watch her visitor come closer.

"At least I know now why you broke off the morning meeting," Nikol said when she was only a meter from Danai. "You just wanted to play outside."

"I could sit here just like this for the entire afternoon," Danai said, keeping her eyes closed, "and be exactly as productive as I was in that meeting. More, really—at least I would be enjoying myself a little."

She heard Nikol walk around and sit next to her on the bench. "Progress isn't exactly swift, is it?"

"Progress isn't even progress," Danai said. "I can't think of anything that's measurably different than the first day I arrived. But how would your mother feel about us talking diplomacy outside official channels?"

"I don't care how she'd feel," Nikol said stubbornly. "I know how I feel—sick of it all. Let's talk about something else."

"Amen," Danai said.

So Danai talked about her trip to Aldebaran, about the handsome but unctuous Major Anderton and about the satisfaction of chopping a 'Mech in two at the waist. And Nikol talked about the rainy winter, the confines of the Amur Palace and her mother's ever-increasing determination to live up to the Marik name even though, due to her descent from the false Thomas Marik, she didn't really have the blood.

Danai opened her mouth, on the verge of saying, "Well, it looks like we both have ambitious parents," but she stopped herself—barely. She was more open with Nikol than with anybody else, but she wasn't ready to share this information yet. She didn't know when, if ever, she'd tell anyone about the secret of her parentage. That piece of information was a bombshell, and if Daoshen had taught her anything, it was not to detonate bombs lightly.

So she said nothing, and was left awkwardly opening and closing her mouth like a fish while Nikol raised her eyebrows in concern.

"Can I ask you something?" Nikol asked.

Danai smiled, though it felt a little thin on her lips. "Meaning, 'Can I ask you something you may not want to answer?' Sure, why not."

"Is there something . . . bothering you? Something wrong?"

Danai almost laughed. She felt a barking chuckle rising through her lungs, but she knew if she let it out there might be no stopping it, that it might continue on and on into hysteria. And then Nikol would *really* have something to be concerned about.

She managed to keep a decent facade of control. "How do you mean?"

"I can't really say," Nikol said. "I noticed it the first day you got here. Something just seems not right. Something about the way you're carrying yourself. I can't put my finger on it, though. There's just something wrong."

Danai looked at a nearby rosebush, red swirling through the primarily white petals. She stared at the colors until the red seemed to move, to flow like blood through the flowers.

"Danai?"

She didn't answer. Words were starting to come together, she was starting to find a coherent way to tell Nikol what she'd only told Erde and then she'd only managed to say it in a torrent of shouted words caught on holovid.

"Danai?"

"We talked," Danai said, pushing out words that caught in her throat as if they had burrs on their edges. "On Terra, we talked. I mentioned someone. A man. I said he was interesting, but that it was impossible. Between us. Too many barriers."

"I remember," Nikol said.

"I never told you his name."

"I know."

"I met him. Again. Pure chance. On New Hessen. We were fighting. Fighting each other. Then we were both out of our 'Mechs. Alone on the ground. So I helped him."

Nikol clearly wanted to ask who this person was. Danai could see it in her face. But she didn't ask. She rested a reassuring hand on Danai's knee and sat silently, waiting for Danai to speak when she was ready.

"I shouldn't have helped him. Shouldn't have talked to him. But we were alone on the battlefield. And I thought . . . I thought he would be useful.

"He was Caleb Davion."

Nikol did not move. Her hand stayed on Danai's knee, her mouth still a small, sympathetic frown, her shoulders relaxed. But her eyes practically spun. All the shock, all the surprise Danai didn't see in the rest of Nikol's bearing came out in her eyes.

"We were together. On the ground. I was looking for Yen-lo-wang. I had to get it back. We wandered for two weeks, and I found it. It was in my sight. But then the helicopters came, and the missiles, and everything around us exploded. And I ran forward. If I got to my machine—if I could just *get there*—I would be safe.

"But Caleb blocked me. Carried me away. To a warehouse. Put me inside, didn't want to let me out. But I had a rifle. So I pointed it at him. Told him to let me go. Let me get my 'Mech. He wouldn't. I dug the point into his stomach. He told me to shoot. And I . . . and I . . ."

She couldn't see. The world around her had become a moist blur, she couldn't make out anything distinct, but she could see tall, narrow, straight objects to her right, so she stood, she turned, she grabbed and she pulled.

Rose thorns ripped her palms until she got a firm grip, then she tore one entire bush out of the earth and threw it. It flew awkwardly and rustled to the ground.

"God*dammit*!" Danai yelled. "I didn't shoot him! He is a *Davion*! He should be dead! Dammit dammit *dammit*!"

She stood over the uprooted rosebush, shaking, trying to breathe but not to sob. Then she felt hands on her shoulders, lightly guiding her back to the bench. She let Nikol sit her back down, then she buried her face in her hands and fought for her composure. Blood from her palms stained her face. Nikol wrapped an arm around her and waited patiently.

It took a long time.

Then she took a few long, slow, shuddering breaths and felt able to speak. But she didn't raise her head.

"I hesitated. I loosened my grip. On the trigger. He moved, quickly. Hit the gun. Knocked it away. Then he pushed me back. He had a knife. Put it at my throat. Pushed me to the floor. Raped me."

She felt Nikol's fingers stiffen, digging into her shoulder, when she said the word "raped." Then Nikol practically collapsed on top of her.

"Oh my god. Oh my god, Danai. Oh my god."

They sat in the warm sun for a while and didn't say anything. Clouds drifted in and out of view, the sun moved lower and lower, and the roses on the bush at their feet soaked in the last minutes of sunlight as long as they could before they began to wilt.

22

Danai awoke to the all-too-familiar feeling that something was wrong. She sniffed the air, wondering if a whiff of smoke or ozone had made her alert, but the air smelled fresh and clean.

She stepped carefully out of bed, looking one way and then the other, waiting for someone (or, knowing her luck, a puma that had wandered in from the jungle) to pounce on her.

No one was there.

Everything looked perfectly normal, and continued to look normal as she got dressed and prepared for another day of stalled diplomacy. There was no indication that anything at all was amiss. But she had learned to trust her instincts over the years, and she remained convinced that something, somewhere, was not right.

She had to wait another twelve minutes before she found out what it was.

She sat at the table in her room, enjoying the waffles brought to her by the palace staff, when Sandra charged into the room, with Clara close on her heels.

"Bell's gone," Sandra said.

Danai picked up the linen napkin on her lap and carefully wiped the corners of her mouth. "That's a shame," she said.

"No, *Sao-shao*, this is serious! No one has seen him since last night! He's not in his quarters! He's *gone!*"

"Couldn't we all use a break from him?"

"He's not in the DropPort. Anywhere. That means he's in restricted territory, and I can't imagine he received special permission to wander around. He's in danger of being arrested, unless he's already under arrest! Do you know how that will affect the negotiations if one of your command crew is arrested here? Do you know how much leverage you'll lose?"

Now Danai was interested enough to care. "All right, that would be bad." She checked her chronometer. "I'm meeting with the captain-general in forty-five minutes. If she has anything to say about Bell, I'm sure I'll hear it quickly. If not, Clara will send you word that he hasn't been caught yet. You'll need to find him. We can get you a pass off the DropPort so you can track him down before they do. In the meantime, check every comm channel you can, get people stationed by every window that's accessible to us and see if you can spot him."

Sandra bowed quickly, then dashed out.

Danai looked at Clara. "What do you think—is he doing something heroic or stupid?"

"It's Bell," she said. "There's an equal chance of each. There's also a good chance he's doing something heroic *and* stupid."

Danai nodded. She picked up her knife and fork and cut a very small bite of waffle. Suddenly, she wanted the meal to last a long time, and the morning meeting to never come.

Her dread was fulfilled when she went to the meeting. She approached the door of Jessica's private office, only to be told by one of the guards standing next to it that the captain-general wished to meet Danai in the throne room today.

"That can't be good," Danai muttered to Clara as they hurried through the palace halls.

"Maybe she's having her office repainted today," Clara said optimistically.

Danai's only response was a short laugh.

The throne room, when they arrived, was more packed than Danai had ever seen it. Jessica was there, of course, with Nikol. Philip, who hadn't attended most diplomatic functions, was there today, along with a half-dozen people Danai didn't recognize and another half-dozen guards. Compared to Danai's small party—herself, Clara and Wiggins—the crowd in the throne room was impressive and daunting.

Just because Jessica didn't appreciate our attempts to intimidate her, Danai thought, *it doesn't mean she's above a little intimidation of her own.*

Three empty chairs were set up in front of Jessica's throne. Danai walked to them, but remained standing. The increased formality of the situation seemed to demand it.

Jessica started speaking as soon as Danai stopped moving.

"I'm certain I made the rules concerning your people quite clear," Jessica said. "I believe I even provided a detailed map explaining where they could go and when. And I am positive I explained that I would have no tolerance for any adventurism by your military personnel."

She stopped speaking. Danai assumed she was supposed to say something.

"Yes," she said.

"That, then, makes last night's incident all the more intolerable. Jacyn Bell, your sergeant at arms, was arrested last night in the restricted area. He is in our custody."

Danai kept her face expressionless, but her mind was running a long stream of curses, all of them directed at Bell.

"What's more," Jessica continued, "he was arrested in the middle of an illegal activity. What was the charge again, Major Casson?"

"Solicitation," a dour-faced man said with clear satisfaction.

Dammit, Danai thought. *I should have castrated Bell as a condition of him being on the command crew.*

"A good commander must control those who serve under her," Jessica said. "And with your Canopian upbringing, I had thought you would have a stronger handle on the members of the weaker sex in your command."

Philip did not seem to appreciate the end of Jessica's remark, but he remained quiet.

"I suggest you meet with this Bell and inform him of the full extent of the trouble he has gotten himself into," Jessica said. "And then, perhaps, you may take some time to yourself to determine why men give you such problems before we meet again."

Danai heard the last line all too clearly. "Men," Jessica had said, not "this man." She knew something. She had to. And there was only one way she could have found it out.

Danai kept herself from looking at Nikol, but she could feel cold poison pouring over her heart. Nikol had told Jessica. Danai had told her about Caleb, something she had only managed to tell Erde, and Nikol had promptly run to Jessica with the information. Danai's fist clenched, her nails digging into her palms, maybe drawing blood, but the pain didn't matter. The icicle in her chest had grown, freezing her entire body, and she didn't feel like she could move or even breathe. This planet and these people who had appeared to treat her so well, were a nest of vipers. She should have landed in Yen-lo-wang and come into Oriente firing. It would have been better. So much better than *trusting* anyone. *Ever.*

She fought to make her jaw move. Her teeth grated, and it sounded like her mouth was full of gravel.

"Where's Bell?" she finally managed to say.

"Major Casson will take you to him." Jessica paused, then seemed struck by a new idea. "Tomorrow," she said. "It would probably be beneficial for both of you to have a day alone with your thoughts. That will be all for today.''

Danai's thoughts were the last thing she wanted keeping her company, but she didn't seem to have a choice.

She didn't want to be alone, and she didn't want to talk to anyone. Words had gotten her nowhere. Words were toxic.

Zi-jin Chéng, Sian
Capellan Confederation

Erde had enough experience to know that the message with her name on it should not be opened in public. Casual letters were not generally sent via command circuits in diplomatic pouches. This was of some significance.

She hoped it was business. Danai had been through enough personal issues to last her for a good long time. With any luck, it was a note asking for some urgent advice on matters of diplomacy.

It was not.

It was a brief, handwritten note, not even a dozen words. But they were enough to tear at Erde's heart.

> Great-aunt Erde,
> I know who my father is. Did you?
> Danai

Daoshen. Daoshen had done it again. How could Naomi, her beloved older sister, produce such a vile offspring?

Sun-Tzu Liao's genes must be powerful, she thought, to so overwhelm anything her sister contributed to that child.

He must have told her. Who else would know? The secret had been closely guarded for decades—Daoshen didn't even know that Erde knew, though he had to suspect. They had tried to keep Naomi and Erde separate in the months before Danai was born, the better to set up the secret right from the start. But Erde had been involved in court intrigue for too long, she was too good at noticing inconsistencies and picking up on dropped pieces of information to be kept in the dark forever. She'd known the secret since Danai's first year of life, and she had yet to determine the right way of breaking the news to Danai. She had worried that if she delayed too long, Daoshen would beat her to the revelation, and now it had happened.

The timing seemed particularly cruel. Danai was suffering from too many burdens to have another one added, and Daoshen hadn't even had the grace to tell her while she was still on Sian, where she was still within the reach of Erde's consolation. He had told her when she was alone, isolated. When she would have to deal with the knowledge herself.

Which was, she knew immediately, the whole purpose. Daoshen was running Danai through the gauntlet while, in his own twisted way, trying to bind her closer to him. If she made it through all this with her head held high, she would emerge as more of a Liao than she ever had been. She would be on the path to becoming the daughter Daoshen envisioned.

But Danai was not just a Liao, though Erde appreciated that side of her every time she watched holovid coverage of Danai's adventures on Solaris VII. She was also a Centrella. And she deserved more than Daoshen gave her. She deserved someone who could show her that a parent and a sovereign did not have to behave as Daoshen did. That a ruler could increase the security and power of a nation—as Daoshen certainly had—and still be considered a failure. Erde had her own bits and pieces of information that she could use, but she knew how to reveal them in a way that would build Danai up rather than tear her down. Danai needed to see that service to the state did not demand the complete destruction of her character. Quite the opposite, really.

She had wanted to be back in the Magistracy long ago. But now, it seemed, she had yet another journey in front of her.

23

Amur, Oriente
Oriente Protectorate
11 April 3136

Bell was being held, oddly enough, in the lower levels of Amur Palace. The dungeon. Oriente had never been through a feudal stage, and so the palace had never held a real dungeon, but apparently the building's architects thought the medieval allusion was appropriate. The walls of the corridor Danai had to pass through to reach the holding area were rough-hewn stone, and the maintenance staff even let moss grow on a few rocks for effect. They wanted anyone who walked this hall to know they were in considerable trouble.

Of course, Danai was fairly certain the real might of the walls was hidden behind some fake stones. Any attempt at escape, or to smuggle a weapon, would trigger the sensors that were likely hidden throughout the masonry. Alarms would sound, gun barrels would emerge and all of a sudden the corridor would look decidedly modern.

Danai hoped to avoid seeing that aspect of it. It helped that she had no desire to break Bell out.

She was led through a series of sliding metal doors

and placed on a metal stool in front of an exceedingly thick sheet of ferroglass. Even Yen-lo-wang, had Danai somehow managed to get it through the cramped corridors and low ceilings of the basement, would need a few chops to break through it. The small room on the other side looked smudged and blurry.

A door opened on the other side, and for a moment Danai saw only darkness beyond it. Then Bell, wearing gray coveralls, sauntered into view. His central role in a brewing diplomatic incident seemed not to affect him. His hair was impeccable, his grin insolent. He was completely himself, which irritated Danai to no end.

"I shouldn't have to remind you of this, but anything we say will be recorded," Danai said. A hidden set of microphones in the stone walls carried her words to Bell through an equally hidden set of speakers.

"Really?" Bell said. "Good quality sound, do you think? Maybe I should sing something."

"Bell . . ." Danai said.

Bell sang.

> *"One night on Laiaka,*
> *I took my baby for a drive,*
> *But I took the top down—*
> *'Fraid she didn't survive."*

"Bell!" Danai yelled. "What the hell is the matter with you?"

"Okay, maybe that wasn't my best effort, but all things considered . . ."

"A *call girl*?" Danai said. "A *prostitute*? You went into the restricted area after a *prostitute*? How stupid, how *male* can you be?"

"What do you think?" Bell said, and the arrogance dropped out of his voice.

"You don't want to ask me that," Danai said. "I could go on for hours about how stupid I think you could be."

"I'm sure you could. But you think I'd go into the restricted area on a foreign planet after a prostitute?"

Danai had another furious response ready to go, but

she swallowed it. He was right. She'd been thinking about it for a day, and she had already concluded that he probably wasn't guilty. On Aldebaran she had thought he was a major pain in the ass, but he was also where he was supposed to be, every time. Every assignment she'd given him, he carried through until it was done. He could be annoying, but she had been forced to admit that he was not, in fact, that stupid.

However, she wasn't willing to let go of her anger that easily.

"I've seen you hit on me at exactly the wrong time. Twice. You're more than capable of thinking with your groin."

"Did I break any laws hitting on you?"

She sighed. "No."

"And in all fairness, *Sao-shao*, I don't think there's been a moment since I've known you that might have been considered the *right* moment to hit on you. So you see my problem—I haven't had a lot to work with."

He was right, and she resented that like hell. "This isn't about me," she snapped. "And I'm under no obligation to make myself available to your advances."

"Of course," he said mildly. "I'm just pointing out that there's a big gulf between the bad judgment I've shown and the bad judgment I'm being accused of."

"All right. You want me to believe you're innocent. Tell me what happened."

"I wasn't going after a prostitute, for starters," he said, and then some of his customary insolence returned. "There are some things a man shouldn't have to pay for."

"So what where you doing?"

"My job," he said. "And I can speak freely about this, because they already know all of it anyway.

"I was in a restaurant," he continued. "In the part of the restricted area we can go to in the daytime. It's a good place to be—DropShips loading and unloading all the time, people coming and going. You get a good feel for what's happening in the Protectorate, and even in the surrounding areas.

"It was getting late, about an hour before I needed to be back in quarters. I met a woman. Yes, she was good-looking, and yes, that's why she first caught my eye, but I wouldn't have spent the last hour I had out with just anyone. No matter how cute she was." He put on his cockeyed grin. "Even if she was as cute as you."

"Bell!"

"Oops. Wrong time again?"

Danai, in spite of everything, couldn't help but smile a little. "Yes," she said.

"My mistake. Anyway, she had a badge on. Irian Technologies. A courier, but someone a little more important than a regular messenger. Someone who was going to meet with Philip Hughes and know what she was talking about, you know? So I thought it would be worth seeing if she'd been anywhere interesting lately.

"She hadn't—she was just coming in from Irian. But she was friendly, I was charming and we talked a little shop. I said I'd been on Aldebaran, seen a little of the fighting last year—I didn't tell her, of course, that I'd *done* a little of the fighting there—and said I'd left the planet to get away from the chaos.

"She told me it was a good thing I didn't flee outward. If I had hit Menkalinan or Kyrkbacken, I might have been right back in the middle of the chaos. But then she corrected herself. She said some machines were supposed to go there, but they went to Park Place instead.

"I thought that was interesting. Something you should know. So I made my excuses and stood up to go. I reached for some bills to pay for the meal, but she waved me off. Said she was already charging it to Irian. I thanked her and left.

"I walked out of the restaurant, went about twenty meters, when someone grabbed my arm. A big guy in a suit, with sunglasses. He asked me if I was forgetting something, I said no. He told me I hadn't paid for my food, so I told him the nice young lady I was sitting with was taking care of the bill, and he responded that the nice young lady had just skipped out herself. I told him

I was sorry about the confusion and I'd be happy to pay, so we went back to the place.

"I was at the front of the restaurant, getting out some cash, when the woman I'd been eating with ran up. And let me just say that the way she was running drew the attention of every nearby male with a pulse. She was full of apologies—to me, to the security guy who'd grabbed me, to the maître d', to me again for good measure—and that went on for a while. She'd forgotten to sign for the dinner, she said, so the maître d' produced a noteputer, she signed her name, and everything was taken care of and I still had all my cash.

"Trouble was, I had ten minutes to get back out of the restricted area and a seven-minute walk ahead of me. I needed to move. So I pried myself away from the woman—she was still apologizing—and started to jog off.

"I was making good time, getting across all the streets, and coming close to the DropPort. I was feeling good about the progress I'd made, so I slowed to a walk. Then a car pulls in front of me, the passenger door opens and damned if it's not the woman from the restaurant climbing out. And she's still apologizing. She's sorry she didn't pay, sorry she followed me, sorry she's keeping me from going where I need to be. She just wanted to see me one more time, to maybe make another date. Well, she was pretty cute, but the tailing me for a few blocks and jumping out at me set off an alarm or two, so I said no thanks. But she kept grabbing me, making it tough to get away.

"I finally said that I *really* had to go, and I hated to do what I was about to do, but I had to do it. I gave her a gentle shove so I could get away.

"Turned out I didn't shove her hard enough. She had enough balance and presence of mind to trip me. *Trip* me! And while I was stumbling, she gave me a shove, right into the front seat of the car, and she tried to close the door.

"I wasn't having any of that. I stuck my leg out, and

she closed the door on it. I've got the bruise to prove it." He rolled up a leg of his coverall, revealing a straight black-and-blue mark across the back of his calf.

"I struggled out, pushing the door all the way open and tried to step away, but she tripped me again. This time I went down on the ferrocrete. I heard her footsteps behind me as I fell, so I turned, lying with my back on the street, to fend her off.

"She fell on me, but it wasn't an attack. Her hands were all over, rubbing and her lips pressed right into me. I was surprised. And I've gotta say, it wasn't entirely unpleasant. But I didn't forget what I was supposed to be doing, so I pushed her off.

"She didn't resist much. She rolled off me, then sat down. I noticed she had some cash in her hand, and I guessed she'd taken it from me while she'd been on me. But I didn't care. She could have it.

"I started to get up when some hands grabbed my shoulder, pushing me back down. There were a couple of MPs behind me, telling me that the woman sitting next to me with my cash in her hand was a known prostitute and that I was in a restricted area and I was under arrest. And here I am."

Danai sat silently for a minute, trying to absorb Bell's story. He sat still, arms folded, waiting.

"You expect me to believe that?" she finally said.

"Yes," he said. "For one of two reasons. Either you know I'm essentially honest, or you think I'm too dumb to invent a story that convoluted. You can pick your reason, but yes, I think you should believe me."

Danai shook her head. It was incredible. A sloppy story. But as she thought about it, it actually made sense. It started to come together.

"You were set up," she said.

"This is what I'm telling you."

"They planted this woman. Gave her an IrTech badge. Had her schmooze you. Made sure she had some interesting information to drop to keep you interested. Then did absolutely everything in her power to get you arrested."

"Right."

"Park Place really was attacked," Danai said, still thinking out loud. "That's all over the news. But they set this woman up with information that Menkalinan and Kyrkbacken were supposed to be the targets but that was changed. So either that's what happened or that's what they want us to think happened."

"There's one other tidbit there," Bell added. "Not a shock, but good to have confirmation of the rumors—IrTech's making 'Mechs for the Protectorate."

"If the woman was telling the truth. But we'll assume she was. Which means Oriente was originally planning to go deeper into Prefecture VI, but didn't." A light went on in Danai's head. "That's why Daoshen was so mad. That's why he pulled us away so quickly. It wasn't that I screwed up. He wanted the Protectorate to put more pressure on New Canton, but they didn't. So he gave up, not only because he thought we couldn't handle the full brunt of Triarii forces, but because he was mad at Jessica and wanted us to get some kind of payback." She knew Jessica would hear those words soon, if she wasn't listening right now, but she didn't care. She figured Jessica must already know all this, or she wouldn't have given the information she did to Bell.

"So we know what ticked him off," Bell said. "But why let us know this now?"

"Because it doesn't matter. At least we know the situation, but we have no real leverage—nothing, at least, to compare to what Jessica got by arresting you. It's a power play. She's showing the strength of her position."

"And what are you supposed to do?"

"I have no idea."

Later that night, she still didn't know. But she'd decided one thing—she was sick of being played. She was sick of being a step or two behind all the machinations, sick of being tossed on the winds of diplomacy. She needed to get some control back.

She had a weapon. A big weapon. The Duchy of Andurien was about to become a partner with the Magistracy of Canopus, which made it a de facto ally of the Capellan Confederation. That was a nice, big stick and she was about to swing it.

She'd been in the middle of these diplomatic games long enough—her whole life, in fact. She had spent her life learning Daoshen's rules, Jessica's rules, everyone else's rules. Now it was time to make some moves of her own.

24

Amur, Oriente
Oriente Protectorate
15 April 3136

Jessica strung her along for a few more days, making her wait for a meeting. *More games*, Danai thought. *More reason to do what I'm going to do.*

Her situation had not changed. Bell was still in jail, and Danai was not inclined to press for his release—if she received any concessions from Jessica, that was far from the first one she wanted.

Finally, five days after Bell's arrest, Danai was granted another meeting. She was told it would be in the private office, which she hoped represented a thaw in relations.

She arrived with her customary companions, and was met by Jessica, Nikol and their implacable stenographer. Greetings on all sides were strained. The long, fruitless meetings combined with the recent turmoil hadn't made any of the parties involved too happy with each other. Danai's "hello" with Nikol was particularly awkward, as they hadn't spoken since the last meeting. The sting of Nikol's betrayal still froze Danai's heart.

Danai had rehearsed her opening lines repeatedly over the past few days. What she intended to say was this: "I'd first like to offer an apology for the actions of my sergeant at arms. I have no excuse for what he did. He certainly should have known his own boundaries, where he could go and where he should not. Because if you do not know your borders—if you don't know what's going on in your most crucial, most vulnerable areas—then you have trouble indeed."

It sounded perfect. Vaguely threatening, specific enough about borders while being vague enough to not say *which* borders she was talking about. It would get Jessica's attention and start her guessing about what Danai knew. Then the game would be in force.

But she had to wait before she could deliver her salvo. "Thank you for coming, *Sao-shao* Liao-Centrella," Jessica said. "I regret the gap in our meetings, as well as the difficult situation of recent days. I hope to use this meeting as an attempt to get past those troubles and move productively forward."

Danai nodded, then prepared to move to take some control over the situation.

"All right. You want to move forward? Great. No more games."

Danai stopped. Had she just said that? She checked her memory. Yes, that sounded like her voice. But that wasn't what she intended to say. In fact, it was quite the opposite—she was going to *start* playing games, not end them. What an odd thing for her to say. Time to get things back on track.

"We're not going to get anywhere unless we're straight with each other. I know you set up Bell. I know why you did it. And it's fine. He could use some time in the brig. But we're not going to communicate through strange women or veiled threats. We're going to talk. We're going to ask each other straight questions, and we're going to give each other straight answers."

Dammit, that wasn't right either. She was getting further and further off message.

"I'll start. The attack on Zion. Yes, I ordered it. But only because I didn't know the details of your agreement

with the chancellor. He didn't see fit to tell me. Naturally, if I had known, I would never have attacked. It
was a move to try to draw New Canton's attention away
from Aldebaran—similar to the intent of your move to
Kyrkbacken and Menkalinan, the one that didn't happen. I'm happy to leave Zion alone if that's what you
want. My intent was never to interfere with the Protectorate."

Jessica exchanged a glance with Nikol. The captain-
general looked troubled, but Nikol looked amused. They
held a brief whispered colloquy, then Jessica returned
her attention to Danai.

"I have to say, this is an approach to diplomacy I
haven't seen much. And it's . . . pleasant. But how would
this work? How many questions do we get? Do we have
to answer all the ones we ask?"

"This isn't another game," Danai said impatiently.
"There is no set number of questions. There are no
rules. If you need to not answer a question immediately,
I understand—you don't spend as much time as I have
with Daoshen—I mean, Chancellor Liao—without understanding that some things can't be revealed. But if
that's the case, we say so. Directly. We don't play coy.
We just talk. Like we're normal people."

Jessica laughed. "But we're not."

"I know. But for the time being, we're going to pretend we are."

"All right. Let's see how long we can keep it up.
Seeing as how you've already provided me with an answer, perhaps it's your turn to ask a question."

"Fine. You were going to go to Kyrkbacken and Menkalinan, but then you decided not to. You knew this
would aggravate the chancellor, but you thought it was
worth it. There's only one reason for that—you wanted
him to offer more than you had gotten. So what is it
you want?"

"Security," Jessica said. "I've got too many borders
where the situation is dicey at best. If I could move
troops away from some of these borders, I could concentrate my forces where I want them."

"Where do you want them?"

"That's a second question," she said. "And one I probably wouldn't answer even if it was the first."

"Fair enough. What do you want to know from me?"

"Our border with the Confederation is quite broad, and I intend to leave it fortified until the day I die. But the exact number of troops I commit there is an open question—how much do I have to worry about Capellan aggression?"

"You want a straight answer?" Danai leaned forward. "As long as Daoshen is chancellor, you will *always* need to worry about Capellan aggression."

Her point made, Danai sat back. "That's the long-term reality," she continued. "But luckily for you there's also short-term pragmatics. And grudges. For the time being the chancellor would rather have his border with the former Free Worlds League secure instead of hostile. There are two things he wants more—the Republic reduced as a threat, and the Davions punished for their long years of being Davions. I can't reveal the specifics of where he wants to go, but if you really thought about it you could figure it out for yourself. So for the time being, I think the chancellor would rather have you as a partner instead of an enemy." She paused. "Of course, the chancellor is known to be mercurial."

"That's one way to put it," Jessica said. "But you answered my question fairly. I suppose that makes it your turn."

"Okay. This is a simple one. You say you want your borders to be more secure so you can move your troops where you want them. I assume you'd like Capellan help. Let's say I return to the chancellor, and we find a way to make your borders more secure. Would that motivate you to move where you originally planned—to go into the Republic as far as Menkalinan?"

Jessica didn't hesitate. "Yes. And that's probably something we should get in writing this time."

Danai nodded. "All right. So. Progress. We've made

progress. I'll need to return to Sian, of course. To talk to the chancellor."

"Of course," Jessica said. "In the meantime, I'll just hold on to *Sang-wei* Bell. To motivate you to make your trip as rapidly as possible."

Danai dropped her head a little. "Fine. I'll do what I can."

Jessica stood. "Then I think we've done all we can for the time being. We'll look forward to your return."

Danai rose, grasped Jessica's hand in a firm but not overly warm handshake, nodded curtly at Nikol and walked out.

"We all need to pack and get out immediately," she told Clara and Wiggins as they walked away. "The more we look like we're in a hurry, the better off we'll be."

"*Look* like we're in a hurry?" Clara said. "Shouldn't we actually *be* in a hurry?"

Danai didn't respond, but she walked quickly to stay ahead of the other two so they wouldn't see her grin.

She was ready to go within an hour, but she understood the rest of the preparations would take longer. Since she had no intention of going to Sian, she went to her DropShip so she could talk to the pilot about interesting places to blow a few months. She'd been in a foreign place for almost four weeks, and been either in transit or in battle for untold months before that. It was time for her and everyone else in her company (except, of course, poor Bell) to enjoy a nice, extended leave.

And it had all been made possible by her brain, which had, for some reason, thrown out her well-planned strategy and gone with something entirely different.

Who could guess that after weeks of Jessica trying to maneuver Danai into a corner—and finally succeeding—that Danai would get out of it without any of the manipulations she'd been repeatedly exposed to? It was a revelation; the games Daoshen was so fond of were not, in fact, a necessary part of ruling. She didn't have to play them, and she might somehow be able to avoid Daoshen's fate. There could be something more in her future than being an empty vessel for Capellan ambition. She could be an actual person instead of a—whatever Dao-shen was, and still do her job as a Capellan and a Liao.

It was the most comforting thought she'd had in months.

25

The tremendous JumpShip took longer to recharge at each jump point than any other ship because of all of the lights. Lights everywhere, flashing, red and green and blue and yellow. Spelling out words, casting odd shadows, making skin—and there was plenty of it on display—appear in colors nature never intended. Drinks that were illuminated from within darted through the air on hovering trays, available to anyone who dropped enough chips into the tray's slot. There were dozens of rooms with throbbing lights and deafening music, and all of them had plenty of corners and nooks for pairs or trios or however many people could fit into the small spaces.

There were so many ways to spend money. Gaming rooms, bars, restaurants, acrobats, freak shows and the finest, most open brothels in the known universe.

One cannot spend a great amount of time among soldiers without learning a lot about brothels. You don't even have to go to the brothels, you just need to listen to the others talk about them.

Common complaints about brothels tended to fit into two categories. The first was the quality of services offered, whether concerning the age, appearance or enthusiasm of the professional delivering them. The second was the awkwardness involved in negotiating a transaction, as it wasn't always clear what services were being offered, how much they cost and whether the establishment was in danger of being raided by local authorities.

The brothels in Canopian pleasure circuses took care of both complaints. The high level of income flowing through the establishments enabled them to be particular in their hiring, employing only the best, and the menu of services posted in the lobby made it quite clear what you could get and how much it would cost you. Added to this was the fact that absolutely no one on board one of the traveling circuses had any interest in raiding the brothels.

Danai understood how this made the brothels appealing to some, though they weren't her preferred method of entertainment, but she still didn't quite understand the lengths some people went to visit them. Were the planets from which these people came—along with all the planets they passed when journeying to the pleasure circus—so empty of potential partners?

Maybe they were, maybe they weren't. But being able to get exactly what you wanted clearly held strong appeal, and the fulfillment of this desire brought billions of C-bills to the Magistracy of Canopus through the pleasure circuses each year.

Danai and her company had been holed up in the pleasure circus for about two weeks now. In a few weeks more it would be time to head back to Oriente to continue exercising the diplomatic art. In the meantime, her main responsibility was to make sure she stayed entertained by a most impressive collection of amusements. She didn't even need to keep her company under some degree of control—they couldn't really wander too far away, they couldn't get arrested unless they tried really hard and even if they got incredibly blasted, they'd have a long journey back to Oriente to dry up. The only real risk was that one of the Capellan ships that liked to harass pleasure circuses might show up. The Capellans made a pile of money taxing the circuses more than any other nation, but they often felt the tax burden itself was not enough to display their objection to the general principles behind these establishments, and so they embarked on the occasional raid. Of course, the worst that could happen was that Danai and her company would leave the circus, go back to their own JumpShip and find something else to do until it was time to return to Oriente.

Danai spent a lot of time with Clara and Sandra, dancing and gaming and taking in whatever shows they wanted to see. Other than having to endure the occasional leering customer asking them where their price sheet was, everything went very well.

It was too bad Daoshen would never comprehend the full extent of the coup Danai was currently realizing. She wasn't sure he had it in him to have fun for the sake of having fun. After all, how did having fun advance the Capellan Confederation?

But that was the beauty of this trip—she was, in fact, advancing the Confederation by maintaining the illusion of traveling all the way to Sian. Her entire plan would blow up if she went back to Oriente now. Duty required her to stay put.

The activity for this particular evening was a contest; Clara, Sandra and Danai went to three different blackjack tables and they were going to stay there for three hours—not a minute more. At the end of the time, they would meet and compare stacks of chips, and the loser would buy the others drinks while they sat together and made fun of the other players at their respective tables. It sounded like a good plan to Danai.

After two hours and forty-five minutes, Danai was pretty sure she was going to do the buying. She was down—not much, but she was down. The problem was, she wasn't really paying attention to the game. She was too engrossed in the people walking by: the single people trying to pair up without spending money at the brothels, the sharks patrolling tables looking for marks, the fleet-fingered thieves lifting a few chips off the top of particularly large stacks in front of inattentive players—it was better than most of the shows she'd seen on the ship. Since she wasn't employing any strategy, she was left to rely on luck, which, when it comes to blackjack, usually means losing.

She tried to stage a rally in the last fifteen minutes, and a double-down on an eleven that hit to twenty at least got her back to even. She sputtered with mediocre hands for a few minutes, then hit a blackjack with two minutes left. She had a small handful of chips as her profit, so she decided to call it a night.

A few minutes later she was buying drinks with her winnings as Clara and Sandra flipped a few of their extra chips at people walking by, trying to peg them in the forehead. A waiter eventually came by and politely asked them to knock it off, but they slipped him a few chips, which allowed them to nail a few more passersby before they decided to call it quits.

Danai weaved through the hallway toward her cabin. She wasn't really drunk, but weaving just felt like the right thing to do. Despite her loss in the evening's contest, this whole trip counted as her first real victory in a long time, and she was enjoying it.

She walked into her cabin, didn't bother turning on the lights and sprawled happily in her bed. She rolled around on it a few times to find the most comfortable spot, then settled into it and got ready to sleep for ten hours or so.

After a minute, she noticed something pulsing. A light. She could see it through her eyelids, a faint blinking on and off. She couldn't remember having any blinking lights in her cabin.

She opened her eyes and saw that there was, in fact, a blinking light in front of her. It was set into the small wooden table on the side of her bed, a corner of the surface blinking in soft blue. She groaned lightly and touched the light, wondering who could be leaving her a message here.

The voice that came over the small speakers in the table made her sit upright in bed.

"Danai, it's Erde. I've just arrived on the ship, and I'm told that you're here. I would like you to call on me when you have a moment. No rush—just drop by cabin eighteen when you have a moment. I should be in most of the time."

Like hell there's no rush, Danai thought. She had the lights on and was running a brush through her hair before the message finished playing. She'd deliberately gone into the casino without a comm—she didn't want any members of her company bothering her with petty concerns—and now this happened. The message she'd been anxious about since her arrival on Oriente had finally gotten a reply.

As she ran toward cabin eighteen she had a brief qualm about calling on her aunt at this late hour, but then she remembered that day and night had little meaning on a pleasure circus ship. She'd been keeping herself on Oriente time, since she'd be heading back there soon, but there was a good chance the other patrons were keeping themselves on the times of at least a dozen other planets. Everything on the pleasure circus was open constantly, and there was no notable surge or drop in business from one hour to the next. There were always customers.

As Danai had no way of knowing what kind of schedule Erde was on, she might as well take her at her word and drop by when she had a moment. She had a moment now.

Her heart was pounding when she reached the door to cabin eighteen. She thought about turning back and going to bed, but the questions in her mind weren't about to just vanish after a little sleep. Not when she had the chance to take care of them now.

She pushed the buzzer next to the palmpad for Erde's door, then waited. After ten seconds, the door slid open.

Erde was dressed in her customary sky blue. She looked alert and cheerful, but her face seemed to have gained a few extra wrinkles in the past weeks, and her shoulders seemed to have become more slumped. She looked like she was slowly being worn down.

You and me both, Danai thought.

"Danai!" Erde said, the smile on her face only increasing the number of wrinkles. "So good of you to respond to my message so quickly. Come in, come in."

Danai walked in, almost at a funeral pace. The door slid closed after she passed through it, then her aunt stepped forward to give her a hug. "I'm very glad to see you, Danai. You have no idea."

Danai returned the hug without much conviction, then walked farther into the cabin. It was vast, with a broad screen that showed a picture of the stars and planets outside. It was designed to look like a window, but it wasn't—this cabin was nowhere near the JumpShip's exterior hull. The picture was a reasonable facsimile of a window, though, and unlike the rest of the ship, it helped remind you that you were floating in outer space.

Danai took a seat on a black sofa near the picture, and her aunt sat right next to her. Danai would have preferred a little more distance between them until her questions were resolved, but she wasn't going to tell her aunt that. She'd make do.

"Aunt Erde, what are you doing here?" Danai asked. "It's a pretty big coincidence to run into you here."

"Not a coincidence at all," Erde said. "I came here looking for you."

"Looking for me? Why?"

"I received your note," she said, and as if to prove this she pulled the note out of a pocket in her dress. "I thought it needed a personal response."

"How did you find me here?"

Erde smiled gently. "My dear, the networks I have cultivated over the years would be useless indeed if I could not use them to pinpoint the location of one of my favorite people in the known universe. I sent the proper inquiries to the proper people, and they told me how to find you."

"I'm touched that you would seek me out," Danai said. "Touched and amazed. Glad, too—what I wanted to talk about might go better in person. If you can help me understand a thing or two." Her voice didn't sound right in her own ears, and she hoped that was due to the drinks she'd downed with Clara and Sandra. But she hadn't really drunk that much.

"You know I'll do my best," Erde said.

"All right, then. Good. So you got my note. Do you have an answer?"

"Yes, Danai. The answer is yes. I've known who your father is for quite some time."

Danai exploded off the sofa. "Then why didn't you *tell* me? Why did you bleeding wait for *him* to drop the news on me? If you know—you, the person I've trusted for so long—why couldn't you tell me the truth?"

"And how would I tell you?" Erde said, calmly meeting Danai's ire. "When? How would I deal with Daoshen once he found out I'd let go of a secret he'd been holding onto for years? It wasn't my place to tell you, and even if it was, it is not a simple secret to divulge."

"Not your place?" Danai exclaimed, leaning over her still-seated aunt. "You *raised* me. How could anything that has anything to do with me be considered not your place?"

"You know your broth—your father. You know how he reacts to things. You know what could have happened if I told you before his appointed time. He could have separated us so easily. Made it so I never saw you again. Raised you himself." Erde shuddered. "Do you know what you would have become then? What he would have made you into?"

Danai closed her eyes. She had her impressions of him from her earliest childhood, memories burned into her brain despite the long, relatively happy years with Erde in the Magistracy. If she had spent all her childhood with Daoshen . . .

She didn't want to finish that thought, but Erde did it for her.

"You would be an empty vessel," Erde said. "A duplicate of himself. Daoshen is only the latest living example of the Capellan quirk of believing the state is greater than the individual, that the individual—particularly individual rulers—should be a tool of the state. The truth is that the state is nothing more than a collection of individuals. The state is the tool of those people, not the other way around.

"If I had lost you, Daoshen would have you. You would have become his. Is that what you would have wanted?"

Danai fervently shook her head.

"I wouldn't think so," Erde said. "But now that he has told you, now that he has decided you are ready for that particular piece of information, I can tell you the whole truth. That's why I came to find you.

"The past year has, I imagine, helped you learn much about the kind of person your father is, about the character he possesses and the personality he once had but has since done away with. But I'm not certain you understand the full extent of his obsession—of what some might consider his madness.

"By now you certainly realize that 'God Incarnate' is, to Daoshen, more than an exalted title. He sees it as the literal truth. He is the descendant of divinity, and he is divinity himself. One thing divinity is loath to do is to mix its blood with the common blood of humanity, thus diluting its holiness. The divine line must be maintained at full strength."

A small black hole opened in Danai's gut. She knew what was coming, and the dread of it threatened to overwhelm her. But she had gone this far, and she had to know for sure. She had to hear it from Erde's lips.

"He needed an heir," Erde continued, "but he needed a mate of the right blood. Fortunately for him, there was one close at hand—one for whom he had always felt an illicit attraction. Once he told himself the deed was necessary, he had little compunction about performing it.

"He forced himself on his sister Ilsa and impregnated her. Then, through a combination of threats and cajoling, he convinced her to carry the resulting child to term. You are the product of their union."

Danai sat quietly. The news that Daoshen was her

father had sent her into hysteria, but this latest revelation—one more blow to absorb—weighed her down, numbed her. All thought, all feeling, were sucked away into her black hole. She had no desire to scream, to cry, to even move. All she wanted to do was sit and wait to disappear.

When Erde spoke again, her warm whisper came from near Danai's ear. Her arm was around Danai's shoulders, though Danai hadn't seen her, hadn't felt her draw near.

"There is nothing I can say to make this easier to bear," she said. "You are the only one who can make the pain go away, and it will take time. But I can give you one piece of advice, for whatever it is worth. Any person is more than simply the sum of their parents. As long as you keep some portion of *yourself* about you, something beyond being a tool of the state, you will have at least that advantage over your father. You will be more than an empty vessel."

An empty vessel, Danai repeated silently. Daoshen. A vessel that had raped his sister. Her mother.

When Danai had been recalled to the Confederation after her years in the Magistracy, it was a nightmare. At least for the first few months. She lived in fear of being summoned again into her brother's presence, of trying to bear up under his cold scrutiny, of feeling the animal fear his presence inspired.

He'd called her to the throne room one dark spring morning, her third visit to his lair since her return from the Magistracy. She nearly threw up on the throne room floor after the guards let her enter, but she somehow managed to stay upright. But when Daoshen spoke to her, she noticed that his tone seemed milder than it had been during their previous meetings. He asked about her comfort, her well-being—things he had seemingly not given a thought to before that moment. Then Danai noticed that Daoshen was not the only other person in the throne room. Standing off to his right was Ilsa, looking regal but smiling warmly. Danai could not help but notice that Daoshen threw her the occasional glance, as if ensuring he had her approval. The questions about her well-being, she realized immediately, were not Daoshen's idea. They were Ilsa's.

In that moment, Danai's new life made a bit more sense. She once again saw a woman instilling compassion and thoughtfulness in a man, something she had been taught in her youth was the natural order of things. Even better, she saw that she might not have to fear Daoshen all her life—at least one person in the Confederation managed to exert control over him. There would always be distance between Ilsa and Danai, and Danai could never treat Ilsa as a true sister because of that gulf. But Ilsa was a role model when Danai needed one.

Now, however, all of Ilsa's admirable qualities, her poise, her control of Daoshen, were shown to be hollow, since they all came after a terrible defeat. A defeat that Daoshen's mere presence—not to mention Danai's presence—would bring to Ilsa's mind again and again. She was a victim, sitting there next to the man who raped her, walking with him into formal occasions, again and again and again.

Danai would never let that happen to herself. She would never sit calmly next to Caleb. If she ever saw him again, she planned to rip his arms off and beat him with the bloody stumps.

When she thought that, she felt a surge of anger in her gut. It wasn't a pleasant emotion, but it was something the black hole hadn't managed to take from her. It was something, for now, to hold on to.

26

A month later, she was still running primarily on anger. She'd left Erde back at Shuen Wan, and their parting, at least on Danai's end, was colder than she would have liked. She wanted to muster some warmth, some thanks to Erde for her kindness, but that part of her personality had not returned yet. Her aunt's words, though, had at least given her hope they would return someday.

During the journey to Oriente, Danai had recovered enough presence of mind to use her anger constructively. She knew how she would approach Jessica Marik, and hopefully be off-planet quickly with everything she wanted.

Her landing and reception this time had been far less formal. She hadn't assembled a party to march into the palace; instead, she'd sent most of her company back to their quarters in the DropPort while she and Clara traveled to Amur Palace to let the captain-general know they had arrived.

Jessica, naturally, made them wait before she met with them. It was a ruler's way, Danai knew, to try to avoid ever having anyone believe they were the sovereign's top priority. So she patiently waited, then appeared in Jessica's office at the appointed time, ready to get to business.

The main difference in this meeting was Nikol's absence; one of her older sisters took her place. Danai felt a bit of regret about the deterioration of her friendship with Nikol—she hadn't bothered to say good-bye to her friend when she had left Oriente in April—but since anger was her dominant emotion at the moment, the ire she felt at Nikol's betrayal far outweighed any other feeling.

She exchanged a few pleasantries with Jessica, and then the captain-general got to business.

"I suppose the first matter is to discuss how your meeting with Chancellor Liao went," Jessica said.

"My meeting?" Danai said, allowing wrath to color her voice. "The one where I had to ask the chancellor to give additional concessions on an agreement he thought was already in place? Well, let me first say that the chancellor was not thrilled to see me arrive without a signed agreement in hand. And when I told him the terms needed to be renegotiated, he was somewhat . . . less happy."

"I'm sorry to hear that," Jessica said mildly. "I'd be even more sorry if Chancellor Liao's happiness was my top concern. Should I take it by his displeasure that he was not willing to grant what I asked?"

Danai scowled. "He certainly wasn't initially. But I pressed him, tried to get past his wounded pride to see the benefit of doing what you wanted. He didn't like the precedent, and if you try to plateau bargain with him again he will be inclined to cut off all discussions, but eventually I convinced him. The Duchy of Andurien will not trouble you."

"Then I'm sure the forces of the Protectorate will be happy to move deeper into Prefecture VI."

"If you don't mind, this time I believe we'll put it in writing."

Jessica smiled, looking much like Danai assumed the

fairy-tale Goldilocks had appeared when she tasted that third, perfect bowl of porridge. "Of course," she said.

The next few hours were gobbled up by wrangling over the finer details of the treaty, making Wiggins and the Oriente stenographer type up draft treaties, compare the versions, revise them and so on repeatedly. Both Danai and Jessica had minor riders they wanted attached to the agreement—for example, Danai asked for Bell to be released and all charges to be dismissed, while Jessica included a provision stating that, "No official of the Capellan Confederation would publish rumors concerning the alleged relationship between Irian Technologies and the Oriente Protectorate until such time that the rumors could be indisputably proven true." Danai did not think it would take long for the Confederation to acquire such proof, with Irian 'Mechs likely to be on the move throughout Prefecture VI in short order, but in the meantime Jessica would have enough time to spring whatever surprise attacks she wanted against targets other than the Confederation.

Finally, the negotiations ended, and a final version of the treaty was produced and signed. Danai's first diplomatic mission, a three-month effort, was officially a success. And in all that, she hadn't had to say a word about Ilsa's pending marriage to Duke Humphreys.

The tedium of the negotiations had helped mute Danai's anger, and she was surprised, when she wrote her name on the bottom line, to feel something else. It wasn't strong, just a sense of contentment. But it was more pleasant than anger, and was the first real sign that what Erde had said might come true, that her personality might recover from all the blows. She might not ever be normal again, but she could at least discover a new normal.

The job complete, Danai saw no reason to stay on Oriente any longer. She wanted to report to Daoshen, and then see what he might give her for a job well done. She sent Clara to make preparations for a launch, then went to reclaim Bell. After that, she had one other matter to take care of.

*   *   *

Bell, while not entirely thrilled at having sat in jail for two months while his entire company enjoyed a pleasure circus, was still in good spirits when Danai found him. He'd been treated well, he said, and even been allowed to use a simulator on a few occasions, though he suspected that was because his captors wanted to study Capellan tactics rather than help keep his skills fresh. To throw them off the track, he purposefully engaged in the wildest, most suicidal strategies he'd dreamed up while in the field. He'd had a lot of fun, plus he hadn't shown his captors anything of use.

Danai dispatched Bell back to the DropPort, while she opened her comm and dialed a number she'd received a year ago on Terra.

"Hello?"

"Nikol? It's Danai."

"Danai! You're talking to me! Are you here? On Oriente? Where are you?"

"At the palace. Heading to the gardens. Would you like to meet me there?"

"Of course! Give me . . . oh, just go there. I'll be there first."

And she was, sitting on the same bench they had occupied when Danai told her what Caleb had done to her. The rosebush she had ripped out had carefully been replanted, but there were still a few bare spots where Danai's hands had ripped away leaves and petals.

Nikol sprang to her feet as soon as she saw Danai, her eyes dancing, but she didn't step forward for a hug. "Danai! I'm so glad to . . . well, I'm just glad."

"I'm glad to see you too," Danai said, measuring the words in her mouth to see if they were true. They seemed to be.

"Sit down," Nikol said, but Danai balked.

"Not yet," she said.

Nikol shrugged, and she remained standing also.

"I gathered that you were mad at me," Nikol said. "It wasn't that hard to figure out. But I didn't know why."

"Really," Danai said dryly.

"So I thought about it. About when it might have started. And I remembered the look you gave me at that one meeting, and I remembered what my mother said. She said something about you and men. About why they give you such problems. I know my mother; it was an offhand insult, just pulled off the top of her head to make you mad. To play on your Canopian roots. But you heard her say 'men.' And you thought I'd told her about Caleb." She whispered the last name like it was a shameful curse. Which, Danai thought, it was.

She didn't know what to say, what to believe. But she knew she wanted to believe Nikol. And right now a friend would be a very, very good thing.

"You didn't?" she said.

"I would never," Nikol said. "*Never*. Look, I know state matters are important. I know what we have to do sometimes, when we're in ruling families. But there are lines I will not cross. Compromises I refuse to make. I can't let the state determine how I treat people, to make me betray them at the drop of a hat. The state's for us, not the other way around."

Danai started. It was almost an exact echo of what Erde had told her. Either Nikol and Erde had been in secret communication, or the unseen powers of the universe were being none too subtle about delivering a message.

"Okay," Danai said. "Okay. I believe you."

"Can you sit down now?" Nikol said.

Danai almost smiled. "Yes."

They talked. It wasn't like old times yet—Danai's head was still too full of secrets that she wasn't ready to divulge—but it was friendly. Better than that, it was warm.

At one point in the conversation Nikol reached out and grabbed Danai's hand. "I didn't even tell you! Guess who's here!"

"Who?"

"The man you saved me from back on Terra! Frederick Marik!"

Danai whistled. "Wow. Persistent, isn't he?"

"Apparently. But at least here there's plenty of other members of my family around to distract him, so he doesn't have to focus on me. I was hoping mother would tell him what he could do with his proposal, but apparently she's more tenderhearted than I give her credit for. She hasn't booted him off-planet yet."

"Maybe she's considering offering you to him."

"My mother would never do that," Nikol said, "since she knows full well I could get my hand on suicide pills if I needed them."

They talked about a dozen other things, including war, diplomacy and, in general details, the problems of possessing certain last names. In the end, the conversation—which Danai had feared would be painfully long—seemed all too short. But the spinning political wheels of the Inner Sphere would not slow down just for Danai, so it was time to leave.

"Guess it's time to go be a *sao-shao* again," Danai said.

"As if you don't enjoy it."

Danai shrugged. "There's good parts and bad parts. Like anything else."

"I know," Nikol said. "You should try diplomacy full-time. One day you're working on treaties with the major powers of the Inner Sphere, the next you're having to explain to residents of a small town that as long as pig farming is going to be their major industry, they'll just have to put up with the smell."

Danai smiled. "Diplomacy's got plenty of unpleasant odors of its own."

"Anything that touches politics does." Nikol grew serious. "Which is why I promise anything we say to each other will never be dragged down into politics. We can be above that."

Danai nodded slowly. "We can try. But when you're a Liao or a Marik—when you're *us*—politics has a way of keeping you in its grasp. Look at our families. Everything they do, every relationship they have, is touched by it. They breathe politics every moment. They haven't found a way to get above it."

"We will," Nikol said.

"How can you be sure?"

"Because it's us! And because we'll promise each other we'll be above it."

"That's it?"

"That's plenty."

"Okay," Danai said. Having a relationship with someone who wanted nothing from her but friendship would be a novel experiment, but one she was more than ready to try.

Nikol stood. "Give 'em hell," she said, and hugged Danai. Danai hugged her back, and at least one thing was right in the universe.

The DropShip lifted off not long afterward, taking the Capellan representatives home. Jessica and Nikol formed part of the official Oriente delegation that saw them off. They sat in a small room on an upper level of the DropPort, with windows all around to watch ships as they came and went. Once the Capellan ship was gone, most of the delegation returned to work, but Jessica and Nikol stayed in the private room. Jessica ordered an early dinner to be brought up, and the two of them sat at the square white table in the middle of the room.

"Where did you run off to earlier?" Jessica asked.

"To talk to Danai. She called me."

"Really? I thought she was angry with you. Does this mean you two patched things up?"

"Yes, Mother, we did."

"May I ask what the cause of the rift was in the first place?"

"No, you may not."

Jessica rested her chin on the back of her hands, gazing at Nikol. Then she apparently decided to let the matter drop.

"Fine, then," she said. "Everything else went well this morning. I'm glad your talk did, too."

"You know, in all we talked about, the negotiations didn't come up. What happened?"

Jessica summarized the agreement for her daughter.

Nikol whistled. "Wow. Just what you wanted." She raised a bottle of cranberry juice, part of the meal that had just been brought in. "Here's a toast to over-reaching."

"We call it 'plateau bargaining,' dear," Jessica said. "But I'll drink to it by any name."

They clinked bottles together, drank and gazed at the thick forest at the edge of the long tarmac.

"This isn't over yet, of course," Jessica said after some thought. "Really, none of this ever is. Danai described the chancellor as angry at our requests, but by her description he folded so easily that he was more petulant than anything else. It seems too easy."

"A little buyer's remorse?" Nikol suggested. "You get what you thought was a good price, only to think you could have gotten more if you'd pressed harder?"

"Something like that. What's clear to me is, despite the openness of our one conversation, neither of us was laying all our cards on the table. Which is fine—there's not a table big enough to display our collected secrets and machinations. But I think some of the Confederation's maneuvering has something to do with Andurien. Just because I think we have the upper hand now doesn't mean we'll keep it. We need to keep our eyes open."

"Don't we always?" Nikol said. "But we took a step forward. The Marik name just got a little bigger in the Inner Sphere."

"As it should be," Jessica said.

27

Gongs sounded across the Forbidden City, deliberately staggered and arrhythmic. The courtyard in front of the Celestial Palace burned in the hot sun as the echoes of the scattered instruments vibrated in the air. Banners of Liao green hung limp on the windless day. With the noise and the stultifyingly humid air, the courtyard was not a comfortable place to be, and most residents of the Forbidden City wisely stayed indoors.

That made the courtyard the perfect place for Danai. She sat on a small bench on the west side of the courtyard, sheltered by a brown roof that stretched out for five meters around the perimeter of the large open area. Sweat trickled down her neck, down her back, even though she had done nothing more strenuous for an hour than sit perfectly still.

Daoshen was expecting her. She knew she was supposed to report to him as soon as she landed, and she had followed instructions precisely right up until the moment she entered the courtyard. She saw the doors of the Celestial Palace across the way and froze. She knew what was behind there, who was behind there, and even though she had worked hard on the long journey home to make herself ready, she wasn't. Even on the best days, during the times she thought he was her brother, he held an odd sway over her. Now that she knew the truth about him, that power had grown even greater. He could intimidate her when he was nowhere near her.

That was no way for a warrior to feel. So Danai had sat, finding a shady spot in the courtyard where she could gather and strengthen her will.

She tried to remember Kai. There was a brief overlap in their lives, a mere four years, and when Danai imagined his face she couldn't be sure if it was based on her own memories or of the countless holovids she had seen of him. But just as her earliest memories of Daoshen came with a kick of dread, her thoughts of Kai Allard-Liao came with feelings of warmth and strength. He would certainly know how to be his own person and stand up to Daoshen. And though she'd been a small child, he had seen something in her, regarded her highly enough, that he left her the greatest gift she had ever received in her life. She still didn't understand why he had done that, but the thought that he had that faith in her was a great comfort as she prepared to face the chancellor one more time.

After an hour of meditation, she felt somewhat better. She knew she would still feel intimidated in Daoshen's presence, but she might at least be able to keep her knee from shaking.

Her heart racing, she stood. She walked slowly but with stateliness.

The equipment around the doors performed its array of tests as she approached, and the doors opened silently as she came near. They were Liao green, giant wooden double doors with a series of ever-diminishing rectangles carved into each one. They opened outward, and Danai stood still so they wouldn't hit her as they moved. Then she entered.

She walked through the corridors that led to the

throne room, and when the herald asked who she was she said her rank and name, nothing else. The herald showed her in immediately, without checking with Daoshen.

She stayed at the far end of the throne room when she entered, her back practically pressing on the door. She saw Daoshen ahead, the dark shadows of his brow completely obscuring his eyes. He was motionless— Danai thought he might be unconscious, but then he spoke.

"You know better than that," he said. "Approach the throne."

She jerked forward as if he had yanked on strings attached to her knees. It was the most graceless stroll she had made since she was a toddler, but it took her to the middle of the throne room. She bowed, long and deep, mainly so she could avoid looking directly at him.

"We have awaited your return," Daoshen intoned. "We assume that, after all this time, your diplomatic mission is complete. We also assume you have succeeded, for you do not have the bearing of one returning in complete disgrace."

"Yes, Chancellor," Danai said. "I have a new agreement. Signed by Captain-General Jessica Marik. You may inspect it."

"Bring it here."

She walked forward, her right arm stiff in front of her, holding out a copy of the document. She saw his face more clearly and felt a stabbing in her chest, seeing him in the flesh as her father for the first time. But her legs held steady.

His fingers, long and thin, nimble as snakes, snatched the paper away. Danai retreated once the paper left her grasp.

Daoshen's head bent, casting even longer, darker shadows over his face as he silently scanned the document.

"Why was one of your officers arrested?" he finally asked.

"It's a long story," Danai said. "But it came down to a simple misunderstanding. That's why Marik was willing to let him go without any charges."

"The arrest of an officer reflects badly on a commander," Daoshen said, and he sounded as if he expected Danai to immediately write down what he said, word for word, and remember it forever.

She didn't. She remained in place, waiting for him to finish reading the agreement.

Then he spoke again. "You told the captain-general that Andurien would not be a threat, which, thanks to activities far outside your control, is true. She then offered to attack the planets she had agreed to move against as part of our previous agreement."

"Right," Danai said.

"Then neither of you really gave the other anything new. You simply put the general terms of the verbal agreement into clear writing."

"Yes."

"That is acceptable," Daoshen said. "It seems that, on this occasion, you did not fail to live up to the trust we placed in you."

That, Danai knew, was as close as she was going to get to a thank you. From Daoshen's perspective, she had merely done what she was supposed to. He would no more thank her for her mission's success than he would thank a flower for blooming. Both events were merely indications that the universe was traveling in its proper course.

Daoshen let the hand holding the paper fall onto the armrest of his throne. Danai knew she was about to be dismissed. But she wasn't ready to leave yet.

"I should tell you," she said quickly, before Daoshen could announce that the meeting was over, "that the Mariks know nothing of the pending wedding of Ilsa and Duke Humphreys. I didn't have to reveal that tidbit to make them feel safe."

Daoshen sat impassively.

"That means you still have that as a weapon," Danai said. "Or a wedge or a lever, whatever you want it to be. For the next seven months or so, it's yours to do with as you please."

Daoshen remained expressionless. But somehow, the room seemed to brighten a touch. The atmosphere grew a fraction less oppressive. She had the distinct impression she'd pleased him.

"That exceeds expectations," he said. "It perhaps has earned you the commendation of the Confederation."

"I don't want a commendation," Danai said bluntly.

"Then what is it you want?"

"Aldebaran."

Daoshen raised a single narrow eyebrow.

"I want to go back there. No games, no politics. Just me and my entire battalion. I want to go there and show them how Capellans fight."

"Should you go, you will receive no additional assistance from me. No reinforcements. And to ask for such assistance would indicate a grave failure, which is a particularly serious matter on a mission you specifically requested."

"I won't ask you for anything," Danai said. "I just want to take my whole battalion there and do that planet right. And once we've got that, we'll take Zurich for good measure."

Daoshen then—smiled? Did he smile? Did Daoshen ever smile? If he did, Danai thought, that might have been it, a serpentine curl of the lips. Then he nodded.

Danai bowed deeply and left the throne room. She needed no other response.

The meeting, all told, had been a bracing success. No long lectures. No criticism. And she even gained a concession from him, slight though it was (Daoshen, like most Liaos, did not need much persuading to approve a mission of conquest). Still, though, something about the meeting had seemed odd. Daoshen had been Daoshen, as he always was and always would be, but something about his manner felt off. It took Danai a long time to put her finger on it.

Then she had it. Not once in the course of the meeting had he mentioned his message to her. Not once had he called her his daughter, his child. Her world had been turned upside down, but as far as Daoshen was concerned, nothing important had changed.

That thought made Danai's skin crawl, and it made her grateful to be leaving the palace and leaving Sian. Leaving her father behind for a good, long time.

28

The last arrangements had been made inside the trailer that Gartin Krauss had positioned next to his gambling hall. A crude hallway connected the two, and Krauss had just finished stuffing the walls with enough insulation to prevent cold drafts from blowing through and disturbing his customers.

Most of his old gaming equipment was going into the trailer—that is, most of the equipment besides the stuff he'd put into storage. He had a few card tables in there now, a row of slot machines and a craps table. It was a little cramped, but since it didn't draw much of a crowd, it was acceptable.

His main hall, with its new royal blue carpet, café tables, wrought-iron chairs and fully stocked bar (with hot sandwiches and pastries available along with the liquor), was now ready to handle all the action the citizens of Wen Ho were willing to give him.

He hadn't, of course, taken that first bet nearly a year ago, when the Capellans first came to Aldebaran. He'd been too busy following government instructions to evacuate in case of invasion. But he'd been allowed to return once the Capellans were chased out of Jifang Po, and he had found, to his surprise and relief, that his modest hall had survived the Capellans' passage. Not only had it survived, but a customer had been standing patiently outside, waiting for it to open. It was the same lumpy man who had been trying to place a bet on military maneuvers when the sirens had announced the Capellans' arrival.

"You should've taken my bet," the lumpy man had told him when Krauss unlocked the front doors. "I was going to bet on the Oriente Protectorate."

"The Protectorate?" Krauss had scoffed. "Who in the hell would bet on the Protectorate?"

"I had some inside information," the lumpy man had said.

That had started wheels spinning in Krauss' head. He still had some moral issues with taking bets on war, but he also had moral issues with not eating. People hadn't been playing for fun lately, but maybe he could interest them in a little blood sport as long as the Capellans were still on the planet. He needed to make a buck while he could—the whole planet might fall, then the Capellans would take over, and who knew what they'd do to the place.

So he'd talked to the lumpy man a little bit, and eventually took his first military wager—fifty C-bills saying the Capellans would beat back the Triarii.

When the outcome of the fighting finally became clear, Krauss collected money not only from the lumpy man but from a number of other patrons who had shown up, interested in making a little profit off of the planet's misfortune. He'd paid some of the money out to a second group of people who'd put their money on the Triarii but, as was always the case with a knowledgeable bookie, the vigorish came to a nice sum.

With a growing crowd of willing bettors, Krauss expanded to matters political as well as military. How long would Legate Juk hold on to her command? Would Governor Sampson be deposed, resign or serve out his term? Who would be the next governor of Zurich? Some people had wanted to put money on the total number of casualties from the fighting on Aldebaran, but Krauss drew the line there. You could bet on winners and losers, he said, but not deaths.

It was enough. His new bookmaking business surged. People came from across Wen Ho, and even from Daipan once that city's population returned from evacuation. Before long the new patrons were bumping elbows with those engaged in more traditional games, and Krauss couldn't help but notice that the new patrons outnumbered the old. He pushed the traditional gamers into an ever-shrinking corner of his hall, until he'd finally come up with the trailer idea. He'd have two halls in one—a traditional gaming hall for the old-timers, and his new current-events betting parlor, which was the source of most of his profits these days.

He checked the latest odds. Five to one that Capellan troops would return within half a year. Twenty to one that they wouldn't return at all. Fifty to one that Legate Juk would stage a military coup. Thirty-five to one that the Triarii commander, Major Anderton, would. Five hundred to one that someone from outside Prefecture X would go into that walled-off area and return to tell the tale. Twenty-five to one that the Republic would rise again from its shrunken borders. A thousand to one that it would do so in the next twelve months.

He'd hired new staff, all off site, a team of number crunchers who could gaze into their terminals and tell him which odds looked like good bets and which he'd be likely to take a bath on. They had saved his life—in general, he had little idea about what was going on outside the doors of his own parlor, and was quite ill equipped to lay accurate odds on the affairs of the surrounding systems. He still didn't understand much about what was going on out there, but his number crunchers did, and that was all that mattered.

The lumpy man was in the hall today, like every day. He'd become the perfect customer—showing up nearly every day, bringing in more and more friends, betting often, losing almost as often. Losing didn't seem to affect the man. He appeared more interested in making interesting bets than in actually winning anything. Krauss had no idea where the man's money came from, and he didn't care as long as it kept flowing into his pockets.

"Five-to-one odds the Cappies will return," the lumpy man was saying. "It's a joke. Is there anyone out there betting they *won't* return? That shouldn't even be an even-money bet. Should be a hundred to one that they won't come back, not five to one that they will soon. In fact, I think you should be taking action on the date they'll get here. I've already got November fifth circled on my calendar."

Krauss liked the idea. He fired off a quick message to his number crunchers, who got odds back to him within ten minutes. They were true wonders, those boys.

"I can give you forty-five-to-one odds for November fifth," he told the lumpy man.

"Forty-five to one? You've got a deal."

"How much am I putting you down for?"

The lumpy man waved a handful of bills in front of Krauss. "How's a hundred fifty C-bills sound?"

A piercing wail cut through the air. Its pitch rose, then it held a high note and throbbed. Krauss felt the inside of his skull turn to jelly.

Everyone in the hall was still. Most of them were looking up, as if the plaster ceiling of the gaming hall could tell them anything about the noise they had just heard.

The wail fell a little, then returned to its high banshee cry. Krauss lowered his eyes and saw that the lumpy man remained frozen, looking through the air at nothing. His handful of money remained in front of Krauss' face.

"I'll take that bet," Krauss said, snatching the cash. "You lose."

In truth, Danai had no intention of bothering with Wen Ho or Daipan this time around. She'd seen how willing the defenders had been to give up on them during her first invasion, and she didn't think the situation would be any different even with Triarii assistance.

They'd concentrate on Jifang Po City, so she would focus there as well.

She'd landed northeast of Wen Ho this time. She planned to charge north, skirting Daipan, and move toward the capital. By the time she got there, the defenders should not only know she was coming, but they should realize she was ready to hit much harder this time.

She was pacing herself, staying in the middle of her force with the rest of her command lance. When push came to shove, she'd make sure she was right in front doing the pushing, but for now she needed to direct the action, to set it up so that her eventual participation would be as meaningful as possible.

The reconnaissance company was leading her battalion forward, but they didn't have the primary responsibility for locating the defenders. She had her aero squads with her this time, and she was going to use them.

She was ten kilometers outside of Jifang and closing in at a moderate speed. It wouldn't take them long to reach the outskirts of the city, so she would soon need a detailed description of the defenders' numbers and positions.

At exactly the right moment, her comm came to life. "*Sao-shao* Liao-Centrella, *Sao-shao* Liao-Centrella, this is *Sao-wei* Feng, do you read, over?"

Danai rolled her eyes. Donny Feng talked like a character in a military holovid, the formality of his words balanced somewhat by the enthusiasm of his delivery. He was like a boy playing soldier with the absolute best toys in the universe.

"I read you, Feng. What've you got?"

Feng's voice sounded disappointed when he replied— he was always much happier when people played along with him and echoed his tone.

"The enemy appears to have you on their sensors and are mobilizing in response. Repeat, the enemy appears . . ."

"I got it the first time," Danai interrupted. "Who's mobilizing where?"

"Sensors show a smaller force, mostly artillery, smaller vehicles and battle armor units remaining downtown while the larger units have moved east. Repeat, larger units have moved east."

"How many larger units you got?"

"We read six companies of 'Mechs and fourteen of armored vehicles, along with nearly a battalion of infantry. Sensors cannot detect all units within the city, but we estimate another battalion of infantry and several artillery units to be ensconced therein. Over."

"Okay. Go after the ones heading east. Wait until they're clear of the city, then sweep by on a few runs until we get there. Keep them occupied, but don't get yourself into any trouble. Break off before things get too heavy."

"Roger, confirm that aero units are to engage defenders moving in easterly direction away from Jifang Po City. Will make first run in approximately seven minutes. Over."

Danai decided it wouldn't hurt her to humor Feng a little bit.

"Confirmation received," she said. "Proposed timeframe is acceptable. Execute plan and report. Over and out."

"Roger and out," Feng said with abundant joy.

Danai didn't want anything to do with the units downtown. First of all, the big fish, most likely including Anderton, were in the group heading east. Second of all, the defenders had had almost a year to devise defenses around town, traps that would make the building they'd blown up in Daipan seem like child's play. It was time for some nice, open-field slugging.

She shifted her units so they were moving almost due east, roughly parallel to the city's northern boundary. She hoped it looked like she was trying to get around the defenders' flanks, but it didn't matter if her maneuver fooled the defenders of Aldebaran. In the end, she'd charge them straight on to see if they could take it.

Exactly seven minutes later Feng's voice came over her comm again. "*Sao-shao* Liao-Centrella, this is *Sao-*

wei Feng reporting. We are commencing our first strafing run on the enemy battalions. Repeat, strafing to begin immediately."

"Roger, report received and noted. Proceed, over and out."

Talking like that could be habit-forming, she thought.

She counted to fifteen in her head, then decided the combined Triarii-Aldebaran forces outside the city might now be a little distracted by Feng's two squads roaring overhead. She had most of her battalion turn again, heading north, running hard, charging toward the enemy lines. She had Bell lead one company of 'Mechs that continued east, hopefully far enough to get out of sensor range. Then it would be up to him to find a good way to come back in.

She started running forward, eager to move faster as she saw smoke rising in the distance, but Yen-lo-wang wasn't yet warm enough to move at its top speed, and she shouldn't break a hundred kilometers per hour yet even if she could. Outnumbered on open land, it wouldn't be wise to separate from her battalion. Yet.

The smoke rose higher, blending into the autumn gray above. There wasn't enough of it. For all Danai knew, the planes had just set some grass or some old barns on fire. It wouldn't be difficult—apparently the area hadn't had much rain since they left, and the grasslands were a tinderbox. There wasn't enough to indicate that the enemies ahead had been badly damaged. The first aero run had likely been little more than a brief distraction.

The enemy was now close enough to start showing up on her sensors. Typical of the Triarii, their march out of the city had been tight and orderly. They appeared to be divided into five groups, each with a mix of 'Mechs, infantry and vehicles. None of the groups were sitting still, waiting for Danai to hit them. They were fanning out, making an inverted vee whose point was charging toward the Capellans—though they didn't appear anxious to engage Danai's battalion. Their advance was about the slowest forward motion she had ever seen. She would make up for it with speed of her own.

"Artillery, set up," she ordered. "Get ready for a long afternoon—I think they're going to keep us at arm's length as long as they can."

Right after she gave the order, the first artillery shots soared into the air, but from the wrong direction. The Triarii artillery was firing.

The shots were poorly aimed, landing short of Danai's forward units. Still, since these units were the lightly armored reconnaissance vehicles, it would be best to get them moving before the defenders' spotting improved. She ordered them off to the flanks so they could keep an eye on any surprises Anderton might want to bring up.

The next minute was a good one. The artillery behind her fired into enemy lines, while Feng led his units on another run. Danai, watching her sensors, was impressed that, except for minor evasive maneuvers, the Triarii maintained their formation. She was certain some of the units ahead must be part of the militia, but in the past ten months Anderton had apparently instilled some discipline in them, so much so that they were all now essentially Triarii. Whether he'd managed to give them some fighting skill along with the parade discipline remained to be seen.

She was now close enough to see flames at the base of a couple of smoke columns. Sure enough, it looked like the landscape was burning instead of the Triarii. Hopefully the second aero run had done more actual damage.

Her fingers danced over her control sticks, waiting for the chance to fire at something. The anticipation had her heart racing, and she almost felt happy.

Then, in an instant, the confrontation went from minor artillery skirmish to full-fledged battle. As if on some unspoken signal, PPCs, gauss rifles and autocannons on each side opened fire. The air sang with speeding rounds, but most of them hit dirt. The shots were more for intimidation than for damage.

Danai still hadn't fired. She had a whole line of Capellan 'Mechs and vehicles in front of her and no clear view of the enemy. She checked her sensors and gave obvious orders to keep herself occupied.

"All companies press forward but keep your heads up. Don't let them concentrate fire in any one place. Keep them moving back so they don't get their feet under them."

"Two plus two is four," Bell said.

"What?"

"Oh, I'm sorry. I thought we were saying things we had learned in the first year of school."

"Very funny," Danai said. "Where in the hell are you?"

"Making my way, making my way. I'll be there—when you need me most. When the situation is direst, when you call for help but no help seems available, then will I sweep forward and wipe the field clean of offending elements . . ."

"Yes, right, fine, shut up. Don't wait for the damn last moment. Get in here."

"Of course, *Sao-shao*."

She looked ahead. The fire was getting heavier, both sides shooting lasers through the smoke as well as shells and slugs and cannon rounds. Danai caught one gleam of golden fire erupting in the enemy lines, a fusion engine breached by a lucky shot. She took it as a good sign.

The smaller Republican 'Mechs, *Locust*s and *Spider*s, were darting back and forth on the front lines along with armored vehicles, hitting larger targets with quick shots and then scooting away. In front of Danai, Rang Yu Company scattered a little to avoid enemy fire and get off shots of their own. Their movement opened up a hole in front of Danai. She quickly got an Artemis lock on a Kelswa tank and fired her LRMs, twenty parallel sets of contrails marking the path to their target. She followed up with a laser shot at a retreating *Locust*, searing its back just as the LRMs made contact with the Kelswa in a rapid series of explosions. The tank skidded to a stop, where other elements of Danai's battalion hammered it into oblivion.

It was a nice takeout, but the enemy fire was getting heavier as the legs of the enemy's vee spread and more units drew into firing range. Danai couldn't afford to get into an open-field slugging match with the Republican forces—they could bring their superior numbers to bear, and the Capellans, superior warriors or not, wouldn't be able to withstand that barrage.

She knew what she needed to do. It would work if Bell was fast enough.

"Bell! I'm getting impatient!"

"You and me both," he replied. "I didn't get into this thing just to jog around all day. But we're coming. I'm going to guess you want me on the east leg of their formation?"

"Wow—you really *did* read a book on tactics once, didn't you? Yes, that's where I'd like you. That's where I'd like you *now*."

"Be there before you know it."

That was that. The next thing she needed to do was hold her lines under the increasingly heavy fire while keeping the Republican troops occupied.

"Clara, Sandra, I'm moving up. I'll be doing a lot of back-and-forth. Cover me."

"Yes, *Sao-shao*."

"You got it, Danai."

She dashed forward for five steps, then veered to her right—in the nick of time, it turned out, as a volley of metal and energy flew into the spot she'd just left. She loved her ax and shield, but she also knew they made her a visible and obvious target.

Let them come, she thought.

There was a cluster of 'Mechs and vehicles a good half kilometer in front of her, bunched too tightly in a formation more suited to parades than combat. She blasted both her long-range weapons at them, then turned left as their return fire darted toward her. A gauss slug slipped over her shield and caught her shoulder, not quite penetrating to the joint's actuator but getting deeper into Yen-lo-wang's body than she liked.

Then fire came from her left, and things suddenly got

too hot to handle. At least a half-dozen weapons had her in their sights. She tried to plant her left foot and push off to the right, but it was difficult to make fifty tons of metal stop on a dime. She slowed up enough that most of the latest volley of fire missed her, but a few autocannon rounds peppered her shield. She tried to get into a run to her right, moving back a little, but the group that had made such an inviting target earlier was now a considerable threat, moving forward, squaring up for their shots. Their next volley would be a doozy.

But it didn't come. 'Mechs, vehicles and infantry troopers alike turned around instead of firing, wheeling to meet the company of 'Mechs closing in from the northeast. Bell's *Yu Huang* anchored the attack, fists and chest guns blazing with fire as he slugged away with his full complement of weapons. He laid down enough fire for three 'Mechs as he advanced, which just made the blasts from his supporting troops more devastating.

"All units hit the right *now!*" Danai called, then led the charge forward.

The right side of the Republican lines, which had been advancing with steady confidence, wavered. The fire hitting them from both sides ripped vehicles in two, splintered entire infantry platoons with single blows and sent their 'Mechs reeling into the dry grass of the battlefield. Dust rose each time one of the big machines thumped to the ground, while shells cut the air over the fallen behemoths. At some points enough fire poured into one spot that the air itself seemed to catch fire, igniting and then imploding around the poor victim caught in the middle.

Danai sped ahead, the hard earth letting her move at top speed. Her laser cut a path in front of her, while selected volleys with her missiles picked off anyone who threatened to get in her way.

Then she was at the enemy lines, ax swinging, catching a tank as it hurried into retreat, the force of the blow sending it tumbling into a cluster of infantry. Lasers flashed in front as well as behind her, and cannon slugs buried themselves in her exterior. So far her armor was doing its job, though some of the close-range shells were coming perilously near vital spots.

Just as quickly as she hit the lines, she was through. She could see the horned helmetlike top of Bell's *Yu Huang* less than two hundred meters away, smoke trails drifting out of the pyramid-shaped missile launchers hunched on his shoulders.

"Everyone keep moving northeast. Bell, that includes you and your company. Let's see what kind of damage we just did."

Danai stayed near the Republican lines, sweeping her ax down near her feet to crush scurrying infantry and battle-armor troopers, long enough to make sure her entire battalion came through. Sandra, naturally, came with the last of the stragglers, but she laid down a ferocious volley of gauss and PPC fire to dissuade the Republicans from attempting to close on the Capellan rear. Then, mainly for effect, she fired her jump jets, and both sides were treated to the sight of the bulky *Marauder II*, with its heavy arms and squat, headless torso, rising into the air. Danai was surprised that the force required to lift the behemoth off the ground didn't knock the entire planet off its normal orbit.

She ran forward as Sandra approached the ground, monitoring her sensors to see what they had accomplished.

It was devastating. They'd shattered at least a third of the right leg of the vee, and the rest had lost their Triarii discipline and were in full retreat. Danai knew this was a moment to capitalize on, when the enemy was demoralized and disoriented. This was when the battle would become a rout.

"Let's give it to 'em again," she said. "Feng, any chance of another run?"

"Negative on that, *Sao-shao*," Feng reported. "Their aero units have engaged us and are pressing us hard. Repeat, they have engaged and are pressing hard."

"Can you handle them?"

For two words, Feng changed his tone, letting some arrogance creep in and sounding more like an actual human being. "Well, yeah," he said, as if insulted by Danai's question.

"Good. Have fun. Roger, over and out."

"Roger over!" Feng said cheerfully, and got back to work several hundred meters overhead.

"Okay, we're doing this without aero. That just means you won't have to look out for misaimed bombs falling on your heads. Let's keep them on the run."

The Capellan battalion turned and began blistering the retreating Republican units. Danai, feeling no need for restraint, ran ahead with the light 'Mechs, ready to mix it up in close quarters now that the numbers were a little more equal. She got a laser blast off, hitting a *Cougar* in its broad chest. It kept moving after she hit it, but she knew that at least she'd melted away a good deal of armor.

The *Cougar* dropped back to assess its damage, while other 'Mechs scattered under the wilting fire from Clara and Sandra. Then, in the middle of the group, a 'Mech stepped forward to rally the troops, desperate to turn around the disorderly retreat. It fired a volley of missiles to distract Clara and Sandra, then turned to fire a gauss shot at Danai. It was a *Thunderbolt*, and the poise and precision of its pilot brought the surrounding troops out of their panic at the Capellan barrage. Danai couldn't see it clearly in the cloudy light and battlefield haze, but she suddenly knew that if the sun had been shining, the *Thunderbolt* in front of her would be gleaming.

It was Major Anderton. Suddenly Danai had a singular focus in the battle.

29

Danai didn't know how the Republican forces would react to losing their commander, but she knew how she'd react to taking out Anderton, and that made the task worthwhile. He had a good crowd around him, but Danai could deal with that.

She ran toward him, her triple-strength myomer giving her unholy speed for a 50-ton machine. Her feet tore up the grass below, and she watched the *Thunderbolt* turn toward her.

She was already turning, moving right, but Anderton had been waiting for it. A gauss slug ripped into her left leg, tearing away armor, digging into the machinery beneath. She kept running, waiting for a limp to develop, but it didn't. The leg held. By a thread, probably, but it held.

Behind her, Sandra plodded ahead, blasting at Anderton with everything she had, while Clara charged at the surrounding company and tried to keep them dispersed with her lasers. They got some assistance from a pair of

Enyo tanks, keeping pace with Clara and leveling fire forward as the bigger targets drew the enemy's attention.

Anderton moved forward, one step, two, three four five, then jump jets fired from his feet and he was in the air.

"Keep on the grounded 'Mechs," Danai ordered Clara and Sandra. "I'll take care of our shiny friend."

She pivoted her torso to keep eye contact on Anderton as he flew, then made her legs come around until she was walking backward, leaning back a little. She got a missile lock on Anderton and fired an LRM volley at the rapidly descending machine. He must have jammed it—most of the missiles flew wide, and the rest struck well clear of vital regions.

The *Thunderbolt* had its right arm lowered as it came down, firing a gauss slug at Danai's head. Knowing that Anderton knew how to lead her, she slowed and leaned forward. She was rewarded with the sight of the slug passing harmlessly overhead.

He was coming in for a landing three hundred meters in front of her. She charged ahead. He was too smart, though, to rush into a melee with her. He moved back, slowing her progress with gauss and missile fire. Danai steered clear of the slug, but most of the missiles hit their mark, one of them catching her already-wounded left shoulder. This time it wasn't harmless. Warning lights flashed, telling Danai her left shoulder actuator was damaged. It would move, but be less responsive than she liked.

The *Thunderbolt* was moving directly backward while Danai had to weave and change speeds to avoid fire, so despite her far superior speed she couldn't gain much ground on him. She couldn't let him keep moving backward or he'd be too deep into his lines for Danai to make a successful charge. She couldn't wait for an opportunity to arise, so when Anderton took another shot at her leg, she made her own opportunity.

The slug hit her above her knee while she was in midstep, and the joint froze in that position. The hip actuator still worked, leaving Danai to walk in a half-hopping motion. She immediately went into a slow retreat, her myomer doing little to increase the speed of her backward limp.

Anderton took the bait. He didn't go into an immediate charge—he'd seen enough of Danai's long-range weapons at work to know a feeble Yen-lo-wang remained dangerous—but he stopped his retreat and moved forward, taking a diagonal path that would bring him closer to Danai without running into the teeth of her arsenal.

Danai fixed her position and let some LRMs fly at Anderton. At least half of them made contact. Explosions sprinkled across the torso near the head, but he kept moving. She hadn't struck a critical blow.

She would have liked to give him a heavy laser shot, but she'd been using that weapon a little too freely recently. One more shot, combined with the occasional laser bolt that managed to hit her, would put her in danger of shutdown. Danai knew Yen-lo-wang's cockpit was hot, but it didn't register with her. After all, that was how battle was supposed to feel.

Then she had trouble. Anderton had brought friends— a *Ghost*, a *Spider* and an *Ocelot*—to bring her in line. Her ruse would have worked against one 'Mech, but against four she was a sitting duck. Time to move.

The two smaller 'Mechs darted beams of energy at her as they ran forward, one to her left, the other to her right. So she moved back, dropping her affected limp for a full-speed backward run. When they turned to get a bead on her, she moved rightward, running roughly parallel to the advancing Capellan line.

The machines pursuing her were fast, even the 50-ton *Ghost*, but they couldn't keep pace with her. Danai left a trail of gigantic footprints in the parched ground as she pounded along. Laser fire from her pursuers passed behind her; they hadn't adjusted to her speed yet.

They also had failed to watch the rest of the lines. Danai knew that Sandra, reliable Sandra, would be planted in the middle of the Capellan troops, keeping an eye out for trouble and launching long-range fire at it. Sure enough, glowing rounds from Sandra's PPC flew out and caught the *Spider* on one of its broad, winglike structures. The force of the blow turned the machine. It was flush to Sandra now, where it met two gauss slugs in the face. The *Spider* fell.

Danai veered to her left, turning her torso in an attempt to get an LRM volley off at the *Ghost* or *Ocelot*, but they were wheeling around as well, staying in her six, and she wasn't ready to turn and head directly at them yet.

She turned a little more, moving back toward the Republic lines, making her pursuers turn and draw fire from their backs if they wanted to keep up their pursuit. They did, and a run at Capellan lines by two companies of Triarii assault tanks kept them from absorbing much damage from the rear.

Then Danai saw Clara, and she realized she was lucky to only have 'Mechs on her tail. Clara had moved into the fray and was going after support vehicles and infantry with a vengeance, the guns at the end of her *Tian-Zong*'s hands staying low and ripping up the ground near her, as well as any units unfortunate enough to be there. She kept moving, turning, twisting, using a few well-aimed kicks to complement her gauss rifles and lasers. She consistently leveled blows at units just as they had her in their sights. She was a one-woman demonstration of why and how 'Mechs ruled the battlefield.

Danai turned back to her right a little, the better to allow Clara plenty of room to continue her task, while she tried to decide how to deal with the three 'Mechs chasing her. She couldn't keep running—not only was it un-Capellan, but if she kept moving at full speed she'd leave Anderton too far behind and lose him, and she didn't want that.

If she meant to turn, she might as well do it now, while the *Ghost* and *Ocelot* had some separation from Anderton. She made her turn wide and irregular, straightening it out or sharpening it as the Republican 'Mechs fired. She trampled the sort of path a gigantic drunken snake might leave.

The pursuing 'Mechs had slowed as she turned, looking for a good shot. Since they were squared at her, she didn't dare charge head-on, so she kept her weaving pattern going.

Closing to within 150 meters, she raised her ax. She pointed herself at the *Ghost*, then at the *Ocelot*, then back, keeping them a little off balance, but not enough. Their shots were getting closer. A few wore away armor on her shield, one blast even taking off a big chunk of the lower left side. One shot from the *Ocelot* came in low, and Danai had to stoop Yen-lo-wang as she ran, blocking the shot with her truncated shield so it didn't pass through and hit her damaged leg. That slowed her up enough for the Republican 'Mechs to let loose with their most intense barrage yet, a blast of beams Danai had trouble seeing because they were heading straight at her. She dodged to her left, but knew she had a problem. Even if a few of these shots missed, there'd be more where they came from.

But the enemy 'Mechs didn't fire again. Instead, both machines leaned backward in unison, reflexively looking up. Danai immediately knew what was going on. Opportunity had come around again, and she intended to grab it by the throat and make it stay awhile.

She charged forward at full speed as Bell's *Yu Huang* came down from the sky, blasting death from the ends of its arms. The *Ocelot* was already in full retreat, but the *Ghost* had thoughts about getting in some shots at Bell before he fell back.

It didn't work. Bell had selected the larger 'Mech as his primary target, and he fired three guns—two from the arms, one from the chest—at the *Ghost*. None of them missed. The *Ghost* staggered, then spun as a PPC round hit its shoulder when it was off balance. Bell's autocannon rattled off twenty rounds, peppering the *Ghost* across its body, but mainly in its chest. Bell kept the barrage coming until the red-and-brown metal of his opponent's chest was drowned in smoke and flame, and the *Ghost* fell where it stood.

Danai ran past the toppling corpse in pursuit of the now-panicked *Ocelot*. It was fast, but not fast enough, and Danai caught it. She drew almost even, looked down, saw the cockpit and crushed it with the ax. The *Ocelot* listed to the right, then fell when a sweeping blow caught its legs, tearing them out from under it. The 'Mech fell and rolled, scattering nearby infantry who were in midflight from Clara.

Then there was Anderton. She admired his tenacity. He stood three hundred meters away from her, holding his ground, firing a gauss round into her shoulder-mounted laser. Lights and alarms went off, warning her of damage to her most powerful weapon. That was okay, though—she didn't plan on using it.

At her top speed she could close on Anderton in a mere ten seconds, so she did, running at a tilt, smoke and dust swirling around her as the no-longer-immaculate *Thunderbolt* loomed ahead. Anderton blasted away with his lasers, breaching Danai's shield and doing further damage to her shoulder laser, but not enough to slow her. She raised her ax and watched the *Thunderbolt* crouch, preparing to dodge her blow.

She lowered the ax, holding it out wide, and Anderton did what he had to—he moved to her left to avoid its wide sweep. Just what she wanted.

She had her shield arm bent, and she thrust it out as Anderton made his dodge, moving it early to compensate for the bad actuator. She went left too, and her shield caught the *Thunderbolt* solidly in the chest.

Anderton's 'Mech outweighed hers by fifteen tons, but she had speed on her side and the force of her blow knocked the *Thunderbolt* over. The weakened shield shattered, chunks of armor dropping on Anderton's fallen 'Mech. The blow staggered Danai too, but her own moves on the pedals coupled with the workings of Yen-lo-wang's gyros kept her upright.

She turned as Anderton struggled to get his machine on its feet. She wasn't about to let that happen. She swung her ax again as she pivoted her torso, a giant, level blow that crashed into the LRM launcher by the *Thunderbolt*'s head. The launcher and its ammunition went off like fireworks, explosions coming one after another, blowing through the cockpit and even doing some damage to Yen-lo-wang's arm.

Anderton's last words, she imagined, were, "Gracious! How unpleasant!" Or something to that effect.

Jifang Po City
15 October 3136

"Where are you people going?"

"To our DropShips, Legate."

"To your *what*? Since when does a battalion retreat to its DropShips in the middle of battle?"

Major Tyla Pruett, recipient of a recent battlefield promotion, ran her hand through the tight curls of her black hair. A few hairs stuck to her hand, pulled out near an ugly burn a little above her right ear. She shook her hand, letting them fall on the otherwise spotless floor of Legate Sophia Juk's underground command center.

"We're no longer in the middle of battle," she said. "That battle ended yesterday."

"I'll say it did," Sophia said, even more irate with this tall woman than she had been with the late Major Anderton. "It ended with you fleeing into my city in a rout. But the fight for Jifang Po is just beginning."

"For you, perhaps. Our work here is finished. We are to return to New Canton."

"What?" Sophia thought about standing on a chair so she could stare at Pruett eye to eye. "When did those orders come down?"

"I'm not at liberty to say."

"You're not at liberty to say? Who the hell do you think I am? I'm commanding the defense of this planet—there's *nothing* you're not at liberty to say to me."

"Nevertheless."

Sophia took a step back, hands on her hips. "Do you

even *have* an order?" she asked. "Or are you scarpering because you got beaten so badly yesterday?"

Pruett then did something Sophia had not seen Anderton do in the year he'd spent on Aldebaran. She got angry. A rush of blood gave a reddish tinge to the dark cast of her face, and she leaned over Sophia like a tree looming over a squirrel.

"We are not *scarpering*! We are not *fleeing*! We have *no more battalion*! Do you understand that? We are in tatters! We have no choice!"

Pruett's anger had an oddly calming effect on Sophia. "What do you expect me to do when you're gone?"

Pruett's answer came in more level tones. "That's up to you. My responsibility is to my unit right now, and committing it to battle would be condemning every soldier in it to death. I'm sorry, Legate Juk. The Triarii are done here." She offered Sophia a quick salute, but did not wait for it to be returned.

Sophia sank into her command chair as if firm hands were pressing her down. By all accounts she had heard, Pruett might well have been right about the damage experienced by the Triarii battalion. The Capellans had been ruthless, pursuing the routed Republicans right to the borders of Jifang Po, dismantling any 'Mechs unlucky enough to stumble on the way. When the battle started, the combined defending force had outnumbered the Capellans by more than two to one. If the battle recommenced—and given the fact that the Capellans were even now moving through Jifang Po's outskirts, that seemed quite likely—the odds would be exactly reversed. And not many of the surviving troops were of a mind to take on the Capellans again.

But she no longer had a decision in the matter. Once Pruett had made her choice (if, indeed, she even had one), Sophia was left with one course of action.

The weight on her back grew even heavier. She was about to write her name in Aldebarian history books in a very unwelcome way.

30

Jifang Po City, Aldebaran
Capellan Confederation
30 October 3136

The meeting was a formality. Her troops had already laid down their arms. The news had already been broadcast across the planet. For all intents and purposes, Aldebaran was once again a part of the Capellan Confederation. But for some reason, the savagery of the recent battle could only be officially ended with the niceties of words and protocol, and that was what Legate Juk had to endure now.

She stood in front of the governor's mansion, watching dark clouds build on the horizon. Maybe it would finally rain, she thought. Finally tamp down some of the endless dust the battle had kicked up, finally wash some blood back into the earth.

Governor Sampson stood next to her, a morose figure. He did not seem anxious to become a Capellan. He had been in government so long he might not have known how to do anything else, but he was not about to serve as part of a Capellan administration, even if they would let him. She expected him to be on a

DropShip heading for someplace, anyplace else, as soon as tomorrow.

Part of her had expected the Capellan commander to walk up to the mansion in her 'Mech, the fearsome ax-wielding machine she had heard so much about, and do a little victory dance on the lawn, but instead a series of ordinary transports arrived at the mansion's circular driveway, and a large number of uniformed personnel climbed out. Most of them formed into three long lines in front of the vehicles, but a dozen or so of them marched forward.

Four of them, three women and a man, were in dress uniforms, black capes flowing behind them as they walked stiffly. One man wore civilian clothing and carried a noteputer. The others wore field uniforms, proudly displaying the Liao green accents on their sleeves.

One woman, barely taller than Sophia but lithe and leaner, walked ahead of the others. She removed her helmet as she approached, and long black hair fell to her waist. Her eyes were green, and they seemed to absorb her surroundings while remaining fixed ahead. She had all the confidence of a victorious warrior, which, Sophia thought, was only fitting.

Troops standing behind Sophia and the governor—green troops, some of the only militarily trained individuals on the planet who were not wounded—drew themselves to ragged attention as the Capellan soldiers approached. Sophia knew they were trying to be helpful, but the sloppiness of their display likely did nothing to make the Capellans think any more highly of the planetary militia. Of course, the recent routs, combined with the way the Capellans had swept through three cities in the battles a year ago, had probably told the invading force all they needed to know about Aldebaran's defenders.

The dark-haired woman bowed, a motion practiced and graceful.

"Governor Sampson. Legate Juk," she said. "I am

Sao-shao Danai Liao-Centrella, commander of the Third Battalion of McCarron's Armored Cavalry of the Capellan Confederation. I was told you requested my presence."

Yes! Sophia screamed silently. *You blew the living hell out of us and we need to see what to do to get you to knock it off!*

Governor Sampson said much the same thing, only he delivered it in politician-ese. "Yes, *Sao-shao*. After the actions of the twenty-seventh and your subsequent movement on the city, we feel it is advisable to surrender to your forces. While we deeply regret the action, and while we abhor the Capellan aggression that makes it necessary, we have little choice."

Sampson, Sophia knew, threw in that last sentence just to get a minor protest on the official record. The Capellan commander seemed to take no offense at it. In fact, she became oddly jocular.

"Well, that's the nature of battle, isn't it?" she said. "One side always regrets it."

Then Liao-Centrella became more formal. "We are pleased to reclaim a world that has ancient ties to House Liao. We know that periods of transition such as the one Aldebaran is facing are worrisome, but we have confidence the planet will prosper and that many residents will eventually gain full citizenship in the Confederation."

Then, abruptly, she threw up her hands. "Blah blah blah," she said. "Wiggins, add some more stuff so that the official record makes me sound magnanimous and graceful while also full of Capellan nationalism, all right? Good. Now. Governor Sampson, I know this isn't easy, but it's the way things are at the moment. You'll understand if I don't directly apologize for anything. Or maybe you won't understand. Either way, you're not getting an apology. And Legate Juk, you did what you could with what you had. The building in Daipan last year was a nice touch, and I imagine you had a few more surprises waiting for us if we came into Jifang Po."

"Not enough," Sophia said curtly, not at all warmed by Liao-Centrella's dropping of formality.

"No, I suppose not. And you're mad at me because of the way things went, because you lost. That's the way it should be. Hate me if you need to. I understand. I'll understand it even more once I arrest you."

Liao-Centrella raised her hand as Sophia started to protest. "Now, now, now, it's not like that," she said. "But you understand that it's bad practice to just let the military commander of a conquered planet run around free. It's only house arrest, your house or the governor's mansion—your choice. And if you decide you'll be happier away from Aldebaran—either of you—we'll make the necessary arrangements. After last week's battle, we really don't need any bitter reprisals, do we?"

Sophia was confused by the Capellan commander's tone—not just the jocularity, but the directness of it. She was not used to anyone in diplomatic circles speaking so plainly, and if it hadn't been a victorious Capellan employing the technique, she might have appreciated it more.

"Now, before the two of you head off, I'll need one more thing," Liao-Centrella continued. "I'd like to get a message to whoever's in charge of Zurich since Gulvoin flew the coop. If you two could discuss what happened here, that might spare us the necessity of going to Zurich and doing the same thing—only more easily, since they have neither the Triarii nor a decent militia. I'm sure that with your help we can make him see the light."

Sophia couldn't stay silent now. "You want us to help you convince another world of the Republic to surrender to you? What on earth do you think would make us want to do that?"

Again, Liao-Centrella took no offense. Her equanimity was unnerving. "Because you'll be saving lives," she said. "Zurich will be mine. We both know it. The question is, what will it cost?" She smiled. "Come on," she said. "I'm sure you'll feel better about it with a few guns pointed at your head."

Sophia's faced drained of all color as her fists shook.

Liao-Centrella held up her hands. "Joke, joke. Just a joke." She turned toward the man who had walked forward with her. "You see, Bell? Some jokes, in the wrong context, just aren't funny."

It had taken the rest of the day to prepare the communiqué for Zurich and to negotiate the finer points of Aldebaran's surrender, but finally it was night and Danai was relaxing in one of the concessions she'd wrangled for herself. She'd taken over the Winchester Arms, the hotel she'd commandeered during last year's invasion, as her temporary battalion headquarters. She planned on stuffing the hotel full of as many battalion members as it would hold.

The hotel had been nice before, but it was much nicer with electrical power and functioning room service. She'd ordered a crab leg dinner sent up to her room, and she cracked each leg and sucked out the meat with gusto. She planned on meeting Clara and Sandra later, but for the moment a private dinner in her hotel room felt good.

Victory on the battlefield wasn't a cure-all, but it was still awfully good medicine. The lives of Capellans lost on the battlefield, the humiliation Caleb had handed her, the torments Daoshen had put her through (she still avoided thinking of him as her father) and the revelation about Daoshen's rape of Ilsa still weighed on her—the icicle in her chest hadn't completely thawed, and she had doubts it ever would—but she had learned to live with it. She remembered once hearing of a man in one of Terra's ancient wars who received a fatal wound in battle—except that the wound took fifty years to kill him. Obviously not fully convinced that he was supposed to die, the man served as a university president and, if Danai remembered correctly, some sort of political official until his wound finally claimed him, making him the last and certainly most drawn-out casualty of that war.

Maybe the wounds she had received this past year would kill her. If it wasn't that, it would be something else, since life itself was fatal. Until the wounds finally succeeded in snuffing her out, though, she determined to follow the example of the primitive soldier and live as if she didn't know she was supposed to die. She didn't have to turn into her parents (*please, please*, she thought, *don't let me turn into my parents!*). She did not need to forfeit who she was in order to serve the Confederation. She only had to follow her great-aunt's advice and hold on to herself. And victory on the battlefield was one thing that felt very much like herself.

Something else would've felt right, too, but she wasn't sure what it was. She took another bite of crab, another sip of mao-tai. Neither of those filled the bill. *Oh, well*, she thought, *maybe I'll come up with it later*. She finished her dinner, then decided to head to the hotel bar to meet Clara and Sandra.

As she approached the elevator (now that aero attacks were no risk, she'd taken a room on the top floor of the hotel, the better to get a view of her newly conquered planet), she saw a tall, wavy-haired man in a black dinner jacket and matching pants standing by the elevator doors. She couldn't help but admire the shape of his shoulders and hips as she walked toward him. This planet seemed to have its share of good points.

Then the man turned, and Danai stopped in her tracks as she realized she had been ogling Jacyn Bell's backside. *Damn civilian dress trips me up every time*, she thought.

She approached, waiting for him to say something insolent or smart-assed. But he just smiled and nodded and remained silent. She looked at his face an extra second, just to get a mental picture of what he looked like without his mouth moving. With his long face and amused eyes, he actually looked pretty good.

The doors to an elevator opened, they both entered and still he said nothing. They went down twenty-five floors in silence. The doors to the lobby opened. They exited quietly.

Danai turned toward the bar, while Jacyn looked about to head out of the hotel. Then she turned back to him.

"What?" she said. "What did I do?"

He raised an eyebrow. "I don't know," he said. "Did you do something?"

"I must have," she said. "No smart remarks? No casual put-downs? What did I do to deserve that?"

"You're not actually telling me you *wanted* me to do any of those things."

"No. Well, yes. Maybe." She sighed. "Look, we didn't get off on the right foot for a lot of reasons, and plenty of them are your fault, but some are mine. But somehow, we got to a point where we have this thing, which is you make fun of me or say stupid things, and I sometimes make fun of you back or I treat you like an idiot. And that's kind of working for us, right? I mean, look at how the battle worked."

A little bit of the familiar smirk showed on Bell's face. "I suppose it's kind of working for us, yeah."

"So why are you changing it now? Why the silence, which is one thing I never associate with you?"

He thought, and as he did so Danai saw an extraordinary thing—the face of Jacyn Bell became completely serious. No cocked eyebrow, no smirk, no eye that looked like it was about to wink. It was unnerving.

"I thought of a lot of things to say, actually. I started to say a few of them. But then I stopped and thought and realized I probably shouldn't say any of them."

"Why?"

"You don't want to know."

"Yes, I do."

"Trust me."

"No."

"Yeah, right," he said, lapsing back into his sardonic tone. "Why start now? Okay, look, you want to know? Really?" She nodded. "Fine. Here it is. You come to the elevator, and I'm ready to kid you about something, so I look at you, and you're out of uniform, and you've got the silk that's clinging to you there"—he pointed to one part of her dress—"and there, and your eyes are doing that thing that your eyes do when things are going well for you."

"My eyes do a thing?"

"Yes. So I'm me, right, and being me, that means there's only a few things I can think to kid you about when you come out looking like that. So I get ready to kid you. But then I think about the last time I tried to kid you like that, and I think about how much a broken nose hurts and how I might not get lucky enough to have my beautiful features unmarred if I try it again, so I shut up. That's why I didn't say anything."

A thought struck Danai. A thought about what it was that she had been missing, what her old self might do in this circumstance.

"Try it," she said.

He eyes widened. "What?"

"Try it. You finally had decent timing, and you choked. But you get another chance. Try it."

"Oh. Okay. Um, wait, hold on a minute." Jacyn fell silent.

"Come on!" Danai said after a minute. "What the hell's the matter with you?"

"It's a lot of pressure, being witty on demand, okay?"

"Oh, you're never that witty anyway."

"Not helping!"

"Be a man! Suck it up! Just *do* it!"

Then, in an abrupt switch, he was fully Jacyn Bell again, eyebrow raised, mouth twisted in a smug grin. "Nobody orders me around like that unless they're wearing a mask and holding a whip," he said. "Do you have either?"

She grabbed his hand and pulled him back to the elevator. "Come on," she said.

"Does that mean yes?"

"Get in here." Elevator doors opened, and they disappeared inside—the only two in the car.

She was on him in a flash, catching him in a kiss that was artless but passionate. But then they made a few adjustments, moved legs here and hands there, the cool fabric of their clothing growing warmer as their bodies pressed against each other, and the second kiss worked out better.

She pushed him back against the elevator wall and he gave way gladly. The elevator suddenly felt humid.

Then the elevator door opened. Danai turned to leave, but they were only on the tenth floor. Some other people were coming aboard—three members of an infantry platoon.

Luckily, she had pulled herself off Jacyn quickly, and she thought they looked normal unless someone looked closely and saw the flushed skin at the top of her chest or the fabric moving on top of her rapidly beating heart.

The troopers saluted, and she briefly returned the salute even though she was out of uniform. She and Jacyn stood awkwardly, looking at their toes, until the doors opened again and the troopers walked off.

Jacyn turned to her, one hand outstretched, but she held him off for a moment.

"I want this to be clear," she said. "We're not going to do this because you're so damn charming that you swept me off my feet. We're not going to do this because war is terrible and we want to experience something good. We're not doing this to gain any sort of advantage on each other, to force commitment or loyalty or anything. We're doing this because we want to."

Jacyn furrowed his brow. "Doing what?" he asked innocently. "What are we doing?"

"Shut up," she said, and then she let his hands—along with the rest of him—move forward.

The elevator reached its destination soon, and they practically fell out of it, panting. They staggered down the hall and into Danai's room. The door closed behind them, their hands moved toward each other's clothes with specific purpose and Danai let her body take over. Which was good, because it knew quite well how to get what it wanted.

He didn't stay long afterward, by her request—explaining fraternization to the rest of the battalion was a lot more difficult than pretending it didn't exist. As she lay on her bed in a pleasant haze, she thought maybe she had been wrong—what she had just done, nice as it was, hadn't been what she wanted. It had been plenty good, and she felt as lively as she had in years, but it hadn't been everything. She still wasn't sure what the rest of it was, but at least now it seemed like something that could be confused with sex.

She thought about Jacyn, wondered where things would go from here, reminding herself of his unfortunate tendency to be a horse's ass. *It doesn't matter,* she thought. *It will go where it will go.* And that thought—the idea of two people deciding for themselves where something would go, based on their own wants and needs, instead of trapping themselves in a long dance of maneuvers or evasions to force the issue one way or another—was deeply satisfying.

31

Jojoken, Andurien
Duchy of Andurien
1 March 3137

There must be a million weddings in the Inner Sphere every day, Danai thought. *Joyous weddings, happy occasions where two people decide to get married because they love each other. Not ridiculous shams where beautiful women marry squat mushrooms for political advantage. Must be nice to live in that other world.*

Then she looked around at the Jojoken Gardens, with early spring flowers blooming in every imaginable color, bright blue and red birds circling overhead, white silken banners edged with gold fluttering in the breeze and a tremendous cake that had enough buttercream in its frosting alone to cause cardiac arrest in an entire regiment. She had to admit there were some advantages to living in her particular stratum of society.

And this wasn't even to be a grand state wedding. The duke and Ilsa both wanted things kept secret until the right time came to reveal their new partnership, which sounded more accurate than calling it a marriage. It hadn't been difficult for the duke to set aside a portion of the gardens for an unnamed private government function, then make sure prying eyes were kept far from the tent where the wedding would take place. The cake itself had been shipped in a large—very large—crate.

Danai had landed yesterday and traveled alone to a hotel near the gardens. She had no official accompaniment and she received no official welcome. As far as regular diplomatic channels were concerned, she wasn't there.

Daoshen was lucky—not only was he officially not there, he was not there in truth as well. Danai might be able to slip into Andurien unnoticed, but the Capellan chancellor could never pull it off. Assuming, of course, that Daoshen would ever be willing to travel like a normal person instead of like the God Incarnate. Which he wouldn't.

His absence was for the best, though. Even if it was a sham of a marriage, Daoshen, with everything he had done to Ilsa, should be nowhere near it.

She hadn't seen Ilsa yet. She had not seen her, talked to her or communicated with her since talking to Erde last summer. She didn't know what she would say to her. How do you start that conversation?

"So, I understand you're actually my mother . . ."

"Is it really true that the guy I thought was my brother but is really my father raped you?"

"I thought, when you're about to marry a man for whom you care nothing, we should talk about other ways in which our family is completely screwed up."

None of the approaches seemed adequate, and avoidance looked better all the time. She had fought hard in the past year to gain some sort of equanimity, and this one encounter threatened to blow it all to hell.

But today was the day. The wedding would happen in five hours, and Danai would have no choice but to see Ilsa then. When she saw her mother for the first time since learning who she was, her reaction would be unpredictable, and it was generally a bad idea to fly completely off the handle when heavy security was in the area. She would have to talk to Ilsa, and it would probably have to be now.

She lingered in the gardens a little longer, smelling a few flowers, marveling at the size of some of the Andurien bees.

Then she went off to have a nice family chat.

"I'm sorry, you can't see her."

"Of course I can. I'm not the groom. He's the only one that's prohibited from seeing her. Not me. Let me in."

"She's preparing for the wedding. Unless you're here to help her with that, you can't see her."

"But she'll want to see me."

"I don't think . . ."

"She'll want to see me! Just tell her I'm here, and she'll have you show me in."

"I don't think so."

"She will! Go in there."

"No. She won't. She knows you're on-planet. She's told me that she can't see you."

That was quite enough. Danai had steeled herself for this meeting, and she was not going to be put off.

"Like hell," she said, and took Ilsa's dressing assistant down with a leg sweep and a shove on the back of her shoulders. She pulled the door open behind the assistant and charged in.

And there was Ilsa. In her wedding dress. It was unzipped in the back, so it hung loose at her shoulders. She stood on a small platform, the relatively simple white dress trailing a single meter behind her. The room around her was filled with flowers, which had been tossed onto tables and chairs without much thought for aesthetics or for preserving the blooms. Her arms were folded, her eyes lit with cold fire and she seemed utterly unsurprised at Danai's arrival.

"I knew I should have put more people at the door," she said conversationally. "Hello, Danai."

"Hello, Mother." She put a full load of venom into the last word.

Again, Ilsa looked nonplussed. "I had heard Daoshen told you he is your father. I wasn't sure he had told you the rest of it, but I supposed you would put it together yourself before too long. So. Now you know."

"That's it? That's all you have to say?"

Someone grabbed Danai's arm. She turned to see a very determined assistant behind her, pulling fruitlessly on her elbow. Danai rolled her eyes.

"Never mind, Mei," Ilsa said. "She made it this far, no thanks to you. She might as well stay. Zip me up, please, and then you may go until I summon you back."

Mei, head bowed, moved forward, grabbed the zipper, pulled it to Ilsa's neck, then shuffled out of the room.

Zipped, the dress was quite modest—high-necked and flowing rather than clinging.

"I can't imagine Humphreys picked that dress out himself," said Danai, momentarily forgetting her anger and treating Ilsa like her sister again.

"The duke didn't pick it out," Ilsa responded. "I need the poor man to be able to focus enough to get through the ceremony. He'll have plenty of other chances to see me in other sorts of dresses."

Which brought them right back to the point at hand and ruined the small moment of rapport.

"How can you marry him, Ilsa?" she said. "Don't you understand what kind of life you'll be condemning yourself to? After all you've gone through with Daoshen . . . how can you do this?"

Ilsa, oddly enough, seemed on the verge of smiling. "Well, you suddenly seem to have learned a lot about my life. I don't want to sound ungrateful, but before you offer me advice we should talk over a few matters." She sat at a dresser with a large oval mirror and started trying on earring after earring after earring. She had at least two dozen pairs lined up. "I heard about your diplomatic mission to the Oriente Protectorate last year," she said. "By all accounts it was a grand success. Do I have that correctly?"

"It went well," Danai said guardedly.

Ilsa inserted a set of pearls into her ears. "So well, in fact, that I believe you were able to ask for a favor and have it granted."

Ilsa clearly had good sources, but Danai would expect nothing less. "Yes," she said.

"You took Aldebaran, and then got Zurich to surrender as well. A fine coup for the Confederation. You have gained praise throughout the realm, and I'm quite proud. I would like you to remember, though, what made all that possible. You could sign a treaty with the Oriente Protectorate because you could promise them that Andurien would not be a threat. And the only reason you could promise that is because of my arrangement with the duke."

Suddenly she turned, a pair of dangling earrings swinging as her head moved. "Everything you've accomplished, your grand conquest, your diplomatic victory, happened because of what I am doing today. You would have had *nothing* without this. You owe me *everything*, and you stand here asking how I can do what I'm doing? Have you learned *nothing* from your time in the Confederation?"

Danai's anger rose to meet Ilsa's. "How are you so loyal to the Confederation? To Daoshen? After what he did to you? If I were raped"—she almost said "when"—"—I would *never* cooperate with the man who did that to me! He would be dead to me! I couldn't stand the sight of him, much less walk next to him day after day after day. Do you see what he made you? And now, to serve his will, you're doing *this*! What did Daoshen ever do to earn this loyalty?"

Muscles eased in Ilsa's body, starting with her neck. It relaxed, her shoulders fell and her entire body slumped slightly. Then she gave an amused smile.

"Raped? My, my. Who told you that?"

"Aunt Erde."

Ilsa laughed, a cruel sound. "That explains it." She sat back down and resumed making her way through her earrings. "Danai, you are an excellent warrior and have served the Confederation well, but you still clearly have much to learn. Daoshen never raped me. I'm sure you know of the power women have—I've seen you wield it yourself. I've seen how men look at you, how they follow you. Haven't you seen that look in Daoshen's eyes when he looks at me? If you haven't, you would be the only noble in the Inner Sphere not to notice.

"I first saw that look when we were teenagers, and it didn't take me long to learn how to use it to my advantage. Daoshen was at my beck and call. Like a puppet on a string. At first it was just games, child's play, but then I saw how serious his feelings were, and just what I could get from him. I could preserve the Magistracy, keep it safe from Capellan aggression for decades. Better yet, I could make it the Confederation's closest ally. All I needed to do was give Daoshen the two things he wanted most—myself, and an heir. I succeeded in both counts, and you see the results. The Magistracy is more secure than it has ever been, and it is poised to grow stronger.

"You ask me how I could do what I have done. How could I not? I have been as dedicated a servant as the Magistracy could hope for. I have led the leader of the Capellan Confederation by the . . . nose, I suppose I should say, and in exchange for occasionally granting him small favors I have received vast concessions. I regret nothing."

Danai stood over her mother, watching her put on earring after earring after earring, going through all the pairs, then going through them again. To her own surprise, Danai felt strangely unmoved by the conversation. The nerves, the unrest she had felt before this meeting had faded. Instead of anger, she felt pity. Her mother was more like her father than she had guessed. In the pursuit of a stronger political realm, they had parted with their souls decades ago, and neither now had any interest in regaining what they had lost, because neither was capable of feeling the void inside them. They were mere tools, serving political ends and machinations that had been set in motion by people long dead.

Danai loved her nation, and she would continue striving to be a worthy servant of it. But she would do it her way, with her whole soul, instead of with an empty shell. She would never again think of herself as her parents' child.

Acknowledgments

Jason M. Hardy

As always, plenty of help came from various quarters on this book, and the biggest challenge is remembering everyone I owe a debt to. If I forget anyone, it's because my mind isn't always good, not because you weren't helpful.

- I have to thank Randall Bills, and not just because I always thank him on general principle. Without his creativity and support, I couldn't have done anything on this. He was very generous at a time when I really would have understood if he wasn't.
- At GenCon 2005, I not-so-subtly hinted to Sharon Turner Mulvihill that I'm always available for work she might want to throw at me. Her reply was along the lines of, "Why do writers always say that? I love my writers! Of course I'll give them work!" A few months after GenCon, this book came along to prove her point. I'll never doubt her again. I should also add that the book would have suffered greatly without her guidance and comments.
- BattleCorps.com members SkuggiSargon, Tenaka-Furey and Paul all were helpful when I wandered into BattleChat or AIM with various questions. I'm incredibly grateful for their cheerful assistance. And just think—if *you* were a BattleCorps member, you might see *your* screen name acknowledged some day!
- My brother who shall remain nameless for my own secret purposes helped on some of the Chinese phrases that appear in the book, though cursing was not his strong suit.

- While writing this book, I was also reading Shelby Foote's three-volume work on the Civil War, and it greatly increased my understanding of tactics and military thinking (not to say that I'm in any way an expert or even accurate). Oddly enough, the one direct reference to a Civil War person in the novel is a story not contained in Foote's work.
- My wife, Kathy, is an absolute treasure in all ways. Period.
- My son Finn's pretty good, too.

Randall N. Bills

First and foremost to Sharon Turner Mulvihill, for always helping me pull out the best story possible in a book . . . and, this time around, for her forgiveness as life kept getting in the way of this book.

To Jason Hardy, who as ever was willing to step in with a monster-sized helping hand and write one incredibly good book.

Finally, to my wife, Tara, and children, Bryn Kevin, Ryana Nikol and Kenyon Aleksandr: All too often I live in so many realities. Thanks for grounding me in the most important one (and for your forgiveness when my realities collide).

About the Authors

In the course of writing this book, JASON M. HARDY thought way too much about how to destroy things with a very large ax, so if you see him on the street in the near future, it might be wise to give him a wide berth. He is the author of the *MechWarrior: Dark Age* novel *The Scorpion Jar* and the recent *Shadowrun* novel *Drops of Corruption*. He also contributes short stories to BattleCorps.com.

He lives in Chicago with his wife and son.

RANDALL N. BILLS began his writing career in the adventure gaming industry, where he has worked full-time for the past decade. His hobbies include music, gaming, reading and, when he can, traveling; he has visited numerous locations both for leisure and for his job, including moving from Phoenix to Chicago to Seattle, and numerous trips to Europe, as well participating in an LDS mission to Guatemala.

He currently lives in the Pacific Northwest, where he continues to work full-time (and then some) in the adventure gaming industry while pursuing his writing career. Randall has published six novels and two Star Trek novellas; this is his seventh novel.

He lives with his wife, Tara Suzanne, and children, Bryn Kevin, Ryana Nikol and Kenyon Aleksandr, along with an eight-foot red-tailed boa named Jak o' the Shadows.

MECHWARRIOR: DARK AGE

A BATTLETECH® SERIES

THE ULTIMATE IN
SCIENCE FICTION AND FANTASY!

From magical tales of distant worlds to stories of
technological advances beyond the grasp of man, Penguin has
everything you need to stretch your imagination to its limits.

penguin.com

ACE
Get the latest information on favorites like
William Gibson, T.A. Barron, Brian Jacques,
Ursula Le Guin, Sharon Shinn, and Charlaine Harris,
as well as updates on the best new authors.

ROC
Escape with Harry Turtledove, Anne Bishop,
S.M. Stirling, Simon Green, Chris Bunch, Jim Butcher, E.E.
Knight, and many others—plus news on the
latest and hottest in science fiction and fantasy.

DAW
Mercedes Lackey, Kristen Britain, Tanya Huff,
Tad Williams, C.J. Cherryh, and many more—
DAW has something to satisfy the cravings of any
science fiction and fantasy lover.
Also visit dawbooks.com.

*Get the best of science fiction and fantasy
at your fingertips!*

Roc Science Fiction & Fantasy
NOW AVAILABLE

DEATHSTALKER CODA by Simon R. Green

0-451-46024-3

As prophesied, Owen Deathstalker has returned to
save the Empire from the mysterious entity known
as the Terror—leaving his descendant Lewis
with the task of leading an army against the legions
of the madman who has usurped the throne.

SHADOWRUN #3: FALLEN ANGELS
by Stephen Kenson

0-451-46076-6

Welcome to the Earth of 2063—a world of
magical creatures and cypernetic-weapon duels
to the death. Kellan Colt is drawn into the paranoic
elven homeland of Tir Taingire, where she must
unravel the most difficult riddle of all:
who can she really trust in the shadows?

Roc Science Fiction & Fantasy
Available September 2006

THE PROTECTOR'S WAR by S. M. Stirling

0-451-46077-4

Ten years after The Change rendered technology
inoperable throughout the world, two brave leaders
built two thriving communities in Oregon's
Willamette Valley. But now the armies of the
totalitarian Protectorate are preparing to wage war
over the priceless farmland.

FIRESTORM:
Book Five of The Weather Warden
by Rachel Caine

0-451-46104-5

Putting aside the personal chaos that has plagued
her, rogue Weather Warden Joanne Baldwin must
rally the remnants of the Weather Warden corps
against a double threat—the Djinn who have
broken free from Warden control, and a cranky
Mother Earth who's about to unleash her full fury
against the entire world.